The Search

For the

Stone of Excalibur

Book II – The Chronicles of the Stone

Fiona Ingram

Biblio Publishing

ISBN: 978-1-62249-218-3 (pbk)
ISBN: 978-1-62249-219-0 (Kindle) Fiona Ingram

Cover design and internal graphics by South African artist Lori Bentley. All rights reserved.

Published by
The Educational Publisher Inc.
Biblio Publishing
Biblio Publishing.com
Columbus, Ohio, USA

ABOUT FIONA INGRAM

Fiona Ingram's earliest story-telling talents came to the fore when, from the age of ten, she entertained her three younger brothers and their friends with tales of children undertaking dangerous and exciting exploits, which they survived through courage and ingenuity. Haunted houses, vampires, and skeletons leaping out of coffins featured in the cast of characters. Inspired by a family trip to Egypt, *The Secret of the Sacred Scarab* began as a little anecdotal tale for her two nephews (then 10 and 12), who had accompanied her on a trip to Egypt. This short story grew into a children's book, the first in the adventure series *Chronicles of the Stone*. From then on, more adventures were inevitable and the second book, *The Search for the Stone of Excalibur,* developed.

Although Fiona does not have children of her own, she has an adopted child from an underprivileged background, who has discovered the joys of reading for pleasure. Fiona's experiences with teaching her daughter to read and appreciate books have sparked her interest in the fight against illiteracy, and she has written many articles on getting kids to love reading.

www.FionaIngram.com
www.chroniclesofthestone.com

iii

DEDICATION

For my wonderful mother, Wendy, who inspired the adventure;
for young explorers everywhere;
and for anyone who has ever dreamed of saving the world.

ACKNOWLEDGMENTS

I would like to thank several special people who helped so much in bringing this book to fruition—my late mother, for her support and her enduring faith in my abilities; my wonderful friend Lisa Carr whose encouragement and wise counsel kept me from giving up; gifted artist Lori Bentley for a beautiful cover and superb interior illustrations (as always); and my editors Lynn Everett (USA) and Jenny de Wet (South Africa) for editing and guidance.

Special thanks: whenever an author delves into the past, it is vital to engage the assistance of experts. My thanks go to swordsmith Jake Powning for his help with details of Dark Ages warfare and weaponry. In addition, thanks go to David Nash Ford for his invaluable information on early British kingdoms and much detail about Arthur and the history of the Dark Ages. A big thank you goes to children's author Wendy Leighton-Porter for her Latin translations.

So much has been written about Arthur that it is hard to decide which resources have the right idea about Arthur's origins. For my part, I prefer the theories put forward by authors Steve Blake and Scott Lloyd in their books, *The Keys to Avalon* (Element), and *Pendragon: The Definitive Account of the Origins of Arthur* (The Lyons Press). Interested readers will also find Christopher Snyder's *Exploring the World of King Arthur* a fascinating read (Thames and Hudson).

For readers who see a distinct similarity between Dunrobin Castle in Scotland and my fictitious Strathairn Castle, they are right. The beauty and mystery of Dunrobin played a large part in creating the atmosphere of this book. For readers who spotted the resemblance of the ruined chapel to Rosslyn Chapel, they are also right. Rosslyn has a haunting quality that is nigh impossible to describe.

For young adventurers who want to learn more about King Arthur and Excalibur, there are some details at the back of the book. However, for much, much more, read *The Young Explorer's Companion—The Official Illustrated Guide to The Search for the Stone of Excalibur: Chronicles of the Stone Book 2*. If you'd like to be updated on Adam and Justin's next adventures in the *Chronicles of the Stone*, please email me at fiona@fionaingram.com to put your name on the mailing list for previews and special offers. You can also email to let me know how you liked this adventure and please feel free to leave a review on the purchase or any social book site.

CONTENTS

Black is the way of the Dark Brothers,
Dark of darkness, not of the night;
Travelling o'er earth, they haunt Men's dreams
Putting their hopes to flight.
It is they who are filled with Blackness
Always seeking to quell the light;
But others are filled with glory
And have conquered the bondage of Night.
Seek not the Kingdom of Darkness,
For evil will surely appear;
'Tis only the Master of Brightness
Shall vanquish the Shadow of Fear.
Know that light is thine heritage,
Know that darkness is only a veil;
Sealed in thine heart is brightness eternal,
Waiting to turn night pale.

–From the writings of Thoth, *The Book of Dreams*

A journey with King Arthur

The Second Adventure Begins

"Oh. My. Gosh!" Justin said in utter disbelief. "This is so not happening."

Surrounded by their luggage in the departure lounge of Johannesburg Airport, Adam and Justin Sinclair stood with their mouths open, staring at their Aunt Isabel racing toward them, frantic. She had an African girl with her and clutched the child firmly by one hand. The girl, who looked about ten, held a small travel bag in her other hand. Thin black plaits flew around her head as the two dashed along.

The cousins had been waiting twenty minutes already for their aunt. It was surprising she was late because with Aunt Isabel things were organized. Going on a trip with her was an experience in efficiency, as they had discovered just a few months ago when they had visited Egypt with her and Gran.

Egypt. Adam's lips curled into a satisfied smile. What an adventure. Egypt was where the whole quest had actually begun with the discovery of the first Stone of Power and meeting Ebrahim Faza, the Egyptologist who knew so much more than anyone else about the Seven Stones of Power. They had found the tomb of the Scarab King and rescued James Kinnaird, their archaeologist friend who had been abducted by the evil Dr. Khalid. They had also helped the Egyptian police crack Dr. Khalid's smuggling ring. The Egyptian government gave them medals for their efforts, which was pretty cool. The only bad part was that Ebrahim suspected Dr. Khalid had survived when the tomb of the Scarab King collapsed into an abyss, and that he would also be hot on the trail of the remaining Stones of Power.

1

Now the cousins were about to fly to London and then on to Scotland for the next stage in the quest—finding the second Stone of Power and the Scroll of the Ancients. The words of James' letter danced in Adam's mind.

"Dear Adam and Justin," James wrote. *"I hope you're both ready for some action because things have been happening faster than I'd expected. I think the second Stone of Power has been discovered, but I can't say more. I've enclosed your air tickets. I'm sure Isabel will persuade your parents that an educational trip to Scotland will be just the thing to fill your July vacation. Looking forward to seeing you both. Your friend, James."*

Amazingly, Aunt Isabel had had no problems convincing their parents because they had been so proud of the boys' role in cracking the smuggling ring. Justin's father had also remarked several times about how mature the cousins now seemed. Adam's father had also agreed that travel broadened the mind and said that of course the boys should visit Strathairn Castle, James' home in Scotland. Their parents knew nothing about the quest, the Seven Stones of Power, or the Scroll of the Ancients. Just as well, too. Adam could imagine his parents totally freaking out if they knew the real danger involved in the quest.

Adam frowned. Who was the girl? It was supposed to be just the three of them—Aunt Isabel, Justin, and him. He wasn't keen on sharing their adventure with a stranger. Maybe she was just some kid lost at the airport. But as the two drew nearer, Adam had the sinking feeling she was coming with them.

Justin's face wore a black scowl. "If she's coming, I'm not going."

"We don't know that. Maybe she's lost and Aunt Isabel is helping her."

Justin glanced at Adam. "Yeah, right. Very likely, I'm sure."

Adam thought again. Justin was right. The girl was coming with them.

Isabel pounded up to them, pulling the girl in front of her as she came to a halt. Adam couldn't quite find the right words to describe his aunt's state. He had never seen her like this. Aunt Isabel was always in control, always so strong. Even when they were kidnapped in Egypt and faced serious danger at the hands of the ruthless Dr. Khalid, she had confronted their enemy with courage and strength. Now she was wild-eyed and seemed desperate. Her auburn hair was untidy and her face was red as she gasped out her next few words.

"Boys! This is Kim Maleka. She's going with you." Isabel swallowed and tried to catch her breath.

"But—" Justin protested.

"No buts." Her voice was stern with a strange undercurrent Adam had never heard before. "There's no time to tell you everything. In fact, the less I say the better."

Surprised, Justin blinked and then subsided into silence, not even trying to conceal his resentment as he gave his rucksack an angry kick. Adam glanced at Kim. She seemed uncomfortable. Adam grinned, trying to be friendly. Kim returned a small, sad smile.

"I can't stop events now so just listen."

Their aunt's intensity grabbed their attention, making the cousins suddenly alert. There was a lot at stake. The discovery of the first stone had begun stirring the ether; now they must hurry to find the remaining six Stones of Power before the confluence of the planets and before Dr. Khalid and his master got to them.

Isabel spoke in a low voice, the torrent of words tumbling out as if she couldn't speak fast enough. She ran her fingers through her mop of auburn curls in an exasperated gesture. "James has been hurt. He was in France on a field trip and something happened at the dig. We think it was instigated by …"

She didn't finish the sentence, but of course she meant Dr. Khalid. He must have survived falling into the abyss when the Scarab King's tomb collapsed—just as Ebrahim had thought.

"Now, don't worry," she continued, "James is recovering, but I must fly to Paris to see how he is and find out what's going on. Before he left for France, he said he had new information about the second Stone of Power and would tell us everything when he saw us. The three of you can go on ahead and I'll meet up with you later. Hopefully, James will be well enough to fly back with me to Scotland."

Adam found his voice. "But, Aunt Isabel, we don't know where to go or what to do." He hated sounding so small and weak, but that's exactly how he felt.

Isabel gave him a quick, reassuring squeeze. "Don't worry. I'm not just abandoning you. It's all been arranged or, I should say, rearranged. James called Gran and left specific instructions. I have them somewhere, but I'm not sure how accurate they'll be. You know your whacky grandmother."

Whacky sounded just like Gran.

Isabel dug in her handbag for a crumpled piece of paper. She squinted at the spidery writing and even turned the page around to see if she had it the right side up.

"I can barely read this. Your gran's writing is terrible. It says something about you'll be met at Heathrow Airport by someone called Ink Blobb and then you'll take the bus to Oxford."

Isabel tried to decipher more squiggles. "James is insistent you meet with someone called Humpleby Twiddle. Twiddle?"

Adam sniggered. *Imagine having a name like that.*

"Imagine having a name like that," Isabel said, echoing his thoughts. "I'm sure your gran's got it all wrong. Anyway, this person is a … pagli-bolo-pher. She must mean a paleographer, someone who studies old writing, I think."

Old writing? The Scroll of the Ancients. Adam's heart thumped with excitement. He nudged Justin, who ignored him.

"So that's it." Isabel sounded calmer now. "You'll catch the flight to London and then take the bus to Oxford with this … er … Blobb person. You'll stay with Mr. … um … Twiddle, who's obviously a friend of James, until I tell you what to do next. I'm sure it'll all work out fine."

Justin made a flapping gesture with one hand to attract Isabel's attention and then indicated the girl standing next to them.

"Oh, yes. Kim. You're so quiet I almost forgot about you." Isabel gave Justin a sharp look. "Justin, you're in charge now because you're the eldest."

Justin had a strange, pained expression as if struggling between pride at being put in charge and annoyance at having to babysit.

At last, he said with forced cheerfulness, "No problem, Aunt Isabel. Just as long as they both do exactly as I say."

Adam opened his mouth to object, but his aunt cut him short.

"Of course they'll listen to you," she said, giving Adam one of her stares, brimful with meaning. Adam shrugged as if he didn't care.

Trust Justin to want to boss us around.

Isabel held Kim close for a few moments. "Sorry I haven't had much time to tell you everything, my dear, but I'm sure Adam and Justin are just dying to fill in the gaps. They're heroes, actually."

Kim widened her large brown eyes. "Really?"

"Really and truly. They even have the medals to prove it. The Order of the Guardians of Ancient Egypt or something fancy like that."

Isabel handed Kim's air ticket and passport to Justin. "Here's Kim's documentation. A flight attendant will look after you on the plane and this Blobb person will meet you at Heathrow and take you to Oxford."

Her tone softened as she said, "I know there's been quite a drastic change of plans, but I trust you boys to see it through. Take care of Kim and make the best of things. You're both old enough to manage. I'll be in touch as soon as I can."

She walked with them to the British Airways departure gate, hugged them, and then strode off to go fly to France.

Adam looked at his companions. The silence was crushing.

"This is a bit of a double whammy for you guys," Kim said.

What could they say to someone who was clearly not welcome? She'd just get in the way of the action.

"I mean, here I am, a girl, and guess what? You're stuck with me. Looks like I'll mess up your plans and they sound pretty exciting." Tears glistened in her eyes despite her bravado.

Now realizing how unwanted she felt, Adam broke the ice by awkwardly sticking out his hand. "Hi there. I'm Adam. This is my cousin Justin. Yes, we had an incredible adventure in Egypt a few months ago and that's the reason we're going to Scotland—well, Oxford first. Anyway, you're welcome to come along."

Kim gave a shy smile as she shook hands.

Justin mumbled a reluctant hello and then said, "This is a stupid question, but where did you come from? We were at my aunt's house before we went to Egypt and you weren't there."

"I know. I'm kind of a problem kid." Kim laughed at Justin's shocked expression. "Not *that* kind of a problem kid. I was living with my mother in a township and it was hard to study properly."

Adam had some idea of just how tough it must have been for her. There were plenty of newspaper reports about life in the townships in South Africa, where many of the country's poorer black population lived. They were not pleasant places for children to grow up, let alone study and do well at school. Many of the houses were mere shacks made of tin, plastic sheeting, and cardboard, with no running water, proper sanitation, or electricity. Most of the roads were dirt tracks that turned into churning mud troughs when it rained. Crime was high and countless children ended up in street gangs, or lured into drugs and worse.

Adam thought of his comfortable house in Durban, their hometown. He had his own bedroom and his dad had just bought him a new computer with fantastic programs. He felt sorry for Kim.

Kim started again. "I mean I couldn't keep up at school, so my mother—she works for Aunt Isabel as her housekeeper—asked if I could stay with your aunt and get some help with school and homework. Life's much better now. I have my own room, plus a computer, and my mother stays in the cottage behind the house so she's happy."

"What's it like actually living with Aunt Isabel?" Justin asked, with a sideways glance at Adam.

Kim chewed her bottom lip, thinking. "Um … how can I explain this? Some people would say she's strict. I think she's firm, but fair. You know exactly where you stand with her."

Kim had hit the nail on the head. Their unconventional aunt was loads of fun, but she had rules about how she expected her nephews to behave.

"School comes first," Kim continued, "if you know what I mean. I'm a grade behind already so it's all about me catching up and getting a proper education."

Justin frowned as if he didn't really understand how someone could fail an exam, let alone a whole grade. "What's the problem at school?"

Kim looked downcast. "Math and English are my worst areas. I just can't get the hang of it."

"I'm top of my class in math and Adam's the whiz at English, so maybe we can give you some help if we have time during the trip."

Kim brightened. "Cool. I really want to hear about your adventure. Egypt sounds totally amazing."

Justin glowed and opened his mouth to say more, but a crackle of static interrupted him and a loudspeaker called their flight. They saw a smiling flight attendant heading in their direction. It was time to go.

Justin grabbed his rucksack. "Let's get on board and then I'll tell you all about it."

Adam gave a wry grin; Justin loved being the center of attention. Adam slipped his hand into his pocket to hold his golden scarab. Even though it was only a replica, it made him feel safe, just as the real sacred scarab had done.

Maybe it's just because I got so used to it in Egypt.

Familiar with air travel after their Egyptian adventure, they reassured the terrified Kim that the plane wouldn't fall out of the sky. After the flight attendant had settled them comfortably, Justin told Kim the whole story about their previous trip, including the Seven Stones of Power, the secret of the sacred scarab, and the way Dr. Khalid's men had ruthlessly hunted and kidnapped them, taking them across the desert to the Scarab King's hidden tomb. Then Adam described the destruction of the tomb and their realization that the sacred scarab—containing the first Stone of Power—began their quest to find the remaining six stones, which had been scattered throughout the ancient world and lost in the mists of time.

"So now you guys have to find the next Stone of Power?" Kim asked.

"That's right," Adam said, "but that's not all. Our mission is also to find the Scroll of the Ancients. James' ancestor, Bedwyr the Curious, was a thirteenth-century monk and he somehow managed to find it and then hide it away somewhere."

Justin added, "This ancient scroll contains all the clues to the remaining Stones of Power and how to use them to read the *Book of Thoth*, the most powerful book in the world."

Remembering their friend Ebrahim Faza's warning about future danger, they didn't tell Kim too much about Adam's importance in the quest.

Kim's big brown eyes grew even bigger as she listened, breathless with excitement, to the most extraordinary tale she had ever heard.

"So this means we'll be involved in another adventure? I'll get to be part of it, right?"

Adam and Justin exchanged uneasy glances. Justin struggled for a tactful reply.

"Uh … I guess so. I'm not being mean, but I don't understand why Aunt Isabel included you on this trip. She knows what we went through in Egypt. We could've been killed a few times. No kidding."

Kim's face fell. "I don't think she had any choice. My mom had to go sort out a family problem. Then the people who were supposed to take care of me while Aunt Isabel was away said they couldn't at the last minute. I think it was easier for her to take me along."

Adam said, "Aunt Isabel thought she was going to be with us, but things are different now that James has had this accident."

"So, it's just three of us," Justin said. Then he added in a bossy tone, "Remember what Aunt Isabel said. *I'm* in charge. You're quite little, Kim, so stay out of trouble and do as I tell you."

Kim turned up her nose at Justin. "I'm not so little, you know. I'm a small-sized person, but I don't need anyone to look after me."

Justin raised his eyebrows. "Really? So exactly how old are you?"

Kim glared. "I'm nearly thirteen."

Justin sniggered. "O-ho, then you just keep quiet, little girl, because nearly thirteen actually means you're still twelve, the same age as Adam. I'm older than both of you and that puts me in charge, just like Aunt Isabel said."

Adam just rolled his eyes, not wanting to get involved in the argument.

Kim smiled sweetly. "Don't worry, Justin, I'll listen to you. You can still be in charge, seeing as it's so important for your supersized ego."

With that, she gave Adam a mischievous wink. He grinned back. Justin was going to have a hard time ordering a determined girl like Kim around. Justin subsided into his seat with a cross expression and pretended to read the in-flight magazine, ignoring Kim.

When Justin went to the bathroom, Kim asked, "Is he always like that? So bossy?"

"I guess so," Adam said. "He likes to be in charge. It makes him feel important. Don't misjudge him, though. He saved my life twice."

Kim gave him a disbelieving stare. "Really? How?"

"Once when we were in the desert, trying to save someone from sinking sand—actually, one of the men who kidnapped us. Then another time, when Dr. Khalid was about to shoot me while the tomb of the Scarab King was collapsing. Justin hit him in the eye with his slingshot. Justin just likes to feel important because he's older, so don't worry too much about what he says."

Kim smiled. "All right then, I won't. You were telling me about this sacred scarab. What does it look like?"

"I can show you." Adam took the scarab out of his pocket and pressed the tip of the head. Gold pincers emerged, holding a round crimson jewel. Golden wings shaped like those of a vulture, sparkling with green and blue gems, shot out from the sides of the body. Legs emerged from the base, each clawlike foot clutching a gleaming green stone.

Kim caught her breath when the jeweled wings opened. She gently touched one. "It's magnificent. How can you own such a valuable thing? I thought you said you gave it back to your friend Ebrahim."

"Yes, I did. I gave him the real scarab. This is just a replica. When we got our medals from the Egyptian government, they also gave me this as a reward for saving the real sacred scarab. Justin got an incredible snake stick with genuine crystal eyes."

"You brought the scarab with you?"

Adam jumped at the sound of his cousin's voice.

Justin sat down next to Adam. "What for? What happens if you lose it?"

Adam quickly pressed the tip of the scarab's head again, retracting the scarab's glittering wings, pincers, and feet. He put it back into his pocket. "Nothing. No reason. I won't lose it."

Justin cocked his head to one side and raised a disbelieving eyebrow.

Adam felt his cheeks redden. "Okay, I brought it along because it makes me feel more secure."

"It doesn't work, you know," Justin said. "It's not like the real one."

"That doesn't matter," Adam retorted stubbornly. "It's mine and I want it with me." He folded his arms and glared at Justin, who shrugged and said, "Suit yourself."

Kim looked puzzled so Justin explained, "The real sacred scarab is a pretty powerful artifact, only we didn't know it at the time. It's safely locked up in a vault underneath the Bank of Egypt in Cairo now. This is just a replica." He glanced at Adam. "But it's also quite valuable. I bet Uncle Mike and Aunt Jennifer don't know you brought it with you."

At the mention of his parents, Adam scowled even more. Kim hastily changed the subject, remarking that the cousins looked like brothers because they both had red hair and freckles.

"No way," Adam sputtered. "We're *completely* different."

Adam pointed out their different eye colors—his eyes were brown while Justin's were blue—and Justin's bigger build.

Adam added, "Justin's the action guy. I'm the—" He stopped, suddenly remembering they hadn't told Kim everything about his role in the quest. "I'm more of a geek," he finished lamely, shooting a warning glance at his cousin.

Justin picked up on Adam's cue. "When we were in Egypt, that's how things worked out. Adam did all the clever things. I just had to keep saving everyone from certain death."

Early the next morning, the plane landed at Heathrow Airport. They disembarked and retrieved their bags with the help of the friendly flight attendant. She herded them through passport control and finally to the exit gates, saying, "Off you go now. There's the person who is collecting you." She gave them a cheery wave good-bye.

Adam stared at the sign bobbing above a sea of faces. It read *Attention Adam and Justin Sinclair*. A lanky youth appeared, holding the sign. He was about nineteen, tall and skinny, dressed in black jeans and a black T-shirt with a white skull and crossbones on it. The most striking thing about him was his shock of jet-black hair standing up on his head, in distinct contrast to his pale face.

He gave them a wide grin. "Hi, guys. My name's Benjamin Blott, but you can call me—"

"Ink!" the three kids chorused loudly.

He stared. "How did you know?"

Kim and Adam sniggered while Justin said, straight-faced, "Lucky guess?"

It wasn't hard to see why Benjamin was nicknamed Ink: his black hair was the color of ink and with a last name like Blott …

Ink laughed. "Yeah." Then he said to Kim, "Hello. This is a surprise since I wasn't expecting you as well, but welcome to England."

Kim gave Ink a tentative smile.

Ink picked up the two biggest suitcases. "Let's go." Not waiting for a reply, he strode through the crowd, leading the way to the bus station. The kids followed him, clutching their remaining bags, and hurrying to keep up with his long-legged stride. Ink bought three bus tickets to Oxford and gave them to Justin.

"You look like the eldest so you're in charge."

Justin said, "Aren't you coming with us? We have to meet someone called Humpleby Twiddle, the paleographer."

"Actually, it's Humphrey Biddle," Ink replied as he helped the driver load the suitcases into the luggage compartment underneath the bus.

"Uh … yeah," Justin said. "Do you know him?"

"He's my dad. I'm going to Oxford as well, but not in the bus. I'm riding my bike." He pointed to a gleaming black and silver motorbike parked nearby.

Justin's mouth hung open. "Wow! That's yours?"

Adam couldn't see what was so exciting about a motorbike. He preferred Ink's skull and crossbones T-shirt.

Ink seemed amused by Justin's obvious admiration. "Like it?"

Justin nodded.

"I'll give you a ride sometime," Ink said, with a careless pat on Justin's shoulder. "Get on board now. See you in Oxford."

He put on his crash helmet and took a black leather jacket from one of the bike's panniers. Adam climbed onto the bus with Kim and Justin and they watched the huge bike roar off into the distance. When Ink disappeared from view, Justin lay back in his seat, looking rather dazed. Adam and Kim giggled softly. Not many things left Justin speechless.

The journey from London to Oxford took about ninety minutes. Once the bus had passed from the city outskirts onto the highway, they enjoyed the pleasant views of green fields dotted with peacefully grazing sheep and cows, distant villages, and a sapphire blue sky. Adam opened the nearest window. The air felt moist and fresh, with gentle sunshine filtering through to warm their arms.

Adam winked at Justin. "Better than Egypt?"

Kim asked, "How hot is it there?"

"It was blazing," Adam said. "We couldn't go outside without loads of sunscreen or else we'd have fried. Everything felt so dry."

"But how did you survive? I can't imagine being stuck in a desert and having to ride a camel for miles."

"I don't know," Justin said solemnly. "When I think about it now, if I had known what was coming, I'm sure I would've run away rather than face something like that. But once you're in it, once you know there's no turning back and you have to keep going because so much depends on you … well … you just do."

Adam quickly began talking about something else because Justin looked so serious. "So, have you met Gran yet?"

When Kim nodded, he asked, "What does she think about you living with Aunt Isabel?"

Adam felt a tiny stab of jealousy at sharing their beloved aunt and grandmother.

Lolling back in her seat, Kim giggled, remembering something amusing. "Oh, Gran's so funny."

Then she sat up and put on an expression just like the boys' grandmother. She pursed her lips, screwed up her eyes, and, peering at Adam, tapped him on the chest.

"She said, 'I suppose I now have another grandchild to keep in line.' When I said, 'Yes, Ma'am,' she said, 'Don't call me Ma'am, call me Gran, and if your school marks don't improve, you'll have to tell me why and it won't be a pleasant experience.'"

"She's only kidding," Justin said. "I mean, she wasn't being—"

"I know what she means," Kim interrupted. "She's such a cool person for a grandmother. I love her nails and all her bling."

Adam thought of their eccentric grandmother, with her long red fingernails, constantly changing hair colors, and loads of glittering jewelry.

"You should've seen her in Egypt," he said. "She was so brave that when we were kidnapped in the Valley of the Kings, she drove all the way from Luxor to Cairo with two Turkish carpet salesmen in a beat-up old cab and made the British ambassador send the Egyptian army to rescue us."

Kim's mouth formed a perfect *O* in surprise. "Wow! So you guys actually were in serious danger in the desert."

Justin said, "I wasn't joking when I said we nearly died there."

Adam thought about James' letter again. Had the second Stone of Power really been found? Where should they start looking for the Scroll of the Ancients? Which one was the most important right now?

There was no time to ponder possibilities because the bus had pulled up to the station and the passengers were already grabbing their bags and getting off.

Kim peered out of the window. "There he is," she said.

Adam caught a glimpse of Ink perched on his motor bike, waiting for them. Ink waved and beckoned them toward a cab. Once the luggage was in the trunk, the cab whizzed off. Obviously, the driver already had his instructions.

The center of Oxford was charming; its narrow cobbled streets crammed with quaint shops, mediaeval architecture and, of course, the famous university colleges with their intricate wall carvings and equally famous spires stretching skyward. The sun glowed on the saffron-colored Cotswold stone. Most of the old colleges were made of this yellowish limestone, giving the buildings their distinctive, aged appearance.

"I hope we have time to explore." Adam craned his neck to see as much as possible out of the cab window. "This looks like a cool place. Lots of mysterious old things here, I bet."

As the cab turned a corner, Adam glimpsed a flash of sunlight on water through the fronds of several weeping willow trees. "Hey, a river. We can go boating."

"Let's see what Aunt Isabel and James have planned for us first," Justin said, sounding serious.

After a few twists and turns, the cab pulled up outside a pretty thatched cottage. It had a shop on the ground floor and living space on the upper level, judging from the floral curtains fluttering in the second-storey windows. Ink roared to the back on his bike and reappeared a few moments later to give them a hand with their luggage.

"Welcome to Humphrey Biddle's Amazing Antiquarian Bookshop," he announced with a small bow. "Prepare to be amazed."

The shop bell tinkled as the front door flew open. A plump little man appeared, beaming a welcome. Dressed in a tatty old green cardigan and worn brown corduroy trousers, Humphrey Biddle resembled an elderly, rumpled hobbit. He was balding, with fluffy white tufts clustered around his ears, and a wispy salt-and-pepper beard straggling down the front of his cardigan. Instead of regular glasses, Humphrey wore an old-fashioned pince-nez perched on the end of his button nose. Adam noticed extremely shabby bedroom slippers on the old man's feet. A sock-clad toe peeped through a hole in the front of one slipper. Humphrey's sharp gray eyes were piercing, as if they could see right through you. Adam liked him immediately. Humphrey had the same quality about him as their Egyptian friend Ebrahim Faza, even though Ebrahim was the picture of elegance and Humphrey the exact opposite.

Humphrey gave them all vigorous handshakes while propelling his guests into the tiniest, most cluttered bookshop Adam had ever seen. Books, books,

13

books! They were everywhere: teetering on the edges of small tables, bursting out of glass-fronted cabinets, clustering in piles on the floor, and lurking on the tops of cupboards. Their covers were a variety of faded colors, with curly gold lettering on the spines. There were rolls of old parchments and ancient-looking scrolls all over the place, maps galore, and some yellowing globes of the world.

A fine film of dust lay over everything. The shop smelled of old paper and history: a mixture of sunlight on warm, freshly mown grass, a hint of vanilla, and dried flowers. Adam felt as though they had stepped back a hundred years or more. He sniffed in appreciation.

This is the most incredible bookshop in the world.

Kim just stared, her brown eyes goggling. She wrinkled her nose. "Ugh! Smells weird," she whispered.

Justin wore a similar expression. "Ditto."

At last, their host stopped bustling around to peer with interest at his visitors. "Let's all sit down," he chirped, leading the way through the shop. At the back was a small living room cluttered with loads more books.

A large sofa with fat cushions took up most of the room. Two tapestry armchairs squeezed in on either side of the sofa, and an old television set sat in one corner. In front of the sofa was a long, low coffee table, untidy with used cups and saucers. On the walls hung several faded maps, along with a number of dark landscape oil paintings in gilt frames. At the far end of the room, Adam noticed a fireplace, the ornate mantelpiece crowded with dusty ornaments and figurines. Tarnished brass fire irons lay on the hearthrug. Evidently, Humphrey wasn't too fussy about cleaning up.

"Get cake and refreshments," Humphrey said to Ink, as he shoved several piles of books off the sofa to make space. "We might need an extra chair or two. We don't often get so many visitors all at once."

He fussed about the room, moving books and papers, and pulling the armchairs to form a circle with the sofa. Then he patted the worn cushions invitingly, releasing a cloud of dust. Kim sneezed.

Humphrey looked apologetic. "Sorry. Never seems to be much time to dust. Amelia always complains because I seldom let her in here with the vacuum cleaner."

He shook his head determinedly. "I say to her, 'Amelia, I am an antiquarian book dealer. Old books are my business. What is an antiquarian bookshop without dust?' Besides, I think vacuuming is bad for the manuscripts."

He plonked himself down on a nearby armchair and immediately leaped up again as an angry yowl came from beneath him.

"Dear me, Bismarck? My apologies."

A large, yellow-eyed marmalade cat shot out from under Humphrey and leaped onto the windowsill behind the sofa. After shooting several scornful glances in their direction, it began washing itself.

Humphrey leaned forward, his eyes shining behind his pince-nez. "Such excitement," he whispered. "Now, what's this I hear about the second Stone of Power?"

A STRANGE AND UNWELCOME VISITOR

humphrey burst out laughing. "Ha-ha! I thought that would surprise you. You thought I didn't know about the Stones of Power."

Justin and Adam exchanged panicky glances. How much *did* he know?

Kim said nothing; she just stared at Humphrey.

Still giggling to himself, Humphrey mopped the corners of his eyes with a large grubby handkerchief. Then he put on a serious expression. "Now, children, I'm just teasing you. There is much to discuss."

Just then, Ink came into the room, carrying a tray loaded with food and mugs of steaming cocoa, which he placed on the coffee table.

"Dad," he said, while clearing away the dirty crockery. "They're not used to your nutty sense of humor so give them a break."

Ink winked at Adam. "Dad's just kidding. He's actually quite sane when he wants to be."

Suddenly, with Ink's grin, things seemed normal again.

They began eating while Humphrey fished in his pocket for something. "Aha," he announced in triumph, waving the something in the air. "Here it is. A letter from my good friend, Ebrahim Faza."

Adam sat bolt upright. He almost choked on a large mouthful of cream bun as he hurriedly tried to swallow it and speak at the same time. "You know Ebrahim Faza?"

Humphrey waggled his eyebrows at Adam. "Of course I know Ebrahim. That's why you're here. We go back a long way. I saved his life once in Egypt. You know how seriously they take that sort of thing."

Adam knew just how important that sort of thing was because he had saved Ismal's life in Egypt. Ismal was one of their kidnappers, who had almost been swallowed by shifting sand when they were crossing the desert. That incident had turned events in their favor because later Ismal had helped them escape when the Scarab King's tomb collapsed.

"What happened?" Adam asked, biting again into his bun. A blob of cream squirted out of the side and landed on the front of his shirt. He carefully scraped it off while listening to Humphrey.

"It was years ago. I was walking late one night in Cairo." Humphrey warmed to the telling of the tale.

"I don't know why, but I decided to take a shortcut down an alley to get back to my hotel. I saw three thugs attacking a man. I shouted and ran toward them, and—like most cowards—they fled. Ebrahim wasn't badly hurt, just a few cuts and bruises. I hailed a cab and took him back to his house. Given my kind of business, the antiquarian book trade, and … er … Ebrahim's interests, it was natural for us to become friends."

Justin lowered his voice before asking, "Do you know who was behind the attack?" His eyes were wide as he waited for an answer.

Humphrey nodded. "Yes. Ebrahim thought it was …" His voice died away, but his beetling eyebrows waggled expressively.

Adam and Justin glanced at each other. Kim frowned, looking left out.

"It was the evil guy I told you about," Adam whispered in her ear. "Dr. Khalid, our enemy."

Kim glanced nervously behind her. "He seems to be pretty powerful."

"It's who he works for that's the biggest problem. Someone even more powerful and dangerous."

"Anyway," Humphrey continued, "our friendship began, and the rest is history as they say."

Justin leaned forward. "So, you know all about …" He sketched a vague gesture in the air.

Humphrey's white tufts quivered as he nodded.

"And since you're a pal-e-ographer," Justin said, pronouncing the word carefully, "Ebrahim must have told you all about the Seven Stones of Power by now?"

Humphrey smiled. "I've known about the Stones of Power for a while. Although Ebrahim hasn't shared all the details with me, and I do not expect him to do so, I've been of great help to him in his research. You may speak freely."

"I suppose *you* should tell us why we're here," Adam said. "I mean, James sent us a letter saying he thought the second Stone of Power had been found. I guess you probably know what happened with the first stone."

"Speaking of the first stone," the old man said, "Ebrahim mentioned that you have something you might like to show me."

Adam wiped a sticky hand on his pants before he felt in his pocket for the scarab. When he laid it on the coffee table, everyone stared. Ink gave an admiring whistle. Adam pressed the head to open the jeweled wings and was pleased to hear the intake of breath from Humphrey and Ink.

"It's not the real thing," he assured them.

"No?" Ink raised his eyebrows. "It looks real enough to me."

Justin interrupted with a small laugh. "Obviously, Ebrahim wouldn't give something so important to us—I mean, to Adam—even though Adam was the bearer of the real sacred scarab in Egypt. It's far too valuable. The real thing is safely locked away in the vaults of the Bank of Egypt. They have the latest antiterrorist technology to protect it so even Dr. Khalid couldn't bomb the place open. This is just a replica."

Humphrey muttered, "Is it?"

Adam looked sharply at him.

The old man reached out for it. "May I?"

Adam placed the scarab in his palm. Humphrey turned it over several times, examining the golden creature. After a few minutes, he gave the scarab back to Adam.

"Wonderful. Perfect workmanship. An extraordinary piece."

"It *is* a replica, isn't it?" Adam asked as he pressed the scarab's head again to retract the wings.

"Oh yes, yes, my boy," Humphrey replied with a warm smile. "No need to worry. You're not walking around with the fate of the world in your pocket."

A mixture of relief and disappointment flared up inside Adam, a feeling he quickly squashed. Naturally, Ebrahim would not entrust something as precious and significant as the genuine sacred scarab to the care of a mere boy. Yet, Adam wished he still had the real artifact with him. He put the scarab back into his pocket and looked at Humphrey.

"You were telling us about Ebrahim's letter?"

Humphrey peered at the letter. "Now, where was I?" He scanned the lines.

"Ah, yes. Apart from some gossip about acquaintances in the book trade, Ebrahim says, '*Be warned, my old friend. The enemy is on the move and sooner than we expected. As I thought, Dr. Khalid survived falling into the abyss when the Scarab King's tomb collapsed. There have been several attempts to break into the Egyptian Museum, so he must think the first Stone of Power is hidden there. Instruct Adam and Justin to take the utmost precautions when tackling this next stage of the quest. Peril will be hard at their heels. Their lives may be in danger. Trust no one. I will join them as soon as I can, but I cannot say when. There is still much to do here in Cairo with our investigations. We believe the recent archaeological find may indeed be the second Stone of Power, but let us not jump to conclusions. Time is of the essence and we need to track down the Scroll of the Ancients as soon as possible. From what Dr. Khalid said in the tomb of the Scarab King, it is clear to me that he thinks the scroll is lost and he will possibly be unaware of this part of the children's quest. He is relying on Bedwyr's document, the Chronicles of the Stone, which he stole from Strathairn Castle for his information. Let me know your thoughts once you have more information on this recent find. I remain your brother in the quest, Ebrahim.*'"

Adam remembered James telling them in the Scarab King's tomb how Bedwyr had written a long, illustrated poem describing the Seven Stones of Power, and also confirming that he had hidden the original scroll safely away somewhere. Dr. Khalid had stolen the poem, which Bedwyr called *The Chronicles of the Stone*, when James' father had put Bedwyr's writing and illustrated manuscripts on display one year when the castle was open to the public.

Humphrey folded the letter and put it back into his pocket.

Justin and Adam exchanged uneasy glances. Ebrahim, who never exaggerated, had definitely said peril would be stalking them. Adam wished Ebrahim could be with them soon. The quest would be so much easier if he were here.

Ink stared at Humphrey with wide eyes. "Dad, I thought this was just about archaeology, but it sounds like a whole lot of danger. Do you think you should be getting involved in something so risky at your age? What about your heart?"

20

Humphrey squirmed a little; he looked embarrassed. "I've been meaning to tell you the whole story and I will—later. And don't bring up the subject of my heart because there's nothing wrong with it."

"Oh yes, there is." A soft but determined voice came from the doorway.

Everyone looked up. A woman stood there, a shopping bag dangling from each hand. She had one of the most pleasant, smiling faces Adam had ever seen. Dressed in a navy suit and small flowered hat, she gazed at them with sparkling blue eyes and smiled.

"I am Miss Amelia Sudsbury, Humphrey's assistant and secretary, but please call me Amelia. Miss Sudsbury sounds so schoolmarmish."

She put down the shopping bags and came into the room. Amelia Sudsbury was petite and trim. Although she wasn't a young woman, it was hard to guess her age. Her light brown curls under the flowered hat sat precisely in place, and anyone could see why the dust in Humphrey's bookshop and living room drove her crazy. Miss Sudsbury was as neat as a pin, from the top of her head to the tips of her sensible shoes.

Advancing on Humphrey, Amelia wagged a stern finger. "I don't suppose you told the children that you've recently had a minor heart attack and that your doctor advised you to rest?"

Her expression radiated strong disapproval. "Now, from what I hear, you're going to be jaunting off on a dangerous expedition that could damage your health."

Humphrey seemed to shrink into his cardigan. He twisted a loose button nervously, but replied with some bravado, "It wasn't a heart attack. It was a heart *palpitation*. I can assure you that I'm taking the utmost care of myself, and besides, I'm not going to run about the countryside solving any archaeological mysteries. These three young explorers will do it for me."

He waved one hand in their direction. Again, Adam felt a brief pang of fright: they would be alone.

Kim pulled a mock ferocious face and clenched her fists. "I love the idea of adventure. Bring it on. Grrr!"

Justin turned on her. "You're just stupid if you think it's going to be so easy. This isn't some kind of picnic. We almost died in Egypt when we were alone in the desert. Do you think we want to get involved again in something so dangerous without any help? Plus, we have to look after *you*."

Kim stared at him, stunned. "Don't call me stupid."

Justin scowled. "Well, you are."

Kim's lips trembled and her eyes filled. She pressed her lips together and blinked furiously to hold back tears.

Adam couldn't keep quiet. "Justin, don't be like that. We were fine in Egypt. We won't be alone."

"You just heard him." Justin pointed at Humphrey. Then he jumped up and headed to the window where he began stroking Bismarck. Adam was surprised. Justin never showed fear or weakness, except for once in Egypt when they were crossing the desert with their kidnappers.

"Justin," Humphrey said softly, "of course you won't be alone. I meant that I won't be able to do any running around, but I'll guide and advise you three each step of the way. I have to hold the fort here and receive new information from Ebrahim. Why don't you sit down and we can discuss things further."

Amelia picked up the tray. "And why don't I fill up these plates? Is anyone still hungry?"

"I wouldn't mind more cocoa," Kim said. "And maybe some of that yummy chocolate cake."

Amelia nodded and left the room.

Justin came over to Kim. "Sorry. I think I'm just tired, probably jet-lagged. I didn't mean it. You're not stupid."

"That's okay," she said. "I could never have gone through what you and Adam experienced. It sounds so exciting, but I bet it was terrifying."

Justin perked up; he loved praise. "Actually, there were a few really scary moments."

"When we have some time," Kim said, "I'd love to hear more about the desert and the Scarab King's tomb."

Justin put on a brave smile. "When I think about it, this'll probably be easy stuff after what Adam and I survived." He looked at Humphrey. "So what's next?"

Before Humphrey could speak, the shop bell tinkled.

"Bother," Humphrey said. "Just when we're about to get to the interesting part. Excuse me a minute."

He went through to the front shop as Amelia returned with a laden tray.

"Have you worked for Humphrey a long time?" Justin asked, stuffing cake into his mouth. "Hey, this is so good. I wish my mom could bake like this."

22

Sounding muffled as he tried to speak through a mouthful of chocolate cake, he continued, "She just gets cake from the supermarket. Doesn't taste half as nice."

"I've been with Humphrey for quite a few years," Amelia said. "I suppose that's why I boss him around so much."

"She has to bully him a bit," Ink cut in, with a grin in Amelia's direction. "I don't know what Dad would do without Amelia. He really doesn't take enough care of himself. He gets so caught up in his old books and manuscripts that sometimes he even forgets to eat."

Justin stared at Ink, his mouth sagging open. A crumb fell out. "How could anyone *forget* to eat?"

Ink laughed. "He just does."

Kim shushed them. "Hush! Can you hear something?"

Adam wrinkled his nose in disgust. "No, but I can smell something."

They all sniffed and pulled faces. There was a faint but horrible stink. It was intermittent; sometimes Adam could pick up the scent and then it seemed he had just imagined it.

Justin asked, "What does it remind you of?"

"Rotten mushrooms?" Kim mused.

Amelia nodded. "Some kind of mold."

"Wet earth?" said Ink.

"A graveyard?" Adam and Justin chorused.

With one accord, they all tiptoed to the door and tried to get a peek at the visitor who had entered the shop … because that was where the smell was coming from.

Adam couldn't see the person properly because he, or it might have been a she, was enveloped in a long, flowing garment, like a cloak with a hood. The person must have been sweating under the thick fabric in such warm weather. Then he heard Humphrey's voice.

"What kind of document are you looking for?"

Humphrey sounded abrupt, even rude, which was odd because Humphrey seemed like the kind of person who would gladly help anyone interested in an old book or manuscript.

"Where did you say you were from?" Humphrey asked suspiciously.

Then the person spoke. It was the most spine-chilling, frightening sound, conjuring up memories of nightmares and horrifying sensations of terror and dread.

"I am a member of the Ancient Association of Antiquarian Book Collectors," the voice hissed.

The words seemed to slither out of the person's mouth. Adam's skin crawled, as if he had touched something disgusting.

"Never heard of it." Humphrey's voice was gruff. "And you're looking for ancient Egyptian texts?"

"Or mediaeval manuscripts specifically discussing ancient Egyptian texts," the voice whispered, each syllable singing in hideous sibilance.

"Nothing," Humphrey snapped. "I've had nothing like that for a long time and I'm not expecting anything similar in the near future."

"Such a pity," the voice oozed. "But if you do receive any such material, will you keep it aside for me? I will return soon."

"I can't promise." Humphrey's reply was cautious, as if he were afraid of something.

Then came a laugh; a low, hollow sound, like the faint clang of a church bell. Adam peered around the doorjamb a few inches more, just in time to glimpse a pallid face so skeletally thin that it seemed fleshless, like skin stretched over bare bone. It was a man. He didn't seem human; he seemed more like a creature from some frightening old fairytale. A lean white hand saluted Humphrey, showing long bony fingers with blackened nails. Under the shadow of the hood, a pair of dark eyes flamed briefly with a demonic light. Then the heavy eyelids closed for a few seconds. When they opened again, the man glanced in Adam's direction. Adam ducked behind the doorjamb, feeling strangely breathless, as if that fleeting look had sucked the air from his lungs.

The shop bell tinkled as the cloaked man swished out into the street. Adam ran to the shop's front door with Kim and Justin. Ink and Amelia followed close behind. They looked outside. There was no cloaked man in sight. Just a few casually dressed tourists strolling along and chatting to one another.

"Where'd he go?" Justin asked. The man seemed to have disappeared into thin air.

"Dad!" Fright tinged Ink's voice. He caught Humphrey just before the old man toppled over, and then lowered him into a chair. "What happened? Are you all right?"

Humphrey waved a feeble hand. "Feeling a bit dizzy, that's all. Don't make a fuss." His face was pale, with beads of sweat pearling on his forehead.

"I'm going to make you a strong cup of tea," said Amelia, as she dashed to the kitchen.

"Dad," Ink urged, "let me help you to the sofa. I think you'd better lie down. Maybe you should take your medicine."

Humphrey nodded and allowed Ink to half-carry back him to the living room. Once Humphrey was comfortable and had swallowed a few mouthfuls of hot, sweet tea, he was able to speak. Color returned to his face as he tried to sit up.

"I feel better now," he whispered.

Ink eased Humphrey gently back against the cushions. "You should rest. I can take the kids out to see some of the sights while you sleep."

Amelia gave a stern nod, but Humphrey was adamant. "No, no," he said, heaving himself upright. "Just put a few cushions behind my back … there … that's better."

He smiled and the anxious group could see Humphrey was reviving.

"I need to tell the children as much as possible, but—" he caught sight of Ink and Amelia's expressions "—I won't overdo it."

"Who was that stinky guy?" Justin asked, screwing his face up in disgust.

"Someone or something rather strange," Humphrey muttered. "I shouldn't say this, but almost otherworldly, if you know what I mean. I felt a kind of hypnotic sensation creeping over me while I was speaking to him, as if I was in the grip of some kind of …" He gave an awkward laugh, as if a little embarrassed to say the word. "Spell!"

Justin and Kim nodded in understanding. Adam could see they had both felt a strange and unpleasant sensation. Only Ink and Amelia seemed unaffected by the man's presence in the shop, apart from the initial moldy smell. Amelia then excused herself, saying she had letters to type in the back office and would see everyone later.

Humphrey waited until Amelia left the room. "Well, Justin asked what was next."

They all stared at Humphrey, waiting for him to continue, but he did not say any more.

"So what about the second stone?" Adam prompted him. "Ebrahim mentioned a recent find. Has something been discovered?"

25

He watched Humphrey. Justin, Ink, and Kim leaned forward in anticipation.

Humphrey eased the words out with care. "It ... er ... might be embedded in a sword."

Justin raised his eyebrows. "A sword? What kind of sword?"

A tremor of excitement rippled through Adam's body. His arms went all goosebumps and the answer popped into his head before Humphrey spoke.

"The sword of the greatest king of myth and legend," Adam blurted out. "I'm right, aren't I?"

Justin and Kim stared at Adam.

Ink frowned. "You can't mean—" he stammered in disbelief.

"I can and I do," Adam said, glancing at Humphrey for confirmation.

Humphrey gave a slow nod, with a reluctant half-smile on his face.

"The sword of Arthur," Adam said. "And he's not just a legend. My history teacher said Arthur could have been a real king."

Humphrey nodded again. "Yes, there's more than enough evidence to pinpoint the existence of a significant historical military leader who could have been Arthur."

"King Arthur?" Kim said. "I didn't know he was a real person."

Justin looked taken aback. "*The* King Arthur, the once and future king?"

Adam gave his cousin a smug grin. "You know as well as I do that there's only one King Arthur."

Ink raised his voice above the others. "Dad, is this possible?"

"Yes, my boy," the old man replied tiredly. "I know what you're thinking. If it's true that Arthur's sword has been found, then this is indeed an event of mixed fortunes."

Adam had a strong sense of danger. It was all very well to say that Excalibur might have been found, but such a discovery could have serious consequences.

"I see what you mean," Ink said. "Some maniac could steal it for his own purposes."

"These fanciful conjectures cannot leak out to the press," Humphrey said sadly, "even if it's not Excalibur. We have Dr. Khalid to contend with, and we could have many crackpot groups eager to use what they *think* is Arthur's sword to achieve their own crazy ends."

His face brightened. "But first we have to determine if indeed the find is from Arthur's era, and since all we have is news of the find, no details yet, the press won't be reporting on it for a while. Only a few people know of the discovery."

"What do *you* know about it?" Justin asked.

"In a recently drained bog somewhere in Wales, a group of archaeologists has discovered what appear to be the remains of the war regalia of a military leader, possibly dating from between the fifth and sixth centuries."

Adam was disappointed that James had not made the discovery. Then he realized that although James had found the clues to locating the first Stone of Power, the sacred scarab, it might not be possible for him to find all the stones.

"So what exactly is there?" Adam asked.

Humphrey wagged a finger at Adam. "You must know by now that in any new dig, there is never *exactly* anything. The entire area must be fully investigated before anyone can announce details to the academic world. Experts must examine and date the remains as accurately as possible. One has to be sure of the facts before making sweeping statements that could change the face of known history."

"But do we have to go all the way to Wales to see this stuff?" Kim asked. "I thought Adam and Justin had come here to look for the Scroll of the Ancients."

"Thank you for keeping us on track, Kim." Humphrey smiled at her. "As you heard from Ebrahim's letter, we can't be diverted. We must focus on the purpose of the trip. So, the best thing to do is simply look at the remains, keeping their appearance in mind while you hunt for the scroll."

Justin looked confused. "Everyone keeps telling us that's what we're here for, but no one's bothered mentioning where to start looking."

Humphrey seemed surprised by his remark. "In Scotland, of course. Somewhere in Strathairn Castle. That's the last place Bedwyr, James' ancestor, would have been able to hide anything before he died. The reason you didn't go there first is that James isn't home yet and we had news of this find. Ebrahim and James wanted you to see the relics before you continued with the scroll search, anyway, so it has all worked out rather nicely."

Now it was Adam's turn to be puzzled. "You say Strathairn Castle is the place we should look for the scroll?"

Humphrey nodded.

"But what about the monastery where Bedwyr spent most of his time? Isn't it more likely he hid the scroll there?"

Humphrey shook his head. "Highly unlikely, Adam, and remember he lived roughly seven hundred years ago. Bedwyr's monastery no longer exists. Any remaining ruins would have been fully excavated by now. Another thing, Bedwyr suspected his life was in danger. That's possibly why he didn't make a huge announcement about the scroll to his superiors, even though doing so would've allowed him to go down in history as the monk who *made* history."

"So what happened to the monastery?" Justin asked. "Why is it no longer there?"

Humphrey thought for a minute. "A number of reasons. By the early fourteenth century, there were as many as five hundred different religious houses in Britain. Then came the effects of the Black Death."

"That's the plague, isn't it?" Adam interrupted. "With horrible boils and stuff."

"Yes, in 1348 the plague dealt the monasteries a serious blow, depleting the population of monks and nuns. Most of the monasteries never fully recovered. King Henry VIII also had a hand in their demise. When he broke with the Roman Catholic Church in the 1530s, his first targets were the rich monastic houses. The big cathedrals and abbeys survived because they could bargain with the king. However, Henry stripped the smaller churches of any wealth, such as money, land, and their gold and silver. He had most of them demolished. The way people viewed religion also changed as more people became educated and could read and make their own decisions. As a result of all of this together, the number of monasteries gradually decreased."

Kim raised a hand. "Hello there. Anyone listening?"

Four heads turned in surprise.

"Thank you. Now, do we have to go to Wales to see these remains?"

Humphrey laughed. "Sorry, Kim. You see how easy it is to get sidetracked when it comes to ancient history. No, you don't have to go anywhere. The remains are already here in Oxford, at the Ashmolean Museum. They arrived yesterday."

"Is that normal?" Justin asked. "I mean moving precious stuff around."

"No, it's not usual procedure," Humphrey replied. "But it just so happens the world's leading authority on fifth and sixth century British history, Archibald Curran—also known when we were students as Currant Bun because of his

28

impressive appetite—lives here in Oxford. He's been asked to examine the remains first and give his expert opinion. Archie used to be the Keeper of Anglo-Saxon and Mediaeval Antiquities at the Ashmolean Museum."

"When can we see the stuff?" Adam asked.

"Not right away, of course," Humphrey said, "and generally it would be months before the public could see the relics, but James and Ebrahim asked me to pull a few strings. Archie's going to look at the relics first with the museum authorities. After that, I'll arrange a private visit so he can explain the historical details to you."

"Why didn't he just go to Wales to examine the relics?" Adam asked.

Humphrey winked at him. "Since he hates traveling, utterly loathes it, the object comes here to him whenever he has to give his opinion. The official reason he doesn't travel is poor health, but that's not strictly true."

"When do we meet him?" Kim asked.

"Later today. He's coming to tea. You can trust him—he's one of us—but don't let on too much. The less people know about why you children are here, the better. He thinks you're here for an educational holiday. He's an expert on Roman Britain so you can ask him any questions you like. He loves talking about Arthur so we probably won't be able to get him to shut up."

Ink caught Adam's eye and winked. "Dad, why don't the kids clean up and change. Then, if they don't want a … er … nap, we can explore Old Town."

Humphrey wasn't fooled. "I think they're a bit too old for afternoon naps. What you mean is that *I* should have a nap."

Ink reddened. "I'm only thinking of you."

Justin interrupted. "That's a brilliant idea. We all need a shower and clean clothes, and we'd love to explore Oxford."

Kim and Adam nodded eagerly.

Humphrey said, "You'll actually be staying with my widowed sister Pandora Brocklehurst. Ink will take you there later. So have your shower, but don't unpack too much. Perhaps Kim should go first."

"Come on," said Ink, leading the way. "The bathroom's upstairs."

Justin made exaggerated sniffing noises in Kim's direction until Adam punched him on the arm to make him stop. Kim stalked out of the room ahead of the boys, ignoring Justin.

Once Ink had shown the kids the way upstairs to the bathroom and the spare bedroom where they could put their luggage, he came back down to sit with Humphrey.

"I know what's on your mind," Humphrey said, "and, yes, I'm going to ask you to accompany the children to Scotland."

"That's okay, Dad. I was going to suggest it anyway." Ink's face was solemn. "But this isn't just about rummaging in Strathairn Castle for some old scroll. There's something special about Adam. I can feel it." He paused. "It's going to be dangerous, isn't it?"

Humphrey patted his shoulder. "Yes, and that's why I have to tell you everything … well, almost everything … so you're prepared for the worst. They're going to need you."

the Stone in the Sword

Soon they were ready in clean jeans and T-shirts. Humphrey called up the stairs, advising them to take jackets in case it rained. Kim's clothes were all brand new. Even her sneakers looked as if they hadn't been worn much.

Adam stroked the sleeve of Kim's denim jacket. "Nice. Where did you get this?"

"Aunt Isabel bought it for me," Kim replied, zipping the jacket up halfway. "I'm so lucky. You know she doesn't believe in designer labels for kids."

Adam nodded because that was true.

Kim continued. "But when she said I needed new stuff—wow, she bought me such fantastic things. I don't feel embarrassed now when my school has a civvies day. The kids used to say, 'Kim, you're so boring. You've only got one smart outfit.'"

Kim straightened her collar. "Now they say nothing. But I know they're jealous."

Adam and Justin glanced sideways at each other. It was clear Kim had come from a poor family. Although neither of their parents splashed out on ridiculously expensive things for them, the boys always had decent gear. Never having experienced anything like poverty or hardship, they found it difficult to relate to someone who had.

"How do you know they're jealous?" Justin asked.

Kim seemed uncomfortable; she hesitated before answering. "Some of the kids call me a ... a coconut."

Justin frowned. "That's so weird. Why a coconut?"

31

Kim shrugged. "I live with a white person now so they think I live a rich life. They say I'm black on the outside and white on the inside like a coconut."

"Are these kids ... er ...?" Justin hesitated.

Kim gave a wry smile. "You mean are the bullies black or white?"

Justin nodded.

"They're black like me," Kim said quietly. "Many of them also live in the townships."

Adam was shocked. "But how can ...?" He stopped speaking.

"You mean how can black kids act so jealous when they should be happy for me?"

"Yeah. I don't understand."

Kim sat on the bed. She smoothed out a wrinkle in the quilt. "I don't either." Her head drooped. "It's been so difficult for me to deal with their attitude that I almost gave up."

"Why didn't you?" Justin asked.

Kim lifted her head and looked straight at him. "Because living with Aunt Isabel is my only chance. It's up to me to work hard and get excellent marks to make a better life for myself. My mom didn't even get to high school so she can't help me with schoolwork and studying. She wants me to be more than a domestic worker cleaning people's houses. If I keep failing, or if I give up, that's all I'll ever be."

"I also get bad marks sometimes," Adam said cheerfully. "You know, tests don't always go well."

"So what's a bad mark for you?"

"Um ... I got only eighty-five percent in the first term for history."

Kim burst out laughing. "What? You call that bad. I call that stupendous."

Adam shrugged. "I don't want to brag, but I usually—"

Justin cut in. "What Adam means is he's brilliant at history and usually gets about ninety-five percent or sometimes even higher."

"I'd give anything for ninety-five percent," said Kim, with an awed expression.

"Then get in the zone," Justin said. "It's up to you. You can do it. Aunt Isabel will help you."

"I know she will. She's very encouraging." Kim gestured at her clothes. "She's given me so much already."

"Well, you look cool." Adam grinned. "Not like a coconut. You shouldn't keep quiet. Call them something back." He thought for a moment and then named a popular candy bar. "I know. Choc Chunks."

Kim was taken aback. "Choc Chunks?"

"Yeah, they're dark on the outside and thick on the inside for saying horrible things to you."

Kim burst into peals of laughter. Adam was pleased he'd managed to cheer her up.

Then Kim's smile faded. She fiddled with the jacket zipper. "But that's not really the answer, is it? I'll have to find a way of dealing with them. Have you ever been bullied?"

"Yeah," Adam said. "It was terrible before we went to Egypt. Wilfred Smythe is the class bully back home and he's huge—the size of a house. He used to make my life so miserable, calling me a freckled rat and rubbing my face in the dirt."

Kim's mouth fell open. "So what did you do?"

Adam glanced at Justin and they both laughed.

"Nothing. It was the weirdest thing. When we got back to school, I had to give a presentation to my history class about the trip to Egypt. After everyone heard the story of our adventure and saw our medals from the Egyptian government, Wilfred decided I was someone special—not a little rat. For some reason he respects me. Now he beats up the kids who give me a hard time."

Still laughing, they went downstairs and met up with Ink at the front door. Ink suggested that they walk into the center of Oxford.

"It has some great things to look at. I don't know how much you kids like history."

"This whole quest is a kind of a history mystery," Adam said, "so it's just as well we like it."

Justin agreed.

Kim looked uncertain. "I haven't done anything like this before, but I want to see as much as possible."

"We're in for lots of digging into old places and things if we're going to find the Scroll of the Ancients," Justin told her, "so this is good training for you."

As the group strolled down St. Giles Road toward the Old Town area, Kim rather cheekily asked Ink to tell them about himself.

33

"There's not much to tell," he said. "I've lived here in Oxford all my life and I'm reading Classics this year so I can follow in Humphrey's footsteps. I know he'd like me to take over the business, even though he keeps dropping hints about a career in London. He just wants me to be successful so I guess he thinks London has more opportunities."

"Do you want to go to London?" Adam asked.

Ink shook his head. "I love Oxford. It's my home. I can't imagine living anywhere else. London's okay for visits, but it's too big for me."

"What happened to your mother?" Kim asked. "Did she die when you were young?"

"Actually, I don't know my real parents," Ink replied. "Humphrey's not my real dad. I'm adopted."

He laughed at their stunned expressions. "Didn't you wonder why his last name is Biddle and mine is Blott?"

"Well, I did think it was strange," Justin said, "but it seemed rude to ask."

"I was found in the park—in a basket, actually—so you could say I'm a foundling."

"That's terrible," Kim whispered.

"Gosh," Adam said. "Like in a movie? What happened to your real parents? Do you know who they were?"

Justin frowned. "I think it's dangerous to leave a baby alone in a park. How did Humphrey find you?"

"It's not that terrible." Ink shrugged as if it were no big deal. "You see, my mother wrote a note and put it in the basket with me. She was careful to leave me next to the bench where Humphrey sat most Sundays to feed the pigeons. He soon noticed me when I started screeching my head off. That's the way he always tells it. I think she'd been watching Humphrey, figured out he was alone in life, and decided he was the best person to raise me."

"What did the note say?" Kim asked, fascinated.

"It was short and quite clear, typewritten so no chance of tracing the handwriting. It said that my name is Benjamin Blott. My father Bartholomew was a respected Classics scholar who was killed in an unfortunate accident while doing research abroad. I guess my mother gave me up because she couldn't keep me. Anyway, she also wrote that Humphrey had a kind face and hoped I would bring him happiness, and that he could be as much of a father to me as if he'd been my natural father."

"Did your real father have any family?" Kim asked. "Maybe you could try to trace them and find out where you come from. Do you have your birth certificate?"

Ink shook his head. "Apparently my father was an orphan. My only remaining connection would be my mother, and I have no way of discovering who she is or was, because she didn't include a birth certificate. She might even be dead for all I know. I haven't done any searching for my birth parents. I guess I might eventually. But right now, it's not that important. Humphrey registered me in the name my mother put in her note. Child's name—Benjamin Blott; father—Bartholomew Blott; mother—unknown."

"What an incredible story," Justin said.

"I can't imagine what it would be like *not* to have parents," Adam said slowly, "even though mine are quite strict. Were you angry with your mother for abandoning you?"

"But she didn't abandon me," Ink said cheerfully. "She could've dumped me in an orphanage. Instead, she left me with the best father a boy could ever want. Humphrey had no children of his own so he adopted me and brought me up as his son. I think of him as my dad. I only hope my poor mother managed to make some kind of life for herself because she certainly gave me the best chance in the world."

They walked in silence for a few minutes.

Then Kim piped up, "Do you have a girlfriend?"

"Kim!" Justin bugged his eyes at her. "That's enough. Stop asking so many personal questions."

Kim tossed her head. "Ink can ask me anything back. I have no secrets."

Ink blushed beet red. "No, well, I haven't exactly got a girlfriend, but ..." He glanced at them, seeming embarrassed to say more.

"Go on," Adam prompted.

"There is someone special. She just moved here. I like her a lot," Ink muttered, "but ..."

"But what?" Kim asked. "Does she know you like her?"

"That's the problem," Ink sighed, his expression dejected. "I don't think she knows I even exist. Miranda." He breathed her name with reverence. "Her name is Miranda Swann."

Kim smiled encouragingly at Ink. "That's a beautiful name."

"Does she live nearby?" Justin asked.

Ink stopped walking and pointed across the road. "You see the flower shop over there?"

Three heads swiveled. Adam saw a shop sign with the words *Flower Power*.

"That's where she works," Ink said.

"Here's the perfect excuse for you to introduce yourself to her," Kim said. "Why don't you go in and get a bunch of flowers for Amelia and just chat with Miranda."

Ink looked hopeful for a moment. Then his face fell. "But what about taking you kids sightseeing?"

"We'll keep walking and you can catch up with us," Adam suggested. He had an idea Miranda was one of the reasons Ink didn't want to leave Oxford.

Ink looked doubtful, but when three faces smiled persuasively at him, he grinned back. "Okay."

"Just be yourself," Kim advised him. "Girls prefer it."

"See you later!" Adam ran off before Ink could change his mind.

The others raced after him. They slowed down once they were far enough away from the flower shop and then stopped to catch their breath. Adam turned a corner somewhere and they found themselves standing in front of the Ashmolean Museum. The elaborate façade and soaring columns flanking the entrance gave the building an impressive, stately appearance. It looked as grand as the Egyptian Museum in Cairo.

"Hey," Adam said. "Here's where the relics are kept. Do you think we could see them?"

"Not a chance," Justin replied in a dampening tone. "You heard Humphrey. No one's allowed to see anything before Archibald Curran does. Anyway, if the museum thinks the regalia belonged to King Arthur, I bet there'll be a lot of security. We're wasting our time even trying."

"Why don't we just go in anyway now that we're here," Kim suggested. "There could be some information on a notice board mentioning a new find."

Adam remembered the incredible discovery under the Egyptian Museum, when they had stumbled upon the secret room in the basement and found Dr. Khalid's men packing stolen artifacts into boxes.

36

Then Justin winked at Adam. He had a sly grin, as if he were also remembering the basement cache. "Why not?"

Adam grinned back. "I guess it can't hurt to try to see the stuff. What about Ink? Won't he look for us? He doesn't know where we are."

Kim looked smug. "I bet you that when we go back to the flower shop, he'll still be there talking to Miranda."

"How can you be so sure?"

Kim turned up her nose with a superior-sounding sniff. "Because I'm a girl and I know what girls are like." She trotted confidently up the steps to the museum entrance.

Justin shrugged. "I guess she knows what she's talking about." Following Kim, he said, "Let's see what we can find out in here."

Adam ran up the steps to join them. A wave of exhilaration rose in his chest. What would the regalia look like? Would he feel any sensations if the second stone were there? The sacred scarab had tingled and burned in his hands when he touched it. Although he hadn't known it at the time, the sensations were a clear sign that the scarab was the first Stone of Power.

They reached the entrance together. A stern-faced security guard stepped forward as they pushed open the huge door.

"Sorry, kids. Museum's closed."

Kim pointed to the sign displaying opening and closing times. "It says here the museum doesn't shut until five."

"Yes, missy," he replied. "But there's a special function this evening. The museum has to be closed for a few hours because they'll be preparing for it."

"Is it to do with an exhibition?" Adam asked. From Justin's expression, he had the same thought: the museum was closing early because someone would be examining the regalia.

The guard's face went blank. "I can't say, but sorry, no visiting today."

Kim's eyes filled with tears. She gave a loud sniff.

"What's the matter, little girl?" asked the man.

"No, it doesn't matter," she whispered with a breaking sob in her voice.

The guard looked disturbed. "Now then, there's no need to cry." He patted her shoulder awkwardly. "Is there something special you wanted to see?"

Kim nodded slowly. Adam and Justin exchanged disbelieving glances. Kim had gone from cheerful and spunky to sad and tearful in a matter of seconds.

Amazingly, it was having the right effect on the guard. He was no longer being bossy. In fact, he was being downright sympathetic.

Kim fumbled in her jacket pocket and pulled out a folded piece of paper. "Here," she whimpered. "We have to look at this for a school project."

She gave it to the guard. "It's famous and I have to write a report on it for term marks."

The guard unfolded the paper and glanced at it. "The Alfred Jewel? Yes, it's famous, very famous indeed. It's from the ninth century. But you can come back tomorrow and see it, dearie."

Adam nudged Justin. There was definitely something important going on, but the museum didn't want any publicity.

Kim sniffed. "No, I can't come back tomorrow."

"Why's that?"

"B-because we're only on holiday here. We're leaving tomorrow to go thousands of miles all the way back home to Africa and it'll be too late," she wailed.

All the way back home to Africa! Adam nearly burst out laughing. Surely, the guard wouldn't believe her. Adam winked at Justin, who was also enjoying the joke. To Adam's surprise, the guard frowned and pursed his lips while he thought.

"All right. You and your mates nip upstairs and have a quick look. But be back down here in ten minutes, is that clear?"

They flashed him winning smiles before they darted into the museum.

"It's in the 'England 400—1600' gallery on the second floor," the guard called after them. "Head up the stairs. Follow the signs and hurry up."

As they followed his directions, Justin said, "Africa? What a joke. I didn't think he'd believe you."

Kim looked pleased. "Why not? I am African and we do have to go back home. Just not tomorrow."

"Uh, yeah … that's right," Justin said.

"Why are we looking at the Alfred Jewel?" Adam demanded. "We have to find where they've stored the Arthur regalia. And how do you know about the Alfred Jewel anyway?"

The Alfred Jewel, a world-famous Anglo-Saxon artifact, the most precious relic of its age, dated from the ninth century AD. Adam was extremely proud of his good general knowledge, especially in history. Although he liked Kim, he didn't enjoy being shown up by a girl.

Kim stopped and stamped one foot impatiently.

"The guard only let us in because he felt sorry for me when I said we needed to see something special. What better excuse is there than the most famous thing the museum has?"

Adam couldn't argue with Kim's logic.

"I only know about the Alfred Jewel," Kim continued, "because Aunt Isabel printed something off the Internet about it when she was helping me with a history project. I suddenly remembered she said it was stored at this museum. Believe it or not, it was a complete accident I even had that piece of paper in my pocket."

She glared at Adam. "Satisfied now? I mean, you both did *want* get into the museum, right?"

"Yes, of course," said Justin.

"And it's not likely these relics would be kept in a gallery about Ancient Greece or Rome or Egypt?"

"Uh, no, I guess it would have something to do with Britain," Adam admitted.

"Come on then," she said, "we're wasting time. We only have ten minutes." Kim darted off to the gallery with the cousins trailing behind her.

"She sort of takes over, doesn't she?" Justin muttered.

"But she has a point," Adam replied.

So far, Kim wasn't the drag they had thought she would be. In fact, she had good ideas and seemed to be working out situations before he and Justin even had a chance to think. It didn't feel the same as when they had done things together in Egypt. Adam still wasn't sure how he felt about sharing this adventure with someone else. He glanced at Justin, but couldn't read his cousin's expression.

Kim disappeared through a doorway so they hurried to catch up. When they did, Kim was looking around the gallery, frowning.

"What's up?" Justin asked. "Run out of clever ideas already?"

Kim ignored his sarcastic tone. "We haven't much time. Where do you think the museum would keep new relics? I mean stuff that still has to be restored."

"Not in a public gallery like this," Adam said, glancing about at the various display cases. "It'll be in a separate room, probably locked away."

"Let's split up and look," Justin suggested.

39

They scattered in different directions, scouring the gallery until Adam found a closed door with a sign that read *No Entry*. The door was locked, but someone had carelessly left in the key. What a stroke of luck if this was the right place.

"Hey," he called softly to the others.

They stood in front of the door, not daring to touch the key.

Justin prodded Adam. "Go on, open it."

They would get into serious trouble if they were caught tampering with and maybe even contaminating a recent archaeological discovery. But they were here now. Adam turned the key and they crept into the darkened room.

Adam reached for the light switch, but Justin caught his hand.

"No, don't put on the light. That guard may come looking for us. Leave the door open so the lights from the gallery shine in."

Justin was right. Light streamed in from the main gallery, illuminating the pile of objects on a large brown carpet square in the center of the room. The items were neatly sorted into smaller groups. Around the edges of the carpet were rope cordons with *Do Not Touch Museum Property* signs hanging from them.

Adam stared at the relics. Although a coating of hardened mud obscured the outlines of most of the smaller pieces, he easily picked out the main items. There was a tarnished shield, a broken knife, a reinforced leather breastplate, a helmet with a battered crest, a heap of crumbling leather thongs that might have been reins, a spear, something that could have been an old cauldron, a damaged battle horn—and then he saw it. The long distinctive shape could only be a sword. Adam went to where the sword lay near the carpet edge and knelt to examine it. Kim and Justin followed, kneeling next to him.

"What do you think?" Justin whispered.

Adam didn't answer right away. To be honest, he felt disappointed because it wasn't anything like he'd expected.

"I'm not sure," he said, looking more closely at the sword.

The hilt was crusted with dirt, but he could make out a faint design. It looked like the heads of two beasts, possibly dragons, facing inward on the crossguard of the hilt, with a round stone or gem set between the beasts' mouths. The sword was so filthy that it was impossible to see any details clearly. The sacred scarab had also been dirty and insignificant at first. When the peddler slipped the ancient scarab into Adam's pocket in Egypt, the artifact looked like "a piece of old rubbish," as Justin had said. Only later, when Adam was Dr. Khalid's prisoner in the tomb of the Scarab King, the dirt disappeared: the sacred scarab transformed into an amazing artifact made of gold and gems. If this was Arthur's sword and the other items were his war regalia, perhaps the same thing would happen as with the scarab. Adam slipped one hand into his pocket to feel for the replica. A shock jolted him. He had left it behind at Humphrey's cottage when he changed his clothes! He lost his breath for a moment, stunned he had forgotten something so precious.

Kim touched his shoulder. "What's the matter?"

Adam felt the blood draining from his face.

"You're so pale," she said. "Do you feel sick?"

"My scarab's not here. I must have left it at the cottage."

"So what?" Justin said impatiently. "It's only a replica. No one's after it like they were the real one. Concentrate on this stuff."

Clang! Had someone kicked over something downstairs?

Three heads snapped round and three pairs of eyes stared fearfully at the open doorway.

Bang! Someone slammed a door shut somewhere.

"Hurry." Justin poked Adam in the ribs. "I think the guard is closing up. We don't have much time."

"I'm trying. Give me a chance." Adam tried to focus his thoughts, but his head swam and he felt a little dizzy. Out of the corner of one eye, he saw a dark shadow hover briefly in the doorway. Were the lights in the gallery flickering or was it just his imagination? There was a slight shuffling noise outside the room and then the whiff of a faint but horrible smell. The others hadn't seemed to notice anything. Maybe the mud simply smelled moldy and he had imagined the rest.

"Why don't you hold the sword to feel if you have any ... um ... sensations?" Justin hissed. "Just touch it."

"Why should he feel anything?" Kim asked, her eyes widening.

When Justin hesitated, Adam knew he was trying to avoid telling Kim too much about their strange experiences with the powers of the sacred scarab.

"Because," Justin finally said, glancing at his cousin, "Adam's pretty sensitive to ... uh ... vibrations and things. So he might feel if there's something special about the sword."

His excuse sounded rather lame. Kim pulled a face and rolled her eyes doubtfully. Adam reached under the rope cordons and grasped the hilt of the sword.

41

It felt rough and gritty from the hardened mud. He raised the sword off the carpet a few inches; it was heavy. He imagined whirling it around his head, thrusting and stabbing at the barbarian hordes as they rushed at him. He wondered about Arthur, more a famous legend than a solid figure up until now. *Had* he been a real king? Was this really his sword?

"Feel anything?" Justin murmured encouragingly.

Adam shook his head. "Nothing. It just feels cold and hard. How did the warriors actually fight with these swords? This weighs a ton."

Justin's next words sounded despondent. "I was hoping you'd get some kind of sensation if it was the real thing. Looks like it isn't." He stood up.

Adam laid the weapon gently back on the carpet and released the hilt. He gazed at the stone between the beasts' heads, waiting for a gleam, a shimmer, anything to give him hope that this was the second Stone of Power. But the stone remained dull and lifeless. It was just an ordinary archaeological find, probably exciting for the experts who would soon be examining it, but of no use to Ebrahim and the people dedicated to locating and protecting the Seven Stones of Power.

He slid his finger along the blade. Some of the dirt rubbed off, revealing a bluish gleam of metal. He was amazed the sword hadn't rusted away after hundreds of years in a bog. He could make out a portion of detailed embossing, or perhaps words engraved on the blade. The letters looked strange. If they were words, he didn't recognize them.

Kim checked her watch. "Hey, guys. Ten minutes have passed. We'd better get out of here before that security guard locks us in."

She and Adam scrambled to their feet and the trio exited the room. Adam hesitated before closing the door behind them.

"We'd better turn the key," Justin said. "Leave everything exactly as it was. If someone forgot the key in the lock, it's their problem, not ours."

Something made Adam rub his sleeve over the door handle and the key.

Justin sniggered. "I think you've been taking lessons from your dad about breaking-in techniques." He nudged Kim. "My uncle's a cop and Adam comes up with all kinds of clever ways to throw the baddies off our track."

Adam stared at him, unsmiling. "But my ideas work."

Justin looked shamefaced. "Yes, they do. Sorry. I was just kidding. Let's go."

They ran down the stairs and peered into the empty foyer. There was no sign of the guard and the main door stood ajar.

Kim was indignant. "You'd think he'd be here to lock up, after all the fuss he made."

"Just be glad there's no one here," Adam muttered, suddenly uneasy about the situation.

Something nagged at the back of his mind as if a dark shadow was stalking him. He gave a mental shake. It was his imagination, of course. Probably from being around all of these old things.

NEW DEVELOPMENTS

The weather had changed while they were in the museum. Slate-gray storm clouds darkened the sky and it began to rain hard. As large pelting drops chilled their faces and slid down their necks, they turned up their jacket collars and dashed back in the direction of the flower shop.

Kim suddenly stopped. "What's that noise?"

Justin and Adam stopped as well. A faint scrabbling noise came from an alley where garbage lay in heaps.

Adam pointed to a trashcan. "Rats."

Kim shook her head. "No, it was a squeaking noise."

"Rats squeak," said Justin with exaggerated patience. "It must be coming from that pile of trash."

"This was more like a puppy or a kitten squeaking," Kim said, walking determinedly up to the trashcan.

Justin and Adam rolled their eyes at each other behind her back, but they followed her. Girls. Once they had some idea in their heads, they didn't give up.

Kim peered behind the trashcan at a small pile of garbage. "There's something here," she cried. "I can see an animal."

"Don't touch it," Justin advised her. "It might have a disease."

Kim ignored him. Crooning softly, she crouched down and pulled away some pieces of soggy newspaper. Underneath the paper lay a small, shivering mound.

"Look, a dog."

"Be careful—" Adam began to say, but he was too late.

Kim scooped up the filthy creature and held it to her, stroking the trembling little body. From under drooping ears, brown eyes shone, and a tiny pink tongue emerged, giving Kim grateful licks on her face. Adam knelt next to her, patting the dog's head. He loved animals as much as Kim evidently did, and he missed Velvet, his German shepherd back home.

Justin wrinkled his nose in disgust. "Very cute, I'm sure, but what are we going to do with a stray? It probably has truck loads of fleas as well."

Kim strode on ahead, clutching the dog, while the boys ran to keep up with her. The cousins exchanged resigned glances, although Adam was sure he wouldn't have left the dog behind either.

They met up with Ink as he emerged from the flower shop, a happy, dazed expression on his face.

"How did it go?" Justin asked.

Ink grinned. A silly love-struck grin. Ink was definitely smitten. "Brilliant! We're going to—" Ink suddenly snapped back to reality. "Hey, is that a dog?"

"Of course it's a dog," Kim announced. "And don't try to make me leave it in the garbage heap."

"I wasn't going to," Ink said, looking mystified by her attitude. He glanced at Justin and Adam. They both shrugged. Ink nodded. *Girls.*

Justin nudged Adam. "I bet Humphrey will say she can't keep it. Anyway, how can we go on this mission with a flipping dog? I like animals too, but it must go to an animal shelter. There's nothing else we can do for it."

To their surprise, Humphrey was as enthusiastic about the dog as Kim. Within twenty minutes, the small black, white, and tan Jack Russell terrier was bathed, fed, and examined for injuries, before it finally curled up on a cushion and fell asleep.

Kim decided to call him Smudge because he had a white face with a black smudge over one eye. "I know I can't keep him, but I couldn't leave him there to die of hunger. How could anyone be so cruel as to dump a poor helpless animal?"

"You did the right thing," Humphrey said in a comforting tone. "Don't worry, Smudge can stay here if no one claims him. Bismarck will just have to get used to him."

Bismarck retreated to the windowsill after a fit of furious hissing and spitting, which Smudge ignored.

Humphrey fixed Adam with a keen gaze. "So, did you see anything interesting on your walk?"

Kim and Justin remained silent, shooting expectant glances at Adam. Adam's face went hot. Should he should tell Humphrey what happened in the museum? He didn't want to lie. It was better to tell the truth to maintain trust between them.

"Actually," he said slowly, "we ended up at the Ashmolean Museum and we did see something."

Adam related the details of the sword to Humphrey. "But it didn't look like anything unusual."

His voice faltered when he saw a frown appear on Humphrey's face, and the way his beetling brows drew together. Ink also looked quite serious, although he didn't comment. Adam wondered how much he and Justin *didn't* know. It always seemed that other people knew more about things than they did; yet he and Justin were the ones directly involved in the quest, facing Dr. Khalid and his evil plans, both in the past and again in the near future.

"Hmmm," Humphrey mumbled. "So you didn't see or … er … feel anything out of the ordinary?"

Adam blinked at the strange question. He had thought Humphrey would scold them for entering the locked room. But Humphrey seemed unconcerned about their actions and more interested in what they had experienced. Adam glanced at Justin, who also looked surprised.

"No. The stuff is dirty so we couldn't see anything definite." Adam didn't mention the noises they had heard, or the smell, or his feelings of uneasiness.

"But what did the sacred scarab look like when you were given it?" Humphrey asked.

Justin cut in eagerly. "I thought it was just a piece of junk at first, but it turned out to be the first Stone of Power."

Humphrey continued to look at Adam. His clear gray eyes signaled understanding, but Adam remained silent.

47

"Humphrey," Kim chirped from the sofa where she was stroking Smudge. "What did the sword of Arthur actually look like? I mean, obviously anything that's been in a bog for a long time is going to look rather mucky. I guess it would be difficult to imagine a fantastic sword while you're looking at something very dirty."

The shop bell tinkled before Humphrey could answer Kim.

Humphrey's face lit up. "Just in time. The expert who'll be able to explain everything to you and answer your questions far better than I can."

He put his fingers to his lips. "Not a word about going to the museum."

Humphrey disappeared into the front shop and reappeared a few minutes later, ushering the strangest looking person into the room.

"Children," Humphrey beamed, "let me introduce Archibald Curran, our resident expert on Anglo-Saxon Britain and foremost authority on the legendary King Arthur."

Archibald Curran bowed and then minced into the room, waving a red silk handkerchief that he occasionally raised to his nose. Clearly, he liked to make a dramatic entrance. He looked like a large version of Humpty Dumpty with an egg-shaped body and incredibly skinny legs encased in tweed trousers. His belly stuck out from under a fancy yellow waistcoat. He also wore a tweed jacket and a floppy blue-and-yellow spotted bowtie. Adam was convinced the patch of gray fluff perched on top of his head was a wig. Archibald Curran wore large square glasses with unusually thick lenses that magnified his pale blue eyes, giving him the appearance of a startled owl. He spoke in a reedy voice, at odds with his solidly plump body.

"Good day to you all," he trilled.

The kids immediately jumped up to greet him and shake hands. Their manners won the visitor's approval since he allowed himself a prim smile and instructed them to call him Archie. He found himself a comfortable place in the largest armchair available. Amelia appeared in the doorway, pushing a tea trolley loaded with small sandwiches, cakes, scones, cookies, and a large teapot.

Archie giggled, rubbing his hands in delight at the sight of the delectable eats as he teasingly scolded Amelia. "My dear Miss Sudsbury, you do indulge me. Oh yes, indeed you do. I shall just have a teensy morsel to keep my strength up."

With that, he dived into the feast and managed to demolish a fair amount of the goodies in a remarkably short space of time.

Adam nudged Justin. "He's worse than you."

Justin scowled. "What do you mean? I'm nowhere near as bad as that."

Kim muttered, "There won't be anything left for us."

"Help yourselves to whatever you want," Amelia advised them, with a meaningful lift of one eyebrow.

"Dig in before it's all gone," said Ink, leaning over to grab a piece of cake.

They spent the next twenty minutes devouring the delicious spread while Archie mumbled between mouthfuls to Humphrey. Humphrey nodded enthusiastically, spraying his guest with crumbs in what seemed an interesting conversation. Adam strained to hear the discussion, but the two old men kept their voices down.

Finally, Archie sat back in the armchair and patted his lips delicately with his handkerchief.

"Now, my dear Humphrey, we all know why I am here and I know why your guests are here, so ask away."

Humphrey folded his hands over his stomach. "Over to you three."

Justin and Kim both stared at Adam to begin the discussion.

Adam said, "We were wondering, sir, if this latest archaeological find is really Arthur's war regalia, and how you'll know if it belonged to him."

Archie pursed his lips as he placed his fingers in a steeple. His bushy eyebrows swished together.

"Well, since no one has examined this recently discovered sword properly yet, or knows what the sword actually looked like in all its glory, I would hesitate to announce to the world that it is indeed Arthur's sword. We need a thorough investigation of the relic and the place where it was found. Then we match it up with archaeological and historical knowledge of the time, as well as any primary written reference."

Adam felt his cheeks burn at Archie's remark about no one having examined the sword yet. Out of the corner of one eye, he noticed that both Justin and Kim also appeared uncomfortable. He hoped that touching the sword hadn't contaminated the relic.

"*Is* there any written reference?" asked Ink. "Surely the whole idea of Arthur and a magical sword is just an old legend?"

Archie tut-tutted his disapproval at Ink's disbelief. Then he got up and scoured Humphrey's bookshelves with a searching gaze. He pounced on a small red-bound book and flipped it open to the page he wanted.

"I do not subscribe to the notion that Arthur's sword was magical in any way, but it certainly was special," he said in a tone clearly reserved for nonbelievers. "Let me read you a description of Arthur's sword. Then you'll see what we hope to uncover beneath the centuries of dirt."

Striking a dramatic pose, he cleared his throat several times. "This is from the *Mabinogion*, a collection of mediaeval Welsh poems."

He read aloud, "*Then they heard Cadwr, Earl of Cornwall, being summoned, and saw him rise with Arthur's sword in his hand, with a design of two serpents on the golden hilt; when the sword was unsheathed what was seen from the mouths of the serpents was like two flames of fire, so dreadful that it was not easy for anyone to look.*"

Archie closed the book and held it against his chest as he studied his audience. His glasses magnified his pale blue eyes to what seemed the size of saucers.

"It is described as having a gold hilt, studded with topaz, diamonds, and jacinth. It is supposed to shine with the strength of thirty flaming torches and blind one's enemies. The words '*one edge to defeat*' are engraved on one side of the blade and the words '*one edge to defend*' on the other."

He gave a smug smile. "So you see, dear young people, why the figure of Arthur has been shrouded in magic and mystery for centuries."

Adam felt a pang of disappointment. The sword in the museum hardly looked like the elaborate description he had just heard. Yes, there was some kind of inscription on the blade, but the book described a sword with snakes on the hilt. Archie had said *serpents*. Adam had seen something like dragons on the hilt.

Then Archie said, "Of course, the serpent and the dragon were intertwined in Celtic mythology, the dragon being in essence a large serpent with legs and wings."

Adam looked up at Archie with mixed feelings. He could now see how the beasts' heads could be dragons' heads. But what about the stone between their mouths? It looked so ordinary that he couldn't imagine anything glorious about it. Certainly, it didn't seem capable of sending out fiery beams.

"It sounds incredible, sir," he said, a note of doubt creeping into his voice, "but weren't the people back then too primitive to make anything like that?"

"Too *primitive*?" Archie blinked and looked offended. "Do not for one moment think the Celtic swordsmanship was of a primitive nature, my boy," he scolded, wagging a reprimanding forefinger at Adam. "Celtic warriors were renowned swordsmen who placed an extremely high value on fine weaponry. They decorated their sword hilts with amber, ivory, and gold leaf. The same goes for their scabbards, helmets, and shields."

Kim said, "But this sword was found in a bog. That's a kind of swamp, isn't it? Why would anyone throw away something so valuable?"

When Archie turned his pale blue stare upon her, Kim shrank back against the cushions, as if frightened of her boldness.

"Good question, young lady." Archie replaced the book on the shelf before plopping down into his armchair. "No, it was not *thrown away*. The sword has long been a symbol of kingship, of prowess, of a leader's role in society."

He shook his head vigorously. "To let it fall into the hands of an enemy would be unthinkable and symbolize defeat. Thus, often the Celtic people would throw their leader's weapons or regalia into a sacred lake or river. They would rather honor the goddess of the water than surrender such important items to a victorious enemy. Does that answer your question?"

"Yes," said Kim.

Archie smiled and then looked at his watch. "Is that the time already?"

He heaved himself to his feet and saluted Humphrey. "My dear old friend, I must be off. Giving a lecture on Roman Britain this evening at the museum. I want to cast an eye over the find before the others get there. We're going to examine the relics properly tomorrow, but the press wants a Q-and-A tonight and a few photos of the relics before we clean them up."

Humphrey steered Archie, still talking, to the door.

"You know what these journalists are like, Humphrey. Must keep them happy, but not tell them too much."

Archie turned to say good-bye. "Never fear, dear young people. Tomorrow I will have even more exciting news for you so keep your other questions until then. Cheerio."

With a wave of one hand, the egg-shaped figure disappeared.

"There was so much more I wanted to ask him," Adam said.

51

"Me too," said Justin. "I didn't even get a chance to open my mouth. He never stopped talking."

Kim gave a huge yawn. "We'll see him tomorrow."

Humphrey came back into the room, with a thoughtful expression. "Ink, take our guests over to your Aunt Pandora's place. I think they look just about ready for bed."

A ÔREAM OF ARThUR

Adam snuggled beneath the quilt, his eyelids slowly closing. Justin's gentle snores came from the other bed. Justin had fallen asleep almost at once. After meeting Pandora Brocklehurst and her two cats, Wellington and Napoleon, they had eaten a light supper and tumbled into bed. Much to Kim's disappointment, Humphrey had suggested Smudge spend the night at his cottage. However, one look at Napoleon and Wellington was enough to convince Kim it was the right decision. The two enormous tabbies were extremely territorial, and likely to beat Smudge up if he ventured through the garden gate.

When they reached Mrs. Brocklehurst's cottage, she was out, but Ink said she would be along soon. He had a key to let them in and then said he had to get back home. The kids didn't wait long. Ten minutes after their arrival, the garden gate clicked open and a startling sight materialized. A statuesque woman of about sixty, draped in many brightly colored, floating shawls, surged into the room like a galleon in full sail. Pandora Brocklehurst flung off her shawls, revealing a plump body encased in shiny purple fabric. Her hat had clusters of dyed feathers attached to the brim with an enormous jeweled pin. A large red handbag landed on the floor with a thump as the lady tossed it carelessly aside.

She turned steely blue eyes upon the amazed trio and boomed, "Welcome, de-ah children."

Justin stepped forward. "You must be Humphrey's—I mean Mr. Biddle's sister. We're pleased to meet you. Thank you for putting us up while we're here in Oxford. I hope we won't be any trouble."

Pandora Brocklehurst clearly had a fondness for young people with good manners, and took to them instantly.

"De-ah children," she bellowed again as she sank heavily into a large armchair, sending several cushions and her two cats flying. "Call me Pandora."

Adam slipped his hand under his pillow to feel the familiar shape of his scarab. He had quickly retrieved it as soon as possible, vowing never to forget it again. He settled deeper into the puffy pillows. Their plans all seemed to be working out rather well. He wasn't sure how long they would have to stay in Oxford, but no doubt James would contact Humphrey when he was recovered from his accident and let them know about going to Scotland. Oxford was also a fascinating place and he was eager to find out more about the relics at the museum. Imagine if the sword had belonged to Arthur. Imagine if the stone in the hilt was actually the second Stone of Power, even though it didn't look like much. Justin gave a few drowsy grunts, reminding Adam that he should also go to sleep.

Although Adam fell asleep, it seemed that he had fallen awake … awake in another age. He was standing at the edge of a forest. Behind him loomed murky darkness where trees, shrouded in mist, stood side by side like rows of silent sentries. Faint sounds broke the eerie stillness—the rustle of small creatures scuttling in the undergrowth, the occasional soft hoot of an owl, and the whispering of the wind as it shook leaf-laden branches.

Adam shivered in the chilly air. It was hard to tell if it was early morning or late evening because the moon was still visible, a pale disc hanging in a dark gray sky. Ragged shreds of clouds scudded across the moon's face, casting strange shadows on the ground in front of him. Mist floated around his ankles and swirled in soft eddies when he moved his feet. In front of him lay an open field, grayish green in the dim light. Farther away, he saw the mound of a huge hill. Adam got the feeling he had fallen through a hole in time—back to the Dark Ages, back to Arthur's era.

He heard a faint howling noise in the distance. Wolves? Adam froze with fear. He desperately tried to remember whether there had still been wolves in England during the Dark Ages. There must have been because there was no other sound quite like the howl of a wolf. The hairs on his arms rose as he heard the howl again. Although he pinched himself to wake up, it was no good; he remained in the dream. At the sound of distant hoof beats, he shrank back against a large tree trunk. There was no time to run away because suddenly the drumming hooves were all around him. Then came the faint melancholy wail of a battle horn and the tinny sound of chinking metal. He could hear the crisp *snap-snap* of fluttering pennants and when he turned, he glimpsed banners waving among the trees. The surge of spectral riders halted and one man, seated on a white horse, appeared at the head of the cavalcade.

The eerie figure came closer, the horse lifting its feet carefully, clip-clopping right up to the trembling boy. The horse was huge, its trappings gleaming with pinpoints of metal rosettes, its long tail and mane hanging like ghostly cobwebs in the pale moonlight. The beast snorted and stamped restlessly. Adam saw the burnished glint of a helmet with a dragon-shaped crest topped by a red plume. Although the cheek pieces of the helmet obscured the man's features, the shadowy figure was looking right at him. A red cloak swirled around the warrior's body and, as the fabric swung aside, Adam saw the gleam of chain mail and the dark shape of a breastplate on the man's chest. The warrior's armor seemed more Roman than he expected. A banner flapped from the spear of a man behind the warrior: a red dragon on a white background. The warrior raised one arm, and a roar erupted as the sounds of cheering burst from what seemed to be thousands of throats. Although Adam heard strange words in another language, somehow he understood what the voices said.

"Hail the Pendragon!"

Adam was so close that he could have reached out and touched the rider. The spectral figure drew his sword from its scabbard and held it aloft. It seemed to Adam that he saw every detail with strangely magnified clarity. It was the same sword from the museum, but it looked so different now. The metal gleamed with a peculiar bluish sheen. Curious characters embossed the length of the blade. At the top, just under the crossguard, was a small circle with a seven-pointed star inside it. Sparkling gems decorated the hilt and pommel, with two dragons' heads facing inward on the crossguard. The stone between the dragons' open mouths glowed brilliant red. Suddenly, a fiery, almost blinding light shot from the stone, dazzling him. The white horse reared on its hindquarters. The radiant beam lit up the forest as the warrior whirled the blade around his head several times. Adam fell to his knees, shaking with a mixture of terror and excitement as he realized the second Stone of Power was embedded in the sword of Arthur. But the stone in the museum sword was nothing like this one.

Then the figure leaned forward and spoke in a deep voice. The man spoke in the same strange language, but again, somehow, Adam understood the words.

"Restore the Stone of Caledfwlch, lest the land descend into ravening darkness!"

Adam looked up into the man's face, still shadowed by the helmet. Adam opened his mouth but couldn't speak, so he simply nodded. As the warrior raised his sword in salute, Adam glimpsed what seemed to be blue snakes wound around his wrist. For a second or two, the writhing creatures appeared real in the flickering light, and then Adam realized the snakes were tattooed in blue dye. The warrior shouted again; an answering cry came from his men. The ghostly cavalcade galloped past Adam, melting into the mist as they thundered onto the plain.

Adam closed his eyes and then opened them when he felt a hand on his shoulder. He looked into Justin's face. He was back in the bedroom at Pandora Brocklehurst's cottage. Justin was staring at him with a puzzled expression.

"You weren't having one of those weird dreams again, were you? Like the ones you had in Egypt?"

"No, not really."

Adam didn't want to tell Justin about the dream just then. Perhaps it meant nothing. Perhaps it was only because they had been to the museum the previous day and heard so much about the sword.

"Breakfast's ready." Justin prodded him. "Pandora called us a few minutes ago."

Adam jumped out of bed and headed for the bathroom.

"Be right with you. Don't eat all the toast," he yelled over the sounds of running water and furious scrubbing from behind the bathroom door.

Justin snorted. "As if I would."

Adam joined them a few minutes later, his hair still wet from the shower. He quickly crammed buttered toast into his mouth and gulped down his tea. Pandora, a severe frown on her face, was engrossed in the morning paper and didn't seem to notice he was late. Long strands of gray hair straggled onto her shoulders and several hairpins fell into her breakfast plate just as another curl came loose. She drained her teacup, and then surveyed the table and her three guests with an ominous expression.

"Is anything wrong?" Adam finally ventured, disturbed by her expression.

"Yes, there is." She folded up the newspaper. "If you've all finished, we'd better get over to Humphrey's right away."

She rose from the table, bundled her hair into a coil, wrapped several voluminous shawls around her shoulders, jammed her hat on her head, and secured it firmly with a long hatpin. Then Pandora Brocklehurst threw open the front door with the energy of an explorer facing uncharted territory. She breathed in and out deeply, savoring the fresh morning air, and then marched down the garden path. The others trailed behind her, Justin sensibly shutting the front door and garden gate after them.

It took only a few minutes to walk to Humphrey's cottage. They didn't dare ask Pandora what the matter was; they could tell just from her stern face that something terrible had happened. Justin and Adam exchanged worried glances. Adam thought it had something to do with their visit to the museum. Kim appeared unconcerned, but Adam felt it was because she didn't fully understand the situation. Perhaps it was just as well. If he and Justin had known from the beginning what faced them in Egypt, they would never have had the strength and courage to survive the first adventure.

When they entered Humphrey's cottage, Ink was waiting for them in the front shop. With a worried expression, he mouthed the words, "There's trouble," before showing them to the living room. Archie Curran lay slumped on the sofa, his face hidden in his red silk handkerchief, plump shoulders heaving. Amelia sat next to him, trying to coax him to drink a cup of tea. In that instant, Adam knew the something terrible had everything to do with the sword in the museum.

Archie raised his head as they entered the room. He leaped to his feet, dramatically pointed a shaking finger at them, and screeched, "Vandals! Villains!" Then he collapsed back onto the sofa, burying his head in the cushions. A feeble moan—"Vipers!"—escaped from under the cushions.

Adam gazed in horror at Humphrey, who was reading the front page of the newspaper, shaking his head.

Pandora, who had stopped to collect Humphrey's letters from the mailbox on the gate, snapped at Archie, "Oh, do pull yourself together, Archibald Curran. All these histrionics are quite boring."

58

Justin and Adam fidgeted as they stood in the middle of the room, feeling as if they were facing their headmaster Mr. Fry back home. Kim sneaked off to a chair in one corner of the room and began gently stroking Smudge.

Justin gave a polite cough and said, "If someone could just tell us what's wrong?"

Archie lifted his head from the cushions with a moan, pointing to the newspaper. Humphrey turned the newspaper so they could see the headlines.

Bold black letters leaped out: *The Stone of Excalibur Stolen!*

who stole the stone of excalibur?

A dam gaped at the newspaper headlines, utterly shocked.

"You can't think … but we didn't," Justin sputtered.

Adam stared at the adults' solemn faces. Even Ink looked grim.

"Humphrey," Justin said. "We told you everything. I promise we didn't take the stone." He nudged Adam. "Go on. You tell them."

Adam nodded, finally finding his voice. "It's true. I was the only one to hold the sword and I didn't do anything to it."

Kim joined Adam and Justin. "Besides, it was my idea in the first place. Adam and Justin wouldn't have gone into the museum if I hadn't suggested it. If anyone's to blame, it's me."

Finally, Humphrey said, "It's my fault, Archie. I knew the children had gone into the museum and that Adam had touched the sword. I didn't want to tell you because I thought you would get upset. I know that was wrong—"

Bristling with indignation, Archie bounced out of his seat before Humphrey could finish. He spluttered for a few moments, unable to speak properly. His eyes bulged and his face turned red as he danced up and down on his toes. He looked ready to explode.

"You … what?" he screeched, flapping his hands in the air. "You knew they had been to the museum and touched … I should say *contaminated* the artifacts? All the time I was telling them about Arthur's sword, you knew they had already seen it. When not even *I* had seen it?"

Almost crying with rage, Archie balled his podgy hands into fists and waved them under Humphrey's nose. "Trying to make a fool of me, were you? Eh? Eh?"

Humphrey looked uncomfortable. "No one tried to make a fool of you," he said, pushing Archie's fists gently aside. "It's just that there is something ..."

Adam knew why Humphrey hadn't finished his sentence. Humphrey was trying to protect him. Humphrey glanced at Adam and, when the old man gave a slight shrug, Adam knew Humphrey would take the blame.

Before he could say anything, Pandora intervened. "Now just sit down and shut up, Archibald Curran," she bellowed. "You were a dramatic little boy years ago and I can see nothing's changed. Still the prima donna. Stop screeching and wailing this minute, and let's see what's in the newspaper report. Then we'll get a clear idea of exactly what happened."

Waving her hands for everyone to sit down, she gave Archie a disapproving look. "How could these young people possibly have the skill or even the wish to steal part of an archaeological find?"

Settling back in her chair, Pandora accepted a cup of tea from the quietly hovering Amelia and gestured to her brother in a commanding manner. "Go on, Humphrey. Read it to us."

Humphrey cleared his throat and peered through his pince-nez at the *Oxford Times* article. "It says here, '*Alarm and confusion reigned yesterday evening at the Ashmolean Museum when museum officials and security officers discovered that the recently excavated artifacts awaiting inspection by Archibald Curran, Britain's leading specialist in the field of Anglo-Saxon history, had been tampered with by a person or persons unknown.*'"

Archie, who was sulking among the sofa cushions with a cup of tea, brightened, smiling proudly when he heard his name. He opened his mouth to comment, but a frosty stare from Pandora silenced him.

"'*Apparently, when the caterers arrived yesterday afternoon to prepare for the press function, they found the museum door ajar and the security guard locked in a broom cupboard.*'" Humphrey frowned as he read a bit more. "Interesting. Someone had knocked the guard unconscious with a heavy blow to the head, and then bound and gagged him. I can't imagine three rather short individuals being able to knock out someone at least six feet tall."

He looked up at Adam. "Was there any commotion at the museum?"

"We did hear a noise," Adam said. "It sounded like someone kicking over a bucket."

"And a loud bang," Justin added. "We thought it was just the security guard locking up the museum."

"When we left," Kim said, "there was no one in sight. I wondered why he wasn't there to close the door behind us because he made such a fuss about letting us in at all."

"Listen to this," Humphrey continued. "'*Museum authorities were horrified to find that the door to the storage room, which had been locked, was standing open and that someone had tampered with the artifacts. When asked for his comments, Florian Boldwood, the present Keeper of Anglo-Saxon and Mediaeval Collections at the Ashmolean, said it was a devastating loss for the museum and that his fears regarding sloppy security had finally come to fruition.*'"

Archie gave a disgusted snort. "Florian Boldwood! That effeminate, pathetic, undereducated, overdressed scoundrel. He was only ever any good at public relations, and then it was mainly at selling his singular lack of talent, fooling people into thinking he was the way forward in the field of archaeology."

"Now then, Archie," said Humphrey. "We should give him a chance."

Archie scowled into his teacup. "So much for the new and fresh ideas he promised would transform the museum. What about all the educational exhibits he was supposed to arrange? I haven't seen any substantial changes."

He growled a few more insults under his breath. "He stole my job, do you know that?"

Pandora snapped, "What nonsense. You were due for retirement anyway, and he managed to charm the museum directors into giving him the position."

Archie looked even angrier. "I'm telling you, if it weren't for him I would have stayed on until they found a more suitable replacement."

Humphrey tried to smooth Archie's ruffled feelings. "But they asked *you* to examine the artifacts, didn't they? Not him."

Archie was only slightly placated. "Yes, well, that's true. But when I arrived yesterday, he was already prancing about, showing off as usual by trying to answer reporters' questions and even telling the police what to do."

Archie sank his chin into his hands, pursing his lips. "He was also saying some quite outrageous things about the sword. Speculating wildly. Bound to create problems for us."

Humphrey sat up, suddenly alert. "What did he say?"

Archie waved one hand at the newspaper. "How do you think the press got hold of all this 'Stone of Excalibur' nonsense? Sounds like yet another rubbishy, completely inaccurate movie title. It was Florian, of course."

He looked at the circle of faces and gave an emphatic nod. "Florian just wants publicity for himself. He should have said it was a discovery from about the fifth century. That's what we agreed with the museum directors and among ourselves to say to the media and the public. But no, he had to go and say it's possibly Arthur's sword."

"We don't know what he said," Humphrey replied. "Let's not jump to conclusions."

Archie clicked his tongue in irritation. "He's broken all the rules. You never say something so controversial until you have your facts in order. It would be the same as announcing that someone had found the Holy Grail, or the Ten Commandments, or even the Loch Ness Monster." He snorted. "Why not Bigfoot?"

Ink and Humphrey exchanged solemn glances. Adam and Justin also looked at each other. Obviously, the last thing anyone should have done was proclaim to the world that the sword had possibly belonged to Arthur.

"What do you three know about Arthur anyway?" Archie demanded, as if suddenly noticing them.

"Um." Kim shifted uneasily in her seat. "I know Clive Owen played King Arthur in the movie." She glared when Adam and Justin sniggered and then tried to pretend they were coughing.

Archie put his head in his hands in a despairing gesture. "Hollywood history," he groaned. "No wonder creatures like Florian Boldwood flourish in the halls of academe."

Ink glanced at the cousins and they bit their lips to stop laughing.

Humphrey continued reading. "Listen to this: '*For readers unversed in British history, experts now recognize that the historical Arthur was a great and skilled war leader, who performed many brave and epic deeds in battle. He was most likely a nobleman of Roman-British ancestry. His probable birth date was circa AD 478. It is possible that he was between fifteen and eighteen when he came to power, explaining why legends persist in labeling him a boy-king.*'"

"Fifteen? But isn't that too young to fight battles?" asked Justin, sneaking another cookie off the tea trolley.

64

Adam poked his cousin in the ribs: it was not the time to gobble cookies.

"Of course not," Archie said impatiently. "In those days, a boy became a man the moment he could wield a sword. There was no time to play games, not with the Saxon hordes baying at one's heels."

Humphrey coughed at the interruption. "Where was I? I've lost my place ... oh, here we are. *'By AD 500, after the Roman withdrawal, circa AD 407 to 410, Britain had split into a number of smaller kingdoms. Arthur possibly originated from the kingdom of Powys (now the West Midlands and Central Wales), at that time the largest and strongest of these kingdoms. An era of bitter feuding and civil war erupted. This heralded the beginning of the Dark Ages.'*"

Kim put up her hand. "I have a question."

Humphrey peered at her. "Yes?"

"Why did the Romans come here in the first place? I mean when did they arrive?"

Humphrey sat back in his chair. "Interesting question, young lady. Why do *you* think the Romans traveled long distances across far seas and hostile territory to conquer other countries?"

"Uh ... for wealth?" Justin suggested. "For property and maybe slaves?"

"Because they needed more stuff like food and precious metals, and maybe the other territories had something they did not?" Adam guessed.

"They were ambitious," Kim said.

Archie nodded at each idea. "Yes, all of your suggestions are valid." He seemed to be recovering from his temper outburst.

"I won't go into too much detail," Archie continued, ignoring Pandora's muttered "Thank heavens!" with a scornful smile. "The Romans arrived in 55 BC under Julius Caesar, but that was something of a flying visit. In AD 43, the emperor Claudius resumed the work of Caesar by ordering the proper invasion of Britannia, as they named it, under the command of Aulus Plautius."

He looked up at Amelia, who was hovering nearby with the teapot. "More tea? Lovely." He held out his teacup.

After several long sips, Archie said, "Now, what was I saying? Oh yes, the Romans. After nearly four hundred years of rule, they pulled out, leaving Britain at the mercy of foreign invaders."

"Why did they decide to leave after coming all that way," Kim said, "and after staying so long?" A puzzled frown creased her forehead. "It doesn't make sense."

"The Roman Empire began to go downhill, and it cost a lot of money to maintain their military might. They also needed the army to help with the enormous problems they were having with other restless colonies and conquered territories," Archie replied.

He helped himself to the plate of cookies Amelia had quietly replenished. "Barbarian groups such as the Goths, Visigoths, Vandals, and Huns were pressing on Rome's borders. Rome simply didn't have the resources or manpower to waste on a small, out-of-the-way colony like Britain."

Justin had been thinking while listening. "That must have come as a surprise to the British people after having the Romans there for so long."

"Yes, it did," said Humphrey, smoothing out his newspaper. "A nasty one, too. As you can imagine, by then the people had absorbed the Roman ways—their laws, customs, language, education, and culture. They had become quite Romanized. They also depended on the military might of Rome to protect them from marauding barbarians like the Saxons, the Picts, the Scots, and other invaders. Then suddenly—" he snapped his fingers "—the Romans were gone."

Archie interrupted, waving his teaspoon to emphasize his point. "One problem Britain had after the Romans left was that the various Celtic kingdoms didn't know how to work together. Various kingdoms would join forces, but then they would quarrel and any alliances they had made would break apart. A country divided is prey to invaders. Finally, the time came for a charismatic leader to emerge and change everything for the better. Arthur!"

Adam leaned forward, fascinated by the story of a real hero, one who had lived and died to save his country.

"That's right," said Humphrey. "In fact, listen to this." He held up the newspaper and read, "*Arthur was one of the last British leaders to make a successful stand against the Anglo-Saxons that threatened in the fifth and sixth centuries. Before that, the country had suffered from infighting among the various kingdoms, after the death of a previous strong leader who was possibly Ambrosius Aurelanius, or else his brother, Uther, who was Arthur's father. Arthur used his extensive knowledge of Roman military strategies and warfare against the Saxon hordes and united Britain in the struggle. It is believed he was killed at the Battle of*

66

Camlann, circa AD 537. Arthur's historical origins are clouded by the glamorous myth and legend added on by later historians of the Middle Ages, but he is rooted in fact.'"

Humphrey's face became grave. "So as you can see, Arthur was not a mediaeval king in shining armor, but a Celtic warlord struggling against foreign invasion. And because of him, Britain, alone of all the conquered territories in the Roman Empire, achieved independence."

He carefully folded the newspaper. "Naturally, the sword of the greatest battle leader would be a find of tremendous value for any museum."

Pandora put down her teacup with a clatter. "I can see now how talk of Arthur's sword could be dangerous. Imagine, in this world of confusion and uncertainty, how a renegade or terrorist group could try to use it to their advantage."

Glum nods from Archie and Humphrey signaled their feelings on the matter.

"What do they say about it being Arthur's sword?" Justin asked.

Humphrey picked up the newspaper again and turned it to face them. "Archie, this should interest you. Your friend Florian says here that they are convinced, given the description from Welsh mediaeval texts, that the sword is Excalibur and that a possibly rare stone in the hilt was gouged out."

Archie pointed to the newspaper. "What an idiot. He looks like a playboy on the French Riviera. How can anyone take him seriously?"

Everyone's gaze swiveled to the photograph of Florian Boldwood standing on the steps of the Ashmolean Museum. Several female museum employees stood on either side, gazing adoringly at him. In his early forties, with sculpted blond curls, a fake tan, and a dazzling, movie star smile, Florian Boldwood was elegantly dressed in a designer suit. Clearly, he loved the media attention. Adam stared at the man's face. There was something phony about him. Was it the fake polished smile; was it the carefully arranged hair, swept back from a broad forehead; or was it because his eyes were set a tad too closely together, giving him a sly look?

Justin nudged Adam in the ribs and Adam knew his cousin had spotted the same clues. Florian Boldwood reminded them of Dr. Faisal Khalid, their mortal enemy.

"He's creepy," Kim announced. "I don't like the look of him. You can see he just loves himself to bits."

"See?" Archie looked at Humphrey, delighted by Kim's negative response to his rival. "Children always know. Out of the mouths of babes. The man is a complete fraud. How can he make such statements without a proper examination of the actual sword? He just poses for the camera and gives meaningless interviews to trashy tabloids. He'll say *anything* for publicity."

Adam couldn't take it any longer; he had to speak up. When he cleared his throat, everyone looked at him.

"But he's right," Adam whispered. Then he repeated himself, louder this time. "He's right."

"Who is right?" Archie sounded even more irritable at the idea of anyone except him being right.

"Florian Boldwood," Adam said. "Maybe he said it just to get the press all eager, but he's right about it being Arthur's sword. And there is a stone in the crossguard, between two dragons' heads. It burns brightly like a fire. I think it must be a Stone of Power."

Archie put down his teacup. "What?" he spluttered. "You're just an ignorant little schoolboy. How could you possibly know anything about Arthur's sword? *I* am the expert, in case we are forgetting ourselves here." He finished his sentence with a dramatic flourish of his handkerchief and sat back in outraged indignation.

"Adam, you don't have to say anything," Humphrey began, but Adam interrupted him.

"Yes, I do," Adam said. "I didn't feel anything unusual in the museum when I touched the sword, but last night I had an incredible dream. I saw King Arthur. I saw his army ride across a field, heading for a hill. I saw the sword as it would have been centuries ago."

Archie burst into a hoot of scornful laughter. "You saw Arthur? Don't make me laugh." He glared at Humphrey. "My friend, if you believe the ramblings of a tiresome schoolboy who had too much cake before bed, then I don't know what the academic world is coming to."

Everyone else stared at Adam in astonishment.

"You *did* have a dream last night," Justin said. "I knew it."

Adam nodded.

"So what? So he did have a dream." Archie imitated Justin's voice and pulled a sour face. "What's so special about that?"

68

Justin struggled to keep his temper, but managed to say politely, "Well, sir, I'm not sure how much you know about the quest or the Seven Stones of Power, but when we were in Egypt, Adam was the bearer of the first Stone of Power. Adam had dreams and visions that all came true." Ending his sentence on a note of triumph, Justin looked especially pleased when Archie gaped in amazement.

"The Stones of Power? You can't tell me a mere boy is that important." Archie made strange gobbling sounds, rather like a turkey. "Humphrey, I thought these children were just … I thought you were simply humoring them … a fun holiday abroad … a bit of archaeology thrown in … a favor to James … I did not think—"

"You did not think that one of them could be vital to finding the Stones of Power before Khalid does?" Humphrey nodded slowly. "Would you like to tell us more about Egypt, Adam?"

Adam told them about his dream of the great golden doors in the crystal cavern, the doors that had opened into the Forbidden Chamber containing the Pyramidion and the Stone of Fire. He also told them about his vision of Thoth, the Egyptian god of wisdom, at Edfu; and how Thoth's words had provided the clue to opening the chamber. Expressions of amazement, disbelief, and shock struggled for victory on the adults' faces.

Pandora looked at Adam with an expression bordering on awe. "And last night you dreamed of King Arthur?"

"Yes," Adam said. "He had these blue snakes tattooed on his wrists. I saw them in the moonlight when he raised the sword."

Adam turned to Humphrey. "What does that mean?"

Archie interrupted before Humphrey could answer. "Well, since *I* am the expert," he said, shooting a hurt glance in Humphrey's direction, "allow *me* to enlighten you. The snakes are ancient Celtic symbols of kingship or leadership, tattooed in blue woad, a type of dye. They symbolize the king's bond with the land. He must be prepared to sacrifice himself for the good of the land, should it come to that."

His words reminded Adam of the sacrifice the Scarab King had made. The king had died to protect the first Stone of Power and Egypt from Seti, his evil stepbrother.

Archie stared at Adam, his eyes rolling like oversized saucers behind his thick glasses. "Did you say you saw a hill?"

69

"Yes, sir," Adam replied. "I had my back to the forest, quite a dark and scary place. The army came out from the trees and raced across a plain to the hill."

Archie muttered to himself, "*Mons Badonicus, Mynydd Badon*—the Battle of Badon Hill, Arthur's greatest battle. The boy may be right, even though my better judgment says otherwise."

"Why did the newspaper say he was a Celtic warlord?" Adam asked. "His armor looked sort of Roman with a breastplate and helmet."

Archie nodded. "Yes, of course it would. Once the Romans cleared out, the Celts gradually reestablished their tribal Celtic identity—that's why the various kingdoms began to quarrel—but they kept what they'd learned, such as knowledge of Roman military techniques, warfare, weapons and armor, and ways of improving upon weaponry."

"Tell us more about action and fighting. What happened at this battle?" Justin asked.

Archie smiled happily at Justin's interest. "The Battle of Badon Hill took place circa AD 516. It was perhaps Arthur's greatest victory and one that stopped the Saxon advance for at least half a century."

"What about the sword?" Humphrey asked Adam. "You saw the sword as it will look when it has been restored."

Adam was beginning to feel uncomfortable with all the attention on him.

Justin, on the other hand, made the most of it. "Go on, tell us."

Kim grinned, looking proud to be associated with Adam and Justin.

Adam described the whole dream from start to finish. Archie and Humphrey were especially interested in his description of the sword.

"Can you draw this sword, Adam?" Humphrey asked. "It would help us immensely."

"Of course he can," Justin boasted. "Adam's brilliant at drawing."

Ink produced paper and a pencil, and Adam quickly sketched an accurate picture of the sword. Humphrey and Archie put their heads together over the picture, muttering to each other. They questioned Adam closely on the exact details of the weapon, asking him about the embossed words and the circle with the seven-pointed star. When Adam mentioned the bluish sheen, Humphrey and Archie slowly raised their eyebrows.

Humphrey looked thoughtful. "Interesting," he said, polishing his pince-nez with the edge of his cardigan. "You see, the bluish tinge to the metal indicates the iron content. Legend holds that Arthur's sword was thrice-forged from meteoric iron. Ancient people called iron from meteors 'star metal.' Thus, a weapon of meteoric iron was said to be 'star-forged.' The Egyptian word for the metal is *ba-en-pet*, meaning 'not of this earth.' Such weapons were rare and precious."

Archie allowed himself a moment of reverie, his eyes going dreamy while he pondered. "It's said that the sword of Arthur is faerie-forged, made in the time before time," he mumbled, almost speaking only to himself. "Forged by the hand of Gofannon, the Celtic god of smithcraft. It's said that a warrior has only to thrust the sword into the ground and Gofannon will come to his aid."

Then he snapped back to reality, giving his head a little shake. "Just stories … old legends. Sentimentality has no place in science."

"But wouldn't his dad … uh … whatshisname?" Justin frowned as he struggled to remember the name from the article.

"Uther," Archie reminded him.

"Yeah, Uther. Wouldn't *he* have given Arthur his sword?" asked Justin. "Didn't kings usually pass on their weapons to their heirs?"

"Remember I told you the Celts liked to offer their weapons to the goddess of water. They also believed in reincarnation," said Archie. "So in Uther's case, his sword would have been melted down and poured into a lake. The idea was that Gofannon would then forge it anew in the underworld, so that it would be ready for Uther's reborn soul."

"I thought King Arthur pulled his sword from a stone," Kim chirped. "That's what the legend says."

Humphrey replied, "In the fifth century, many times leadership disputes were settled by two warriors in single combat. The victor would draw the sword granting him leadership from a stone altar. That's how the legend came about of the sword drawn from a stone. I suppose the story was embellished over time to make it sound more mysterious."

"There's one thing I'm puzzled about," Adam said warily, not wanting to upset Archie a second time. He squirmed as all eyes once again focused on him.

"Go on," said Amelia. "You've obviously had an inspired dream or vision. Don't hold back now."

"He didn't call it Excalibur. The sword, I mean."

"What?" Humphrey's eyes goggled. "You mean the person … er … Arthur actually spoke to you in the dream?"

71

Adam nodded.

"Good heavens," Humphrey said. "What did he say?"

Adam hesitated because it was going to sound extremely weird. "It was another language, but I understood the words."

Even Justin stared at him in disbelief. Adam had never told Justin about speaking in ancient Egyptian when he had used the sacred scarab to open the golden doors of the Forbidden Chamber. This was something even Adam had never understood. How could he comprehend a language that had died out centuries before?

A strange excitement seemed to grip Archie. "Go on." He reached out one hand to Adam as if to drag the words from him. "What did he say? Can you remember what he said?"

"The words as I understood them were, 'Find the Stone of *Caledfwlch*, lest the land descend into ravening darkness.'" Adam stumbled over the unfamiliar syllables, but was surprised and pleased that he remembered them. He repeated the words. "The Stone of *Kah-led-vulgh*. That's what it sounded like."

"But why didn't he say Excalibur?" Justin asked.

"Caledfwlch is the true name of the sword," Archie almost shouted. He beamed when Humphrey nodded in agreement. "The Excalibur and the Lady of the Lake nonsense only came much later when mediaeval historians and poets got hold of Arthur's story in the 1100s. Caledfwlch became Caliburn, which in turn became the fancy sounding Excalibur."

Archie slapped one knee indignantly, an angry hiss escaping from between his teeth. "Of course, Florian would use the more familiar name just to scrape up some ghastly publicity."

"And the dragon?" Adam asked. "There was a dragon on a banner—a red dragon—and when his men cheered, they said, 'Hail the Pendragon' or something like that. What's a Pendragon?"

Archie gave a smug smile. "The word *Pendragon* is a title, meaning a chief or leader. Arthur's father, Uther, added it to his name so he became *Ythr Pendragwn*—meaning 'Uther, the terrible or fearsome Head-Dragon, or Chieftain' in Old Welsh. He did this after a dragon-shaped comet appeared in the sky at the time of his brother Ambrosius' death."

Humphrey gazed at Adam. "And even though you don't understand the language, you understood the words?"

72

Adam nodded. "It's weird. My ears heard the language, but my brain understood the words."

Archie jumped up, scattering cushions, his arms raised as if in praise. "Humphrey, my dear friend, this is a miracle. Tell me how a young boy from another country can understand and translate Old Welsh, a language that no longer exists?"

He stared at Adam, who shrugged modestly.

"Something like that happened to me in Egypt as well." Adam then told them about speaking in ancient Egyptian to open the golden doors of the Forbidden Chamber.

"You never even told me that you spoke in ancient Egyptian," Justin burst out. "I thought you spoke English."

Adam was flustered. "I—I wasn't sure if I just imagined it, and then with so much happening and the tomb collapsing …"

"It's okay," Justin said abruptly, but Adam knew it wasn't.

"I'm sorry," Adam whispered, trying to make Justin see that he meant it. But Justin simply scowled and turned his head away.

Archie was overjoyed. He paced the room, muttering excitedly to himself, and then put his face close to Adam's and said, "And you say this ability manifested *after* you were given the sacred scarab in Egypt?"

"I think so," Adam replied, a little cautiously because he wasn't sure. "Nothing happened at first. After I'd had it for a while, I began to feel sensations, like vibrations and heat, and then I had the dream of the crystal cavern with the golden doors."

Archie felt in his pockets. "Maybe I have an ancient coin you can practise with." He looked about the room. "Humphrey, haven't you got something here that's at least two or three hundred years old? An old map, perhaps?"

Humphrey looked blank. "What are you talking about?"

Archie's face lit up; his eyes shone with elation. "Don't you know what this means? This boy is an *archaeomancer*, a living link to history. He can see the past simply by touching an artifact and then waiting for the answers to come. We could use his skills to accomplish great things … *incredible* things."

Archie grabbed Humphrey's arm. "This boy could tell us everything about the ancient past," he gabbled. "It's amazing. No more fumbling about in the dark, thinking up theories only to have them disproved later."

73

There appeared a star of wonderful size and brightness, with a single ray, on which was a ball of fire extended like a dragon, out of whose mouth proceeded two rays, one of which seemed to extend its length beyond the regions of Gaul, and the other, verging towards the Irish Sea, terminated in seven smaller rays. Struck with terror at this sight, Uther anxiously inquired of his wise men what this star portended. They made answer, "The star and the fiery dragon under the star are thyself; the ray, which stretches towards the region of Gaul, portends that thou wilt have a very powerful son, who will possess the extensive territories which the star covered; the other ray signifies thy daughter, whose sons and grandsons shall successively possess the kingdom of Britain. Hasten, therefore, most noble prince; thy brother Aurelius Ambrosius, the renowned king of Britain, is dead; and with him has perished the military glory of the Britons."

from the Annals of Roger de Hoveden (1174—1201),
12th Century chronicler of the history of England

Humphrey shook his arm free. "No!"

"But—" Archie stepped back and looked at Humphrey, bewildered. "This could give us the edge over the competition. We could rewrite history—correctly this time." He rubbed his hands in glee. "Ha! Just imagine Florian's face. The worm. He'll be so jealous."

"Florian is the last person who can ever know about this." Humphrey's voice was thunderous. "The man is a chatterbox and bursting with ambition. Heaven knows what he'd do with this information or who he would tell."

Adam stared, shocked by Humphrey's outburst. Justin and Kim looked equally horrified.

Glancing at his friend's stunned face, Humphrey softened his tone but his voice remained stern. "Archie, I hate to disappoint you. However, there are things to consider."

Archie gazed vacantly at him.

"Anyway," Humphrey continued, "this boy's gift relates *only* to the Stones of Power. He is not a freak show one can trot out at exhibitions. This quest is of the utmost importance. It should come first. Secondly, secrecy is paramount. You know that even as we speak, the enemy is on the move, trying to find the remaining six stones in what little time is left before the planets align."

Adam suddenly realized that was the reason Ebrahim and Humphrey had wanted him to see the relics at the Ashmolean: only the person who had experienced the mystical energy of the first stone would know if the newly discovered sword contained the second Stone of Power.

Archie sounded apologetic as he mumbled something about missing a marvelous opportunity. Deflated and disappointed, he sank back onto the sofa and twiddled his handkerchief aimlessly between his fingers.

Humphrey patted his friend's shoulder. "Yes, I understand how you feel, but unless we stick to the original purpose there won't be much opportunity left to us, will there? We also don't want to put Adam in any danger."

Adam and Justin exchanged troubled glances. Being an archaeomancer sounded pretty cool, but Adam was especially disturbed by Humphrey's comment. It seemed that their quest was steadily becoming more sinister. Adam remembered how he had felt before the trip to Egypt—wanting to be someone special and achieve fantastic things. His wish had come true when he became the bearer of the sacred scarab, but ever since then things seemed more frightening than exciting.

Now they couldn't turn back. They had to find the Scroll of the Ancients and restore the second Stone of Power to the sword of Arthur.

Pandora Brocklehurst rummaged in her handbag and took out a large, shapeless mass of gray wool that could have been anything from an oversized sweater to a blanket.

Her knitting needles clicking furiously, she said, "I hate to cut the history lesson short, but no matter the name of the sword and no matter if it belonged to Arthur, someone gouged a stone out of the hilt for a possibly wicked purpose."

Pandora stopped knitting and fixed them all with a steely stare. "But who?" Her question cracked like a whip, making Adam jump. As she continued, her voice boomed in the small, crowded room. "Who is this person and what does he want with something as unimportant as a stone from an old sword?"

Pandora shook her head in disbelief. "If they were part of some crazy group, it would've been easy enough for them to steal the whole sword, given the lax security at the museum. But they stole just the stone. Why?"

She looked back down at her knitting and picked up several dropped stitches. "Only a particular knowledge about that stone would give them reason to steal it. I don't know much about the Stones of Power, but I think the Stone of Excalibur has fallen into the hands of an enemy."

Archie made a strange sound, like a muffled wail. "It's not … who I think it is?" he quavered, wiping his forehead with his handkerchief. His eyes went glassy and his pudgy face turned pale.

"I couldn't go through that horrifying experience again!" Archie leaped from the sofa and clutched at the air. His eyes rolled wildly as he collapsed on the floor in a dramatic heap. "No, no. I couldn't."

Adam gazed at him curiously. Had Archibald Curran possibly experienced an unpleasant encounter with Dr. Khalid? Adam knew firsthand the kind of terror that the evil Dr. Khalid could inspire. He also knew Dr. Khalid would sacrifice anyone to obtain the Stones of Power.

Ink and Amelia both rushed to help Archie to his feet.

"There, there now." Amelia soothed him. "You won't have to go through anything. How about more tea? A cupcake? What about a nice fresh muffin with strawberry jam?"

Briefly distracted by the thought of food, Archie allowed Amelia to help him back to the sofa where he submerged himself in the cushions, chewing a fingernail in his anxiety. Amelia glanced at Ink and they began clearing the cups and plates from the table.

Ink winked at the boys. They smiled back, but Adam felt sick to his stomach. If the pompous Archibald Curran could be reduced to an oversized jellyfish of fear at the mere mention of Dr. Khalid, how much more dangerous would their enemy be now? Dr. Khalid had already lost the sacred scarab because of Adam and Justin's efforts to outwit him in Egypt—but had he successfully stolen the second stone? The answer came right away.

"It's not Khalid," Humphrey announced, quickly scanning the rest of the article.

"How do you know, Dad?" Ink asked, poised at the door with his hands full of crockery. "You told me it's his life's work to find the stones. Who else would suspect that a stone in the hilt of a grubby old sword could be a Stone of Power? Who else would be looking for them?"

"I can't answer that," Humphrey replied, "but there's one thing I'm sure of—it's not the work of Khalid and his master."

Ink's face fell. "There's someone else as well?"

Pandora put down her knitting. "Not Khalid?"

Archie sat up, hope etched on his face. "Not Khalid?" he echoed.

"More likely some other organization," Humphrey replied. "I can't imagine a single individual knowing much about the significance of the stone in the hilt, or even wanting to steal it."

Justin asked, "Then who could it possibly be? Someone as powerful as Dr. Khalid and his master?"

"And is this someone working with, for, or against Khalid?" Pandora wondered aloud as she counted the stitches on her knitting needles.

Goosebumps appeared on Adam's arms and he shivered. The threat of Dr. Khalid and his master was bad enough. He didn't dare ask if there might be someone else even more powerful and ruthless after the stones.

"Just reading the remainder of this article tells me a lot about the thief," Humphrey replied, peering closely at the page. "It's interesting the kind of 'signature'—for want of a better word—a criminal leaves behind. It reveals a lot about the individual and the motive."

Adam found his voice. "What do you mean?"

"The evidence doesn't reveal the actions of an expert thief like Khalid. It says here, '*Several clues carelessly left behind at the scene of the crime have baffled the police. A few threads of what appears to be a kind of roughly woven fabric prompted detectives to speculate that the thief brought along a bag to carry off the sword, but was interrupted and left the sword behind, taking only the stone. They have also discovered smears of a strange, unidentified brown substance on the floor, on the sword itself, and on the metal poles holding up the rope cordon surrounding the relics. A partial thumbprint may lead to the identity of the criminal, but it is too early to expect full forensic results. There is also an incomplete footprint of a soft-soled, pointed shoe.'*"

Humphrey looked up from the newspaper at the faces gazing expectantly at him for an explanation. "What I mean is that Khalid is smart. He would have carefully removed the stone from the hilt and substituted a replica. This thief has barged in and clumsily gouged the stone out of the hilt."

He dropped the newspaper to the floor. "Khalid wouldn't want to draw any attention to himself. In fact, after your adventure in Egypt, I think he'll be even more careful to conceal his activities."

"What about Ebrahim's letter?" Justin said. "He mentioned something about increased danger and peril. Maybe he knows something we don't."

"I'm not sure," Humphrey replied. "We'll have to wait for more information to be released. Now the press has the story, the police will be under pressure to speed up their investigation."

Amelia looked at her watch, tut-tutting about how late it was, and how she had to catch up with her filing. Then everyone burst into a flurry of activity. Humphrey remarked that, since there would be no more information until the late edition of the newspaper, Ink should take the kids sightseeing for the remainder of the day.

Archie proposed they all meet again at Humphrey's cottage later that afternoon to watch the early news on television. Then he marched off, muttering something about "having it out with that pretentious dummy, Florian."

Pandora rushed off, saying she was going home to feed the cats and tidy up as Humphrey vanished into a back room, mumbling something about cataloguing manuscripts.

With the adults now all gone, Ink said, "Come on, kids. I think we should take Smudge to the local vet anyway and get him checked out. Let's do something normal for the rest of the day."

Adam felt a rush of warmth. Ink was such a great guy. He treated them as if they were his peers, even though he was older. Soon they were walking down St. Giles Road, heading for the city center.

Humphrey was glad to have the others out of the way for a few hours. There was information to find and letters to write, the most important of which was to go to Ebrahim, using their system of false names and addresses to protect their identities. Ebrahim was always trying to persuade him to use email, but Humphrey didn't trust computers and cyber space. One heard such terrible stories about people called "hackers." He wondered how things would turn out and whether the children, especially Adam, would be up to the task ahead. Humphrey felt so helpless, suddenly so old and feeble, and not in the least prepared for what awaited. He stroked Bismarck's sleek head, receiving a deep purr in return. He fumbled in his pocket for Ebrahim's letter. There was one page he had not read aloud, the page containing frightening information, details he dared not share with anyone, not even with Ink—not yet. Humphrey read Ebrahim's words of warning again, the page fluttering as his hands shook with fear.

One word stood out: *Necronomicon*, the Greek name for a terrible book, an ancient book of shadows and death, buried for centuries, forgotten … and yet now there were reports. If it had been found at last, then a dark truth would finally be unleashed. He could not tell anyone. Perhaps the rumors were just stories, half-remembered tales from past ages. Nothing must interfere with Adam's quest.

suspects

The vet said Smudge was a tad skinny, but perfectly healthy. Ink bought him a collar and leash and for the rest of the afternoon Smudge trotted along next to Kim, his tail wagging and a doggy grin on his face. They walked around Oxford, admiring old buildings, historic monuments, and interesting shops until they were tired. Then they stopped at a local café, where they ate the most delicious ice cream imaginable.

"How long do you think we have to stay here in Oxford?" Adam asked, licking pistachio and fudge ice cream from his cone and longing for another double scoop.

"Had enough adventure already?" Ink asked.

"Of course not," Adam protested, feeling his face turn red. He didn't want Ink to think he was chickening out.

Ink laughed.

Justin looked at Ink. "Your dad's great and the whole thing with the sword is so exciting. But we must find the Scroll of the Ancients and I can't wait to get started."

Justin glanced at Kim and Adam, who both nodded vigorously.

"We can't wait for the baddies to make a move," Adam said. "We need to stay ahead of Dr. Khalid and this other bunch of people."

"Whoever stole the stone out of the sword probably won't hang around Oxford," Kim said, looking thoughtful. "Perhaps they're also after this scroll, if it's so important."

Adam gazed at Kim, her words striking horror into his heart. "What are you saying?"

Kim shrugged. "The person who has the stone might come after us, thinking we know something."

Justin's eyes widened. "But how would they even know about us? No one saw us at the museum."

"How do you know? Think about it," Kim replied. "Adam touched the sword and then suddenly the stone in the hilt disappeared on the same day. How do we know someone didn't trail us into the museum, see us examine a dirty old sword, wonder why we found it so special, and then look at it after we left? They could've taken the stone and are now following us to get more information."

She turned to Adam. "How do these Stones of Power work anyway? Are they special on their own or do they only work together?"

Adam replied, "Seven stones were broken off from the original Stone of Fire. Each stone was given to an ancient king to help him rule wisely, so each one must have some special kind of power. Each king would pass on the stone to his heir. Over time, I guess the stones were lost. The Scarab King was the last ruler to use the first Stone of Power. Now, if the stone embedded in the sword hilt is the second stone, then that means King Arthur was the last ruler to use the second Stone of Power."

"But you need all Seven Stones to read the *Book of Thoth*. That's the most powerful book of knowledge in the world, remember?" Justin interjected.

Adam continued. "The book is encapsulated in the Stone of Fire, which is sealed inside an alabaster Pyramidion—that's like a mini version of a pyramid. We actually found the Pyramidion in the Forbidden Chamber, but it fell into a giant chasm in the earth when the Scarab King's tomb collapsed. Dr. Khalid fell in, too, but Ebrahim always thought Dr. Khalid survived and maybe he'll also find the Pyramidion somehow."

Adam felt in his pocket for his scarab as he spoke Dr. Khalid's name. Just holding its familiar shape in his palm calmed him. "The only good thing is that the first Stone of Power is the most important one. No one can read the Book of Thoth without it. Anyway, like Justin said, the first stone is safely locked away so even if Dr. Khalid locates the Pyramidion and the other stones, everything is useless without the first stone."

"So remind me why we even need the scroll." Kim's words sounded muffled through her large bite of ice cream cone.

"The Scroll of the Ancients contains clues to the Seven Stones," Justin said. "If we find the scroll, we can find the stones sooner because we'll know what to look for. And by *we,* I mean not just Adam and me, but also James and Ebrahim."

"There could also be information in the scroll," Adam added. "Details we might need. There's so much we still don't know. We don't even know what language the scroll is written in."

"Okay." Kim said, sounding determined. "So we know that the next important step is to find the scroll. The thief may not know there are more stones or that he needs more facts to find them, but I'll bet he finds out soon enough. Then he'll come after us."

"I think Kim's right," Ink said. "Even though the thief may not know exactly what he has or what he needs, if he really did see you kids in the museum then he'll probably continue to follow our lead, follow *us* to see what we do next."

Justin and Adam looked at each other with gloomy expressions.

"On the plus side, though," Ink said, "if this person has the second stone with him, there may be a chance for us to get it back."

"You're right," Justin said. "It won't be easy. We can't let our guard slip for a single moment." He turned to Adam. "Remember what Ebrahim said in his letter to Humphrey. Trust no one."

Adam looked up at the café window and gasped in horror. Then he dived under the table, pulling Justin and Kim with him. They all crashed into a heap on the floor.

"Ow!" Kim squealed. "That hurt."

She rubbed her elbow while Justin examined his knee.

Justin gave Adam a fierce look. "Are you crazy?"

Ink hadn't moved. He casually finished the last bite of his cone. Then he said in a low voice, "What's the problem, Adam? See something?"

Adam burned with embarrassment, especially since he was still clinging to Kim and Justin, preventing them crawling out from under the table.

"I think there was ... I thought I saw ..." His voice faded.

Justin pulled himself from Adam's grip and scrambled to his feet, banging his head on the underside of the table. "Don't tell me another nameless, shapeless person is following us." He glowered at Adam. "Just like in Egypt."

Adam protested, "I was right all those times in Egypt and you know it."

Justin thumped down in his seat. Kim clambered out from under the table, staring at Adam. He felt dizzy so he sat as well.

"Did you see that strange guy again?" she asked. "The one who came into Humphrey's book shop?"

Adam breathed in and out deeply. He didn't care what Justin thought or said any longer. It was clear now why Justin was so angry and offhand.

"I know you're still upset I didn't tell you about speaking in ancient Egyptian," Adam said to him in a low, controlled voice. "But after all the times you laughed at me, all the times you mocked me and said it was my imagination ... and then it turned out I was right and you know I was. You just don't want to admit it."

The two boys glared stubbornly at each other. Then Justin broke the deadlock.

"Yes, okay. You were right then and you're probably right now. So what did you see *this* time?" His voice still contained a note of mockery.

Ink interrupted. "I'm not trying to play big brother here, but something needs to be said."

Three pairs of eyes swung their gaze in his direction.

"I think the dangers facing us are far more important than who did or didn't tell whoever about whatever." Ink looked at Justin. "Justin, I think by now you should've learned to put any disappointment or hurt pride aside. Is it because you resent Adam? Or because he has extraordinary abilities?"

Justin went red. "Of course not," he burst out. Then he hung his head a little. "I was a bit jealous in Egypt, but not anymore. I know Adam is the special one."

Words of protest crowded into Adam's throat. He wanted to tell Justin how important he was. He wanted to tell Justin that, for all he cared, Justin could have the burden of being exceptional. He wanted to tell Justin that he needed his cousin's support. But Justin's next words saved him the trouble of speaking.

"I'm always doing this. I mean, losing my temper and being sarcastic. Sorry, Adam."

"That's all right. I won't keep things from you again," Adam replied, relieved the tension had passed.

Ink gave a wry smile. "Since I have to go with you kids to Scotland, I'm suggesting a new rule."

Three faces turned to him.

"Every detail is vital to our survival, depending on what dangers we have to face. I propose that from now on we share all information. It could save our lives."

Ink was right, of course.

"So what did you see, Adam?" Ink asked. "Was it the strange person that came into the shop yesterday?"

Adam frowned, struggling to find the right words. "I thought I saw him, but I actually *felt* him more than I saw him, if that makes any sense."

Adam couldn't really describe to the others the feelings he had experienced a few minutes before. Sensations of nameless horrors, nightmares, and darkness; his skin crawling, his nerves screaming silently … and all in a matter of seconds.

The others gazed back at him. Adam could see from their faces they were trying to understand, but didn't quite get what he meant. Obviously, Justin and Kim hadn't experienced the awful feelings this time.

"Do you want to talk about it?" Kim asked.

Adam shrugged. "No, it doesn't matter. I probably saw something dark, like someone's jacket, and thought it was that creature again."

Ink gave Adam a probing stare but didn't press him for details. Adam looked down at where his cone lay in a large splatter of pistachio and fudge ice cream on the floor. Smudge was eagerly licking up the remains. Adam didn't feel like any more ice cream. After that awful experience, his appetite had suddenly disappeared. Ink looked at his watch and said it was time to go.

It didn't take them long to walk back to the cottage. When they arrived, Archie and Pandora were already there. Amelia smiled a welcome as she wheeled in the tea trolley.

Kim nudged Adam. "Does Amelia ever get tired of making tea?"

"Lucky for us, she doesn't," Justin said. "Look at that chocolate cake."

Humphrey looked up from his newspaper as they came in. "Ah, just in time. Have a nice afternoon?"

Ink glanced at Adam, who didn't volunteer any information about the strange sighting at the café.

"Yes, great," Adam replied brightly, not wanting to draw too much attention to himself. Right now, he just wanted to fit in and be an ordinary boy.

After helping themselves to food, everyone found their seats. Smudge jumped into Kim's lap.

Ink flopped onto the sofa next to Archie. "Any more news, Dad?"

Humphrey waved the newspaper. "Yes, I was just about to tell you all. The late edition says here that experts estimate the fibers left at the scene to be roughly seven hundred years old."

Everyone gaped.

"Are you serious?" asked Justin.

Humphrey continued. "The police think the thief may be targeting other museums so they've advised those in surrounding areas to check their exhibits. Maybe this person has a thing for fancy dress?"

He chuckled to himself. "Now here's something else. The brown smears at the scene revealed traces of oak gall and gum Arabic, as well as an unusual element that they haven't been able to analyze yet."

"Is there anything significant in that?" Pandora asked.

"Of course there is," Archie announced breezily. "Oak gall? Gum Arabic? The brown substance must be tannin, of course, the main ingredient of mediaeval ink." His face creased into an expression of confusion. "What on earth would anyone want with something like that in the twenty-first century?"

Adam remembered James telling them about his ancestor Bedwyr, nicknamed "the Curious Monk," who had been murdered centuries before, it was said, by poisoned ink. Could there be a connection?

Justin leaned over and whispered in Adam's ear, "Bedwyr. Poison. Remember?"

Humphrey turned on the television. They were just in time for the early evening news. The spotlight was on local events, specifically the break-in at the Ashmolean Museum. The camera zoomed in to focus on Florian Boldwood, his handsome, smiling face filling the screen. When Archie muttered under his breath, Pandora shoved him with her elbow until he subsided into offended silence.

"The latest news coming up on the Ashmolean robbery and the theft of the Excalibur Stone," droned the announcer's voice.

The camera swung to reveal a thin, scrawny man with a balding head, and round, gold-rimmed glasses perched on his beaky nose. He looked like an eager vulture contemplating a lump of raw meat.

"Here we are filming live at the museum where we'll be chatting to Florian Boldwood, the controversial and charismatic Keeper of Anglo-Saxon and Mediaeval Antiquities at the Ashmolean. I'm Nigel Smith hosting your local news slot *On the Spot*. And 'on the spot' with me now, *haw haw*, is Florian Boldwood himself to fill us in on recent developments."

The camera focused on Florian Boldwood's handsome features, his lips stretched in a false smile displaying dazzling, beautifully capped teeth. Florian's blond hair gleamed as he tilted his head at a flattering angle.

"Tell us, Florian, what's the latest regarding the theft of the Excalibur Stone?"

Florian dropped his smile and adopted a suitably tragic air. "Oh, it's dreadful, just too dreadful for words, Nigel." He shook his head sadly. "I cannot believe our history means so little to the criminal element. It appears that, luckily for the museum, the remaining artifacts are untouched. The thief had no interest in any other precious items, including the Alfred Jewel, which is also of immense historical value. I believe the police have managed to lift a partial fingerprint, but no luck with establishing an identity yet."

The camera moved to Nigel Smith, who flashed big horsey teeth in a gleeful grin before overwhelming his guest with more questions.

"What would be the purpose of gouging the stone out of the sword? Why not take the whole sword? Or perhaps the stone is valuable in itself, but no one wants to say how much it's worth." He winked conspiratorially at the camera. "No one wants to commit themselves, hey? What do you *really* think, Florian, your honest opinion?"

He ended his speech with his trademark *haw-haw* neigh of a laugh.

The unexpected barrage of questions took Florian by surprise. He widened his eyes, hesitating a moment before answering. "Er ... I haven't the faintest idea what the thief's motive could be. Of course, it would be difficult to remove the whole sword without attracting attention because a sword dating from that period would be at least two feet long. Although an adult could carry it easily, someone would be bound to notice it."

Florian cocked his head to one side and put on a serious expression. "Then there's the prospective buyer to consider. No one, not even a private collector, would dare touch such an important artifact. Well, not in Britain anyway." He raised his eyebrows. "I don't know about some of the more unscrupulous collectors in Europe and America, however."

"Is that why you announced the sword was more than likely Excalibur, the sword of Arthur?" Nigel purred. His eyes gleamed behind his glasses at the idea of ferreting out his guest's possible motive. "Was it to frighten off potential buyers who would be risking a prison sentence if caught? On the other hand, was it to promote your new book, which I believe will hit the shelves next week? Let's have the name of the book for viewers, Florian. Something about Roman Britain, I think?"

Florian looked uncomfortable. He moistened his lips with the tip of his tongue, staring coldly at the interviewer. "In point of fact, it's a complete coincidence that the book launch and the theft of the sword happened at the same time. And yes, Nigel, of course I hope readers will be encouraged to buy my book—*Signs and Symbols*: *Roman Britain Revealed*—and find out more about our Roman heritage."

Florian glanced at the camera, one hand fluttering toward his tie as if to adjust it. Then he seemed to change his mind and reached for a glass of water on the table in front of him. He took a sip. When he looked into the camera again, his features were composed and his eyebrows lifted at a quirky angle.

"However, I think we should leave the investigation and guesswork to the police, don't you?" he announced breezily, avoiding a direct answer. "I'm sure your viewers will be more interested in what our highly capable detectives on the case have uncovered. I don't think it's my place to comment on criminal motives. After all, I am only an academic, not a criminologist."

Florian flashed his smooth, practiced smile at the camera as he extricated himself from Nigel Smith's cross-examination. Nigel, visibly disappointed he had not managed to put Florian on the spot, announced that next up after the break was an interview with a police spokesperson at the studio. A car advertisement appeared on the screen.

"Book?" A strangled squawk of indignation came from the sofa. "Florian wrote a *book*?" Archie waved a teaspoon at the screen. "The ignoramus. He can barely write his own name. They're *my* ideas. Do you hear me? He stole my ideas, the lily-livered scoundrel, and passed them off as his own. He knows nothing. Nothing."

A chorus of shushes made Archie subside again into sulky silence, with an occasional mumbled complaint.

The camera zoomed in to the ruddy face of the stocky detective on the case. He identified himself as Detective-Inspector Peter Bradley and asked that any member of the public who could assist the police with their inquiries should come forward as soon as possible. He then announced they had security camera footage from that afternoon. A section of the tape would be aired in a few minutes to help jog the memories of any passers-by. He also observed that, sadly, criminals these days had no scruples about using children to help them in their unlawful activities. He hoped that if someone recognized anyone on the footage, they would call the nearest police station right away.

Adam froze with horror. He could hardly breathe. What would his parents say? Justin gasped. Kim clutched Smudge so tightly he whimpered. The video tape began to play on the television screen. Everyone in the room leaned forward, eagerly absorbing each second of the grainy recording. Nigel Smith's voice droned in the background.

"As viewers can see, it's clear that the thieves used the presence of three young people to distract the security guard."

Adam squinted at the screen. He saw the museum entrance, Kim's bobbing head, and the guard shaking his head, then nodding, and then the trio running into the museum. None of their faces was clear because the camera had caught them mainly from the back or side.

"We'd like these three young people to assist the police with their inquiries. Perhaps they have seen something vital to the investigation."

The camera then cut to footage of the security guard in hospital, his head covered in bandages, telling a group of reporters what had happened.

"All I can say is there were three kids, about twelve or thirteen years old, I guess. I can't say exactly because they all looked young to me. Two boys with red hair like carrots and a little African girl. They wanted to see the Alfred Jewel for some school project. I thought it would be all right to let them in for ten minutes. How was I to know what would happen?"

He frowned at the camera. "But there's no way those kids could've hit me over the head like that. They were genuine visitors wanting to see something in the museum. Whoever else is behind this just used them."

Adam and Justin both nervously touched their heads. Red hair like carrots? There was no escaping that color.

Kim's eyes were wide with fear. Little African girl? There was no disguising that fact.

The camera flashed back to Nigel Smith who continued smoothly, "The Excalibur Stone today … perhaps the Alfred Jewel tomorrow. This is a stab at the heart of the nation. Maybe it's time for the government to open its eyes and address the problem of juvenile crime before it's too late."

Adam couldn't believe his ears. *Juvenile crime?*

Kim's eyes filled with tears. "I'm not a criminal. I'm a tourist." Smudge whined and licked her hand.

Justin scowled at the television. "I want to be a prefect next year. I won't be one if this gets back to my parents and the school."

"It's all a horrible mistake," Adam whispered.

Humphrey leaned forward and turned the television off. "I think we've heard enough for today." He smiled at their anxious faces. "We all know you had nothing to do with the theft."

Justin burst out, "But no one else will believe it. What are we going to do?"

"You must leave for Scotland right away," Humphrey said firmly. "I had a feeling things would get complicated so I took some steps while you were out. I called Strathairn Castle and spoke to the housekeeper there, Mrs. Bridget McLeod. James' father is away fishing up in the north, but she's expecting you. You'll just arrive a little earlier than planned. The last thing we need is the police asking you to remain in Oxford to 'help with their investigations,' as they so tactfully put it."

"When must we go?" asked Adam, still reeling in shock from being implicated in unlawful activities.

"Tonight," said Humphrey. "You'll take the seven o'clock train to Edinburgh. The sooner you children get away, the better."

"Tonight?" Adam gazed at Kim and Justin in horror, feeling like a criminal on the run.

"I'll dash home and get your things ready," Pandora said. Archie and Amelia offered to help her, leaving the kids alone with Ink and Humphrey.

"B-b-but what about the Scroll of the Ancients?" Adam cried out, his heart pounding with sudden fear. "We know nothing. We thought we'd have lots of time with you and that you'd explain about ancient parchments and stuff like that."

"We don't even know where to start looking," Justin said.

"Calm down," Humphrey said. "That's why Ink is going with you. Besides, you'll need some help if you're being followed, which I think will be the case."

He shot a piercing glance in Ink's direction. "Remember, whoever has the second Stone of Power probably doesn't know its true value. You must retrieve it. If you get into trouble, Ink will be able to deal with any problems."

"Well, I hope he's a black belt in karate," Justin muttered under his breath.

Ink grinned. "Don't worry, you'll be fine with me."

Justin raised a skeptical eyebrow. Adam stared doubtfully at Ink, whose skinny frame would be no match for Dr. Khalid's thugs. On the other hand, Ink seemed cheerful enough about everything so perhaps he did know something about self-defense.

"Now," Humphrey continued, "we have a little time before you catch the train so I'm going to show you my special manuscripts and give you some tips on handling fragile material."

"But, Humphrey," Justin protested, "it's not going to be as easy as walking into a library and taking out a book."

"I know," Humphrey said. "Come with me." He shooed Smudge back. "Sorry, boy, no doggies allowed where we're going."

He led the group toward another back room. He took a large key off a hook by the doorway and unlocked the door. "Mind your heads, it's a bit low."

The door opened into a narrow passage that led to another door. Humphrey unlocked that door and led the way down a shallow flight of steps into a basement room, painted white. The lighting was dim, Humphrey explained, to protect the ink and illuminations on the valuable manuscripts from fading. All around the walls were glass cabinets containing rolls of parchment, bound books, and flat pages of manuscripts.

"What is this place?" Kim asked.

Humphrey gave a small wriggle, looking uncomfortable. "This is where I keep the real treasures. Upstairs with all the dust and mess … that's just for show. This material is priceless."

91

"So the stuff upstairs isn't valuable?" she asked.

Humphrey laughed. "Of course it is. What I mean is down here the *information* is more valuable. That puts a different light on matters."

Adam decided there was much more to Humphrey than they had thought.

Justin said hesitantly, "So you really are a paleographer, but no one knows about this secret room."

Humphrey gave a mysterious smile. "Only people who should know. Upstairs is the kind of scenario the average person would expect. Loads of dusty manuscripts, bookshelves piled high with tattered volumes of ancient tomes, an equally old retainer poring over the pages by the light of a flickering candle."

He winked at his audience. Ink grinned. Adam shuffled his feet, a little embarrassed because that's exactly how he had imagined Humphrey at first. Kim and Justin looked sheepish.

Adam frowned. "But why do you have to keep them secret? I mean, why would some old documents be so special that you'd have to hide them down here?"

Humphrey indicated the cabinets. "The older the manuscript, the older and possibly more valuable the information it contains. Imagine if a document disproved the existence of the church or an established religious group, for example, or proved the legitimacy of a ruling house that had long been overthrown by usurpers. On the other hand, imagine proof of an ancient civilization that would shatter many accepted theories. Imagine, if you like, proof that someone or something many people believe in is a fake or had never existed—that it was all a lie."

Kim interrupted. "Isn't that a good thing? People *need* to know the truth."

Humphrey fixed her with a steely stare. "Is it a good thing, young lady? Would it be wise to release information that could turn orderly societies into screaming mobs because their belief system had fallen apart, proven to be untrue?"

"I … I don't know," said Kim. "I never thought of it that way."

Humphrey shook his head. "I don't think so."

Adam spoke up, disturbed by Humphrey's words. "But that means some people are manipulating history and lying to the public."

"I think what my father means," Ink said, "is that when potentially dangerous information comes to light, it must be protected and kept away from people like Khalid, people who would have no conscience about starting wars or creating chaos just to gain power or wealth. We already know the Scroll of the

Ancients could be a dangerous document if it falls into the hands of Khalid and his master."

"I see." However, Adam wasn't sure he understood. "Who makes the decisions about what should be kept secret and what should be made public?"

Humphrey sighed. "Alas, governments do, and if one is an ethical historian, one has to inform the government about dangerous finds."

Then he smiled. "Come now. Let's not speculate too soon about the Scroll of the Ancients. First things first. I need to tell you a little about handling old manuscripts. Once you've arrived at Strathairn Castle, Ink will keep me up to date about what you treasure-hunters discover."

Humphrey then led them around the room, pointing out various aspects of the preservation of manuscripts. Adam hardly heard the old man. His thoughts were a mass of confusion. He heard scraps of information as Humphrey's voice murmured in the background, explaining how humidity and heat eroded ancient vellums and parchments; how proper preservation required airtight containers and dim lighting. The thermometer in each cabinet indicated any changes in heat that could damage the manuscripts.

Humphrey gave them each a pair of white cotton gloves to put on before handling anything. The gloves would keep the acid and sweat on their hands from eating into the scroll and damaging it. Now Adam began to pay better attention to Humphrey as he explained that even oxygen was detrimental to the scroll. He gave Ink a special black pouch for storage.

Justin flapped his gloves up and down. "Do we really need these? I mean, the scroll—if it still exists—will have survived this long without any special treatment."

"Justin, the only reason the scroll will have survived is because Bedwyr, as a scribe experienced in such matters, will have taken appropriate steps for its preservation."

"Oh." Justin sounded subdued by Humphrey's stern tone. "Sorry."

Adam looked at Humphrey. "You seem so sure we'll find it."

The old man's voice was firm, confident. "I know you will find what you are supposed to find."

"How do you know?" Kim asked, with a note of panic in her voice. "How can you be so sure?"

Adam said nothing, but he was stricken with anxiety. Imagine if they failed this task. Imagine if this was all just imagination. Perhaps Bedwyr was wrong. Maybe the Scroll of the Ancients didn't even exist.

Humphrey placed one hand on Adam's shoulder. When he spoke, it was as if he had read Adam's mind.

"The Scroll of the Ancients *does* exist. The clues to its location are somewhere in Strathairn Castle because that's the last place Bedwyr visited before his death."

"What's more important?" Adam asked. "The scroll or the stone?"

Humphrey looked into Adam's eyes and the serenity in the old man's expression reassured him.

"Do not worry about the second stone. It will find you. Look for clues to the Scroll of the Ancients—therein lies the key."

A Creature of the Night

Back upstairs, his mind reeling with information and frantic thoughts, Adam found Pandora and Archie in the living room with their luggage. Amelia was in the kitchen, packing a food hamper. Humphrey assured them he would call Mrs. McLeod again to confirm their arrival in Edinburgh the next morning. Archie offered to take them to the station in his battered old car, which he proudly said was an original Morris Minor. Once their luggage was in the trunk, the kids said their good-byes and squeezed into the back seat. Ink sat in front with Archie. As they drove off, Kim suddenly gave a little yelp of fright.

"What's up?" Justin asked.

"Smudge! We didn't say good-bye."

Adam patted her shoulder. "Maybe it's better this way," he said gently. "It might upset him to see us go."

Kim sniffed a few times. "He'll think I just dumped him."

Ink laughed. "No, he won't. He'll think he's in doggy heaven with Amelia spoiling him and Humphrey feeding him steak every night."

Kim's face remained miserable so Ink tried another angle. "When we get to the castle, I'll call Humphrey and he can tell you how Smudge is doing."

Kim muttered, "All right."

After a few minutes, Archie pulled up at the station with a screech of ancient brakes. "Here we are."

The kids tumbled out the back.

Ink picked up a carrier bag and staggered under the weight. "What's in here? Bricks?"

Kim said, "Amelia packed a few blankets for us, in case it gets cold tonight."

Ink went off to secure their overnight tickets while Archie helped them put their luggage in the overhead lockers of a sleeper compartment with four bunks. Adam shoved his suitcase under one of the lower bunks.

When Ink came back, he said to Kim, "I hope you don't mind being a boy for a few hours. It's too expensive to get two separate sleepers."

"'Course I don't mind," said Kim. "I don't want to be by myself anyway."

The shriek of a whistle and mechanical clashing sounds signaled departure time. The kids hung out of the carriage windows, looking up and down the busy station platform.

Archie stepped from the train onto the platform. He then reached up and shook hands with everyone, mumbling, "Er ... my apologies for getting hot under the collar about things in the beginning. Simple mistake."

"Of course, sir," Justin replied politely. "Anyone can see that ancient history is your life. We appreciate all the information you've given us so far."

Adam grinned because Justin sounded so grown-up. He poked Justin in the ribs; Justin poked him back, and a small, friendly scuffle began between them. Kim shook her head and rolled her eyes.

Archie then moved to Ink's side of the window.

"Good luck, dear boy. You just call me any time you have a question," he warbled, thrusting a scrap of paper into Ink's hand. "Here's the number."

Ink nodded in acknowledgment.

A hopeful expression then appeared on Archie's face. "You will ... er ... keep me posted about ... ah ... developments?"

Ink smiled at his father's oldest friend. "Yes, of course we will. I wish you could come with us."

Archie's expression changed abruptly and a shadow of fear crossed his face. He seemed to have trouble breathing; his breath came in short, shallow gasps.

"No," he wheezed. "I ... er ... impossible!" He turned away hastily, and then swung back with a last imploring look. "But call me, any time of day or night if you need assistance."

Ink nodded, a little puzzled by Archie's insistence.

"Good luck, my boy, good luck." Archie hesitated, as if he wanted to say something else, then his eyes shifted toward the cousins who were still scuffling. "Adam ... uh ..."

"I'll look after him," Ink said. "Don't worry. He'll be fine."

"No, I meant ... all right then, good-bye."

With that, Archie shook his head and plunged into the gloom of the station. His egg-shaped silhouette bobbed for a few seconds before disappearing into the crowds of people heading for the exit.

Adam wondered why Archie seemed so nervous. Ink didn't volunteer an explanation, however, and Adam was too polite to ask, so he put the incident to the back of his mind. Besides, the others were busy getting comfortable. Justin, naturally, had already opened the food hamper and was inspecting the contents.

"Oh, wow. Cake. Those yummy little meat pies. Cream buns. Amelia knows what I like." Justin looked up. "Does anyone else want a snack or is it just me who's starving?"

Adam stifled a giggle. Justin's appetite came first most of the time. He held out his hand for a paper plate and napkin. Ink and Kim were already gobbling sandwiches.

"What's the plan?" Adam asked Ink. "I mean, when we get to Strathairn Castle?"

Ink devoured half a ham-and-tomato sandwich in one large gulp. "Well, it's not like a master plan or anything. I know Humphrey couldn't get hold of your aunt or James before we left, but it'll be okay with just us. We'll manage. Humphrey spoke to James before he went to France, and they decided to ask me to go with you anyway. You see, Humphrey is in constant contact with Ebrahim and needs to stay in Oxford to receive information. They have a complicated system of writing letters to each other. I don't understand it and I never will. I think it's in an ancient code or something."

He laughed. "This is where their skills are put to good use."

Adam and Justin looked at each other in excitement.

Codes? Ancient ciphers? Cool!

"Go on," urged Kim, her sandwich lying forgotten on her paper plate.

"Mrs. McLeod, the housekeeper, knows you're all coming for a holiday." Ink glanced at Kim. "She's also been told to expect an additional guest so don't worry about not being invited."

Ink bit into another sandwich, chewed a few times, and swallowed. "Mrs. McLeod knows me well. I've been to the castle loads of times during my school holidays. She thinks I'm a senior student doing a summer research project on the castle and the Strathairn family tree, which goes back hundreds of years. Parts of the castle date back to the time of William the Conqueror."

Silence.

"The year 1066 ring a bell?" he asked.

Adam piped up. "Yes, the Battle of Hastings."

Ink grabbed another sandwich. "Now, here's the sort-of plan. I know James has all the castle drawings in the library, even the ones from way back. Lucky for us, it's the family tradition to keep papers and charts and that kind of stuff."

Justin looked pleased. "So we'll start looking in the oldest parts of the castle? I can't wait."

Ink nodded. "Yes, because the whole estate is so big we could spend days looking in the wrong places. Also, there are areas like the stables, the old mews where the birds are kept, and other outbuildings that were probably important then, given the way of life seven hundred years ago. If we can isolate the areas that were important about the time period when Bedwyr was alive, we'll save ourselves a lot of time."

He looked ruefully at his companions. "Because, as you know, time is what we haven't got."

Adam thought about the look on Dr. Khalid's face as he had plummeted into the abyss in Egypt. Even then, his expression had reflected malignant evil and the intense desire to succeed in his mission, no matter whom or what he destroyed in the process. Time was hard at their heels as Ebrahim had said in his letter. They must find the remaining six Stones of Power and the Pyramidion before the fateful confluence of the planets.

"So where exactly is Strathairn Castle?" Justin asked. "Is it near Edinburgh?"

"It's about thirty miles away, on a hill above a small village called Haddley," Ink replied. "Are you interested in Edinburgh?"

"Yes, of course." Justin's face glowed. "Who wouldn't be? It has the most fantastic things to see, like Edinburgh Castle and the Armory, and the catacombs under the city. I want to go on one of those ghost tours in the dead of night." He waved his hands in front of Kim. "Woooh! All spooky and creepy."

Kim flinched. "Count me out," she replied primly. "I prefer daylight when I go exploring, thanks very much."

After a long and eventful day, everyone began yawning loudly. They washed their faces and brushed their teeth in the tiny bathroom adjacent to their compartment. Justin and Adam took the two lower bunks. Ink pulled down the blinds and turned off the light before clambering into the bunk above Adam. Ink and Justin were fast asleep within seconds; Adam could hear their gentle snores. Kim, being a girl, probably didn't do anything as unladylike as snoring, Adam thought with a drowsy grin.

As he lay in his bunk, he wondered about his dream the previous night. He had forgotten to ask Humphrey and Archie what they thought Arthur had meant when he had told Adam to restore the Stone of Caledfwlch. In the dream, Adam had clearly seen the stone gleaming in the uplifted sword so why did it need to be restored? Adam had dreamed of the eve of one of Arthur's most successful battles, the Battle of Badon Hill, which had turned the Saxons back for almost fifty years. Why then had Arthur talked about the land descending into "ravening darkness?" Had Arthur known the sword contained a Stone of Power and was telling him what would happen to the world if the stone fell into enemy hands? But Arthur had been dead for roughly fifteen hundred years. It was all too much to think about and he was tired so Adam gave a gigantic yawn and settled into his bunk.

The train made an occasional comforting *chukka* noise that soon lulled Adam to sleep. He dreamed of intense darkness enfolding him, but not just enfolding him; soon, the darkness was enveloping and smothering him. A hazy impression of a white face with pale lips stretched in a mirthless grin, and black eyes lit by a demonic red glow danced in his mind. He tried to move, but a powerful stupor pinned him to the bunk. More than the lethargy of sleep, the sensation made his limbs feel as if they were made of lead. He coughed as a fine dust tickled his nose and throat; he heard the others cough as well. Adam fought the sensation and actually lifted his shoulders off the bunk before the paralyzing heaviness dragged him back down again. He heard a cough from Kim and then silence. The dust was thicker now, clogging his air passages. He choked, unable to breathe properly. With a huge gasp, he thrust himself into a sitting position and opened his eyes. As his eyes adjusted to the gloom, what he saw made him scream, but the scream was silent because his vocal cords refused to obey his brain.

A dark shape like a giant bat hovered over Justin. Adam fought the heaviness, managing to drag his body off the bunk by sheer willpower. He crashed to the floor, unable to stand because his legs had lost all strength. The figure swung round and hissed when it saw him, its eyes glowing with an angry fire. Then, raising its arms, it leaped at him with a screech of rage. Adam stared, powerless. Suddenly, a small shape barreled its way toward the figure, thudding into its legs and clamping down hard with sharp teeth. It was Smudge. There was an excited yelp, a growl, and a scream of pain. Adam blinked blearily at the swirling fury of arms, legs, teeth, tail, and cloak, wondering how it was possible. Smudge was having a glorious time repelling the invader threatening his new friends. From the yells, it certainly sounded human. Kim's head popped over the bunk above Justin, who had also sat up. Both of them stared open-mouthed at the sight of Smudge in action.

Ink raised his head, slithered from the top bunk to the floor, and then staggered to his feet. He was weak but still managed to perform an impressive series of kicks, and karate chops with his hands. Smudge darted in and out of the wildly flailing arms and legs, snapping at the intruder's ankles at every chance. The intruder backed off, snarling and spitting, but not before it gouged deep scratches in Ink's arms with long, talon-like nails. Finally, when the intruder whipped out a knife, Ink reached up and pulled the emergency lever.

100

The screaming siren and massive jolt as the train hit the emergency brakes was enough for the intruder. Lights would come on. People would be swarming all over the train. With a frenzied cry of anguish and frustration, it flung itself into the corridor, slamming against the window. It somehow managed to raise the glass and slither out of the window, scrambling down the side of the train before anyone could stop it. Ink fell to his knees, panting. When the emergency lights came on, Adam could see that someone had removed their bags from the overhead lockers and opened each one. The intruder had obviously gone through the contents, looking for something.

Ink found his voice first. "What was that? Something out of *Night of the Living Dead*?"

"It was human, but somehow not," Justin said, shaken. "Look at your arms, Ink. What kind of creature does that?"

Although Ink tried to act cool, his hands were trembling as he crawled onto the nearest bunk. There were long gouges down his arms where the intruder had clawed him. The cuts were bleeding, but the brown smears around the wounds were even more worrying.

"Are you all right?" Adam cried out. "You're bleeding."

"You've got to see a doctor as soon as possible," Justin said.

Ink looked at Kim. "Is Smudge okay? I think he saved us. That thing drugged us somehow."

"Not me and Kim," said Justin. He grinned at Adam. "We're lucky you woke up."

Kim stroked Smudge, who was wagging his whole body in happiness. "How on earth did Smudge get here?"

Justin pointed to the carrier bag containing the blankets. It now lay on one side and the blankets had tumbled out. "There it is—Smudge's stowaway bag."

"You're a clever doggie," Kim crooned, snuggling Smudge in her arms. Then she noticed brown smears on her hand. "Yuck. What's this? It came from Smudge's mouth."

"I think it's poison," Adam said urgently. He had a horrible feeling the intruder had used something venomous against them. "Rinse his mouth. And you should wash your arms, Ink."

Again, thoughts of how Bedwyr had met his fate jumbled in Adam's head. James had told him in Egypt that someone had poisoned Bedwyr's inkwell hundreds of years ago. There must be a connection, but how, so many centuries later? And what would any of that have to do with what this creature had been looking for in their luggage?

Ink washed his arms thoroughly with soap, while Justin and Kim wiped the brown smears off Smudge's jaws and rinsed his mouth out with water.

"Well," Ink said, drying his arms, "that's the best I can do for now. As soon as we get to the castle, Smudge must see a vet and I'll go to a doctor."

He coughed. "What was that stuff? Some kind of sleeping powder? Am I just imagining things or wasn't that the same person at the shop the day you three arrived?"

Adam nodded. "It seemed like it. Or someone dressed the same way."

Kim widened her eyes. "Do you think it could be a … er … vampire?"

Justin shot her a withering look. "Of course not. Vampires suck blood. They don't unpack people's luggage. Anyway, there aren't any vampires in real life, only in books and horror movies."

Kim just stared at him and bit her lower lip.

Then Justin grinned, put one arm around Adam's shoulders, and said in a deep voice, "Don't worry, Bella, I'll save you."

Adam looked into Justin's eyes and pawed gently at his chest. "Oh, Edward," he squeaked as he fluttered his eyelashes. "You're my hero."

They both roared with laughter, especially when Kim flounced back to her bunk, angry at being teased. Even Ink smiled at the gag.

"Hey, we're only kidding," Justin said. "Where's your sense of humor?"

"I think you're making a stupid joke when the person who just attacked Ink could be a killer," Kim said, still cross.

"Whatever it is," Ink said, "why is it following us?"

He looked and sounded so serious that Adam and Justin's smiles quickly disappeared as they returned to reality. Adam exchanged worried glances with his cousin, wondering how they would deal with this kind of enemy. They were already nervous about Dr. Khalid because, although the mastermind had not revealed himself yet, it would only be a matter of time before he did. Now this odd and dangerous creature was stalking them as well. He remembered Kim's thoughts about the person who had stolen the stone from the sword in the Ashmolean: *The person who has the stone might come after us, thinking we know something.* Was it the same person who had just tried to poison them?

Before he could voice this suspicion, there came the sounds of loud voices and heavy boots clomping down the passage.

"Quick!" Ink closed the compartment door and then got into his bunk. "That'll be the train inspector trying to find out who pulled the emergency lever. It's a serious offence in Britain. We'll talk about this tomorrow."

The inspector saw only four sleepy faces when he flung open the compartment door. Four heads shook in answer to his question about who had sounded the alarm.

"And what about the dog?" he inquired. "Someone heard a dog barking and growling."

"Dog?" Kim gave a huge yawn. "I thought dogs weren't allowed on the train." She gently pushed Smudge's head back under the blanket.

The man snorted and closed the door.

STRATHAIRN CASTLE

When they stepped off the train in Edinburgh, an elderly, white-haired man met them. Tall and slightly stooping, he had a firm handshake and shaggy white eyebrows over bright blue eyes. After welcoming Ink, he introduced himself as Augustus Sheldon, butler to James' father, the old earl. He led the group to a mud-spattered station wagon and insisted on loading their luggage into the trunk without help. He addressed them as "Master" or in Kim's case, "Miss." Justin squirmed and suggested he call them simply by their names.

"Of course, Master Justin," Sheldon replied with a kindly smile and a horrible grating of gears as he swerved to avoid a large truck.

"Sheldon won't listen to you," Ink whispered. "He's a stickler for the old Scottish ways. Sheldon's worked for the family most of his life. I think he started as a pantry boy or something like that when he was just a kid, about sixty years ago. He even calls James 'Master James' or 'the young master.' He's a mine of information about the castle, though, and knows lots of old stories."

They traveled along a country road, heading for the village of Haddley about thirty miles farther north. It was colder and bleaker in Scotland, although the purple heather-covered hills were pretty. They looked back at the grim ancient fortress of Edinburgh Castle, perched precariously like a giant bird of prey on the hill overlooking the city. The Old Town, the historical part of the city built of gray granite, was decidedly different from the warm mellow shades and gentle sunshine of Oxford. Ink said there was plenty of time for day visits to see all the sights, however, and suggested they get to a vet and a doctor as soon as possible.

Ink was paler than usual. His skin had turned a grayish color. His face looked pinched and ill, with dark purple shadows under his eyes. Kim cuddled Smudge in her arms so Ink could take a closer look at him. When Ink pulled Smudge's lips back, the dog's gums were white and his breathing sounded strained. Sheldon said they would be at the local veterinarian in just a few minutes. Ink, clearly reluctant to discuss weird cloaked creatures in the night with anyone, mumbled something about food poisoning.

Soon they turned into the picturesque village of Haddley, comprised of slate-roof cottages, a bustling High Street with a variety of quaint little shops, a small post office and an even smaller police station, a market square with a mercat cross, and winding cobbled streets. A large duck pond on one side of the square was home to several pairs with their ducklings, and two swans that ignored their lowly neighbors as they sailed past in regal pride. Sheldon parked the car and hustled the group into the vet's waiting room. He muttered several words to the receptionist. In a few minutes, Ink and the kids found themselves looking into the friendly brown eyes of Bruce Hamilton, the local vet, who took charge immediately and placed Smudge on the examining table.

"Looks like your dog has eaten some kind of poison," he said, inspecting Smudge's mouth and eyes. "What's your name, boy?" The vet stroked Smudge's ears and glanced at Kim for an answer.

"His name's Smudge. We found him the day before yesterday in the street, next to a pile of trash so maybe he … er … ate something then?"

Kim sounded uncomfortable telling Bruce something untrue, but how could anyone understand what they had encountered on the train the night before.

Bruce continued to examine Smudge. "I don't think so. This is recent, within the last twelve hours." He busied himself with a syringe. "I'll take a blood sample right now and then I'll give him something."

He went over to a cabinet, unlocked it, and withdrew two small glass vials of clear liquid. He quickly drew some blood and then gave Smudge an injection. Smudge raised his head weakly and whimpered. Kim patted him, whispering soothing words.

Bruce said to Ink, "You don't look so good either. You'd better sit down so I can check you as well."

Ink swayed a little on his feet before slumping into the chair that Adam pulled forward for him. Despite his cheerful attitude, Bruce seemed extremely disturbed by the condition of both his patients, and a closer look at Ink was enough to make the vet frown. The long, deep scratches on Ink's arms had turned a suspicious dark color, suggesting infection. Bruce rolled up Ink's T-shirt sleeve even higher and took a blood sample. Then he plunged a syringe into Ink's arm.

Ink gave a feeble grin. "Dog antibiotics for me too?"

Bruce laughed. "I'm afraid we don't have a resident doctor. You have to go to the city for serious problems. But since I'm also a homeopath, I can treat humans. I can deal with most aches and pains. Don't worry. What you're getting is also for humans."

Ink laid his head on the examining table, as if suddenly worn out. When Bruce asked him about the scratches, Ink gave a huge yawn and mumbled something about being attacked by a mugger on the train. The vet carefully took a swab for analysis and then cleaned the gouges, applied ointment, and bandaged Ink's arms.

Bruce looked at Smudge again, extremely puzzled by the undoubted case of poisoning. It was possible that the dog and the young man had been poisoned at the same time, although in Ink's case it was by direct contact and in Smudge's case by biting. He wondered briefly if the children had tried to poison the dog themselves, but after watching Kim with Smudge and seeing Adam and Justin's anxious expressions, he decided they weren't to blame.

"I really feel you should go to a hospital," he said firmly to Ink. "You need more tests and a complete check up."

Ink shook his head. "No, I'll be fine. Just give me anything you want me to take."

Bruce frowned, but Smudge seemed perkier already. He was sitting up and wagging his tail. Undoubtedly, the medication was working.

"All right," he agreed reluctantly. "I'll let you go home today on condition that you rest and come back to see me in a day or two."

Ink nodded tiredly.

"Where are you staying?"

"At Strathairn Castle," Ink replied. "We're guests of the family."

"I know James and his father well." Bruce gave Ink a bottle of tablets. "Start taking these today. I want to see you and Smudge as soon as possible. If you feel worse, or you're worried about anything, please call me immediately."

Before they left, Bruce said, "I'll have these blood samples tested today and let you know the results when I see you."

Once the group left, the vet picked up the telephone and dialed a number. Someone answered after a few seconds.

"Hello, Mac? Bruce Hamilton here. I'm sending over some blood samples for you to check. Very strange symptoms shown by a young man and a dog."

Mac must have sounded surprised because Bruce laughed.

"Yes, that's right. I said a young man *and* a dog. I don't think they ingested enough to be in grave danger, but both were in quite a serious condition. The young man more than the dog, though. I've given them a dose of the new stuff you sent me."

Mac said something. Bruce laughed again.

"I know it'll work because it's begun working already. The dog is recovering rapidly."

Mac said something else.

Bruce replied solemnly, "Yes, a fantastic product, absolutely miraculous. Let me know soonest about the tests. Thanks."

Bruce Hamilton put down the receiver and folded his arms. He looked through the window where he could see the kids and Ink piling into the car with Smudge. They were all laughing as Smudge gave a few happy barks. The poison was nothing like he had ever seen before—not in this century at least, he was sure of it. He felt relieved the poison was slow acting and the antidote he had given them appeared to be working.

Antidote.

He had known just by looking at the victims that antibiotics were useless. It was lucky for the young man and the dog that poisons—past and present—just happened to be his specialty. Bruce's last year of studies had included toxicology, dealing with the detection of poisons, the effects, and antidotes. For his own interest, he had delved back into the past to discover ancient and mediaeval poisons, which was how he had recognized the symptoms when faced with Ink and Smudge's condition. The antidote he had just given them was so new that not many people knew about it. It was fortunate his friend Mac, the scientist who had developed this wonder drug, had sent Bruce a few samples.

Bruce felt sure the poison came from a plant. At first, he thought they might have eaten toxic mushrooms such as Death Angel. But the long scratches on Ink's arms worried him. He mulled over conflicting thoughts as he tried to solve the problem. Had the attacker scratched Ink with some lethal ingredient? Perhaps it was a compound, a mixture of two or more toxins. The names of several mediaeval poisons slipped into his mind. It could be anything … some deadly plant extract such as black hyoscyamus from the herb henbane. Maybe it was wolfsbane, also known as monkshood, a common enough poison. Monkshood was particularly dangerous if it got into open wounds. Then again, it might be thorn apple, foxglove, or even black hellebore. He thought of belladonna, or deadly nightshade, which causes its victims to fall asleep permanently, a symptom that could explain Ink's unusual exhaustion. He would only know once the lab sent the results back. Bruce Hamilton was sure of one thing: whatever the poison, the assailant had not had time to administer much of it. He wondered how and why the young man and the dog had been poisoned. There was much more to this than a simple mugging.

As Sheldon drove up the hill, the tops of towers and turrets showed through the trees. Adam glanced at the others. Ink had a bit more color in his face. Smudge stuck his head through an open window, his ears flapping in the breeze, and seemed nearly back to his normal level of excitement. Finally, the car swept around a small slope and Strathairn Castle lay before them. The grounds extended for what seemed miles as the car meandered up the long, tree-lined driveway. On the left-hand side were extensive, flower-filled gardens with statues and a small, decorative folly. Beyond that was a parking area, no doubt for the tourists. On the right-hand side was a wooded area where Adam glimpsed red-roofed buildings, possibly stables or the so-called mews that Ink had mentioned.

The castle loomed into view, resembling something from a fairytale. From a solid stone base surrounded by a moat, the pale gray walls swept up into an elaborate array of towers, turrets, and crenellated battlements. Adam imagined mediaeval archers firing arrows through the narrow loopholes at their enemies, while the castle defenders ducked behind the battlements.

"It's a bit much when you first see it," Ink said. "Wait until Mrs. McLeod raises the portcullis. You'll feel as if you're in another century."

"What's a portcullis?" Kim asked.

Sheldon explained. "A portcullis is a latticed gate made of wood, metal, or a combination of the two. Portcullises fortified the entrances to many mediaeval castles during a time of attack or siege."

He pointed ahead. "You'll see as we drive over the drawbridge and through the gatehouse that there are actually two portcullises—one at the entrance and one at the end of the gatehouse. The one closest to the inside would be closed first and then the other. This was used to trap the enemy in a small space. Often burning wood or fire-heated sand would be dropped onto them from holes in the gatehouse ceiling called murder-holes."

"Cool," said Justin. "Don't forget the boiling oil."

Sheldon laughed as he shook his head. "Oh no, Master Justin. Pouring boiling oil on intruders is just a myth. It was far too valuable and rare at the time to waste. The castle defenders mostly used boiling water. These days, we only use the inside portcullis. We used to raise it by hand, but now it's powered electrically. However, in the event of a power failure, one can still use the old handle."

"The place seems to have a bit of everything, doesn't it?" Kim sounded hesitant as she stared ahead at their destination.

"I know what you mean," Ink said. "The original castle dates back to about AD 1000 and then later Strathairn descendants just added on. So that's why there's quite a mixture of styles."

Justin prodded Adam. "This is what I call a *real* castle. I can't wait to see the place properly."

Once the portcullis was raised, Sheldon drove across the drawbridge, into the courtyard, and parked in front of the main entrance. Two plump, middle-aged women rushed down the steps to greet them, shaking their hands, and twittering cries of welcome. The women hugged Ink warmly and somehow, between laughter and greetings, they managed to introduce themselves as Mrs. Bridget McLeod, the housekeeper, and Mrs. Margaret Grant, the cook. The two women looked so much alike, with the same brown eyes and graying curls, that they could have been twins. While the women fussed with Sheldon, Ink whispered that they were sisters, now both widowed, and had worked at the castle for years. Hovering on the steps was a shy young woman, with dark hair and a sweet smile, twisting her apron corner in one hand. She was Mrs. Grant's daughter Susan, the parlor maid and general helper.

Adam and Justin opened the trunk and hauled out the luggage before Sheldon could reach it.

Sheldon wagged a disapproving finger at Justin. "That's my job. If you keep it up, I'll have nothing to do."

"Sorry, I forgot, Sheldon," Justin said with a grin. "You can do it next time."

The boys dragged their suitcases into the spacious entrance hall, gawking at the sight. Intricately carved wood paneling, gleaming suits of armor, sets of crossed swords on the walls, a gigantic expanse of tiled floor, and a huge staircase with elaborate balustrades met their bewildered gaze. Kim, lugging her bags just behind them, stood with her mouth open, speechless. Smudge pattered at her heels, rather nervous about the new surroundings. A faded Persian carpet lay at their feet. Adam noticed that one of the corners looked frayed, as if large teeth had chewed on it. Maybe Strathairn Castle had a dog—a rather big one.

Justin was the first to speak. "I thought Aunt Isabel lived in a museum, but this is a hundred times bigger."

"Oh, it's not a museum," cried Mrs. McLeod from the front door. "It's a home, a real home. The old master has his own museum if you're interested in curiosities. Some strange things in there. You can see it later if you like."

She briskly ushered them forward. "Come along now. Hamish will take your bags to your rooms. This way to the kitchen. You must be starving."

Mrs. McLeod rolled her r's in a way that drew the r's out long, and it sounded as if she was saying "starrrrving."

"I think the dining room is a wee bit too grand for you," she said as they passed the doorway of an enormous, magnificently furnished room. The elegantly papered walls hung with paintings and tapestries. The long table, seating at least thirty people, fairly bristled with crystal, silver ornaments and dishes, and glassware. The chandelier twinkled as the beams of sunshine streaming through the open windows caught the facets on each pendant.

"So I've laid out everything in the kitchen. We don't even use the dining room when just the old master and Master James are here. It's for formal occasions

111

and when the tourists come. There's a small breakfast room next to the kitchen, which they prefer for meals."

Alerted by the sounds of footsteps in the hall, an enormous hound hurtled down the staircase toward them, his ears and tail flying. He was evidently the carpet-chewing culprit. Kim snatched Smudge out of possible danger, while Justin stepped behind a conveniently placed suit of armor. Only Adam and Ink stood their ground as the gigantic beast galloped up to them.

"Down, Jasper," said Mrs. McLeod sternly.

"What a great dog," Adam said at the same time. "Here, boy."

The animal chose to ignore the housekeeper's command and befriend this sympathetic visitor. Skidding to a halt at Adam's feet, Jasper opened his giant jaws, displaying rows of large, white teeth. A long, red tongue unfurled from somewhere inside the cavernous mouth and delicately licked his hand. Adam knelt and stroked the whiskered face. When Jasper's large brown eyes gazed into his, Adam knew he had a friend for life.

"Look at this magnificent dog." Adam stroked the animal's ears. "Aren't you a friendly boy?"

Enchanted by this affectionate response, Jasper groveled at Adam's feet, pawing his hands gently for more ear stroking.

Sheldon looked down at the dog. A smile tugged at the corners of his mouth although he tried to maintain his severe expression. "Jasper, heel, I say."

Jasper gave Sheldon a sheepish look, but didn't budge.

Sheldon shook his head in disbelief. "I'm amazed you're not frightened of him, Master Adam. Visitors are usually terrified of his size."

"You mean the size of his teeth," Justin called out from behind the suit of armor.

Adam got to his feet. "He's just curious, not aggressive. I have a big dog at home so I'm used to them."

He looked down at the large, gray mound, now rolling on his back to encourage his new friend to try some stomach scratching.

"He seems quite young," Adam said. "He's so playful."

"There's always been a Jasper at Strathairn Castle," said Mrs. McLeod. "Ever since I can remember. This one must be Jasper the Hundredth by now. My great-grandfather said the family liked the breed. He's an Irish wolfhound, but they're not particularly fierce with intruders as you can see with Jasper."

112

Adam gave the dog a last pat.

"He pines for Master James," Mrs. Grant stated firmly. "There's no good in having a dog if you aren't here to spend time with the animal."

Mrs. McLeod shushed her, but Adam thought she had a point. Mrs. Grant opened the door to the old-fashioned, much cozier kitchen. Rows of bright copper pots and pans hung from the ceiling. Bunches of herbs and dried flowers hung next to the windows. Large work counters were piled with bowls and crockery, and a delicious smell of baking permeated the air.

Justin looked around with delight. "This is food heaven," he whispered to Adam.

Kim stooped to put Smudge on the ground and spent a few minutes introducing him to Jasper. They became friends after several tentative sniffs. Adam was right: Jasper was curious and, from the way the two animals were soon frolicking about, obviously lonely as Mrs. Grant had said. Mrs. McLeod shooed them into the scullery and tossed two meaty bones after them.

"Now," she said, with a satisfied glance at the guests, "let's see about something to eat."

The scrubbed pine kitchen table was loaded with food—fruit, pies, cakes, sandwiches, and cold meats—inviting the hungry group to sit and eat. As they dug into the delicious spread, Mrs. McLeod chattered on, with Mrs. Grant interrupting occasionally to add details. Susan just smiled and passed various dishes around the table.

"Then there's Terence Burns who manages the estate. You remember Terence, don't you, Ink? Of course you do, such a nice man—had a family tragedy earlier this year—and there's Hamish who looks after the birds. He took your bags to your rooms a few minutes ago. He's not that sociable so don't expect too much of a welcome from him."

Mrs. Grant shook her head and frowned. "Keeps himself to himself, he does."

Justin eagerly asked, "Are there lots of falcons and hawks here?"

"Oh, yes," Sheldon replied, "and owls too. Flying demonstrations are popular with tourists, so there are various birds of prey on most of the big estates in Scotland. The old master's conservation-minded as well. He has a breeding program going with a pair of Golden Eagles. Hamish is in charge of the birds. He's the expert." He winked at Mrs. McLeod. "The castle falconer, I should say, to give him his proper title. Grumpy old soul is our Hamish, but you should see him all dressed up in his kilt for the tourists. Rather impressive."

"Can you touch the birds?" Kim asked.

Sheldon gave a short laugh. "Only if you want a finger taken off." Then he gave her a stern look. "Now remember, wild creatures are wild creatures. Just because they agree to stay and do as someone asks doesn't mean it's the same as having a pet cat or dog. So you be careful when you visit the mews."

Kim nodded as if she weren't sure about seeing hawks or falcons if it meant her fingers were in danger of being pecked off.

The guests then learned that the old earl, who was away fishing as Humphrey had said, would be back in two weeks. No one had heard from James since he had left for France, but since he regularly disappeared on such expeditions, this was nothing to worry about, Mrs. McLeod said cheerfully. Obviously, they weren't aware of James' accident. When Adam glanced at Ink, he shook his head to signal they should say nothing about it.

Mrs. Grant said, "The castle is closed to the public until August so there's plenty of time for Master Ink's research project. You're free to explore as much as you like."

Mrs. McLeod winked at the butler, who was loudly slurping his tea. "I suppose you'll be telling the children all the ghost stories, Mr. Sheldon?"

He peered over the rim of the cup and waggled his eyebrows menacingly. "I suppose I might, but only if they've got stout hearts and are willing to brave the frighteners of the night."

For a brief moment, Adam thought he was serious. Then he saw the mischievous twinkle in Sheldon's eyes.

"Or maybe they're far too grown up for such childish fancies," the butler said. "They look too big for kiddy stories."

Adam eagerly butted in. "No, we're not too old for ghost stories. I want to hear them."

Susan spoke for the first time. "I also like ghost stories," she said, "and Sheldon knows how to tell a fearsome tale."

The two older women giggled together. Mrs. Grant said in a mock scolding tone to Susan, "Now don't you wake up screaming in the middle of the night because of some ghost story. You'll get no sympathy from me."

Susan smiled and said to Adam, "I think the best time to hear a good ghost story is just before bedtime because it's more terrifying late at night."

"Are there any stories about the monk?" Adam asked. "I mean Bedwyr, James' famous ancestor?"

There was a sudden silence. Then Susan gave a little squeak and looked at Mrs. Grant.

"Oh no, dear." Mrs. McLeod's lips trembled for a moment. Then she blinked nervously. "We can't talk about him. He's family and all."

"Where's he buried?" Adam hoped Bedwyr's grave was somehow connected to the scroll. He didn't receive an immediate answer.

Sheldon and the three women exchanged solemn glances before Mrs. Grant replied, "There's a memorial stone in the old crypt, beneath the ruined chapel."

She sounded reluctant to speak about it.

Adam felt a thrill of excitement—after their Egyptian adventure, when the earl had invited them to Scotland, he had mentioned the ruined chapel in the middle of a lake.

Justin pushed for more details. "But has he been seen by anyone? If there are ghosts here in the castle or stories about sightings, then surely someone like a well-known ancestor would've appeared as well."

Sheldon looked down into his teacup, seeming to study the brown liquid. "Well, I won't lie to you. There have been some sightings over the years, but always before something happens. That's why we don't mention him. Just in case talking about him … er … rouses him, if you know what I mean."

"Why are you afraid?" Justin persisted. "I mean, he's a family member so he won't harm his descendants, will he?"

Sheldon stared at Justin, as if lost in thoughts he certainly would not express. "I can't explain right now, Master Justin," he said in a bland voice, "but I'll be happy to tell you about the Gray Lady, the Headless Horseman, or the Wandering Knight later on."

Adam gave Justin an impatient kick under the table to signal that his questions were making Sheldon uncomfortable.

Justin got the hint. "That was a great meal, Mrs. Grant. May we help you clear and wash the dishes?"

When Justin stood, Kim and Adam also jumped up to help.

"What? Bless my soul. Of course you won't clear and wash the dishes," Mrs. Grant spluttered, half-indignant but rather pleased by their courtesy. "You young people go on upstairs. Susan will show you to your rooms. Then you're free to run about and enjoy the place. We'll see you at four for tea."

"*More* food?" Justin whispered to Adam, as Susan led the way up the huge staircase and along what seemed to be a never-ending corridor. "I'll be as fat as a pig by the time we go home."

Adam prodded Justin's stomach. "Hmmm? What's this? A spare roll or two? No more cake for you."

"Shut up." Justin laughed as he slapped Adam's hand away.

Susan came to a halt in front of the boys' bedroom. Adam and Justin stood in the doorway, gazing in amazement. The elaborate furniture was certainly antique. A huge four-poster bed dominated the room. There were a few elegant, embroidered chairs, a large carved wooden chest of drawers in the corner, a few portraits of young men in clothing from several hundred years ago, and an enormous wardrobe. Adam immediately christened it the Narnia wardrobe, after the one they had seen in the movie *The Lion, the Witch and the Wardrobe.* Lead-paned casement windows overlooked the wooded area they had seen on their way up the drive. The boys ran to the windows and peered eagerly out, exclaiming at how far they could see.

Susan escorted Kim to her bedroom adjoining the boys' room. There was an interleading door between the two rooms. When Kim turned the handle, she found the door locked.

Susan said, "There's a key hanging on a hook in the other room so that anyone can go through to this room if they wish."

Kim's bedroom, although smaller and containing a daintier four-poster bed, was equally impressive, decorated in cream, gold, and pale green. Delicately painted patterns of gold leaves adorned the ceiling and several wall panels. Portraits depicted young girls dressed in long pastel gowns, holding puppies or kittens or baskets of flowers. Even the tapestry-covered chairs were smaller and looked more fragile. Definitely a room for a girl.

Susan explained, "This room belonged to one of the daughters of an earl who lived a few centuries ago. It's used as a guest room now."

"How can so few people do all the cleaning for such a huge place?" Kim asked.

Susan blushed and giggled. "Most of the rooms are closed up right now, so some of the staff members have taken a bit of a holiday. We usually have two footmen and three extra maids. We only open the castle in August and visitors come right through to December. The old master loves to have a grand Christmas and New Year's party. Then we get in help from the village, so it's no bother at all. But the gardens need a lot of attention. I expect you'll see the gardeners when you go on your walk later. We've got four regular people from the village and a casual chap comes in when there's more work to be done."

Kim pointed to a dressing table laden with crystal jars and fragile ornaments. "This stuff looks so old and valuable. What happens if we break something?"

Adam and Justin stood in the open doorway, listening to Kim. Clearly, they had the same thought.

Susan burst into peals of soft laughter. "There's no chance of breaking anything, I'm sure. All this furniture goes back hundreds of years and no one has managed to damage anything yet. It's a home, like Mrs. McLeod said, not a museum. You just enjoy yourselves. The bathroom is down the passage, right at the end. The taps are a bit stiff, however, and you'll have to wait a few minutes for the water to heat up."

She gave them a shy wave and left the room.

"She's right." Justin looked around the room. "People used this stuff every day so nothing's going to fall apart overnight. I think we should be extra careful though, just in case."

"Where's Ink?" Adam asked.

"I think he's having a nap," Kim replied. "He went off down the passage in the opposite direction. Maybe he has a room he always uses when he visits."

Justin nodded. "He was still looking a bit sick in the car. Let's leave him and explore on our own for a bit. We can shower and unpack later."

Since they were in an old castle with valuable items, they walked sedately down the stairs and found their way back to the kitchen. Mrs. McLeod was helping Mrs. Grant peel potatoes, while Sheldon polished a silver coffee pot. Jasper and Smudge lay curled at his feet, snoozing. He looked up as they entered.

"Want to go off and explore, then?" Sheldon got up and took two folded pieces of paper out of a drawer. He gave one each to Kim and Justin. "There you are." He rummaged in the drawer again and then handed Kim a dog leash. "It's one of Jasper's old ones from when he was a pup. You don't want your doggie getting lost on the estate now."

Justin peered at it. "What's this?"

"A map of the estate."

Adam smiled. "Don't worry, Sheldon. We don't need any maps. We're just going to wander about for a bit."

Sheldon shook his head in warning. "This is a big place, laddie. Mark my words, you'll need a map, especially when you get to the Star Maze. Best not to go in alone. Wait for Master Ink or Terence to go with you. You may be trapped and not get out again." He drew his eyebrows together in a severe frown.

"Has that happened before?" Kim asked breathlessly. "People getting trapped?"

"Aye, it has." Sheldon's tone was gloomy. "With unpleasant consequences. Just like back in 18—"

"Now stop frightening the children," Mrs. McLeod scolded him. "There was only one time a tourist refused an estate map and the silly creature was stuck in the maze for hours, bleating away like a lost sheep. Finally, we had to get Terence to climb the tall ladder so he could guide her out."

"I only meant—" Sheldon tried to continue, but Mrs. McLeod shushed him.

"I know what you meant and you're not telling the children that tale, do you hear?" She gave him a look that quite clearly said "shut up."

Adam wondered what kind of things had happened in the maze. By the looks on their faces, Justin and Kim were wondering the same thing.

Mrs. McLeod continued, "Now Mr. Sheldon, if you need something to do besides filling young heads with old nonsense, there's a window in the Blue Salon wanting a nail in the frame to stop it banging. I couldn't sleep a wink the other night with the racket it made in the wind. And I'm sure someone was trying to get in because what did I see the next morning?"

Mrs. McLeod paused dramatically, her hands on her hips, studying her mesmerized audience.

"What did you see?" Adam asked, since she seemed to be waiting for a response.

"Footprints," Mrs. McLeod announced in triumph. "Scuff marks, like someone was trying to climb the wall with his big dirty feet. And a scrap of sacking caught in the window frame, as well as brown stains on the windowsill. I had to use bleach to get rid of them."

Sheldon looked bewildered. "Nonsense, Mrs. McLeod. What are you talking about? What sacking? What stains?"

"Oh, I know these thieves," she snapped. "He came with a big sack, didn't he now, so he could carry off his loot."

She grabbed a large copper frying pan off a rack above their heads and brandished it in the air. "But just let me catch anyone trying their luck. They'll have me to deal with."

The sight of Mrs. McLeod, eyes flashing, chest heaving, and clutching a dangerous object was enough to frighten everyone into making a quick exit and going their different ways. Jasper bounded down the front steps after Kim and Justin, with Smudge racing to catch up.

Adam thought about what the housekeeper had said. *Footprints ... brown streaks ... sacking.* It was exactly the same trail left by the thief in the Ashmolean Museum. However, the incident Mrs. McLeod referred to had obviously taken place before their arrival. Was it the same person or perhaps a gang of these sinister looking people? Were they— The sounds of Justin and Kim calling broke his train of thought.

"Coming," Adam yelled, dashing after them and forgetting for the moment about hooded creatures.

The Secret of the Maze

When Adam reached Kim and Justin, they were unfolding their maps. "Do you really think we need a map?" he asked. "Most times these are just sketches and aren't even to scale."

Kim studied the map. "I don't know why boys can't listen to advice." She sniffed and raised her eyebrows at Adam.

"Relax," Justin said. "We'll use it just to please you." He glanced at Adam. "Where shall we go first?"

Adam peered over Justin's shoulder. "It looks pretty clear to me. Let's go to the farthest point and work backward. Then we can check out the maze before we return to the castle."

"Sounds good."

"Okay with me," said Kim, attaching the leash to Smudge's collar. "Just remember, we're not supposed to go in there alone."

"Yeah, yeah, yeah," Justin muttered crossly.

"Why don't you let Smudge run about with Jasper," Adam suggested.

"Because Jasper knows where he's going and Smudge doesn't," Kim said. "Sheldon said it's a big estate and Smudge might get lost. I'll let him off when we know our way around a bit more."

They wandered over the drawbridge, taking a moment to gaze into the moat once they reached the other side. Masses of water lilies floated on the greenish water, their round fleshy leaves providing landing pads for insects and frogs. The flowers' delicately pointed petals were a variety of pale yellows, pinks, and blues.

Sunlight sparkled on the water, flashing silver on the curious fish that swam hopefully to the surface, opening and shutting their mouths as if kissing the air. Adam glimpsed moss-covered stones in the shallow water. It was probably only waist-deep on him.

"Sorry, little fish, no food today," Kim said.

They strolled down the long drive, figuring that by turning left, they would be heading through the wooded area they had seen on their way in. A marked path on the map led to the stables and mews. If they walked beyond the stables, they would reach the lake with the ruined chapel.

The estate stretched as far as the eye could see in all directions. Several gardeners were busy snipping hedges and trimming bushes. The warm summer weather ensured trees laden with brilliant green leaves, lawns that looked like crushed emerald velvet, and flowerbeds bursting with jewel colors. Peacocks wandered about the lawns, dragging their magnificent iridescent tails behind them like gleaming carpets. Kim was enchanted. Adam thought it was nice, but could hardly wait to see more exciting things—like the ruined chapel and the maze.

They headed for the woods and found a path leading deeper into the trees. Jasper ran on ahead with Smudge pulling eagerly after him, disappointed to be on a leash. Kim gave in and let him run free. She put Smudge's leash into her jeans pocket. The dogs ran off the path and disappeared into the undergrowth, excited yapping from Smudge and deep baying from Jasper signaling their direction.

After about ten minutes of brisk walking, they broke through the trees and into a clearing. They had arrived in an open area where the stables were situated. It was a clean, attractive setting. Several wheelbarrows, buckets, and spades stood neatly beside the main stable door. A rolled-up hosepipe hung from a hook outside the door.

Justin pointed to the wheelbarrows and spades. "That's for shoveling horse manure, Kim. We have to do some work during these holidays so maybe you can begin there."

Kim narrowed her eyes at him. "Maybe *you* should do it. You need to exercise off all those extra helpings of cake."

He glared at her. "Are you saying I'm fat?"

"I'm saying nothing. You figure it out." She smirked and sauntered ahead, nose in the air.

Justin turned to Adam. "Did you hear that? She said I'm fat."

"You started it," Adam retorted.

Adam ran to catch up with Kim, wishing Justin wouldn't annoy Kim with his barbed comments.

"Hey!" Justin yelled, but Adam ignored him.

Jasper was waiting for them at the main stable door. He apparently knew how to behave near horses because he sat obediently at the feet of a tall man in riding gear. Smudge sat next to Jasper, also gazing up at the man. The man gave first Jasper and then Smudge a snack. He turned at the sound of the kids' footsteps. He had fair hair and a pleasant tanned face.

"Hello there. You must be James' visitors. I'm Terence Burns. I look after the horses and run the estate. This is my son, Billy." He glanced at the stable door. "Come out now, Billy. Come and say hi."

A small, pale face peppered with freckles and topped with a shock of sandy hair peeped around the door and then disappeared.

"His mother died earlier this year," Terence explained. "He hasn't gotten over it yet."

"How dreadful," Kim said softly. "Mrs. McLeod mentioned something like that. What happened?"

"A fire. Billy's mother and I were divorced when Billy was just a baby. She moved away from the village, so he hardly knew me. We live in the cottage nearby the stables. Billy's come to live with me and now he has to get to know me all over again, as well as try to understand why such a terrible thing happened."

Adam asked, "How old is Billy? Is he in school?"

"He's eight, but he hasn't been to school this year because of the accident. Miss Kingston, who runs a therapy group for children with problems, has been giving him extra lessons during this summer vacation to help him catch up."

"Diana." The boy's faint voice echoed from behind the stable door. Billy had been listening, although still in hiding.

Terence's face creased into a warm smile. "Diana Kingston. Wonderful woman. She uses the horses to help kids overcome fears and phobias. They work in a horse paddock just past those trees." He pointed to an enclosure surrounded with white split-pole fencing.

"Can we see the horses?" asked Kim.

Terence led them into the stables. A workspace sat just inside the main door and then there were separate stalls for each horse. Horse bits, bridles, harnesses, and reins hung neatly from hooks, with a saddle and horse blanket slung over each partition. Six magnificent horses, their coats gleaming, hung their heads curiously over the half-doors of their stalls. The place smelled of hay, horses, leather, and soap. Terence introduced each horse. Justin and Adam hung back a little, unsure what the animals' reactions might be. Kim, on the other hand, was unafraid and held out her hand. They snuffled her fingers, as if hoping for treats. Terence gave her a few bits of carrot to feed them.

"The gray is Sirius, the white is Pegasus, the bay is Jupiter, the black is Midnight, the roan is Amber, and the chestnut is Rowan." Terence announced the names proudly.

"My name's Billy."

The group turned. Billy now stood next to his father, a gap-toothed grin on his freckled face.

"I help my dad. I help with the horses. I love Sirius the best 'cause he's James' horse."

Terence looked astounded. Then he quickly patted his son's head. "And what a great job you do, too. Are you ready for Miss Kingston, son? She'll be here soon."

Billy suddenly seemed nervous, as if he had run out of courage by speaking to the strangers, and ran off.

Terence stared at Kim and the boys. "That's amazing. He's hardly said a word for months. Now he's talking. Must be your new faces."

The group wandered back outside.

"I didn't know you could use horses for therapy," Justin said. "I only know about swimming with dolphins."

"It's something original—well, to a small place like Haddley. Quite a few kids come to Diana. Mostly from Edinburgh. She brings them up here a couple of times a week. She's working wonders with them. We also get casual riders during the week and most weekends so the horses keep busy. Where are you kids heading off to now?"

"We want to see the ruined chapel," said Justin. "Is this the way?"

Terence indicated the path. "Yes, you continue on this route. Go past the paddock and the path takes you right to the water's edge. It's a ten-minute walk from here. Generally the lake isn't deep, but it can be dangerous in places, so no wading across."

He looked over their heads. "I see Hamish is busy with the birds right now. I'm sure he'll be happy to row you over any time tomorrow. A thick mist rolls in at night so I wouldn't advise wandering near the lake too late."

A scowling face peered through a window in one of the outbuildings adjoining the stables. Hamish glared at them, looking annoyed at the sight of visitors.

Terence chuckled. "Take no notice. He's really grumpy, but don't be put off by his manners—or lack of them, I should say. Come over tomorrow and I'll make sure you get to the chapel."

He waved good-bye and strode away.

Adam glanced at Justin. "What shall we do now?"

Justin shrugged. "Looks like we'll have to do something else instead."

Kim took charge. "I know. Let's go back and look at the grounds, and then if Ink is awake, we can explore the castle before tea. Maybe we'll find a secret passage behind the wood paneling or a hidden stone stairway down to the dungeons."

Justin looked pained. "I'm sure that *someone* would have found all the secret passages and stone stairways by now, don't you?"

"No, I don't," Adam broke in. "Humphrey's convinced the clues to the Scroll of the Ancients are hidden in the castle so there must be a place no one has discovered yet."

Kim flashed Adam a grateful smile; Justin scowled at him.

When Kim ran ahead, calling for the dogs to follow her, Justin turned on Adam. "I can see whose side you're on."

"What do you mean?"

"You're always sticking up for her."

"No, I'm not," Adam retorted. "You're always getting at Kim. I just think we should work as a team. The scroll must be somewhere in the castle. If it wasn't, then Humphrey and James wouldn't have bothered sending us here."

Justin muttered something under his breath and stalked off. Adam wanted to ask Justin why he was so moody, but decided against saying anything. If Justin wanted to sulk, that was his problem. At the same time, Adam understood that it was hard having someone else around. He and Justin had done stuff together so often that Kim was almost an intrusion. The adventure in Egypt had brought them close, but now it seemed their relationship had changed. Kim was also a stranger to them. They knew nothing about her, apart from the fact that she lived with Aunt Isabel, came from a poor background, and had learning problems. Yet Kim had adopted their adventure as her own. That was okay, but Adam wished she would let him and Justin take the lead more. Then he felt guilty for resenting Kim being there. Pushing all thoughts from his mind, he ran after Kim and Justin's disappearing figures.

"Wait for me!"

They joined up on the driveway leading to the castle. Jasper and Smudge had enjoyed snuffling in the undergrowth for imaginary rabbits and lay panting, tongues hanging out, looking satisfied. Justin examined the map; they were facing the castle.

"Let's turn left," he said, gesturing toward the gardens. "Let's take this path and go through the Ancient Burial Ground, then see the Temple of Artemis and the Rose Garden, and on to the Star Maze. That way we'll see all the marked sights."

Kim and Adam nodded and, with an exchanged glance, silently agreed to let Justin lead. Justin set off with Kim and Adam lagging behind. He seemed to be in a better mood because he was whistling. The dogs raced ahead, Jasper a lolloping gray mound and Smudge a barely visible whitish streak. The Ancient Burial Ground was not half as frightening as it sounded, but they still edged their way respectfully past the moss-covered stone monuments, and crumbling or fallen gravestones. Most of the headstones looked old, jutting out of the springy grass like rotting giants' teeth.

"This must be where James' ancestors are buried," Adam whispered. "I wonder if some of the ghosts live here."

The Temple of Artemis was the folly. It consisted of a circle of marble columns and a domed roof. It seemed rather forlorn as moss and ivy had overgrown the stone bench inside and leaves had blown into the temple. They were glad to reach the maze.

Jasper and Smudge sat at the entrance to the maze, tails drooping and eyes solemn. Adam cleared his throat. He felt uncomfortable, although he wasn't sure why. A glance at Kim and Justin told him they felt the same way. The silence was deathly; the birds they had heard before were now quiet. It had grown darker and the sky had clouded over. A chilly breeze stroked their bare arms, even though the air had been pleasantly warm and still when they had left the castle.

Kim consulted the map again. "This isn't really a star."

126

Adam pointed to the drawing. "There's the star. It's a star shape inside the maze in a different color."

As he indicated the sketch, he noticed a detail that sent a slight shiver down his spine. The star shape inside the maze had seven points. He had a brief flash of the seven-pointed star on Arthur's sword in his dream.

"That's so clever," Justin said, also studying the shape. "It looks as if the maze is laid out in the traditional way, but the star shape comes from the different color plants used in the actual maze."

He laughed at his own joke. "That's why it's called the Star Maze. A-maze-ing!"

His voice died away when the others didn't respond. No one said anything for a few moments and then Kim spoke.

"Uh … guys … this is really creepy. Maybe we should do what Sheldon said and see it with Ink. I don't want to go in there alone."

Adam was relieved she had expressed the fears he was too proud to admit.

"Yeah, you're right. We can go in another time." Justin's tone was casual, as if he didn't care. "There's no hurry. I don't mind waiting for Ink."

Adam's sudden nervousness made his voice squeaky. "Me neither."

Kim turned away with a shiver. "Let's go back to the castle. I don't like it here."

Just then, Jasper gave a long baying howl and raced into the maze with Smudge close at his heels. They heard furious barking and then silence.

"Smudge!" Kim screamed. She ran in after the dogs, as if forgetting her fear.

Justin and Adam looked at each other and made a joint split-second decision.

"Kim, wait for us!" they yelled, sprinting after her.

The air seemed heavier and more suffocating the moment they stepped inside the maze. Adam tried to control his breathing. Surrounded on all sides by an impenetrable mass of leaves and twigs, it was as if someone had instantly woven a trap around the two boys, as if the hedges had closed in on them. Of course, that was impossible … or was it? Adam heard Kim's faint voice yelling for the dogs.

"Where's the entrance?" Justin gasped. "We just came in through the main entrance and now it's gone."

Adam looked behind him. How had that happened? They had run in a straight line, but now they were boxed in. Adam had a sudden memory of Egypt and being trapped in the Crystal Cavern. He slipped his hand into his pocket and clutched his scarab. He knew it couldn't save him the way the genuine sacred scarab had done several times in Egypt, but holding it helped.

"Let's look at the map," he said, forcing a calmer note into his voice.

With trembling hands, Justin held his map so they both could see it.

Adam pointed to the sketch. "We must have gone around the first corner somehow and now we're at a dead end."

They hadn't turned any corner, but what else could he say because there was no other explanation. He looked behind him again. "Hey, there's the way out."

Miraculously, a glimmer of sunlight hinted at a break in the hedge. They ran for the gap. As they turned a corner, Kim raced toward them from the opposite direction.

"Where have you two been? I've been alone in this horrible place and the hedges are full of thorns. It was like a thousand *things* were trying to grab me."

Adam looked at Justin. Were there "things" inside this maze? Was that why Sheldon had tried to put them off going inside alone?

"Where are the dogs?" Adam asked.

Excited barking led them to the dogs digging under a hedge. The animals snarled and snuffled as they burrowed for something. Their frantic scuffles sent large clods of earth flying. Adam and Justin knelt and tried to see what they might be looking for.

Justin said, "Something's been buried. Pull the dogs away."

Adam heaved Jasper back by his collar while Kim gathered Smudge into her arms. Jasper growled, trying to get back to the hole, but Adam dug his heels in and hung on. Justin carefully scooped the earth away and pulled out a bundle wrapped in a dirty old cloth. He laid it on the ground and then unwrapped it.

A brown hessian garment, like a monk's robe with a hood, lay in front of them, as well as a small leather pouch tied with a drawstring at the top. Smudge leaped out of Kim's arms and seized the leather pouch in his teeth, growling as he shook his prize. Kim grabbed Smudge again while Justin took the pouch from him and opened it just a fraction. He sniffed, then wrinkled his nose and coughed.

"It's that stuff the creature used to drug us on the train," he whispered. His face paled. "He's here at Strathairn Castle."

128

They glanced up. The sky was even darker, with lowering clouds casting black shadows all around them. The maze felt oppressive, as if there was no air.

"Let's put it back," Adam suggested. "For all we know, he could be watching us right now."

"Put it back?" Kim said. "Are you nuts? Why? Let's take it so he can't use it to do any more harm."

Justin rolled the bundle up and replaced it exactly as they had found it. "No, Adam's right. We have to let him think he's getting somewhere. If we take his things, he will know we're onto him. Let's leave the stuff, but we must show Ink where it's hidden."

Justin carefully patted the soil down and sprinkled a few leaves on top to look as if nothing but the breeze and fallen twigs had disturbed the hiding place. He placed a small stone nearby to mark the spot. Then they retraced their steps to the entrance.

Surprisingly, they had no problem getting out of the maze. When they emerged, the sun was shining as before, the sky was a clear blue, and birds sang nearby. Adam looked doubtfully at the others. Things were very strange.

They ran back to the castle, the dogs bounding at their heels. They rushed up the front steps and into the entrance hall, almost bowling Sheldon over in their excitement.

"Where's Ink?" Justin asked.

"In the library, Master Justin, and—"

They dashed in the direction of his outstretched arm, not letting him finish.

They paused on the threshold of the library, speechless, their mission briefly forgotten in surprise. The library was enormous, with most of the walls covered in bookshelves. Many of the books had gold lettering on the spines, reminding Adam of the valuable books in Humphrey's shop.

"These must be worth a lot," he said.

A ladder was attached to each set of shelves by a topmost rail. Anyone wishing to look for a book on a high shelf simply climbed up. The ladders ran on wheels at the bottom and could be maneuvered left or right. A narrow gallery with a railing at the top of the shelves encircled the entire room so that visitors could look down into the library from their lofty perch. Sunlight streamed in through a circular skylight in the domed, painted ceiling, where artists of long ago had covered every available inch with images of mythological figures, angels, clouds, and cherubs.

A few comfortable sofas and easy chairs were scattered about, while a huge desk with a shabby leather armchair dominated one section of the room. Papers and books covered the desk so this was probably where James did his research work. A long table took up most of the space in the center of the room, with a few piles of old books on one end. Adam also noticed a large freestanding globe of the world and several framed antique maps. A portrait of an old man, who looked just like James, hung above the ornate stone fireplace.

Justin spun the globe, watching the orb turn in a mass of colors under his fingertips. "Wow, this is some library. Aunt Isabel would go mad for this."

Adam remembered the reason they were there. "Hey! Where's Ink?"

Ink peered over the gallery railing. "Hi there," he called. "I'm feeling loads better. The medicine the vet gave me is phenomenal. Having fun?"

There was no response.

"What's wrong?" he asked. "Has something happened?"

"We … I … er … can you come down?" Justin stammered.

"Be there in a second." Ink nimbly slipped one leg over the railing and stepped onto the first rung of the ladder. He climbed down to the floor and dusted his hands on his jeans. "What's up?"

Adam and Justin both started gabbling the story out at once, their words tripping and spilling over each other.

Ink held up his hands to silence them. "Wait a minute. You've found the stuff the weirdo used on the train?"

"Yes," Justin said. "It's him, he's here, and the sleeping powder is too! His robe is also there."

"You've got to come now," Adam begged. "You've got to see it."

Ink frowned. "I can't believe it."

"It's true," said Kim. "It was buried and the dogs found it. Please come back with us and see for yourself."

Ink ran with them through the gardens to the maze. Adam paused briefly at the entrance and glanced about. This time there was no change in the weather; the air remained warm, the sky was azure blue. Had they imagined all the strange sensations they had felt just minutes before? Kim led the way to where the dogs had dug up the bundle. She looked confused.

"It's somewhere," she said. "It must be here. Justin put some twigs on top of where we dug and a stone to mark the spot."

There was nothing, not even a sign of disturbed earth. It was as if the event had never happened.

"Is this the right section?" Justin asked, looking about for clues to the exact location.

"Definitely," said Adam. "I remember seeing the edge of the colored leaf section forming a point in the hedge and here it is."

Ink looked around. "There are six other points like this one. Maybe we're in the wrong place."

"We can't be." Adam's heart pounded with sudden dread. "We came straight in and then turned the corner to this section. There's no back way out and no other entrance so this must be the place."

They searched but still found nothing. The dogs also seemed less enthusiastic than before. They ran about, sniffing, but didn't show the same frenzied excitement. It appeared that not even they could remember where they had dug.

Ink looked at their distressed faces. "Maybe—"

Then he stopped. He was going to say that maybe they had imagined it, but it was hardly possible to imagine digging something up and actually touching it. He felt disquieted. He hadn't imagined his life-and-death struggle in the train the previous night; nor had he imagined the overpowering sensation of sinking into an enveloping, inescapable blackness. No, the kids hadn't imagined it. They had found something and now it was gone.

"Whoever hid the stuff has come back for it," he said finally. "He must have seen you guys digging it up."

Ink led the way out of the maze.

"What are we going to do now?" Justin asked.

"Are we in danger?" Kim whispered.

Ink stopped and faced them. "Yes, we're in danger," he said bluntly. "We have to locate that darn scroll as soon as possible and find whoever has the second stone. And I must call my dad right now."

The four made their way back to the library where Mrs. Grant had set out cookies and lemonade.

No sooner had they sat than Sheldon arrived with a cardboard box full of papers.

"These are copies of all the documents that may prove useful to your ... er ... research. I hope you find what you're looking for, Master Ink," he said with a solemn expression. "We received a telephone call from Paris a few minutes ago. Miss Isabel Sinclair spoke to Mrs. McLeod and told her about Master James' accident. Nothing to worry about. Master James is recovering well and wanted to know if everything was fine here. He says he should be home in a few days, doctors permitting."

Relieved smiles spread across their faces, though Ink wished James could be back sooner. Sheldon left the kids to start on the food while Ink went to the alcove in the entrance hall where the telephone was situated. As he dialed, he found to his surprise that his fingers were shaking.

"Come on, Dad," he muttered as he listened to the ringing tone.

Humphrey picked up the receiver. "Son? Thank goodness! I was worried when I didn't hear from you. Are you all right?"

Ink quickly summarized for Humphrey everything that had happened to them since they left Oxford. Humphrey gave a loud groan when Ink mentioned the attack on the train. "There was also an attempted break-in at the castle before we got here. We seem to be surrounded by all sorts of strange people."

"Ink, you and the children shouldn't stay at the castle a moment longer."

"But why, Dad?" Ink protested. "There's nothing to worry about. James called and left a message. He's almost recovered and should be home soon. He can take over once he's back."

"Ink," Humphrey interrupted, "there are things you should be aware of—"

Ink injected a firm note into his voice. "Dad, you said we've got to find the scroll so there's no point in giving up now. Leaving the castle would be like admitting defeat. We can't let them win, whoever they are."

Although Humphrey tried to get in a few words, Ink gabbled on, hoping his father would see his point. The last thing he wanted was to hear that they had to come home directly.

"Listen, son. The people who broke into the Ashmolean, the person who attacked you on the train, the visitor who came to the shop, and whoever tried to break into the castle—they all belong to the same group. I wish I could have warned you before now, but Ebrahim's information came too late. His letter only arrived this morning."

"Tell me what? Who are they?" Ink was puzzled. "You only told me about Dr. Khalid. Is he part of this group?"

"I don't think so," Humphrey replied. "These people are infinitely more dangerous than he is right now. You must stay away from them. It would be fatal for you to tangle with them."

Ink laughed, trying to reassure him. "Don't worry, Dad. The weirdo on the train wasn't armed with a gun, just a knife and some sort of powder that he sprinkled on us. We'll be fine."

"No!" Humphrey sounded desperate. "You must get away now! What I'm about to tell you is of utmost importance. They are the Ea—"

The line went dead.

"Dad? Are you there?"

There was no reply. Ink put the receiver down and went back into the library. Three faces looked expectantly up at him.

"Is Humphrey okay?" Adam asked.

"Yes, he's fine. We got cut off. Pity, because I think he was trying to tell me something important about these strange people. He sounded quite worried. I'm sure he'll call back."

Ink looked at the box of documents on the large library table. "I can see we've got some work to do. The castle is full of possible hiding places for the scroll."

As Ink sat down and laid the drawings and plans out in front of them, he wondered what Humphrey had been trying to say. What had started as an exciting mission had turned into something much more sinister. He would never give up, of course, but the responsibility of three children and their safety weighed heavily upon him. Would it be better to pack them on the train back to Oxford? Were they walking straight into terrible danger? On the other hand, Humphrey always worried

133

for nothing. He was probably just exaggerating the level of risk because he was being over-protective.

Humphrey groaned as he replaced the receiver. He had been trying to tell Ink they were being pursued by the most dangerous people alive … a group that had ceased to exist over seven hundred years ago … or had they?

They were the Eaters of Poison. Contact with them could be fatal.

CLUES IN THE CASTLE

Ink took the papers from the cardboard box and spread them on the library table. There was so much material that soon the entire surface was covered. Ink whistled softly as he began sorting the pages.

He shoveled the documents into three piles. "Here are definites, here are possibles, and the rest is no use."

Kim and Adam straightened the growing stacks, while Justin scooped the "no use" pages back into the box.

"Why are these of no use to us?" Justin asked. "There might be something you've missed."

"Bedwyr lived circa 1296. That's our time frame," Ink replied, sifting through the pile of definites. "We need to know the layout of the castle from then until about AD 1320, just to be sure."

"What if Bedwyr hid the scroll in a place that doesn't exist anymore?" Adam asked.

Ink shook his head. "Most times in castles like this one, no one knocked down any walls or structures, except for enemies who might destroy parts of a structure with siege weapons. Instead, the family just built over or around whatever was already there. And if any previous owners had demolished parts of the castle deliberately, then they would have found whatever Bedwyr hid there by now and put it in the family archives. James has been through the library and archives many times. There's nothing there."

After a bit more digging, Ink sat back and selected several pages. He pointed to a drawing. "This is where the stables and mews are now. The stables were bigger then—they had more horses, I guess—and the dotted lines show underground storage bins, possibly to hide food and weapons when the castle was under attack."

"What's this line with arrows leading back to the castle?" Adam asked. "It's very faint."

"Well spotted, Adam. That's the secret tunnel. I remember James mentioning it. He and his cousins used to look for it all the time."

"But can a tunnel go under the moat?" asked Justin.

Sheldon, who had entered the library carrying a tray with more lemonade, leaned over Ink's shoulder. "Ah, the old tunnel. Yes, it could go under the moat when you consider how deep the dungeons are. They're well below the original depth of the moat. These days the moat is only a couple of feet deep because over time it dried out to the level it is now."

"Do you know where the tunnel is?" asked Kim. "Ink said you know just about everything about the castle."

Sheldon gave Ink a small bow of thanks. "Not quite everything, Master Ink, not quite everything."

"Well, Sheldon, *do* you know where the tunnel is?" asked Adam.

Sheldon's expression was blank, as always revealing nothing of his true thoughts. For a split second, however, a shadow of uncertainty flitted across the old man's face. When he spoke, he seemed to choose his words with care.

"The tunnel was built at the same time as the original fortress tower, in about AD 1000. Alas, enemies put an end to the tower a few hundred years later. Castle inhabitants used the tunnel as an escape route from the tower to the stables. The fugitives would exit somewhere near the stables, well away from the castle. Then they would jump on their horses and ride to freedom, without the enemy realizing."

"But wouldn't enemies notice what was going on at the stables while they were making their way toward the castle?" said Kim.

Sheldon shook his head. "That was the point of locating the tunnel exit under the stables. You must have noticed the stables are in a wooded area."

They all nodded.

"Well," he continued, "centuries ago, that area was even more thickly treed. This was to confuse would-be attackers. They would be so busy concentrating on the castle and the riches inside that they wouldn't give a second glance to the woods well away from the castle itself. Later on, some of the trees were thinned out to make room for the paddock and various pathways, but the stables remained."

"Since the stables are still there," Justin said, "the tunnel must also still be there. The exit must be nearby."

Sheldon shook his head regretfully. "That's the problem, Master Justin. Each young heir to Strathairn Castle, including the old earl and Master James, has spent his free time scouring the area, looking for the tunnel. The old master even got surveyors in with equipment, trying to locate it. The mews for the birds, which was added some time in the thirteen hundreds, was built on top of one section of the stables. The exit might be there for all we know, but since the floors are solid stone … I don't think so."

"What about the entrance?" Kim asked eagerly. "Everyone's looked for the exit. What about the entrance, which you say was in the tower?"

"No chance of that, Miss Kim," Sheldon replied, shaking his head again. "If you examine later plans, you'll see additions and improvements were made to the original castle. After the tower was destroyed, many parts of the castle were rebuilt. We wouldn't even know where to start looking."

Ink seemed disappointed. "It's a pity the tunnel was used for only a short period of time."

"There's a saying, Master Ink," Sheldon said.

Sheldon appeared casual as he collected the empty lemonade glasses, but Adam felt sure the old man was trying to drop them a hint.

"They say that when the castle inhabitants are in danger of their lives, the tunnel will be revealed for their safety."

Ink laughed. "I'm sure there was more risk hundreds of years ago. This is the twenty-first century. Not much chance of real danger these days." He grinned at the others.

"I couldn't say, Master Ink," said Sheldon primly. He pursed his lips, seeming almost offended. "I'm just telling you what's been said about it. You never know. We live in strange times."

Sheldon stared at Adam, who instinctively slid his hand into his pocket to grab his scarab. He was convinced Sheldon knew more than he was telling them. But why would he hold back information they needed?

Ink put on a serious face. "Yes, of course. Thanks very much, Sheldon."

"Mrs. McLeod says supper will be served at six because she is sure the young people will be tired and wanting an early night." He bowed and left the library.

Adam looked at the library door as it closed behind Sheldon's stiff back. "Is he angry? He seemed to think you were laughing at him."

"No, I wasn't," said Ink. "And I don't think he was angry. He just likes to add mystery to the castle, like most family servants do. He's been here so long he feels the castle's history is his personal history. Remind him about telling us ghost stories at supper and you'll see how quickly he perks up."

Kim pulled a face. "Why supper so early?"

"You'll be tired," Ink warned her. "All the fresh country air."

"Does it matter if we don't find the tunnel?" Justin asked. He had been studying the plans Ink had selected while the others were talking. "This drawing looks like the library, where we are now, and the other one is obviously the old chapel."

"That's right," said Ink, pulling the diagrams toward him. "We can have some fun and explore the whole castle, of course—we might be the lucky ones to find the tunnel—the library, and the chapel."

"Why those places?" asked Adam.

"The library is part of the original banqueting hall or main hall, which, in those days, was an important gathering place. One of James' ancestors made the banqueting hall smaller. It was divided into the ballroom and this room."

Ink pointed to a sketch. "He then enclosed it in wood paneling, put up the fancy bookshelves, and built the skylight."

Kim looked around the room. "If this room was made separate by adding the wood panels, there might be secret passages behind the panels in the spaces left over."

Ink smiled at her. "Smart girl. My thoughts exactly. It's said that in those days no room had only one way in or out. There was always an escape route."

Justin quickly drew attention back to himself. "And the chapel?"

Ink picked up the chapel diagram. "That's always been a strong possibility. Sections of it are so old that I just can't believe there's nothing important there."

"What about the dungeons?" Justin asked.

"We can have a look, but I don't think they're significant. They've really been cleaned up for the tourists although it's fun to visit. They even have a fake skeleton in chains."

Adam put his chin in his hands, gazing thoughtfully at the plans. "So we've got three important places to check out—the stables, the library, and the chapel."

"As well as exciting parts of the castle," Kim chimed in.

Ink nodded at her. "Let's not rule out any possibilities, and we have to try to find who stole the stone from the sword. The Scroll of the Ancients isn't our only goal."

Adam felt a little guilty that he had almost forgotten about the second stone in the thrill of all the other happenings. In fact, he hadn't even thought about James and Aunt Isabel at all. He spoke up. "You didn't finish telling us what Humphrey said."

Ink's expression turned grim. "Sorry, I should have said so right away. He says there's one group involved. The shop visitor, the Ashmolean break-in, the creature on the train, and the attempted break-in here were all done by the same people."

"What?" Adam croaked. His voice deserted him for a moment.

"But who are they? What do they want?" Justin cried.

"Wait a minute," Kim said. "All these people are together?"

Adam banged one fist on the table as his earlier suspicions returned, this time with greater clarity. "The newspaper reported brown stains and a few bits of hessian in the Ashmolean after the stone was stolen. The guy in the shop wore a hooded robe, made of the same kind of material. The person on the train was dressed the same way, and left brown stuff on Ink's arms when he scratched Ink with his long fingernails—"

"And in the maze, we found a robe plus the same sleeping drug he used on us," Justin interrupted.

"What about the Blue Salon?" Kim said excitedly. "Mrs. McLeod mentioned brown stains on the windowsill and some hessian caught in the window frame."

Ink slowly nodded as each of them spoke. "It's all making sense now. It's one group and there are several people involved, just as Humphrey thought."

"What's the last thing Humphrey said before he was cut off?" Adam asked.

"He was about to tell me their name," Ink replied. "He said something like 'Ea—' before the line went dead. I must tell Sheldon there's a problem with the telephone."

Ink looked at his watch. "Let's move. You guys probably want to unpack before supper and it's after five already." He stood up. "Adam, pass me those drawings. The rest can go back into the safe. We only need these."

Adam leaned over to grab the plans. He picked up the one of the chapel. "Hey! Isn't this a line from the chapel to the stables?"

"What do you mean?" Justin craned his neck to see the drawing. "You mean under the lake? That's impossible."

"Why not?" Adam couldn't disguise his eagerness. "Yesterday, Terence said the lake is quite shallow. It's possible, if you dig deep enough. Think of the Chunnel."

"What's that?" asked Kim.

"It's the Channel Tunnel connecting England and France," said Ink. "It's deep under the English Channel. I see what you're getting at, Adam."

Ink looked at the drawing while Adam pointed to the line he thought he could see.

"It's a rough triangle. Here's the chapel." Adam then grabbed the first page they had looked at, which showed the castle and stables. "And here's the other plan. Maybe it's one drawing that's been cut into two pieces."

Ink scrutinized the plans. "Could be."

Adam traced an imaginary line. "If you go from the castle to the stables, it's a straight line marked with arrows. You can see a faint line from the stables through the lake to the chapel. Then you can draw a line from the chapel back to the castle. See? A triangle."

Ink chewed his lower lip in concentration. "I can't see a plotted line like the one from the castle to the stables, but yes, I suppose you can link the three areas."

"You *must* see it," Adam said. "It's obvious to me."

Ink held the drawing closer to his eyes. "I'm sorry, Adam, it's not clear. It looks more like a fold in the paper." He looked down at Adam. "You have to remember these are all copies of copies so details mightn't be too clear. I tell you what—we'll ask Sheldon if he has a strong magnifying glass. We'll examine it properly to be sure."

140

Adam and Justin went to their room to unpack before supper. Kim disappeared into her room to do the same. While the boys were busy putting their clothes away, Ink popped his head around the door.

"Everything okay?"

"It's great." Justin grinned. "We've got the Narnia wardrobe in here as well."

Ink went over to the huge wardrobe and opened the door. "I also called it that. I read all the books. When I was a kid and visited James during school vacations, I was convinced there was a magic kingdom inside."

Adam hoped they would find something exciting soon like the hidden tunnel or something no one had discovered before—perhaps a secret passage.

Ink smiled at them with a mysterious twinkle in his eyes. "I can show you how to hide in the wardrobe so no one will ever find you."

"How?" Adam asked.

"Turn around and count to twenty. Then open the door and try to find me."

Adam was surprised at Ink's suggestion. Anyone could see there was no place to disappear in there. It was just a big old wardrobe.

"All right," Adam said, glancing at Justin to indicate they should just go along with Ink to humor him.

The boys turned their backs and began counting.

"Twenty!" Justin yelled. "Here we come, ready or not." He rolled his eyes at Adam. His disbelieving expression showed he thought Ink was being childish.

Adam flung open the wardrobe door. Apart from a few heavy coats smelling faintly of mothballs, there was nothing else in the wardrobe. Ink had completely vanished. Justin got inside. He rapped the wooden back of the wardrobe and ran his hands over the sides and base. Nothing indicated a hidden door.

Justin clambered back out. "He's gone."

"That's impossible!"

Justin shrugged. "See for yourself. No Mr. Tumnus either."

Adam climbed into the wardrobe, felt inside, and then emerged, equally baffled. "You're right. He's gone. It must be a clever trick."

"Let's close the door and count to twenty," Justin suggested. "We'd better turn our backs again, like we did before. This is *so* lame."

Mystified, the boys began counting. They turned around just as they reached twenty.

Ink stood in front of the wardrobe, grinning. "How's that for a great hiding place?"

Justin looked cross at being fooled. "How did you do it?"

Ink opened the wardrobe and showed them what they had missed. "Reach up and put your hand to the left side."

Adam felt a tiny insignia carved into the wood.

"Press it," Ink instructed.

When Adam pressed the insignia, he heard a faint click. Then Ink showed them how the base of the wardrobe lifted by way of a hinged trapdoor. He raised the trapdoor to reveal a large crawl space underneath and then persuaded them to get in. Once the boys were inside, he told them where to find a small wooden peg that enabled them to pull the trapdoor down. Another click meant that the bottom of the wardrobe had closed on them.

It was dark and stuffy inside the concealed compartment. Adam had a momentary flashback to their Egyptian adventure, when they were trapped in a secret chamber with a giant cobra. He and Justin were forced to hide in two empty sarcophagi to escape Dr. Khalid's men. The angry reptile had been a nasty surprise.

He heard Ink's voice instructing them how to get out.

"Justin, reach behind your head and feel for another carving. Press it. You'll hear a click. Then you can lift the lid and climb out."

They followed his instructions and scrambled out.

Justin breathed deeply. "That was great but scary."

"How did you know about it?" Adam asked.

"James showed me the false bottom and I think Sheldon showed him," Ink replied. "It's an amazing feeling when you're lying there and you know the other person will never find you."

Adam gave a weak smile, not too sure about the "amazing feeling" part. "Yeah, great."

"Come downstairs when you've finished unpacking. I'll meet you in the kitchen."

Justin and Adam finished unpacking by throwing their clothes into the chest of drawers. Then they went next door to Kim's room. All her garments sat perfectly folded in several small piles on the bed.

"I bet you two just chucked all your stuff inside." Kim smirked as she placed the piles in the chest of drawers.

"No, we did not, Miss Clever," Justin retorted. "And if you've finished winning the prize for neatness, don't you think we'd better go downstairs?"

Kim, not at all upset by Justin's words, sailed out of the room with a supercilious sniff. Adam glanced at his cousin.

"Okay, okay," Justin said. "So we'll tidy up later."

A delicious smell tickled their nostrils even before they reached the kitchen. A stew bubbled in a pot on the stove. Adam could hardly wait to eat.

"It's the Highland air, to be sure," Mrs. McLeod said, ladling out generous portions of meat, potatoes, peas, and carrots in savory gravy onto the plates. "Gives you a good appetite. Susan will be sorry she's missing my stew. She's gone off to visit friends."

Everyone ate more slowly once the edge was off their hunger.

"Do you feel like scaring us half to death just before bedtime?" Ink asked Sheldon.

Sheldon finished mopping up the last of his gravy with a piece of bread. "Perhaps we should have our pudding first."

He winked at Mrs. Grant, who giggled as she placed bowls in front of everyone. For a few minutes, the only sound was that of spoons chinking against china as they all gobbled down apple pie and ice cream.

"I want to hear about the Headless Horseman," Justin said, finally putting down his spoon. "Why was his head chopped off? What did he do wrong?"

Sheldon swallowed one last mouthful before pushing his bowl to one side. He leaned forward, staring intently at his mesmerized audience.

"Aye, the Headless Horseman, Sir Maulsby Dredwell." His eyes rolled with exaggerated fear. "His only crime was patriotism. He supported Bonnie Prince Charlie, the Pretender to the thrones of England, Scotland, and Ireland. When traitors in the community betrayed Sir Maulsby after the Battle of Culloden in 1746, he was executed in the village square for his Jacobite loyalties. They cut his head off at the mercat cross, the place for executions."

The two women twittered together in sympathy.

Adam remembered the monument they had passed on their way to the castle, a stone column with an emblem on top.

"He gallops through the village with his head tucked under one arm, striking terror into the hearts of his murderers, his betrayers." Sheldon rolled his *r*'s ferociously as he warmed to the telling of what was obviously his favorite ghost story. His voice sank to a hoarse whisper.

As he spoke, thunder grumbled in the distance. Adam looked up, startled, as the lights flickered once or twice. Kim gulped, glancing around nervously. A pool of brightness from the kitchen spilled out into the shadowed hall where darkness lurked beyond. Adam shivered, hoping someone would think to turn on a few lights when they went upstairs to bed. Jasper grunted in his sleep and shifted under the table. Adam leaned down to stroke the dog's head. He glanced at Kim, who was clutching Smudge in her arms, gazing wide-eyed at Sheldon. Justin appeared to be unconcerned, but his clenched knuckles betrayed his uneasiness.

By the time the story of the Headless Horseman had ended, Adam's mind was filled with images of screaming victims fleeing for their lives. He could see rivers of blood, and he could hear the hooves of the Horseman's spectral black horse clattering on the cobblestones, along with crazed laughter as the Horseman swung his ghostly sword in the air.

Mrs. Grant said, "There's a storm brewing," as casually as if mentioning it was about to rain. Thunder grumbled in the distance.

She bustled about, clearing the dishes, and getting the cocoa cups. The kettle whistled on the stove, the sudden shrill shriek making them jump.

"Do you lower the portcullis each night, Mrs. McLeod?" Adam asked, hoping she would say yes.

"Oh aye, we do now," she said. "We never used to, but what with strangers about and so much crime these days, it's best to be safe. The old master had it modernized a few years ago. You just press a button to make it go up or down. We don't want to be murdered in our beds by Sir Maulsby either." She finished this remark with a high-pitched giggle.

Mrs. Grant shook her head. "Don't scare the children now, Bridget. Sir Maulsby hasn't appeared for a while. I think the last time anyone saw him was the winter of 1998." Her tone was conversational, as if Sir Maulsby was a neighbor who popped in now and again for a cup of tea.

Justin looked at Adam with wide eyes. Kim made a muffled squeaking sound and squeezed Smudge so hard he whined in protest. A cold shiver ran down Adam's spine. In all the scary books he had read, ghosts could walk with ease through walls, doors, and possibly portcullises. He slid his hand into his pocket and closed his fingers tightly around the scarab.

Mrs. McLeod patted Adam's shoulder. "Don't you worry if the lights go out. We have a generator and Sheldon will go and turn it on if needs be. You'll find candles next to your bed in case you wake up in the middle of the night."

"When the moon is full," Sheldon said, "some people say they see Sir Maulsby Dredwell galloping through the village with his grinning head tucked under one arm. Behind him, he drags the souls of those he killed in revenge for their treachery."

Mrs. McLeod looked at the kitchen clock and said cheerfully, "Is that the time? You'd best be off to bed, children."

After such a chilling tale, Adam didn't want to leave the warm kitchen just yet. Justin looked a little subdued, even though he laughed and said only babies were scared of ghost stories. Sheldon shook his head and suggested they lock their doors that night if they felt frightened, especially since it was a full moon and a storm was brewing.

The lights went out after one particularly loud roll of thunder so Mrs. McLeod escorted the cousins to their room with a lamp. Mrs. Grant took Kim to her room. Mrs. McLeod seemed undisturbed by the darkness and said they would get used to country living before their holiday was over. She turned down the quilt, lit the candles on either side of their bed, told them not to burn the place down, and wished them goodnight.

Adam and Justin quickly cleaned their teeth by candlelight in the bathroom and then scampered back to their bedroom. Adam glanced once at the mass of black shadows at the end of the passage, just to check that they were alone. Once they were back in the safety of their bedroom, they put on their pajamas and jumped into bed. The storm had grown louder, rattling the windows with each roll and crash of thunder. The heavy brocade curtains were still looped back so they could see jagged shafts of lightning sizzle across the stormy sky, crackling with each strike. Rain beat against the windowpanes, the fat drops sliding down the glass.

146

Adam was too nervous to hop out of bed and draw the curtains, so he pretended it didn't matter. He planned to sleep with the quilt over his head anyway. He glanced at the door where a large key stuck out of the keyhole.

"We should lock the door just in case," Adam said, pulling the quilt right up to his chin with a shiver. "You lock it because you're nearest."

"Don't be such a wimp." Justin yawned. "How's anyone going to get into this place? It's like Fort Knox."

He blew out his candle and turned over, yanking most of the quilt onto his side of the bed. With only one candle flame left flickering, the room looked creepy. Enormous shadows threatened from corners that now appeared much darker than in daylight.

Adam pulled some of the quilt back over himself. "Remember one of those hooded guys tried to break in the other night."

"He tried but didn't get in," was Justin's sleepy reply. "We're in a *castle*, for Pete's sake, with high walls and a big fat portcullis. He'd have to be Spiderman."

Adam tried to feel as nonchalant as Justin sounded. Then Justin gave a loud snore. Adam lay back against his pillows for a while, staring at the windows, not at all sleepy. The storm began to die down. There were moments of silence between rolls of thunder. He wondered if Mrs. Grant had been kidding when she said Sir Maulsby hadn't been seen for a while. Ghost stories were usually made-up stories, but what if Sir Maulsby was a *real* ghost and could gallop through the castle walls?

Suddenly, the most unearthly shriek pierced the air and—Adam was sure— his eardrums as well.

"*Gaargh!*"

Adam sat bolt upright in bed, his heart racing, and his chest tight with panic. Then the high-pitched shriek came again.

"*Gaargh!*"

Had someone screamed in pain at the top of their lungs?

Adam grabbed Justin's shoulder, his fingers digging into the quilt.

"You're hurting me," Justin mumbled as he turned toward Adam. "Wassa matter?"

"Did you hear that scream? It's him. It's the Headless Horseman."

The noise came again, loud, agonizing.

Justin gave a drowsy smile. "Don't be stupid. It's just the peacocks."

147

"What?"

"Peacocks. We saw them in the garden. That's what they sound like."

"It can't be. It sounds human, like someone's being tortured."

Adam clutched the quilt, his hands shaking as he dragged it up to his nose this time. He couldn't stop thinking about Sir Maulsby's victims screaming for mercy.

"It's the peacocks, I tell you." Justin buried his head under his pillow. "All these old castles have them. Tradition or something, I expect. Go to sleep."

Muffled snores meant that Justin was already asleep so Adam blew out his candle. The room was plunged into darkness. After a few minutes, Adam's eyes adjusted to the gloom. He could make out the indistinct shapes of the furniture, especially the Narnia wardrobe looming on the other side of the room. There were a few more ear-splitting crashes of thunder and several flashes of lightning before the storm began to rumble away and a soft rain pattered gently at the windows. Adam scolded himself for being so imaginative. He felt under his pillow for his scarab. Ever since their adventure in Egypt, he had become used to hiding the golden replica there each night. It made him feel more comfortable knowing it was close. Clutching it tightly in one hand, he fell asleep and into yet another dream.

This time, he was in a lush green valley with sloping sides covered in wildflowers, bushes, and many trees. A waterfall poured from one hill slope, the crystal torrent tumbling into a deep, blue-tinted pool. In front of him was an extraordinary building. He had never seen anything like it before, not even in history books. It didn't look Roman, or Greek, or even Egyptian. Together with the beautiful surroundings, the temple appeared to be from another time, a more ancient era.

Massive blocks of elaborately carved marble piled one on top of the other formed the walls, with huge statues placed at regular intervals atop the walls. Flanking the sides of the temple, a long line of tall white columns reached skyward. Behind the temple, at the end of the valley, rose a gigantic mountain, its snow-capped peak wreathed in clouds, probing high into the sky.

As Adam gazed at the many steps leading up into the temple, a white-haired man robed in blue emerged from the entrance. Perhaps the man was some kind of priest, or even a king, because he wore a gem-studded gold circlet on his head. Unusual symbols, embroidered in gold and silver thread, decorated his robe. The man raised his arms toward the mountain and began uttering words in a strange language. He cried out, shaking his arms, repeating the words.

As the sleeves of his robe slid back, Adam glimpsed gold bracelets wound around the man's wrists like gleaming serpents. They reminded him of the blue woad serpents tattooed on the wrists of the man he had dreamed about a few nights back: King Arthur, half legend, half mystery.

Then came the deafening noise of a gigantic explosion inside the mountain. An eerie glow appeared behind the temple. The sky turned fiery red as if a blazing sun was setting. Adam knew it wasn't the sunset when he saw plumes of gray smoke pouring from the mountaintop. A roaring blaze turned the sky burnt orange and yellow. Flames leaped from the mountaintop, licking the clouds, tingeing them with gold. An enormous booming sounded under his feet. The ground shuddered and Adam stumbled. This dream was so real he began to feel afraid. Several statues toppled over, and the temple columns shivered and rocked gently.

I should wake up now. Wake up! Wake up!

He pinched himself hard, twisting his flesh painfully between his forefinger and thumb, but, as in his previous dream, it was no use. Things only got worse and he did not wake up. The top of the mountain exploded, shooting boulders, ash, glowing sparks, and flaming rock fragments into the sky. Shocked, Adam stared at the red molten river pouring down the mountainside, scorching a path of destruction as the raging torrent of lava moved toward the temple. A fine rain of ash began to descend, growing thicker and darker with each second, swirling through the temple columns like a massive swarm of angry bees. The man dropped to his knees, coughing, and pointed to Adam, or was it to something behind him? Adam turned, puzzled, and was astonished to find himself in a different place now, a sad and dreary place.

Dark clouds overshadowed the silvered sky. A lone warrior knelt at the edge of a lake. It was Arthur. The battle was over long ago, and the dead and dying lay strewn on the blood-soaked ground. Only the occasional harsh cawing of ravens wheeling and circling over the battlefield, and the faint groans of the wounded broke the heavy silence. The lake was dark and stagnant. The leafless trees fringing

149

the water reflected upside down on the still surface, their bare branches clawing at the sky like gnarled old fingers.

Adam had seen Arthur in his first dream, riding proudly to engage the enemy, but things were now so different. The fierce warrior was weary, smeared with the blood and filth of combat. His hair was matted, darkened with sweat, and plastered on his forehead. His dragon-crested helmet lay forgotten nearby, the brilliant red plumes tangled and dirty. His muddy cloak was slashed in places. The dragon banner lay fallen at Arthur's side, torn and stained. Then Arthur reached for something lying on the grass in front of him. Adam had seen the magnificent sword before. Now dirt dulled its brilliance and the blade was snapped in two. Adam felt his heart turn over. Excalibur was broken. No, it couldn't be true. How was this possible? The sword in the Ashmolean museum wasn't broken. What did it mean? The figure lifted his head and repeated the words Adam had heard in the first dream. Arthur's voice was a hoarse whisper, the words slurring from his lips.

"Restore the Stone of Caledfwlch lest the land descend into ravening darkness."

"But how?" Adam asked. His chest tightened with panic. "I'll do anything, just please tell me how?" He felt so helpless.

The man turned his face away; his head drooped with exhaustion. Adam took a step forward … and woke up.

He sat up in bed, fear turning his blood to ice in his veins. He shook his head to make sure he was awake, trying to focus. Everything was back to normal. The storm was over. In the clear night sky, the full moon rode high in a glittering web of pinprick stars. Pale slivers of moonbeams filtered through the windows, illuminating their bedroom floor in the diamond-shaped pattern of the panes. Then he heard a slight noise outside their room, like the rustle of rough fabric, or the scuffling of a soft shoe. In an instant, Adam knew the person outside was no friend. He grabbed his scarab, shoved it into his pajama pants pocket, and then shook Justin awake.

"Wassa matter *now*?" Justin muttered, still half dazed with sleep. "Is it the Headless Horseman?" He sounded grumpy.

Adam put his mouth right up against Justin's ear. "We have to hide."

Justin reacted instantly to the urgency in Adam's voice. His eyes flew open. "What's up?"

Justin nodded in immediate understanding when Adam pointed to the door and then to the wardrobe. The boys crept to the wardrobe. The door swung open with a faint creak. Adam pressed the carved insignia and lifted up the trapdoor. Justin climbed in first and shifted as far as possible to one side. The wardrobe door swung shut as Adam pulled the trapdoor down. It was amazing that Ink had shown them this hiding place just a few hours earlier. They lay in the hideaway, hardly daring to breathe in case the intruder heard their trembling breaths. The cavity was cramped, probably designed to conceal only one person. Adam had never been so uncomfortable. Justin's sharp elbow poked into his neck, while his shoulders were jammed against Justin's chest. The hard outline of the scarab dug into Adam's flesh through his pajamas. It was so stifling in the cavity that Adam felt they would never get out alive.

He could hear faint sounds—the solid tread of someone larger and heavier entering the room, the swish of the quilt as someone drew back the covers, the occasional squeak of floorboards as the person walked around. Then the intruder opened the wardrobe. There was no escaping the horrible graveyard smell, the reek of rotting bones, the odor of death, decay, and mold.

The intruder sniffed inside the wardrobe. Although he didn't feel the same overwhelming terror as he had the first time they had met one of these creatures, Adam's nerves still screamed at the sound of fingernails scratching on the wood as the creature slid its hands over every inch of the wardrobe, searching for the tiny crack or chink that would reveal a hiding place. Then came a sigh of irritation and disappointment. The wardrobe door closed … silence.

Justin stirred. Adam gripped his cousin's arm to stop Justin moving. Suddenly the wardrobe door flew open again. Hoarse breathing came from whoever stood outside. Finally, after a few long moments, the intruder slammed the wardrobe door shut and left the room. Once they heard the soft click of their bedroom door closing, the boys climbed out of the wardrobe.

When Adam tried to speak, he found he could utter no more than a croak. He looked at his hands—they were shaking.

Justin grinned weakly. "I'm also terrified. My legs feel like jelly."

Adam found his voice. "What should we do now?"

"We'd better follow him and see what he's looking for."

"Are you nuts? He might kill us," Adam protested.

151

"No, he won't. This time he's too close to what he wants. We just need to be careful and very quiet."

"Do you want to wake Ink and Kim?"

"No, let's go alone. We can do it. It'll be like it was before in Egypt—just us. We won't tackle him. We'll only spy on him. See what he's up to."

Justin also wanted to prove to Ink that he was important to the quest. Much as he tried, it was hard to squash his resentment each time Adam received praise or it was clear that Adam was special. Practical action was what Justin did best. So, when the opportunity arose—like now—he wasn't going to let it slip past him. Adam could take the glory for the mysterious stuff. Following the creature might be dangerous, but if they kept well behind, then things could hardly go wrong, could they?

Justin paused at the top of the stairs, almost regretting his moment of bravery and wondering if they were making a terrible mistake. Then he caught Adam looking at him with the same trusting expression as when Justin had taken the lead in Egypt.

Now they had to do it. There was no way they could just cower in their room while an intruder rifled through the castle. They owed it to James to find out what he was after. It was the least they could do.

He grinned at Adam and mouthed the words, "Let's go."

DISCOVERING BEDWYR'S DIARY

They tiptoed down the main staircase. Adam shielded his candle with one hand so the intruder would not see the flame. Shadows leaped out at them, confusing their path. Things looked so different in the dark, somehow unfamiliar and more menacing. The candlelight illuminated the gloomy portraits of past Earls of Strathairn on the walls in brief flashes. Their forbidding faces and stern eyes seemed to be telling the cousins to go back, go back … before it was too late. But it was already too late and they had to keep moving forward.

The great staircase seemed endless, spiraling down into a black void. It was also hard to see anything in front of their feet. The candle flame was pitifully small compared to the huge well of darkness at the bottom of the stairs. Adam couldn't manage the candle and see where he was going at the same time. This made him careless going down the stairs.

"Don't—" Justin whispered, putting out a warning hand, but he was too late.

Adam trod on the "nightingale" floorboard, a loose board deliberately designed to creak. Ink had told them that in the olden days, if an intruder was sneaking up or down the staircase, he was sure to step on it and alert people to his presence. Adam had done just that. The creak of the board sounded abnormally loud. Adam froze in horror, waiting for their enemy to turn back and confront them. Preparing to dash back up the stairs to the safety of their room, Adam vowed that this time he would lock the door himself. But only quiet darkness surrounded them.

In the silence, he could feel his own heartbeat thudding against his chest and hear the rasp of hoarse breath coming from Justin's throat. Perhaps the intruder was so bent on his own mission he didn't realize he was being followed. There were soft sounds ahead of them: the occasional scuffle of a shoe or the brushing of clothing against a piece of furniture. It was impossible for anyone to walk in total silence. Some faint clue would always give them away.

It seemed to be safe so they continued creeping down the staircase. When they reached the bottom of the stairs, Justin stubbed his toe on the huge suit of armor standing guard at the corner. There was a low *bong*.

"Sorry," Justin whispered.

Surprisingly, there was still no reaction from their prey. Perhaps he was farther ahead than they had thought. They followed the sounds until they reached another set of stairs. This led down into what Mrs. McLeod had laughingly referred to as "the old master's Chamber of Curiosities." It was the famous Strathairn Castle Museum, which they had planned to explore the following day. The old earl was a keen collector of antiquities and unusual objects, gathered on his expeditions during his youth. The prowler was obviously looking for something in there.

Adam wished he had brought a weapon, like a poker—just in case.

The faint glimmer in front of them indicated their quarry also had a candle. Adam gripped his candlestick tighter. The light disappeared as the prowler went into the museum, which was evidently unlocked. The boys trod in silence down the narrow stairs and peered around the door. The dark-robed figure moved about as he searched, his candle illuminating the contents of the room. It was difficult to see much more than brief glimpses, but what the boys spied was enough to tell them the place was a collector's dream.

Large glass-fronted cabinets held an incredible assortment of artifacts including knives, early arrowheads, prehistoric stone tools, strangely carved figurines, and even several shrunken heads. On the walls of the room hung animal heads, deer antlers, antique weapons and various pieces of armor, tattered battle flags, swords, and spears. Another upright cabinet housed a full set of samurai armor, including a pair of curved *katana* swords.

The glass-topped cases containing manuscripts and pieces of parchment had caught the intruder's attention. Bending over one of the cases, he opened the lid and began studying the contents, lifting pages between fingers and thumb with care.

Suddenly, the intruder looked up, startled. He held the candle in front of him and peered into the darkness, frowning as he moved the candle back and forth.

154

He was dressed in a hooded robe similar to the person in Humphrey's shop. The flickering flame cast an eerie glow upon his white face, throwing shadows under his eye sockets, turning his face skeletal. His eyes glowed red in the candlelight.

The sight was so frightening that Adam couldn't help gasping. This time the intruder heard him. He spoke in a harsh voice, using a language neither boy could understand.

"*Da mihi librum secretum Arthepii!*"

However, since it was pointless hiding any longer, Adam and Justin stepped forward. Adam had a sickening feeling they were face to face with deadly danger. His stomach turned over in a horrible, queasy way and shivers chased down his spine.

"What are you doing here? What do you want?" asked Justin, his voice wobbling as he spoke.

The intruder spoke again. Adam had a vague idea the words were Latin, but he couldn't be sure.

The intruder took a step closer. When the moldy smell hit their nostrils, the boys backed away, half-afraid, half-disgusted.

"We can't understand you," Adam said loudly and slowly. He shook his head, hoping the intruder would comprehend what they meant. He could see by Justin's expression that he now thought following the intruder had been a bad move. The intruder appeared angry and frustrated. Clearly, he had not found what he was looking for, and now he was cornered because the doorway was blocked.

A noise came from behind them. Adam glanced back, relieved to see Ink's familiar face. Kim, in pajamas and a robe, was also there, peeping around the door. Ink wore jeans and a crumpled T-shirt. His hair was sticking up more than usual so he had obviously just woken up. To Adam's surprise, Ink appeared to understand the intruder because he began speaking to him in what seemed like the same language.

Ink sounded calm and firm when he spoke. "*Quid quaeris?*"

The intruder scowled in reply and then spat, twisting his bloodless lips, "*Da mihi librum secretum Arthepii!*"

Ink shook his head. "*Non habemus quod quaeris.*"

The intruder snarled at him. "*Mendax! Noli conari me decipere. De hoc te dicere audivi.*"

Justin tugged on Ink's shirt. "What's he saying?"

155

Ink frowned. "I asked what he's looking for and he says something about a secret book of Arthepius. I said we don't have it, but he doesn't believe me. He says we're lying because he heard us talking about it."

"Oh no, not *more* books," Justin muttered crossly. "This is exactly how it was in Egypt—*Book of the Dead*, book of this, book of that. It's enough just having the *Book of Thoth* to worry about."

Adam slipped his hand into his pajama pocket and gripped his scarab. The intruder was becoming angrier now, exhaling in hisses, his gaze darting from side to side as if looking for another escape route. Adam couldn't see the poison pouch they had discovered in the Star Maze, but the intruder might have it hidden in his robe. Adam inched backward in case their unwelcome visitor decided to blow the sleeping powder on them again.

The intruder saw the movement out of the corner of one eye and turned to face Adam. His face lit up with recognition as he pointed a bony finger at the boy. His sleeve slipped back, revealing a thin white arm. His lips curled in a snarl as he mumbled strange words.

"*Tu! Exitium templi sancti vidisti. Tu, tu ille electus es et plura videbis. Est tibi notum signi vitae. Tibi non nocebimus. Da nobis quod quaerimus et ceteri tuti erunt, alioquin caveant. Nunc tibi discedendum est.*"

Ink stepped forward to shield Adam. Clearly, he understood the words, even if Adam did not.

Adam looked up at Ink. "Is anything wrong? What's he saying?"

Ink gave him a gentle push. "Go back upstairs now. Wait for me in the kitchen."

Adam grabbed Justin's arm and they edged out of the room, pulling Kim with them. She didn't protest; she just scuttled along, her face tight with fear. They went into the kitchen. The power was still out, so Justin lit a few more candles they found lying on the table. Justin went over to the cupboards and began opening the doors.

"What are you looking for?" asked Adam.

"Just wondering where Mrs. Grant keeps the cookies. Those chocolate chip ones we had at teatime were rather yummy."

"How can you *eat* at a time like this?" Adam sputtered. "Our lives might be in danger. We could be killed."

Justin shrugged. "Then I don't want to die hungry. Bingo! Found 'em."

He hauled a cookie jar off a shelf and opened it. Neither Adam nor Kim could eat a thing. Justin wolfed down several cookies. Smudge woke up and jumped onto Kim's lap. She sat stroking him while Jasper snored contentedly in his basket.

Justin looked down at the heaving mound of fur. "Some guard dog, huh?"

In the museum, Ink and the creature faced each other. Ink wouldn't back down, but he didn't want another fight like the one on the train. He repeated his previous words—they did not have what the intruder was looking for.

"You must leave this place now," Ink added, wondering how the intruder had sneaked through high castle walls, a portcullis, and the sturdy front door he had seen Sheldon lock that evening.

The intruder hissed a few angry words under his breath, and then swirled past Ink in a flurry of hessian robes, disappearing into the darkness. Ink wiped his forehead. He was actually more frightened than he would ever admit. Humphrey hadn't been exaggerating when he had said the quest would be dangerous.

Putting on a big fake smile, Ink walked into the kitchen. The kids crowded around him, demanding explanations. Jasper woke up with the commotion and began barking. Smudge added to the noise. Ink waved his hands at the animals until they settled down. Jasper slunk under the table and Smudge jumped back into Kim's lap.

"Now sit down and relax," Ink said. "Dogs as well. It's all going to be fine. He's gone. The power is still out, but we've got plenty of candles."

Three solemn expressions told him they weren't convinced. Ink sat down at the table.

"Hey, my favorites." He stuck his hand into the cookie jar. "Anyone want one?"

The trio shook their heads. Even Justin couldn't face another snack. He asked his question first.

"What language was he speaking, Ink?"

"Latin. It sounded a bit like mediaeval Latin. I replied to him in classical Latin, but we could understand each other."

157

"What's the difference?" Adam asked. "Latin is Latin, right?"

"Wrong," Ink said, glad to chatter with them so they could unwind. He didn't like the raw fear in their eyes.

"Classical Latin is what we learn when we study the Latin literature of the ancient Romans. Mediaeval Latin is what they spoke in the High Middle Ages, the time Bedwyr lived, circa AD 1296. By then, there were lots of changes in the language because language evolves as time goes by."

Adam frowned. "Why would he speak Latin if we're in the twenty-first century? I mean, he can't be from the Middle Ages—that's impossible."

Kim said, "Maybe it's a group that keeps those traditions alive, the way some people act out battles and historical events. There's a mediaeval society back home, and they love getting dressed up in fake armor and pretending to hack off each other's heads."

"Anyway, what's this secret book of Arthepius?" asked Justin. "I've never heard of it and we definitely don't have it."

Ink shook his head. "Never heard of it. I wonder why he thinks we have it."

Kim said, "I think I know why."

They all stared at her. Ink raised his eyebrows.

"It's because since we got to Oxford, we've been talking about King Arthur the whole time. Anyone eavesdropping may have only heard the 'Arth' part of the word. If these guys are looking for something written by Arthepius, then they heard what they wanted to hear. They heard 'Arth' and thought of their own search."

Ink patted her shoulder. "Well done. Ten out of ten for you, Kim."

Justin scowled at Kim.

"What did he say to me?" asked Adam. "Was it bad?" Half of him wanted to know; the other half did not.

"His exact words were, '*You have seen the destruction of the sacred temple. And as you are the Chosen One, you will see more. You have the mark of the sign of life and we will not touch you. Just give us what we seek and your friends will be safe. If not, they must beware.*'"

Ink leaned forward, resting his arms on the kitchen table. "I think we need to know something more about your dreams, Adam. And what's this about a mark?"

Adam swallowed hard, knowing he must tell Ink everything; they had all promised to share information in order to survive.

"I never knew I had the mark until we went to Egypt," he began.

"Yes," Justin interrupted. "I saw it first. We were swimming in the pool on the cruise boat and I noticed it on Adam's back."

"Will you show us?" Ink asked.

Adam stood up, slipped off his pajama top and turned his back so the others could see the mark in the shape of an *ankh*, the ancient Egyptian sign of life that looked like a cross with a loop on the top. It was on his left shoulder blade.

"It's probably all faded by now. I haven't been swimming since Egypt."

No one said a word. Adam put his pajama top back on and turned to face them, puzzled by their silence. They all looked astonished. Kim's eyes were huge with amazement.

He sat down. "What's wrong?" Cold fear clutched at his heart. His stomach did a weird flip-flop.

"It's not faded," Justin spluttered, pointing at him. "It's glowing, like you're on fire."

Adam slid his hand behind his back, trying to reach the mark. "That's not possible," he said through stiff lips. "It's just a birthmark. It's nothing special."

"Why do you keep on saying that?" Justin burst out. "You *know* what it means."

"Why don't you start at the beginning?" Ink suggested.

Adam hesitated at first, but once he began speaking, it all spilled out at once. He only stopped after he'd told Ink the whole story of what had happened in Egypt—how the peddler had given him the black scarab at Memphis; how they'd solved the clues contained in the scarab; Justin's discovery of the mark; the fortune teller's message that Adam was a Son of Fire and Light; Dr. Khalid's reaction to seeing the mark, and the ancient prediction that only the one with the mark could open the Forbidden Chamber in the tomb of the Scarab King. He also described everything James had told them about Bedwyr and the *Chronicles of the Stone*, a manuscript that Dr. Khalid had managed to steal. After they had all been rescued, Ebrahim Faza and his friend Hamid insisted the boys help James in his search for the Scroll of the Ancients and the remaining Stones of Power. Ink didn't interrupt. Kim sat riveted and Justin only broke in now and again to emphasize a point.

"Well, Adam," said Ink, "Humphrey told me some stuff about the quest, but now this has filled in all the gaps. What a story!"

"You should have been there," said Justin. "It was scarier in real life than it actually sounds."

"Perhaps the mark is more significant than you thought, Adam," Ink said. "Maybe it wasn't just singling you out as the one to open the Scarab King's tomb. The fact that this creature knew who you were and knew about the mark tells me the mark might make you more important in locating the Seven Stones of Power than you think. And if that's the case, then these people, the hooded creatures, must know something about the history behind the Seven Stones."

"It makes sense," said Justin eagerly. "Why else would one of those guys try to break in before we even arrived here unless they know a lot more than we think?"

Adam felt anxious. "Even if they knew about the mark, how did they know I'm the one who has it? I haven't been walking around without a shirt on. It could've been anyone."

"But it's not anyone," Kim said. "It's you." Her words hung in the silence.

Ink turned to Adam. "The creature said you saw the destruction of a sacred temple. What did you see?"

Adam related his dream of the ancient temple destroyed by a fiery river of lava; and then how the scene had changed to reveal Arthur and the broken sword. He recounted Arthur's exact words.

"Excalibur was broken?" Kim gasped. "But that's impossible. The sword in the Ashmolean was dirty, but not broken."

"Perhaps it was mended," Justin said. "I'm sure with all the fighting in those days, swords often got broken."

Adam frowned, propping his chin in his hands. Something was puzzling him. "Arthur said the same thing in both dreams I had about him. Something about the land descending into ravening darkness. What's ravening darkness?"

"Maybe some kind of destruction," said Justin. "It sounds bad."

"How can that relate to now?" asked Kim. "What could possibly happen to this country? There's a police force, an army … people who can take care of things. I mean they have a *queen*, not just a government."

160

Adam didn't want to mention that whoever united the Seven Stones of Power with the Stone of Fire and read the *Book of Thoth* would certainly be able to take control of the world and plunge it into a kind of darkness.

"Hey, I know," Kim said with a meaningful grin. "I just worked it out. Remember what Archie told us? The land *did* descend into darkness because after Arthur's death the Saxons were able to overrun Britain again."

Adam shot a sideways glance at Justin. "Yeah, you must be right."

Justin winked at Adam in silent agreement.

"Were the Dark Ages really that bad?" Justin directed his question at Ink.

Ink helped himself to another cookie. "Yep, I'm afraid so. That's why they were called the Dark Ages. It was a kind of darkness, although not a physical one. Once the Romans left, there was a gradual descent into chaos. Imagine living in a world where the ruling system has collapsed and there's no longer a proper government, schools, libraries, a single currency, or even a common language. Plus there were outbreaks of the plague, the Black Death."

Justin pulled a face. "It sounds terrible." He reached for the cookie jar, shoved a cookie into his mouth and chomped on it, an anxious frown creasing his forehead.

"It gets worse," Ink said. "Bartering replaced money. Cities and towns deteriorated and transportation between them was extremely difficult, if not impossible. Education and literacy collapsed and only the monasteries kept the flame of learning alive."

"But that would never happen again," said Kim, as if trying to convince herself. She cuddled Smudge. "Not in the twenty-first century, hey, Smudge?"

She looked at Adam. "After all, it was just a dream."

Adam wasn't so sure. The image of the defeated king flashed into his mind again. "But Arthur seemed so real. I could've reached out and touched him."

It seemed to him that Arthur's message, although relevant to the period in which he had lived, somehow had meaning for the future—a future that depended on them finding the Seven Stones of Power before Dr. Khalid did.

"Let's not worry about that now," Ink said. "We should go back downstairs and try to find what the intruder might have been searching for."

They followed Ink out of the kitchen. Ink told everyone to go ahead and then pushed Jasper and Smudge back into the kitchen and closed the door. "Sorry, this tour's not for dogs."

They filed down the narrow stairs to the Chamber of Curiosities. Ink had equipped them each with a fresh candle from Mrs. McLeod's store in the kitchen.

When they arrived, Kim gazed around the room. "This is a real Chamber of Curiosities."

Justin and Adam were already inspecting the broken display case.

"Don't touch anything," Ink ordered as he pulled the gloves Humphrey had given him from his jeans pocket. He bent over the case and carefully lifted the pages out. He laid them on a nearby table and began reading, muttering under his breath as he translated the Latin.

Adam and Kim, bored with waiting for Ink to discover something stupendous, wandered behind a painted Japanese screen. They found an old-fashioned writing desk tucked in a corner. Adam remembered having seen something like it in a book about monasteries.

He nudged Kim. "I think this might be Bedwyr's writing desk," he whispered. He lifted the slanted lid and peered inside. It was empty. Disappointed, he closed it. "There's nothing here."

Just then, Justin stumbled around the Japanese screen, puffing for breath as he lugged a large stone with strange designs. "Hey, you two. Look at this amazing stone. It's got Celtic signs carved on it. Maybe the Druids used it for strange and secret ceremonies. Maybe human sacrifices?" His eyes gleamed at the thought.

"Maybe you should put it down before you drop it," Kim advised him. "It looks too big for you to carry."

The stone began to slip from Justin's grasp as he staggered up to them. "I'll put it down here," he gasped. "Phew, it's heavier than I thought."

As he came closer, he bashed the corner of the desk, breaking part of the wood before he dropped the stone onto the floor. In his clumsiness, Justin also managed to knock over the Japanese screen.

Ink stalked over to them. "Will you lot shut up? Do you want to wake everyone?"

Adam almost reminded Ink that Sheldon had said their quarters were on the other side of the castle, but one glance at Ink's face was enough to keep him quiet. Then Ink saw the broken desk.

"Oh no!" His expression grew angrier. "What did you do, Justin?"

Justin turned bright red and hung his head. "It was an accident. I'm sorry. It won't happen again."

"There won't be anything left in one piece by the time you leave if you're not more careful," Ink snapped. "I don't know what—"

"Hey!" Adam knelt down near the broken corner. "Look at this."

They all moved closer to inspect the damaged corner. A section of wood had shifted to the side when it was knocked loose. Underneath was something that appeared to be a secret drawer.

"Wow," said Adam. "The desk looked empty when I opened it."

Ink was astounded. "Well, Justin, maybe something good will come from your clumsiness."

Justin gave a sheepish grin.

Ink fiddled with the loose sliver of wood. "If I can just open this ..."

They stood back to give him room. Adam glanced at Justin, who still looked subdued, and gave him a big thumbs-up. Justin grinned back. Kim squeezed Adam's arm in excitement.

"Aha," Ink cried out. "I think I see ... if I can just move this piece. Justin, hold this bit up."

Justin sprang to help him. Ink carefully eased a bunch of pages out of the secret drawer so as not to tear them on the jagged edges of wood. Once the pages were completely out, Ink stuck his hand back into the aperture and wiggled his fingers.

"Nothing else inside here." Ink then took the loose pages and said, "Let's see what we've got."

As he held the pages near a candle, disappointment registered on his face. The pages were blank, except for an elaborate piece of artwork on the top left corner of each page—an initial about an inch across. Puzzled, he shuffled the pages. Each page slipped behind the next with a dry rustling sound. Ink checked the other side of each page as well. All were clean.

"Why would Bedwyr hide blank pages away in a secret drawer?" Adam burst out. "It doesn't make sense."

He had been almost holding his breath with excitement at the thrill of a real discovery. Now he felt deflated, as if their whole trip had been for nothing.

"Maybe he was planning to write something later on. The monks prepared their pages well in advance of actually writing anything down," Ink replied. "It took ages to get everything ready."

"Why?" asked Kim.

"After preparing the page, the scribe had to make quill pens from goose feathers. Inks and colors had to be mixed. Someone had to copy out what needed to be written, and then an artist had to decorate the pages. So books were a lot of hard work."

He examined the pages again. "Yes, Bedwyr was about to write something. See here how the pages are pricked on the side to help him draw lines on the paper so the writing would be straight. You can also see the lines."

They peered at the pages. There were faint marks down the side, as Ink described, and even fainter lines ruled across.

Kim touched a corner of one of the pages. "This doesn't feel like paper."

"It's parchment," said Ink. "Or it might be vellum."

Adam rubbed one finger on a page corner. "What's the difference?"

"Parchment is usually made from goat or sheep skin and vellum from calf skin. Calf skin was less messy and more popular, but more expensive."

Justin frowned. "How do you turn hairy animal skin into this?"

Ink smiled. "It's a long process. The skins were soaked for a few days in running water, and then in lime and water. Then they were rinsed, stretched on a frame, and dried in the sun. After that, some lucky person scraped all of the fat and hair off the skin. They did this until the skin was clean and ready for use."

Kim wrinkled her nose. "Ugh. It sounds disgusting."

Ink nodded. "Yes, it was rather."

"So it wasn't as easy as just buying a ream of paper?" Adam asked.

Ink shook his head. "No, in fact parchment was in such short supply that often the monks would scrape off the old ink and reuse the sheets. A document made of these reused sheets was called a *palimpsest*. Paper only came along in the late fourteenth century and printing in the fifteenth century, so the monks were very busy before then."

Adam felt a pang of alarm. "Do you think that could have happened to the Scroll of the Ancients? Someone scraped the writing off and used it for something else?"

Ink laughed. "Relax, Adam. I really don't think so. Remember what you said James told you? Bedwyr wrote that the scroll was 'well hid.' We have to keep looking." He glanced down at the pages. "This is definitely not the scroll."

Adam felt that as well. The ancient scroll must still be hidden, but time was running out. Something seemed odd.

164

"Ink, why would Bedwyr draw this insignia thing at the top of the page?"

"It was called an initial. It would be the first letter of the text on a page. It was much bigger than the rest of the text and usually ornately decorated. Some initials even included historical scenes or figures. Others had animals or plants, depending on the theme of what was written. Why do you ask?"

"Because," said Adam slowly, pointing to the pages, "Bedwyr has begun each page with an initial, but how did he know how much space he would use and which word would begin each page?"

"You're right," said Ink. He held one page closer to the candle for a better look. The parchment turned yellow and then brown in places.

"Look out!" Justin made a grab for the page. "You're burning it."

"No, he's not," Adam said in wonder. "The heat is showing up some writing. It's written in some kind of invisible ink."

Spellbound, they watched as strange words appeared on the page. Ink then carefully exposed several more pages to the candle's heat until brown writing covered both sides of each page. The writing did not fade.

Ink laid the pages down. "This is incredible."

Adam stared at the newly discovered text. "What language is it written in?"

"Like most monks, Bedwyr spoke and wrote classical Greek and Latin," said Ink. "These words look like Latin." He frowned. "But they're not. The letters are all mixed up." He scratched his head. "I'm stumped."

"Maybe it's a cipher." Justin lifted a page by one corner and examined it closely. "A secret code. That's why the letters are mixed up. It has to be."

Ink stared at him, and then clapped one hand to his forehead. "That's it. Justin, you're a genius."

"Why would he write in code?" Kim asked. "He was a monk, not a spy."

Excitement spread across Justin's face. "Because Bedwyr was afraid for his life," he babbled, the words tumbling out as if he were thinking faster than he could speak.

"Remember all the things James told us? Bedwyr came back to the castle one year because his father was very ill … he was afraid of something or someone … then suddenly he died. It all fits. Bedwyr wrote in code because he was afraid someone would find out what he knew and then he hid the pages in his desk, safely back home in this castle."

Justin looked pleased at the end of his garbled speech.

"If that's true," asked Adam, "then why did he use such a simple thing like invisible writing? That's a kids' trick. We used to do it when we pretended to be spies in junior school. We used lemon juice."

"It's simple to you, but back then it would have been extremely clever," Ink replied. "Most of the population at that time was illiterate—only a few people could read and write. The monasteries were the only centers of learning, so monks held the key to knowledge through books, writing, and information. Obviously, Bedwyr was trying to conceal information from someone as educated as he was—either a peer or someone over him."

Ink shuffled the pages with care. "Now we just need the key to decode the cipher."

"What about the Caesar cipher?" Justin suggested. "That's a simple one. You just replace the alphabet letters with a shift of three letters. *A* reads as *D*, *B* reads as *E*, *C* reads as *F*, and so on. You can shift the letters any number of times you want, but the idea is the same."

Surprised, Ink raised his eyebrows. "How do you know so much about ciphers?"

Justin grinned. "I read about it. Julius Caesar confused his enemies by encoding his military messages."

"Bedwyr liked history," Adam said, "so maybe Justin's right."

Kim yawned. "I'm so tired I can't think straight. Can we do Julius Caesar and spy codes tomorrow?"

"Good idea," Ink agreed. "I'll keep these pages in my room tonight and we'll tackle things in the morning. You'd better all lock your doors for the rest of the night."

They stumbled to their rooms, exhausted by the night's events.

As the cousins were getting into bed, Adam said, "How on earth are we going to decode something written seven hundred years ago—using a Roman cipher from the first century BC?"

"I don't know," Justin said. "But I can hardly wait to get started."

what happened to humphrey?

The previous evening had been the same as any other for Humphrey, except Ink had not been there. Humphrey sat alone after dinner. Amelia had left at her usual hour, wishing him goodnight. Bismarck jumped onto his master's lap, his yellow eyes gleaming.

Humphrey stroked him. "It's just you and me now, Bismarck, old boy. Lonely, isn't it? Something we should get used to, though. He'll be meeting a nice young lady soon and wanting to leave home, won't he?"

Uncurling his tail, the cat got comfortable and proceeded to lick his marmalade fur. Humphrey pushed him away. "Go do that somewhere else. I don't want fur up my nose, thank you."

Bismarck flounced off to the window while Humphrey mulled over recent events. It was all coming together—the children, the quest—but how would it end? He felt in his pocket for Ebrahim's last letter, a letter of warning that spoke of a far greater threat than they had imagined. A juggernaut of destruction. Malignant forces would be unleashed upon an unsuspecting and unprepared world. Humphrey wished Ebrahim was there to advise him, but his friend was dealing with bigger problems at that moment. Ebrahim had confirmed that the bizarre monk-like creatures were indeed the Eaters of Poison. Their methods were strange, but the results were always fatal.

Not being able to contact Ink again worried him. When he dialed the castle number, the line remained dead. He would try a third time in the morning. Maybe he could persuade Ink to bring the children back to Oxford, where they would be safe until James and Isabel returned from France.

A plaintive *meow* interrupted his reverie. Bismarck sat before him, one paw reaching up as if to say, "Feed me."

Humphrey went to the kitchen, spooned cat food into a dish for Bismarck, and made himself a cup of cocoa, which he brought back to the living room. After setting the cup on the coffee table, he picked up a large buff envelope. Someone had left it on the doormat, with an unusual medallion and chain taped to the outside. This was a real mystery. The words *Hand Delivery* were scrawled across one corner. Odder still, Ink's name was printed on the front as the recipient.

He read the name again. Benjamin Blott. Benjamin. His face creased into a contented smile and his eyes grew a little misty when he thought of the day he had held the abandoned, screaming waif in his arms. His sister Pandora had told him there was no fool like an old fool, but that if he didn't take the child, she would never speak to him again. Benjamin was the name in the note accompanying the baby. Benjamin meant "son of the right hand." Pandora said the baby would be a joy to him and she was right.

The doorbell jerked Humphrey back to reality. He slipped the envelope behind a cushion. "Coming!" He frowned. It was so late, almost nine o'clock. Possibly one of those devoted collectors who lived for nothing but their old books; they often forgot about normal shop hours.

The bell sounded again, impatiently this time.

"Coming!" Humphrey called again, louder.

As he entered the shop, he saw a tall dark shape through the frosted glass pane in the front door. A sudden twinge of fear clutched his heart. *Imagine* … He shook his head. Ridiculous. Probably just an eager client. The shop bell tinkled as he opened the door.

"Can I—"

A heavy blow struck him in the face and he flew backward like a limp ragdoll. Crashing against a bookshelf, he slid to the floor in a crumpled heap, with his pince-nez landing next to him. The intruder stepped over the old man's body, crushing the glass underfoot, and strode into the shop.

168

Just up the road, Amelia and her friend Mildred Perkins were making their way home. Mildred was riding her bicycle while Amelia walked beside her. They had just been to see a movie of Mildred's choice. Although Amelia preferred action and adventure, Mildred adored romantic comedies. Mildred was Amelia's oldest friend since she could remember. Tall, thin, with gray hair twisted into a tight knot and old-fashioned clothing more suited to life a half a century ago, Mildred was the local librarian. She had never married but rather, as she often said, reserved her love for books. Amelia had once thought Mildred had a soft spot for Humphrey. However, since almost twenty years had passed with neither saying anything, who knew? Laughing together, the women were about to pass Humphrey's cottage when Amelia stopped.

"Mildred, wait." She put one hand on the bicycle handlebars. "Look, the front door's open. That's not like Humphrey. He's absentminded, but he'd never forget to lock up."

As they peered through the gloom at the cottage, Amelia saw quite clearly a long shaft of yellow light falling from the doorway onto the garden path. A strange feeling of dread came over her. Humphrey was so habitual and so particular. He would never leave the front door of the shop open, not with so many valuable items inside.

Mildred parked her bicycle in the bushes outside the gate and the two women crept up the path together, each gripping her handbag. They stepped soundlessly over the threshold. Humphrey lay sprawled on the floor. Mildred opened her mouth to utter a terrified squeal, but Amelia silenced her with a hard pinch on the arm. Amelia motioned toward the living room and held a finger to her lips. Pointing for Mildred to check on Humphrey, she then put down her handbag and grabbed the biggest thing on hand—a large, dusty vase. She crept to the door and peered around it.

A tall, dark-robed figure leaned over a small writing desk in the corner. Could this be a thief interested in stealing rare manuscripts? She raised the vase above her head and tiptoed forward until she was right behind him. Then Amelia brought the vase down on the intruder's head with a mighty whack. The vase shattered and the man dropped to the floor, unconscious.

Mildred scuttled in. "Are you all right, my dear?"

Amelia dusted her hands off with a satisfied smile. "Perfectly fine, thank you, but our friend here isn't doing so well. How's Humphrey?"

Mildred's trembling fingers fluttered to her mouth. "Oh dear, Amelia, I hope he's not dead. I think he's all right. I felt the tiniest pulse, but I couldn't be sure. You know how useless I am in … er … situations."

Amelia heard the nervous quiver in Mildred's voice. Once Amelia had checked that Humphrey was indeed still alive, she and Mildred returned to the living room.

"Come on. Let's have a look at him."

The two women heaved the supine body over. The man was unconscious and breathing heavily. With black hair and a thick wooly beard, he looked Middle Eastern. He wore a strange red velvet hat, rather like a fez, and a long cloak of shiny black material. His other clothes—a long dark robe over multicolored baggy pants—also looked foreign.

"Cheeky scoundrel," Mildred snapped, sounding braver now. "Why couldn't he just buy what he wanted?"

"Because I don't think what he wants is for sale," said Amelia slowly.

"What do you mean?" Mildred's small pointed face was frightened and pinched. Her blue eyes peered shortsightedly from behind her wire-rimmed glasses. Wisps of gray hair hung around her ears, giving her the appearance of an elderly spaniel.

Amelia wasn't even sure what she meant so she changed the subject. "Um … we'd better call the police."

Mildred got to her feet and smoothed her skirt. "I tried the shop phone already. It's out of order."

The same feeling of dread came over Amelia again. There had been nothing wrong with the phone earlier because Humphrey had received a call just before she had left that evening to meet Mildred. Clearly, someone had cut the line. This was an odd kind of thief. Why go to all that trouble unless he knew he would be a long time searching for whatever he had in mind?

"Let's tie him up," Amelia said. "There's a roll of washing line in the kitchen."

They tied the man's hands and feet with pieces of washing line and then surveyed their captive.

Mildred blinked at Amelia. "Shall I go to the police station? On my bicycle, I mean. I'll be quick. It's just down the road. Two minutes."

"Would you mind? That would be a great help."

170

Mildred's mouth quivered and she twisted her fingers nervously. "But I don't want to leave you alone here with this … this … ruffian."

Amelia squeezed her friend's hands. "Off you go, and don't worry about me. I'll find something else to hit him with if he wakes up."

Mildred gave a nervous titter. "Don't use the other vase."

"What do you mean?"

Mildred giggled again. "There are two of them and, since they're Ming, I wouldn't smash the other one as well if I were you."

Amelia's heart sank. She looked down at the floor, covered in bits of blue and white pottery. "Ming? Are you sure?"

"Quite. My great-aunt Agatha had one just like it. Worth pots of money."

Amelia followed her down the path to see that Mildred got away safely.

Mildred gave a little wave. "Toodle-oo." She pedaled furiously down the road, elbows tucked in, and her short cape flying out like bat wings. Mildred was a champion cyclist and won the Library Association Ladies' Over-Fifty Cycle Race regularly. She would be back soon. Had the intruder operated alone or was there someone else in the house? Amelia went straight to the kitchen to fetch a large wooden rolling pin, the heaviest weapon she could find. She checked on Humphrey again. His face was deathly pale, but his breathing was regular. Although he had a huge bruise on his forehead, there was no blood. Clutching her rolling pin, she crept back into the living room.

The man had gone. Amelia's heart jumped in fright. The only sign that he had ever been there were the pieces of rope lying on the floor and the shattered remains of the Ming vase. While she was outside with Mildred, the intruder had either regained consciousness and escaped, or someone had taken the body away. Amelia froze for a few moments, wondering if he was hiding behind the curtains. Holding the rolling pin in front of her, Amelia crept around the sofa and stared at the curtains, drawn for the night. A tiny movement of the fabric caught her eye. She yanked open the curtains so hard that the momentum carried her over the back of the sofa. She landed on the cushions, knocking a small table to the floor as one shoe flew off. A heavy, furry mass pressed on her face. Coughing and spluttering, she fought to get free of the strange weight. As she struggled from under the fur, she heard a frightened *meow*. Bismarck dug his claws into her cardigan.

Amelia lay half off the sofa, clutching the cat, and crying with relief. "Oh Bismarck, were you frightened, too?"

171

She slid to the floor, put on her shoe, and then got up, straightening her blouse and skirt. A noise in the shop set her heart racing again. Arming herself with the rolling pin again, she crept to the door and jumped out, waving the weapon above her head.

"Hey, steady on, miss!" A shout halted her wild whirlings.

Facing her were three police officers, two medics, and Mildred. Dropping the rolling pin, Amelia sank to her knees and burst into tears of relief. In the next few minutes, the officer in charge took over, giving orders and checking the cottage. Mildred made tea, and once the medics took Humphrey away, the officer in charge placed the other two police officers on guard at the front and the back of the cottage. He sat Amelia down with a cup of tea and asked her to tell him the whole story from start to finish.

Amelia stared at him as he wrote in his notebook. His face was vaguely familiar. Then she recognized him. It was Detective-Inspector Peter Bradley, the officer in charge of investigating the robbery at the Ashmolean Museum. She had seen him in the television news report about the break-in at the museum. They must have made a connection between the children, Humphrey, and the museum. Although he steered clear of the subject of the museum, the officer questioned Amelia closely about Humphrey's associates: clients who usually came into the shop, regular buyers, international buyers, occasional buyers, and the most common and uncommon client requests.

"I'm glad to say the intruder didn't manage to get into your employer's strong room downstairs," he said, "although it's clear he tried to break the locks."

He gave Amelia a stern look. "I'm assuming that Mr. Biddle's accounts, sales register, and VAT are in order?"

"Of course!" Amelia felt her cheeks turn pink with indignation. She drew herself up. "I do the books myself to trial balance. I can assure you that Mr. Biddle is a highly respected member of his profession. He would never—"

"Yes, I'm sure," said the officer, raising one hand to silence her. "But we have to check every possible source. I'll have two of my men stand guard for the night, just in case the intruder returns. I'll also have a twenty-four-hour police watch put on Mr. Biddle's hospital room."

Mildred tiptoed into the room like a frightened mouse. She edged closer and took Amelia's hand. "Would you like to spend the night at my flat?"

"I think staying with Miss Perkins might be the best idea," said the officer. "I don't want these people targeting you as well, Miss Sudsbury. They might think you know something about Mr. Biddle's business or what they're searching for."

"But I don't know anything," said Amelia.

"They don't know that," he replied. "You might still be in danger."

Mildred's eyes filled with tears. "Do you think we should take dear Bismarck with us as well?"

Amelia decided Bismarck would be better off staying at the cottage where she could feed him every day. The detective-inspector said it was safe for her to come to the shop for work, as he would keep a police guard posted until the case was resolved. The officers loaded Mildred's bicycle into the trunk of a police car and drove the women to Mildred's flat.

Later that night, while she was making up the spare bed, Mildred said, "I think it's marvelous the police are taking this so seriously, don't you? One hears so many bad things about police indifference, but they've been very helpful."

"Yes," Amelia replied almost mechanically, as she was actually thinking something quite different: the same man in charge of the museum robbery was now in charge of this case. And not only was Humphrey's house going to be guarded, but he was also under police watch at the hospital. What on earth was going on?

The next morning, Amelia went to the cottage and found Archibald Curran and Pandora Brocklehurst at the front door, arguing with the officer on duty. Hearing her footsteps, the two turned.

"At last!" Archie bounced up to her with an irate expression. "My dear Amelia, please tell us what is going on. This unhelpful person"—he glared at the police officer who ignored him—"won't let us in and all we know is that Humphrey's been attacked."

"Oh, Amelia." Pandora, looking distressed, grabbed Amelia's hands. "I'm out of my mind with worry. You know how scatterbrained Humphrey is. He possibly forgot to lock the door, or let in a thug who pretended he was a collector or something."

Pandora looked just awful. Her hat, usually worn at a jaunty angle, was slipping down the back of her head, and her shawls trailed untidily behind her. She seemed to have aged overnight.

"Pandora, Archie, I'm as much in the dark as you are," Amelia replied. Then turning to the officer, she asked, "May we go inside? These people are a family member and a close friend of Mr. Biddle."

"Right then, miss."

Pandora and Archie followed her into the cottage. She made tea and they sat down to discuss matters. Although Amelia couldn't tell Pandora and Archie any more than she knew, she suggested that the break-in had something to do with the robbery at the Ashmolean and the quest.

"I knew this would end in tragedy one day." Pandora stirred her tea fiercely, spilling it into the saucer. "Humphrey should never have been involved in something this dangerous at his age. I warned him, but he wouldn't listen."

A tear plopped into her cup, accompanied by a loud sniff.

"He said it was his last chance to do something meaningful with his life. I mean, who worries about that sort of thing at his age?" She fumbled in her handbag. "Oh, drat. Where's my hankie?"

"Now, now, Pandora," Archie wheezed, holding out his red handkerchief to her. "Don't be upset. We are Humphrey's friends and family so it's up to us to do our best for him."

Pandora blew her nose with loud honking noises. She folded the handkerchief and gave it back to him. "Ink must come back right away. Humphrey said the telephone line at the castle doesn't work. He was cut off while he was talking to Ink. I tried Ink's mobile, but that just goes to voice message. Perhaps we should send a telegram."

Amelia shook her head. "We can't risk a telegram. It might not arrive. One of us must go there."

Two pairs of eyes swiveled in Archie's direction. He gasped, choked, and then fell into a fit of coughing. "Not me. I can't go. I'm not well. Listen to this cough."

Pandora clapped him on the back.

"Ouch!" he yelped. "Not so hard."

"See?" Pandora patted his shoulder gently. "You're fine and you are quite the best person to go. Send Ink back home, but you must stay at the castle to protect the children, especially Adam."

Archie looked terrified. He grabbed the corner of Pandora's shawl. "But that man ... you know what happened last time ... I can't do it."

"Yes, you can. You must, Archie. And since you know how that man thinks, you're the best person to keep the children safe until James and Isabel get back from France."

Ignoring Archie's rolling eyes and spluttering protests, Pandora surged to her feet and adjusted her shawls. "I feel quite relieved, knowing this important mission is in the hands of someone so capable."

Archie made little squeaks of denial.

"You'll leave for Scotland tonight, Archie." Pandora said. "I know I can trust you to say and do the right thing. Be strong."

Archie fell silent and simply nodded.

"Good," she said. "Now let's get to the hospital and see how poor Humphrey is doing."

CONFERENCE OF THE BIRDS

The next morning at breakfast, Sheldon announced that Hamish had volunteered to teach them about the birds of prey with a flying demonstration. Adam glanced at Ink, who gave him a slight nod as if to say they must go.

"That's … er … nice of him," Adam said, kicking Justin under the table before he could say no. Justin had already said he couldn't wait to get started on deciphering Bedwyr's diary.

Sheldon raised his eyebrows. "Given that Hamish considers tourists a necessary evil and a constant intrusion into his work at the castle, it's not just a casual invitation, it's a signal honor."

"Um … yeah, right," said Justin as he cut bacon slices into bite-sized pieces. "Signal honor. What time must we be at the … what did you call it?"

"He'll see you at the *mews* precisely at two this afternoon," Sheldon replied. "Be punctual. Hamish is a stickler for time."

Kim looked nervous. "As long as the birds don't bite."

"Don't try to pet them, Miss Kim," said Sheldon, whisking away her breakfast plate. "They really prefer raw meat to human fingers and thumbs."

"Gross," Kim whispered to Adam. "I'm not touching anything dead."

Ink gulped down his tea. "I'm off. Anyone want to help with some old books and stuff?" He winked at Adam as he sauntered out of the kitchen, heading for the library.

Adam and Kim hastily excused themselves from the table and ran after Ink, the two dogs bounding behind. Justin stood, almost knocking over his chair as he shoved the last bit of food into his mouth, mumbling, "Great breakfast, thanks so much, Mrs. Grant."

He hurried out of the kitchen, yelling, "Hey, guys. Wait up."

In the library, Adam could hardly keep still. He was as excited as when he and Justin had managed to translate the Egyptian hieroglyphics underneath the black scarab, before it transformed into the sensational relic later on. He pulled the cotton gloves Humphrey had given him out of his jeans pocket and put them on. Kim and Justin did the same.

Ink grinned. "I'm impressed. You three are proper researchers. I thought you'd all forgotten what Humphrey told you about protecting documents."

They waved their gloved hands in the air.

"No way," said Adam.

"That's good," Ink replied, "because these pages are quite brittle. Please be careful how you handle them." He slipped on his own gloves.

Kim flexed her fingers. "I feel like a real archaeological assistant."

"So, what's the next step?" Justin asked, his gaze straying to the pieces of parchment on the library table.

Ink divided the pages into four piles, one pile for each of them. "I got up early to heat the remaining pages. We all have four pages each. It doesn't look like much work, but it's time consuming to translate the code correctly, so don't rush it."

"How can you be sure it's the Caesar cipher?" Adam asked. "It could be something else."

Ink held up a page. "No, I think Justin's right. It's the Caesar cipher."

Justin shot a smug glance at Kim and Adam.

"The reason I think he's right," Ink continued, "is because Bedwyr used such a basic tool as lemon juice for invisible ink. The Caesar cipher is also quite simple, but it would've been incomprehensible to someone who didn't know as much as Bedwyr did about history."

Kim waved her hand to attract Ink's attention. "Can I just ask something about the lemon juice—how does it work?"

"Easy," Ink said. "The lemon juice contains acid. The acid remains in the parchment after the juice has dried. The acid turns brown when exposed to heat."

Ink passed them each a ballpoint pen and several sheets of ordinary paper.

"I tested a few words and it is a 3-letter shift. Remember, you're writing in Latin, and changing from one set of Latin letters to another. Don't think about English and don't worry about what the word looks like. I'll do the Latin to English translation."

He showed them how to write the Latin alphabet out and then to rewrite it underneath, using the three-letter shift Justin had explained the previous evening. They would have to decode the writing by locating the letters of each word in the bottom alphabet and then changing the letters to correspond to the top alphabet. Once they had each completed a few words, Ink checked to see they were doing it right.

They had been working silently for a while when Kim asked Ink for more pages. Her pile sat neatly stacked to one side.

He looked up. "Finished so soon? Did you do it properly?"

"Yeah, I think so. Check a few words if you don't believe me."

Ink glanced at one of Kim's pages. "Looks okay to me. You're not bad at this."

Kim grinned. "I think I just got the hang of it after a while."

Ink reached over and grabbed two of Justin's pages. "Here, take these. Justin's slower than you are."

Justin said nothing, but he glowered at Kim. When Adam offered him one of his own pages, Justin shook his head.

Later, Sheldon came into the library with a tray of sandwiches and fruit juice, and a reminder about their appointment with Hamish.

"Go on, eat your lunch, and then go see the birds," Ink said. "I can finish up here with translating all the Latin to English."

"Sure?" Justin asked, looking disappointed.

"Yes, I can manage." Ink's nose was already buried again in the parchments. "The birds are worth seeing. Leave your gloves here. Catch you later."

Jasper and Smudge, sprawled at Ink's feet, didn't even look up when they trooped out of the library.

They made their way to the mews where Hamish was waiting. He was short and wiry with bowed legs so that he seemed to rock from side to side when he walked. He wore a long-sleeved, blue-and-white-checked shirt and the shabbiest corduroys Adam had ever seen. It was hard to decide Hamish's age because he looked so scrawny and scruffy. His watery blue eyes inspected them with an intense gaze. His untidy thatch of hair was a mixture of gingery brown and gray, thinning on the top of his head. He had a long, beaky nose, which was red at the tip.

It was obvious he didn't relish his role as babysitter for the afternoon, but his enthusiasm for his craft soon overcame his gruff manner. The mews was a long section added on to one side of the stables, with roomy partitions for the birds and an area open to the outside, enclosed with netting so the raptors could spend time outdoors. There was a kind of loft above the cages, so that Hamish could stand on a walkway and be level with the height of the enclosed area when he let the birds out. Hamish's living quarters were attached to the mews. The door was closed as they passed and Adam wondered what it was like inside.

Kim wrinkled her nose as they entered the mews. "What's that horrible smell?" she whispered to Adam.

He sniffed. There was a musty odor of mice, sawdust, bird droppings, and feathers. It wasn't unpleasant and even Justin, who was quite particular about smells, hadn't noticed it.

"What did you say about a smell?" Hamish turned to stare at Kim. "What smell? There's no smell."

"She said the birds look so well … uh … so healthy," Adam said quickly.

Hamish beamed. "Yes, they are. Best birds in the county. Prime birds. The envy of all the breeders." He leaned toward Adam, a fierce glint in his eyes. "That's why I look out for my aiggs." He wiggled his bushy, sandy-colored eyebrows up and down.

"Aiggs?" Adam asked.

Hamish's Scottish accent was sometimes difficult to understand. Adam glanced at Justin, not wanting to be rude to Hamish who seemed to be warming to them.

"Eggs," said Justin loudly. "Where do you keep the birds' eggs, Hamish?"

"I'll show you later. They're in the incubators, there at the back." He waved toward a padlocked door at the end of the mews. "Out the way of harm and intruders. Protected from thieving devils."

180

Adam remembered Sheldon telling them about the Golden Eagle breeding program, and how anxious Hamish was about egg thieves.

"Why would people want to steal eggs?" Justin asked. "Are they worth anything?"

"Collectors will pay lots of money for all kinds of rare eggs," Hamish replied, his pale stare boring into the boy. "But they'll get what's coming to them if they try anything here. I'm prepared."

He tapped the side of his nose with one finger and gave a secretive grin. "Passive alarms. Beams and all that modern stuff. I'll catch 'em."

"Why is there wire netting in front of each cage?" Kim asked. "There's also netting around the whole place so they can't escape anyway."

Hamish shook his head. "That's to keep animals and predators out of the cages so they can't get to the birds."

"They've got such big beaks and sharp talons," Justin remarked. "Surely the birds would claw and peck other animals in defense."

"Even a cat could hurt a bird," Hamish replied. "You can't be too careful."

Adam went over to another cage. As he leaned forward to inspect the occupant, Hamish grabbed his arm, pulling him back from the cage.

"Don't go too close to Aquila. He can be dangerous."

Adam stared at the huge Golden Eagle, mesmerized by the amber eyes gazing back at him. The bird shifted on his perch, flexing his wickedly long talons. Adam wondered what it was thinking, if birds did think about things. He could see each detail of the feathers' shading, from dark brown along the body to golden flecked with cream on the creature's neck. Each feather was so perfect it looked painted.

"His wings must be huge," Adam whispered. He could imagine the majestic creature soaring free.

"A seven-foot wingspan," Hamish said with pride. "They can take a large animal as prey." He winked at Kim. "Maybe even small girls?"

Kim gave a weak grin and took several steps back. "Uh … this one's cute." She pointed to a small cage with what looked like a ball of fluff snuggled into some straw in one corner.

"Thumbelina, the wee bairn. She's so tame I don't even lock her cage."

The owl was tiny, her grayish brown body lightly speckled with white spots. A white semicircle showed on the back of her neck.

"She's a Eurasian Pygmy Owl that came for boarding two years ago and stayed ever since," Hamish said.

Thumbelina woke up at the sound of their voices.

"Come on, then," he crooned, opening the owl's cage. "Come on, lassie."

Hamish reached out one hand, letting the owl scamper up his arm and hop onto his shoulder, giving several soft, high-pitched hoots. After she gently pecked his ear, he found a few scraps of raw meat in his pocket—Kim shuddered when she saw this—and fed her. He then placed her on Adam's shoulder. The tiny bird sidled up to his ear and nibbled it.

Then, with Thumbelina on Adam's shoulder, Hamish continued showing them the birds. They stopped in front of a cage containing a drowsy white owl.

"Archimedes is a Snowy Owl, an Arctic bird," Hamish beamed, "so the cold winters in Scotland quite suit him."

Archimedes' white feathers were the perfect camouflage for the icy wastes of his native environment.

"He's so cute," Kim said, "just like the owl in *Harry Potter*."

"*Harry Potter*!" Hamish snorted. "Pah! Archimedes is not a movie owl."

Athena, a fierce-looking Eurasian Eagle Owl, lived in the next cage. Orange eyes peered at the visitors and then prominent ear tufts twitched, as if the owl was questioning Hamish.

Hamish stuck some meat scraps through the bars. "Visitors, Athena. They're all right. Say hello."

Tawny-buff feathers speckled with black-brown framed the owl's face. Brown and buff feathers covered the rest of her body. An unusual pattern of dark brown wavy lines crisscrossed the feathers.

"She's very ... er ... handsome," said Justin.

Athena hopped over to the treat that had fallen on the ground. She looked up at Justin as he spoke.

"Do they understand?" he asked.

Hamish's expression darkened as if he were insulted. "Of course they do. No one asks you if *you* understand, do they?"

"Uh ... no." Justin gave a feeble grin.

Adam pressed his lips together so he wouldn't burst out laughing. He walked to the next cage. "Hey! Come look. What a fantastic bird," he called, hoping to deflect Hamish's annoyance away from Justin.

182

Athena

Kim was already standing at the cage that held the unusual bird, about the size and weight of a crow, with dark blue-gray wings and black stripes on its back. It had a pale underside faintly barred with black. Its wings were long and pointed.

"It looks fast," said Justin. "What is it?"

"They are fast," replied Hamish. "It's a peregrine falcon. The falcon's scientific name is *Falco Peregrinus*, which means 'falcon wanderer.' They've been called nature's finest flying machines because they're the fastest creatures on the planet. Peregrines have been clocked diving, or 'stooping,' at speeds of up to two hundred twenty miles per hour."

"What's his name?" Adam asked. The bird stared back at him with an unwavering gaze, seemingly unafraid.

"Horus."

Adam glanced at Hamish. "That's an unusual name for an English bird."

"Who said it was an English bird?" Hamish replied, his pale blue stare fixed on Adam. "The Egyptian god Horus was depicted as a peregrine falcon."

Suddenly, memories of Egypt flooded into Adam's mind. "Of course." He lightly smacked his forehead. "How could I forget?"

"How could you, indeed," said Hamish, but his voice was so low that only Adam heard him. Then Hamish continued speaking, so Adam had no time to think more about his strange words. It sounded like a lecture usually reserved for tourists, but it was interesting, and Hamish's passion for his birds soon captivated his small audience.

"Falconry is an ancient sport. It was practised in China before 2000 BC. Falconry is also the subject of some of the oldest Egyptian wall paintings. At one time, the type of falcon an Englishman could own marked his rank. A king could own the gyrfalcon; an earl, the peregrine; a yeoman, the goshawk; a priest, the sparrowhawk; and a servant, the kestrel."

They continued the tour, with Hamish introducing each bird as if the creature could understand. The owls included Barnaby the white-faced Barn Owl, which was very old now and spent most days snoozing on his perch, and a fawn and brown Tawny Owl. Before Hamish told them the bird's name, Adam glanced down at the nameplate on the cage.

"That says Myrrdin. Does that mean Merlin in another language?"

Hamish raised his sandy eyebrows, so like Athena's prominent ear tufts. "You're a clever lad. How did you know that meant Merlin?"

184

Adam didn't know what to say. "Uh … I didn't know. I mean … I just guessed."

"How strange you can guess when the name is written in Old Welsh."

By now, Kim and Justin had gone back for another look at Archimedes. Adam heard Justin trying, without success, to persuade Kim to give Archimedes a bit of dead mouse. He and Hamish were now alone. Adam stared at Hamish, speechless. Archibald Curran had mentioned Old Welsh, the long-dead language he had understood in his dream of Arthur. But this wasn't the same thing, was it? He licked his lips nervously, trying to think of how to allay Hamish's suspicions.

Adam glanced back at the nameplate on Athena's cage. Those strange letters were familiar from history lessons with Miss Briggs, his class teacher back home. He pointed to it.

"Uh … that's written in Greek, isn't it?" He grinned. "Athena was the Greek goddess of wisdom."

He pointed at Horus' nameplate. "I see now his name is written in Egyptian hieroglyphics. We also learned about hieroglyphics at school. Kinda cool."

Thumbelina woke up and gave a sleepy hoot.

Hamish reached out and took her from Adam's shoulder. "You have a way with the birds. Perhaps you speak the green language."

"Um … no, I only speak English and a bit of Zulu. That's an African language. We learn it at school."

Of course, Adam had also spoken in ancient Egyptian before opening the golden doors of the Forbidden Chamber, but he wasn't going to breathe a word of that to Hamish.

Hamish continued stroking Thumbelina and staring at Adam until he felt uncomfortable.

Adam tried to sound casual as he asked, "What's the green language anyway?" Out of habit, he slipped his hand into his pocket and grasped his golden scarab.

Hamish walked back to Thumbelina's cage and Adam hurried to keep up with him. Hamish's voice was so low that Adam couldn't hear him all that well, but he was too nervous to ask Hamish to speak louder.

"The green language is the language of the birds, spoken by the one who will have mastery over the creatures of the air."

185

Adam gulped, remembering Laila translating the hieroglyphics in the tomb of the Scarab King. Uniting the Seven Stones of Power with the Stone of Fire would enable someone to read the legendary *Book of Thoth*, which contained wondrous knowledge of magic and incantation. The person who read this sacred book could become the most powerful magician in the world. The *Book of Thoth* would enable the reader to enchant heaven and earth, to know the language of the birds and beasts, and to summon the fishes of the seas. He would become ruler of the earth, and master of time and eternity. This was the whole quest.

Adam didn't dare ask how Hamish knew about the language of the birds.

They reached Thumbelina's cage and, after Hamish had placed the bird inside, he turned to Adam. He gripped Adam tightly by his upper arm. Adam looked down at Hamish's hand and noticed something startling. Hamish's long-sleeved shirt had slipped back as he grabbed Adam, revealing strange twisted scars encircling his wrist. For a moment, Adam caught a glimpse of blue at the edge of the scars, making them appear the same as the tattoos in his vision of King Arthur—blue snakes writhing around the man's wrists. Then the image vanished and all he could see were the ugly ridges of puckered flesh.

Hamish followed Adam's gaze. He released Adam's arm and pulled down his sleeve. "What are you staring at, lad?"

Adam looked away. "Nothing. Sorry."

Just then, Kim and Justin came up. Hamish glanced at them with a severe expression. "It's late. You should all go now. I must feed the birds."

"But—" Justin was surprised. "I thought we were going to see them fly."

Kim pointed to the cages. "And we didn't see all the birds. There's still—"

"Tomorrow." Hamish's voice was abrupt. "Tomorrow suits me better."

He disappeared into the mews, calling to his birds in a strange mixture of whistles and hoots.

"Weird. Just weird," Justin said crossly.

They wandered off, back up the path toward the castle. Adam was glad to escape Hamish's piercing gaze, but Justin and Kim looked disappointed.

"I wonder how far Ink got with the translation," Adam said, hoping to cheer up his downcast companions. "There were so many pages, I'm sure he can't have finished already."

Justin brightened up. "Let's hurry back in case he needs some help."

"Race you!" Adam dashed off, leaving Kim and Justin running behind.

When they reached the castle, they headed straight for the library. Justin overtook Adam and burst through the door first.

"Ink, we're back," he yelled.

Kim and Adam crashed into Justin as he came to a standstill. Two people were in the library with Ink. One was Bruce Hamilton, the vet who had treated Ink and Smudge the day they arrived. The other was an odd-looking stranger. He was tall and lean, with stooped shoulders, dressed in a suit that looked as if it hadn't fitted him properly in years. The jacket sleeves and the pants were too short, flapping around his wrists and ankles. Frayed shirt cuffs, revealing bony wrists, jutted out from the jacket sleeves. Although his mop of fair, flyaway hair was streaked with gray, he was still young, probably only in his thirties. His thin face creased into an eager smile.

"Hello, hello, hello to you," he said as he spied the kids. "I'm Dr. Mercury Jones. You can call me Mac. I'm Bruce's scientist friend." His husky, almost whispering voice trailed away as he looked up at the painted ceiling, already lost in thought. "I say, how remarkable, so interesting. What fascinating images."

He sank into a nearby chair and continued to contemplate the frescoes above his head. Then he snapped his head back and stared at the kids with pale green eyes magnified by glasses. Mac pulled the glasses from his face and a large, dirty handkerchief from his pocket, and began polishing; this only smeared the already murky lenses.

"Uh ..." He squinted owlishly at Bruce. "What was I saying?"

"Mac and I have come to check up on Ink." Bruce glanced at Ink, who twiddled his fingers in a sheepish wave. "You look fine. Smudge doing okay?"

Ink nodded. "Yeah, we're great."

"Ah, yes, I remember now," said the scientist, breaking into the conversation. "I ran the blood tests for Bruce and, well, let's just say the poison you had in your system, Ink ... it's incredible. Nothing like it seen in the last five hundred years ... seems to be very old. Have you any idea about how ... er ...?" He gazed at Ink. "I mean to say, how amazing."

"'Amazing' isn't quite the word I had in mind," said Ink. "I can't tell you any more than I already did. Some guy attacked us in the middle of the night on the train and that's it."

Mac slid his glasses back onto his nose. "I know that's what you said, but how this person came to be in possession of something so mysterious is what's puzzling me." His voice trailed away as his gaze wandered back to the ceiling again. He turned his head to follow the images on the ceiling until his whole body twisted in the chair.

"Mac's specialty is antidotes," Bruce said. "In particular, developing a universal super-antidote for all known poisons. Once it's perfected, it will save lives worldwide from insect, snake, spider, marine, and other venoms."

"It's a mithridate," Mac said dreamily. "Something like the theriac of Andromachus."

"Huh?" Justin rolled his eyes at Adam. "Who's Andromachus?"

"What's a mithri … mithirdate?" asked Adam.

Mac untangled himself from the chair and sat up, eager to explain.

"Mithridate. It's a universal antidote, like Bruce said. In other words, a cure-all. The name comes from King Mithridates VI of Pontus—he lived from 114 BC to 63 BC—who was so mistrustful after repeated attempts on his life that he became obsessed with studying antidotes. The result was a fifty-four-ingredient concoction known as the *mithridatum*, which the king took daily. His antidote was so successful that when his enemies defeated him, he tried to commit suicide through self-poisoning, and failed. Finally, Mithridates ordered one of his own soldiers to kill him with a sword."

"And the other guy?" asked Adam.

Mac nodded excitedly. "Even more interesting. Andromachus was a physician to the Roman emperor Nero, and he developed a cure-all even more effective than the *mithridatum*. He removed some of the ingredients of the original concoction and added a variety of other substances, including viper flesh and opium."

Kim made a muffled choking sound.

"It contained about seventy ingredients. As time went by, more and more ingredients were added to the concoction. By the Middle Ages, the antidote was called the 'theriac of Andromachus' and had more than a hundred ingredients. It took years to prepare, and had become solid like treacle or molasses."

He peered at them through his smudged lenses. "You see, the original theriac was a liquid."

"Incredible," said Adam, although he thought it sounded absolutely disgusting.

"So your super-antidote would be a kind of modern-day *mithridatum*?" Justin asked.

"Exactly." Mac beamed happily. He raised a warning finger. "But no viper flesh, I promise."

Bruce interrupted. "Ink and Smudge were given a trial serum of the antidote based on Mac's initial work. It hasn't even been properly tested because it's still at the experimental stage. I just knew it was their only hope." His expression was solemn. "This could have been a tragedy if you hadn't come to me in time and if I hadn't known about Mac's research. Are you sure there isn't anything else we should know?"

There was a heavy silence.

"We need to track down this person or persons," Bruce explained. "We need to find out if they have more of the poison and, if so, what they intend to do with it. The more information we have about poisons, modern as well as ancient, the more we can perfect this serum."

"Uh—ow!" Adam yelped as Justin pressed his foot heavily on Adam's toe.

"Yes?" Bruce looked at Adam.

"Nothing, I mean how come you guys know the poison is so old?" Adam shot an aggrieved glance at Justin, who just shrugged.

"Ah, yes, fascinating, simply fascinating," said Mac, leaning in close. He waved his hands above his head as he spoke. "In Ink's blood sample, I found familiar ingredients used hundreds, even thousands of years ago as both medicines and poisons. But there was one—just *one* ingredient—I've never encountered before."

He brought his arms down, his shoulders drooping in disappointment. "This is the single component that would complete my research. It's the one mysterious factor that would enable me to finalize my life's work."

"That's why we're here," said Bruce pointedly, "to see if there's anything you've forgotten, any tiny detail that might help." He stared at the group, his eyes narrowing with doubt.

Ink shook his head. "Nothing, sorry. But we'll call you if we remember anything."

"All right," said Bruce. "Don't forget to finish the medicine I gave you and please stop off at the surgery for one last check up after that."

Ink nodded. "Sure."

The two men shook hands with everyone and left. As they walked down the front steps on their way to the visitors' car park, their voices floated back to the library.

"I can't believe that four young people saw an attack and can't remember *any* details," said Bruce. "They must be hiding something."

Mac mumbled an indistinct reply and then the men were gone.

Back inside, Ink said, "I hate lying and I'm sure you all do as well, but you know we absolutely can't tell anyone."

Adam turned on Justin. "So why did you stomp on my toe so hard? I wasn't going to say anything."

Justin put on a smirk. "Yes, you were. I could see it on your face. You were just about to blurt out everything."

Adam glared at Justin. "I was not. You know nothing."

"I know you. That's just the kind of thing you'd do."

Ink raised his voice. "Hey! Stop behaving like kids."

Adam scowled.

Justin gave a cheeky grin. "But we *are* kids."

"You know what I mean. *Little* kids."

Justin subsided. "Oh. Okay."

"Did you get any further with the translation, Ink?" Kim asked.

"Yes, I did," he said. "Thanks for asking. Maybe we should focus on the real reason we're here. Sit down."

Ink lifted a newspaper off the library table, revealing papers covered with neat handwriting underneath.

"You finished?" Kim squealed in delight.

Ink grinned. "It wasn't easy, I can tell you, but there's amazing information that puts everything in the picture. By the way, how did it go with Hamish and the birds?"

"He is so weird," Justin grumbled. "We were looking at the birds and then he suddenly decided he wasn't going to do a flying demonstration. He said we should go because he had to feed them."

"And he's crazy about his *aiggs*," Kim said.

Ink laughed. "He's always been a bit eccentric, but now he's completely paranoid about people stealing his eggs. No one's ever tried to steal anything, but he always thinks someone is after them."

"He has passive beams and modern stuff now to trap the thieves," said Adam, imitating Hamish's accent.

Ink picked up the wad of handwritten pages. "Okay. Time to reveal all." He cleared his throat. "Here goes: '*It is the Year of our Lord 1296, and I, Bedwyr, scribe and historian of this monastery, make testament here to the strange and unbelievable things I have seen and heard.*'"

He looked up. "Did you hear something?"

The something was an awful noise—a combination of loud hooting from outside and equally loud wailing. They all heard it.

Ink thrust the papers back under the newspaper. "Sounds bad. Let's go see."

The group went outside onto the front steps. A cab had pulled up and a stout someone was struggling to extricate himself from the back seat. It was Archibald Curran in a tangle of arms and legs. He looked through the cab window and spied Ink staring openmouthed at him.

"Ink, my boy, tragedy has struck. It's your father."

Ink bounded down the steps and helped a disheveled Archie out of the cab. His wiry fluff of hair stood on end, his glasses hung askew off his nose, and half his waistcoat buttons popped as he clambered through the back passenger door, yanking a battered suitcase after him.

"What's wrong with Dad?" Ink shook Archie's arm. "What's happened?"

"Ooooh, don't be so rough," Archie moaned, promptly dropping his suitcase and collapsing in a heap.

"Good grief," said the driver, scrambling out of the cab. "The gen'leman needs a bit o' help there."

Adam and Justin ran down the steps just as Sheldon and Mrs. McLeod appeared.

"Oh, my goodness," Mrs. McLeod screeched in banshee tones. "The man has fainted. Mr. Sheldon, get the wheelbarrow." She yelled behind her into the entrance hall. "Mrs. Grant, put the kettle on. We have an emergency."

Archie raised his head an inch or two from the ground and opened one eye. "Dear lady, please, *not* the wheelbarrow. So undignified for a man of my years and position in the academic community." He fell forward with another loud groan.

Sheldon, Ink, and the cab driver managed to haul Archie up the front steps, across the hall, and toward the kitchen. Jasper and Smudge kept getting in the way, barking and leaping around what they perceived to be a large, bizarre creature with many arms and legs. Obviously, an intruder.

"I don't like dogs," the cab driver kept saying. "He don't bite, does he? I don't like dogs. Can't abide 'em." He gave a few feeble kicks in Smudge's direction.

Encouraged by this display of aggression, Smudge grabbed the cab driver's trouser leg. He hung on as the group shuffled into the kitchen, with the man shouting, "Ow! The dog's got me leg. The vicious brute."

Kim managed to grab Smudge and pull him away. Smudge proudly displayed a chunk of cloth between his teeth, shaking it, and snarling fiercely.

"Bad dog. Very bad dog," Kim whispered, half-giggling at the same time.

Adam grabbed Jasper's collar, and he and Kim shut the dogs in the scullery.

Finally, Archie managed to heave himself onto a kitchen chair where he sprawled, panting, with his head thrown back. He was deathly pale. The cab driver laid his own head on the kitchen table and wheezed, trying to recover from the exertion.

Sheldon grabbed Archie's suitcase. "I'll get our guest's room ready."

Mrs. Grant and Mrs. McLeod looked at Archie anxiously, shaking their heads and whispering.

"He looks quite white, sister." Mrs. Grant frowned. "His heart might give out."

Mrs. McLeod bit her lower lip in agitation. "I'd offer him a cup of tea and some of my best scones with that fresh clotted cream we got today, but I don't think he'll be able to eat a morsel."

The cab driver looked up at Mrs. McLeod. "I won't say no to a cuppa, missus, if there's one going spare."

Archie lifted his head. "Did someone say tea? I'd love a cup. You wouldn't have Indian, would you? But I don't mind China. Er … scones and fresh clotted cream? Yes, perhaps just a tiny mouthful to revive me."

Ink barely concealed his impatience as he asked Archie what he meant about Humphrey. Archie began to recover after shoveling half a scone, laden with a mound of clotted cream and strawberry jam, into his mouth. He gave a few quick munches and swallowed, his pudgy face sad.

"It's tragic. An unknown intruder attacked Humphrey last night and now he's in intensive care at the Radcliffe Infirmary. He has a bump as big as an egg on his head. The doctors think he might have a fractured skull."

"Why didn't you call us?" Ink demanded.

Archie lifted his plump shoulders. "We tried, my boy, we tried. No reply, not even a ringing tone. We even tried your mobile."

"The line here is still down," said Mrs. McLeod. "Sheldon must go into the village to report it."

Ink stood up, knocking his chair over. "I didn't even bother bringing my mobile because of the bad reception. I must go to my father." He pointed to the cab driver. "Don't go anywhere. I need a ride to the station. I'll get my things." He dashed out, heading for the staircase.

"No problem," said the driver. He lifted his cup and winked at Mrs. Grant. "A drop more tea, missus? And another one of them scones will do me fine."

Minutes later, Ink came back into the kitchen, carrying a small overnight bag.

"Don't worry, I'll be back in a little while," he said in a low voice to Adam. He thrust the handwritten pages into Adam's hands. "I already asked Sheldon to lock Bedwyr's originals away in the safe this morning. Make sure you keep these hidden."

"When will you be back?" asked Justin.

"As soon as I know my dad's out of danger."

"What should we do in the meantime?" asked Adam, trying not to sound like a pathetic wimp.

Ink's face creased into a smile. "I'll only be away a day or so. Have fun, go sightseeing, explore the place, but don't get into anything dangerous." He ruffled Adam's hair. "Stay out of trouble."

He pinched Kim's cheek. "You keep the boys in line, okay?"

Tears sparkled in Kim's eyes. "We're supposed to be a team," she said with a sad sniff.

"Yes, we are a team," he said. "This is just a temporary delay."

Ink winked at Justin. "Keep an eye on things for me."

Justin threw his shoulders back and puffed out his chest. "You can rely on me."

Ink ran down the front steps, tossed his bag into the cab, and started to get in when Archie appeared at the front door, his face haggard and a smear of strawberry jam on one cheek.

"Ink, my boy, wait." He tottered down the steps and fell against Ink's chest, clutching Ink's T-shirt to steady himself. "I just remembered something very important."

Ink gently disengaged Archie's fingers. "What is it, sir? I really must go. Dad needs me."

"Take the boy with you. I implore you."

"What boy?"

Archie whispered hoarsely, "You know … Adam, of course. You must take him with you. He's … he'll … he'll be in danger."

Ink smiled. "No, don't worry, he'll be safer here. There are three adults— four including you—and good security. Nothing can go wrong."

Archie hung his head, looking miserable and guilty at the same time. "No, you must take him, please."

Ink became impatient. "I really don't think it's a good idea. Adam's better off here."

He glanced up at the trio standing on the top step and waved. "See you guys soon."

Archie sank onto the bottom step, his head in his hands, heaving piteous sighs.

Sheldon appeared in the doorway and then went to help him. "Come along now, sir, let's get you inside. Your room is all ready and your luggage is upstairs.

You've had a traumatic experience. A little lie-down and some refreshment will help calm your nerves."

Archie looked up, his face brightening at the word *refreshment*. "Yes, that's it. I've had a traumatic experience."

Ink rolled his eyes in exasperation and then he was gone, his last words to Sheldon being that he would return as soon as he could.

As the cab sped across the drawbridge and down the driveway, Adam exchanged mournful looks with Kim and Justin.

Kim folded her arms, her face miserable. "It's not the same without Ink."

"We'll be okay on our own," said Justin. "We don't need help."

"You heard what Ink said," Adam replied. "We mustn't go looking for trouble." Somehow, it felt odd without Ink.

Justin looked smug. "And what if trouble comes looking for us? Like it did in Egypt?"

"We'll … have to deal with it … I guess," Adam said slowly.

"Exactly," Justin said. "Like we did in Egypt."

But Adam had the feeling that somehow this adventure would be a lot more dangerous than Egypt. He wasn't going to let Justin see he had doubts though, so he just shrugged.

Kim nudged Adam. "Let's read Ink's translation. It's safe to do that. I'm dying to know what Bedwyr wrote."

Adam flashed a grin. "Me too. Come on."

They ran back into the library.

BEÐWYR'S ÐIARY ÐECIPHEREÐ

Once they settled into their seats around the big library table, Justin widened his eyes at Adam. "Ink gave the pages to you so I guess that means you go first.

"Yes," said Kim. "You start us off, Adam."

"Okay," he said, trying to sound normal, although reading aloud the thoughts and ideas of someone who died seven hundred years ago gave him a shivery feeling. He began:

> I set down this record now so that those who come after me, those who must put the world straight and make the bad good, will have guidance and direction. I was still a young man, not having seen sixteen summers when my soul recoiled from the wickedness of this world. After I saw there was no hope of repentance for humankind, that they were getting worse day by day, I withdrew from this evil world to devote myself to spiritual service. My parents were well pleased I had chosen a monastic calling, this having been their plan for me, their second son.

> After some six years at the monastery, I found that once I had performed my tasks and my daily devotions, I still had time on my hands. I decided to use it for the study and investigation of natural secrets, which are the shadows of eternal things. I read a great many books in our monastery, written in olden times by philosophers who had pursued the same study. I devoured the classical writings of the ancient sages and

philosophers, the Greeks, the Romans, and even what little was known of those who came before, the Aegyptians, who built great pyramids of stone, now ruined, and abandoned long ago by their pagan gods. How I wish I had curbed my natural curiosity, so that I might have labored in ignorance all day in the garden instead, and not delved too deep, thus uncovering the secret that should have remained hidden from men's eyes and hearts.

Rather, I was so entangled in the web of learning that I began to neglect my daily duties and dreaded punishment. To my surprise, the abbot encouraged, nay, even urged me to continue my studies and to research diligently. Released from menial tasks, I haunted the library, copying out manuscripts every day in the scriptorium and exploring the ancient histories. He also commanded me to write to other monasteries famed for their old books and to beg them, so that I might duplicate the information within. This I did, and our modest collection of books expanded rapidly as our reputation as a center of learning grew. After four years, I was in charge of several brothers, all delegated to copying an ever-increasing number of valuable books.

Kim yawned as she leaned back in her chair, stretching out her arms. "This is a bit boring. It's just about him writing down history."

Justin gave an exaggerated sigh. "You are so ignorant. That's the whole point. Bedwyr discovered the history behind the Seven Stones of Power. We just haven't gotten to that part yet. Be patient."

Kim wrinkled her nose. "Okay, but I hope it gets more exciting. Otherwise, I'll be asleep soon."

Adam glanced at them. "Should I go on?"

"Yeah, yeah," said Justin.

Each day, I examined the ancient writings, reveling in the glory of past cultures, and regretting that so little remained of the wealth of early knowledge. My hunger for information earned me the label Bedwyr the Curious, but I did not complain. In fact, it told me how others saw me—a curious and eager seeker of truth and learning. The abbot, whom I shall not name here, questioned me daily on my achievements. Contrary to other heads of monasteries, he did not object to me reading what others would have forbidden, especially the writings of Greek and Roman philosophers, as well as the books of Eastern religions and ancient myths and legends. He said all literature had merit and instructed me to report anything of particular interest to him. Free to explore where I wished? Surely a scholar such as I could not be happier, being unconstrained when some abbots would lock away what they considered to be heresy.

I should have been happy and, to some extent, I was pleased, yet in the back of my mind lurked doubts, fleeting shadows of suspicion. I wondered why the abbot, himself not a particularly learned man, should encourage me so much. I knew he was ambitious, but that did not disturb me. Then the day came when the abbot's purpose was revealed, not long after the terrible events had taken place. I have been so innocent, so naïve. I was a fool and I have been punished for it. Here is the story of my folly.

Adam looked up from the page.

"What does 'hera-see' mean?" asked Kim.

"Heresy," Adam said. "I think it means stuff that wasn't part of what they learned in the Bible, maybe someone's ideas that were too different or unacceptable."

"Get on with the story," said Justin.

Adam found his place and continued reading.

It was near eight on a summer's evening when the outer bell clanged, signaling the arrival of a visitor. The porter opened the gate and bade him enter. The abbot rushed to welcome him when he heard the caller was a fellow monk, a kind of pilgrim, judging by his ragged and dusty appearance. He told me to attend upon the traveler, offering him company, refreshment, and the use of my cell for his rest. The abbot caught my sleeve as I passed and whispered that I should glean as much information as possible. I knew what he meant, and for some strange reason I went slowly to my task, my heart heavy with an unspeakable dread.

When I entered the refectory where the visitor was finishing a bowl of lentil soup and some of our tasty bread, he rose and greeted me. Dusty and ragged indeed, he was also lean and wiry, his nut-brown face betokening years of travel under a scorching sun. His eyes were the pale gray of a rain-washed sky or the soft plumage of a dove. Light and yet piercing, they seemed to look into my soul. His face displayed a warm smile as he examined me closely, nodding to himself. His powerful presence and natural energy radiated outward as he enveloped me in a brotherly embrace. A strong and wise man, no doubt. I was eager to converse with him and invited him to inspect our library if he was not too tired from his journey. He walked beside me with a spring in his step like that of a young man, although from his lined face I judged him to be perhaps three times my age.

We spoke for several hours. I demonstrated pride in the size of our library and he admired the numerous precious documents. Our most valuable books are chained to the shelves for safekeeping because, even in a monastery, things can go astray. Time fled, the candles were lit, and when the bell sounded for prayers at midnight, I did not budge from my seat, even though I shivered in my thin woolen robe as the sky darkened outside and the warmth of the day faded. I forgot the coldness seeping through my sandals from the stone floor, chilly even in summer. I drank in his words with rapt attention as his eloquence painted a glorious picture of the past. He spoke of a land that once was in the olden days; an island of beauty and splendor destroyed in a single day and night by fiery catastrophe and flood. Something stirred in my brain ... had not Plato himself spoken of this wondrous land?

Adam stopped reading. His mind instantly flashed back to the moment in the tomb of the Scarab King when Laila, their Egyptian guide, had translated hieroglyphics on the walls of the golden room. It was as if he could hear her voice echoing in his brain. This story, like that one, sounded so much like Atlantis that it had to be true. He slipped his other hand into his pocket and held the golden replica scarab, knowing that the real scarab was indeed the key to everything.

"Adam?" Justin shook his arm. "Wake up, you're daydreaming."

Adam blinked. "Sorry. What Bedwyr wrote here—" he indicated the spot on the page, "—just reminded me of something."

"Shall I read now?" Justin reached out for the page.

Adam snatched it away. "No, I'm okay."

Justin shrugged and lolled in his chair, his arms behind his head. "I wonder if it's tea time yet. All this history is making me hungry."

Adam found where he had left off.

Surely, the tale of Atlantis was just a myth, an entertaining story in which the philosopher Plato was testing his audience. I dismissed the thought and listened again as the visitor described the marvelous arts and skills that had enabled ancient builders to raise great blocks of stone like feathers and to lay them tight, without mortar, so not even the thinnest knife blade could slip between the blocks. He spoke of expertise enabling brave men to sail to the farthest reaches of the earth long before the Romans were a great nation. He described how learned men plotted the movement of the heavenly bodies as the great constellations swung across the sky, by placing enormous stones in circles. He spoke of the sages, those wise men of old, such as the Persian magi who read the fate of the world in the stars, of the Aegyptians, of the Chaldeans, and of a people called the Sumerians. He spoke of the prophecies of the ancient Sibyls, the old women who predicted the destruction of Troy, of the conquests of the great Persian King Xerxes and his son Darius, and of those who foretold the murder of Julius Caesar, the fall of Rome to the barbarian hordes, and finally the end of days. He spoke of times and places, and told of great leaders and conquerors as if he had walked and talked with them, shared their food and drink, and been at their side in their greatest triumphs.

Adam glanced up at his audience. Justin and Kim were entranced as they absorbed the monk's riveting tale. Justin hadn't laughed when he'd spoken about Atlantis. Adam picked up the next page.

His words enchanted me, sowing seeds in my imagination that blossomed into splendid visions. I saw the magnificence of Greece. I saw Alexander the Great conquer Egypt. I saw Julius Caesar enter Rome in

201

victory and heard the cheering crowds. I saw so many things that I believe I was drugged by his eloquence. Together, we wept over the destruction of the great Library of Alexandria, once the largest library in the world. Under my guest's spell, I saw the flames leap high and heard the crackling of the fires, the terrible burning smell as past literary glories were consumed by greedy flames, the manuscripts curling and smoking from the scorching heat, and I saw the building crash to the ground, its stones blackened and smoldering. What terrible loss, such devastation. Then my natural curiosity reasserted itself. Wondering how he knew so much, I asked his age. He laughed, telling me he was older than time itself. I took this to be a jest, and thus remarked upon his brown and wrinkled appearance, hinting that he could have passed for a piece of parchment.

Now, dear reader, before I continue, let me say that even in the joy of this brother's intelligent and educated company, my doubts still lurked. Why did he come to our monastery? Why spend these hours with me, a young monk who had no experience or wisdom to offer in return? When his answer came, I fell to my knees and covered my ears. I begged for relief from this burden, asking him to grant it to someone more worthy and brave. He lifted me to my seat again, murmuring encouraging words, and, against my better judgment, I took my hands from my ears and listened.

The visitor reached into his robe and took out a leather pouch from which he drew a tattered manuscript. He said it contained the greatest and most dangerous secret of all time. My curiosity, that old weakness of mine, flared at once. I longed to know what information the manuscript contained. It was older than anything I had seen before, made of some kind of animal skin, but not so fine as the parchment and vellum produced here. I reached out to touch it, my fingers hovering over this precious specimen of antiquity, no doubt containing marvels and mysteries of the past. My fingertips tingled and burned as if seared by flames. Astonished, I withdrew my hand instantly.

The old man smiled, as if he had expected this. He unrolled the document—he called it the Scroll of the Ancients—on a table, and we both *bent over the mysterious writing now displayed to our eager eyes. Some letters I recognized as an early form of Greek, some as Latin, and some even as Aramaic, the lettering of the ancient books of the Semitic people. But the main part of the document comprised strange writing that must have been far older. Painted all around the edges of the manuscript were unusual symbols. I frowned to see them, fearing their meaning. He told me he would explain things for my greater understanding.*

Adam laid the page on the library table. "So it's true. The Scroll of the Ancients does exist." He glanced at the others who were now both leaning their elbows on the library table, staring at him.

"Of course it exists," said Justin. "What do think we're here for?"

"Well, I knew in my head that it existed, but up until now it's been just a story. This makes it more real."

Justin reached for the bunch of pages. "Let me read a bit." He scanned the top of the page and then began reading.

How I wished afterward I had never met the old man. As the tale of ancient times unfolded and the dreadful secrets were revealed, I flung myself into the nearest corner, trembling, begging him to cease his story. How I regretted my inquisitiveness. Such things, I explained to him, are against all my beliefs. It is one thing to admire a collection of old tales; it is something else to believe them. Long ago, he said, enlightened beings indeed walked on earth with men, teaching them and bringing a gift of civilization. Ten god-kings—named in their language the Neteru—came from the ancient island culture of Atlantis, destroyed by fire. They settled in the land of Khem, the black land of the Aegyptians, and imparted their secrets to the children of men in the hope that such wisdom would be well used. When their time was over, a group of semi divine teachers, magicians, and other gifted persons took their place. Called the Shemsu-Hor, the followers of the Way of Truth, their task was to ensure that the teachings of the ancient ones before them survived. However, as I had discovered at a young age, the wickedness of men far outweighs the good in them. Before long, the secrets given to the race of men were forgotten, then lost forever in the mists of time. However, Thoth, the Aegyptian god of wisdom, knowing the true nature of things, had taken steps to preserve his teachings in the Book of Thoth, a book of such terrible potency that even the greatest kings and emperors should tremble to read it. If all this is true, then it is good to fear such power.

Justin looked up. "Laila told us about the Neteru and the Shemsu-Hor, remember?"

Adam nodded. Justin continued reading.

My guest said, "Thoth wrote the book with his own hand and in it is all the magic in the world. If thou readest the first page, thou wilt discover the secrets of all knowledge, which is contained within this book. Thou wilt have the power to enchant the sky, the earth, the abyss, the mountains, and the sea. In addition, thou wilt have dominion over the heavens and the earth; thou wilt understand the green language, the language of the birds of the air, and thou wilt know what the creeping things of earth are saying, and thou wilt see the fishes from the darkest depths of the sea. Thou wilt be Master of Time and Eternity and of the universe."

Adam stared at Justin. Hamish had mentioned the green language when they were looking at the birds. How did Hamish even know about something mentioned in Bedwyr's diary? Hamish had used the exact same words—the green language. Things were becoming very weird.

"Are you okay?" asked Kim.

Adam blinked. "Huh?"

"You look a bit strange," said Kim.

"No, I'm fine," he said.

He decided not to mention it to the others; it sounded too crazy to be believable.

Justin continued reading.

"Immortality is thine and yet if one be killed, if thou readest the other page, even though that one' is dead and in the world of ghosts, he could come back to earth in the form he once hadst. Besides this, thou wilt

204

see the sun shining in the sky with the full moon and the stars, and thou wilt behold the great shapes of the gods."

I was astounded. Impossible! How could the dead be restored to life? I began to see how this book was a source of destruction for humankind. What would happen if it fell into the wrong hands? My friend said that the book would only be read when the time was right. He quoted the words of this so-called god himself, and against all my better judgment ... I believed.

"Laila didn't translate that bit," said Adam.

"What bit?" asked Justin.

"The bit about bringing someone back from the dead. You weren't there. When we were in the golden room, Laila translated the hieroglyphics telling the story of the Scarab King and Thoth, and the Stone of Fire being hidden away. She didn't mention anything about being able to make someone rise from the dead."

Justin shrugged. "Maybe there wasn't enough time. You said Dr. Khalid was in a hurry to find the tomb itself."

Dr. Khalid had certainly been pushing Laila to get on with translating; Justin might be right. Adam just didn't feel sure about it. A spell to bring back the dead sounded horrifying. Imagine all the evil people in the world that Dr. Khalid and his master might bring back to help them in their terrible plans for world domination.

His voice boomed in the library, echoing around the walls and, for a brief moment, it was as if Thoth himself had spoken. "In the Book of Beginnings, I, Thoth, the master of mysteries, keeper of records, mighty king, master magician, living from aeon to aeon, set down for the guidance of those who come after these records of a mighty wisdom which lie in a sarcophagus of stone in the Chamber of Secret Knowledge. O sacred book, writ by my immortal hands, by incorruption's magic spell remain free from decay throughout eternity and unblemished by time. Become unseeable, unfindable from everyone whose foot shall tread the plains of this land, until old heaven shall bring an instrument, the Heroic Child, and give to him the Key of Binding to translate the Mystic Star and unlock the secret

205

contained within." Thus spake Thoth and, laying the spells on the book by means of his works, he shut it safely away, and long has been the time since the book was hidden away.

Justin looked at Adam. "The Heroic Child."

Adam didn't hear Justin at first. Everything seemed to be linked together in a big jumble in his head, as if hidden threads were beginning to draw him into a huge, confusing web.

"Wake up. The Heroic Child." Justin's voice jerked Adam back to reality.

Adam stared at Justin and Kim. "What about the Heroic Child?" Then, noticing their expressions, he said, "Hey, don't look at me. I'm not the heroic anything."

"Of course it's you," said Justin. "The Heroic Child's going to translate this Mystic Star and unlock the secret. That's you."

"Who else could it be?" asked Kim. "I mean, aren't you the one who was given the sacred scarab and made the bearer or something?"

"I am *not* the Heroic Child," Adam protested.

"Yeah, right, of course not. Let me keep reading," said Justin, finding his place again.

When he spoke of these magical spells, I shook my head. I believe in history, not old tales of mythical gods and sorcery. Clearly, if one applies the principles of analysis and rational thought, the situation can be explained. I tried to make sense of what he told me. As I understood it, Thoth, a personage of intelligence and learning, preserved his ultimate teachings—this Book of Thoth—*in a single stone, a stone not of this earth, a stone that fell from heaven, called the Stone of Fire. He did this because men at that time did not appreciate his wisdom. Then Thoth hid this stone deep in the bowels of the earth.*

The old man pressed on with his tale, revealing to me how seven fragments were broken off from the Stone of Fire and given to seven wise men, the Seven Sages, to scour the known world and seek out good and wise kings, the Sons of Fire and Light. Only they could use these fragments, the

Seven Stones of Power, to rule wisely and well and then bequeath the stones to worthy successors.

Then came the worst news: the Seven Stones must never be united, because he who finds and unites all seven fragments with the Stone of Fire will be able to read the Book of Thoth *and use the power of life and death hidden in the Stone of Fire. At the same time, he told me that one day terrible destruction would threaten the human race, which then would have need of a great and wondrous truth.*

I was confused by all this. First, how could a book be preserved in a stone? I wondered if it was not a real book, such as those I am used to reading, but merely a collection of writings, perhaps carved on stone tablets like the ones Moses carried down from the mountain. Second, in one breath, he said the stones must never be united; in the next, he said they would be used to save the world. I asked myself if this was possible. Of course, there is always war, famine, plague, and poverty, but there has been no sign yet of the end of days.

He instructed me all through the long night. He spoke repeatedly of the Seven Stones that will unlock the secret of the Stone of Fire and open the Book of Thoth. *He told me how, without them, the Stone of Fire remains dumb and the book remains shut. My blood runs cold now when I think of the dreadful secret with which he has burdened me. Ah, if only I could pluck this knowledge from my brain and cast out all memory of his words. How strange that I, who have hungered for knowledge as a starving man craves food, now consider this information a curse.*

Alas, there was more horror in store for me as this was not all of which he spake. A malign force, the Dark Brothers, also exists. He called them Old Ones and they represent all that is evil. My heart was chilled and the blood seemed like ice in my veins at these words. He quoted from the writings of Thoth to emphasize the terror inspired by these people, drumming his words relentlessly into my ears.

207

Justin looked up. "The next bit is really creepy. I'm not sure I like the sound of this."

"You can't stop now," said Kim.

Justin continued.

Black is the way of the Dark Brothers, dark of darkness, not of the night; travelling o'er earth, they haunt men's dreams, putting their hopes to flight. It is they who are filled with blackness, always seeking to quell the light, while others are filled with glory and have conquered the bondage of night. Seek not the Kingdom of Darkness, for evil will surely appear; 'tis only the Master of Brightness who shall vanquish the shadow of fear.

Adam shivered. "I wonder if the poison guys are the Dark Brothers?"

Justin frowned at the page in his hand. "I wonder who the Master of Brightness is."

Kim stared at Justin with wide eyes. "Poor Bedwyr. How terrible for him to have to listen to all this. He must have thought he was going mad."

Justin continued reading.

He pointed to the old animal skin covered in strange writing and told me that the clues to the Seven Stones, those precious and vital fragments, were written there. Poetic his words might have been, but I wanted nothing to do with it. Why burden me, an insignificant scribe, with this horrible responsibility for knowledge is a heavy weight indeed. My task, he said, was to preserve this information, this manuscript, so only the Chosen One, the Heroic Child, would find it in time to come. How and when he would find it was not my concern. How he would understand and translate it was also not for me to know. He told me to conceal the Scroll of the Ancients and then place false signs in another document, written in elaborate language, using my skills as a writer. I must name this second document the Chronicles of the Stone, *and he told me what to write. I was flattered, but only half convinced. I pointed to the tattered animal skin. How, I asked, had the Scroll of the Ancients and its secret survived from the mists of antiquity until now?*

"I was wondering about that," Kim said.

Justin flapped a hand at her to shush.

My visitor explained that by 332 BC, when Alexander wrested control of Aegyptus from the Persians, the last members of the true Aegyptian priesthood preserved most of their ancient arts and secret skills in books and manuscripts. In Alexandria, that great city of learning and culture founded by Alexander the Great, a number of Greek scholars, mystics, and philosophers joined the few remaining dedicated Aegyptian priests. They formed a fellowship—the Brotherhood of the Stone—bound by oath never to reveal their special knowledge or its source. Three hundred years later, in 30 BC, Aegyptus fell under the control of the Roman Empire after Octavian, the future Emperor Augustus, defeated his rival Mark Antony and deposed his lover Queen Cleopatra VII. The country became a province of Rome, called Provincia Aegyptus.

Worse was yet to come. In the year AD 296, the Roman emperor Diocletian sought out and burned all the Aegyptian books of magic, science, and learning. He was afraid that the Aegyptian priests and mystics, who knew the secret art of gold and silver metalwork, would amass riches enabling them to fund revolts and rise up against the might of the Roman Empire. Furthermore, when the Roman emperor Constantine declared Christianity the official religion of the Roman Empire in AD 313, he banned all pagan writings. Frightened, the scholars scattered, taking with them what manuscripts had survived. They fled to Persia and the lands of the East, where men of learning welcomed them and their knowledge. The Brotherhood was willing to share their wisdom, but the great secret of Thoth remained hidden, known only to the direct descendants of the true Aegyptian priests.

With the passage of time, the story of the Seven Stones of Power and the Stone of Fire, and the key to unlocking the Book of Thoth *had passed into the realms of myth and legend until now. The descendants of the Brotherhood of the Stone kept the great secret safe—waiting for the time of the Chosen One, the Heroic Child who would use the secret knowledge for*

209

the good of the world. But they were betrayed by a renegade among them who sold knowledge of the secret to the highest bidder. At that time, the bogus priests and charlatans—called the Priests of al Khem—who had ruled the temples of Aegyptus with a corrupt iron hand, sold information to whoever could pay for it; ideas about changing base metal into gold, concocting poisons and so-called magical elixirs said to prolong life, and performing other conjuring tricks. The betrayer of the Brotherhood of the Stone was secretly one of the Priests of al Khem. Thus, the sacred knowledge left Aegyptus and found its way into Europe.

The old man told me he was the last of the Aegyptian priests to survive. I was puzzled because surely he meant he was the last of the descendants of the priests. But I did not want to interrupt him so I kept silent. He then handed me the Scroll of the Ancients, reminding me of my task to hide it well, and to create the Chronicles of the Stone. The manuscript containing the only key to unlocking the Stone of Fire lay before me, under threat of discovery. I asked what the purpose was of hiding something and then creating a misleading reference to it in another document. He silenced me and said the time to reveal the Scroll of the Ancients was not right, the planets had not yet aligned, and the Heroic Child had not yet been born.

This made no sense to me, yet I began to understand that great and majestic forces were at work, eclipsing my beliefs, my existence, and my soul. Dumbly, I bowed my head and nodded. Then he reached again into his pouch. He withdrew a collection of pages bound together with a painted leather covering, advising me to read it carefully. I thanked him for his gift, which I would have to donate to the monastery library since we cannot have private possessions, least of all a book. Even writing this diary violates the abbot's rules.

That night, I could not sleep on my narrow cot although my visitor slept peacefully enough on a mattress on the floor. Just before dawn, I fell into a heavy slumber and only awoke when I heard the bell for prime at six o'clock. I stumbled from my bed, dragging on my robe as I ran to the

210

chapel. There was no sign of my visitor. The abbot approached me as I yawned into my morning gruel, asking about the visitor. I confessed I had not seen him; he must have left during the early hours. The abbot was annoyed, but his face lit up when he heard about the gift. Then suddenly there was a loud noise at the gate. The gatekeeper ran in, his face pale with fear. "Murder! Come quickly!" he gasped, before turning and running back from whence he came.

Adam and Kim jumped as he said, "Murder!" Justin read well and he made the story sound rather dramatic.

We all ran after the man, disbelieving of what we had heard. Murder? Whom? How? Where? Our monastery is perched on the side of a steep hill. Although the path approaching it winds easily up to the gates, the path leading away then falls sharply down the hillside and one must tread with care in order to reach the main road with limbs intact. It was just as we feared. At the bottom of the hill, we spied a pool of blood, a torn robe, an empty pouch, and a leather sandal. Outlaws, those villains who prey upon the weak and unarmed, must have set upon our visitor. But where was the body? I looked fearfully about me. Had he been spirited away by angels, taken up in a fiery chariot like the prophet Enoch? I could see my fellow brethren were disturbed. They clustered in worried groups, nodding or shaking their heads, their faces grim.

The abbot took charge, shooing us back to the monastery like stray chickens. He assured the younger, more tenderhearted brothers that the sheriff would investigate. I could not believe my friend was dead. It was impossible to cry murder without a body. And that was the opinion of the sheriff when he came to speak to me. He had a look on his face suggesting he suspected me at first, but after a few minutes, he patted my shoulder and said there was nothing for me to fear. It was a complete mystery, he told me, one that perhaps we were not meant to uncover. He looked up at the sky and made the sign of the cross. Divine intervention? I doubted it. More like earthly wickedness, in my opinion.

Justin stopped and held out the remaining page to Kim. "Do you want to read the last bit?"

Kim shook her head. "No, you're so good at it, Justin, you keep going. You make it come alive."

Justin beamed. "Yes, I do, don't I? I've just joined the debating society and that's what everyone says."

Adam pinched his lips together to keep from laughing. Justin was … well … he was Justin.

"Are you listening?" Justin stared at Adam with an accusing look.

"Uh, of course I am. I was thinking about what you've been reading," said Adam.

"Stop thinking and listen up. There must be clues in here."

Justin found his place and began reading again.

The abbot recovered quickly from the shock of having a guest disappear outside our gates and asked me about the gift. Glumly, I placed the book in his hands. He paged through it, praising the fine quality of the images, but showed no further interest. He then began to question me at length about my long conversation with the visitor, suggesting that I had perhaps concealed something from him. My guilty thoughts strayed to my cold cell, where I had hidden the Scroll of the Ancients inside the thin mattress on my cot. When I showed a reluctance to speak further, he chastised me, asking whether he had not been a kind and lenient abbot, giving me free time to indulge in my literary pursuits when I should have been peeling potatoes in the kitchen. I knew his question to be unjust and untrue. His desire to find some mysterious knowledge was the only reason for my freedom to study. A brief suspicion fluttered through my mind—was it the ancient scroll the abbot sought? I dismissed the thought at once. How would he, tucked away in a small monastery in the hills, even have heard of it? It would only become clear to me later.

Oh, why did I not trust that small voice inside my head? At that moment, hurt pride took hold of me, blinding me to what lay before my eyes. Yet I could play the same game as my superior. Being the son of a wealthy family, which had endowed the monastery with numerous gifts, mainly money, I was not without respect among the brothers. I put on an injured expression and suggested I could find my spiritual haven elsewhere. Right away, the abbot knew he had overstepped the mark. He put on a kindly smile, embraced me as a brother, patted my cheeks, and told me I should go to visit my family. I agreed because I had just received news that my father was ill, and I had been about to request leave from the monastery to do my filial duty. Then the abbot placed the book in my hands, declaring that something so charming and appealing would make a fitting gift for my father, an ardent collector of all kinds of books. I thanked him because I knew this gift would give my ailing father good cheer.

*I remembered my friend's instruction to read the book carefully, so I went to the library and examined it. I was disappointed. The old man had filled my head with tales of ancient and powerful secrets and a sense of impending doom, and here was something as simple as a bestiary, a book of animals, and in this case, imaginary animals. I looked at the title—*Codex Draconum*—a book of dragons and related mythical beasts. In my opinion, simply something to entertain empty-headed noble ladies who like to exclaim at the possibility of giants and faery folk and other such amusements. I confess my mind was on other matters, and I yawned as I flicked through the illustrations, which meant nothing to me. No doubt, my father would find it interesting.*

I have been unable to push all thoughts of the strange visitor from my mind. I have done as he asked and created a beautiful manuscript with references to the Seven Stones in the ancient scroll, but diverting the reader with obscure and often nonsensical allusions. It is a pretty poem for the lover of literature, but nothing to inspire the seeker of secrets. I have arranged matters to protect the ancient scroll. I have done as I was bade. But it will not end there.

My family was happy to see me, of course, and my father enjoyed the gift. He found nothing disturbing or strange about the book, which led me to believe this is all nonsense. After a few days, my father died peacefully in his sleep. My mother is broken with grief. Is this divine punishment for

213

doing as the pilgrim asked me? My body aches and I feel constantly unwell, my mind filled with fears and fantasies. Dark have been my dreams of late. As I keep vigil in the lonely watches of the night, my mind is wracked with confused thoughts. My prayers afford me no solace. Participating in this undertaking was the most foolish thing I have ever done. There is nothing more here for me, only death. What I have learned convinces me the fate of the world will soon be decided as the dark shadows take shape. I must return to the monastery but I fear ... I fear for my life. There is more to tell, but I have not the strength to continue.

Justin put the pages down on the library table. "That's it. That's Bedwyr's story."

"I wonder if he did go back to the monastery," said Adam.

Kim looked nervous. "What do you mean?"

"Well, he isn't buried anywhere, so where is his body? James told us the monastery sent back Bedwyr's few things. He didn't mention a body and if there were one, wouldn't it be buried here with all the other ancestors? There's a memorial stone, but no proper burial place."

"It's an incredible story," said Kim, "but what can we learn from it?"

Justin burst into scornful laughter. "You obviously weren't listening. There are loads of clues."

Kim glared at him. "Like what?"

Justin gave an impatient sigh. "Oh, please. The abbot, for starters. He's a total scumbag. He was looking for something, and he only allowed Bedwyr to do all that research so Bedwyr could find it for him. The visitor, the pilgrim guy, is a huge clue and the abbot knew it. That's why he was suspicious of Bedwyr after the pilgrim left."

"I don't think the pilgrim died," said Adam. "The clues were there, but without a body there's no murder. I think the pilgrim staged his own death to make the abbot believe he had been robbed of any valuables he might have."

"Hmm," said Justin, "you could be right. The most important thing, though, is that the pilgrim asked Bedwyr to create a fake document and that's the one James' dad put on display, the one Dr. Khalid stole. Now Dr. Khalid thinks he has real information, but he doesn't. Remember, Adam? James told you about it when

214

you guys were stuck in the tomb of the Scarab King. It's just a decoy—a false clue, but Dr. Khalid doesn't know that."

"You're right," Adam exclaimed. "Ebrahim and Hamid were so worried. That's why at the Egyptian Museum in Cairo they said we should focus on the Scroll of the Ancients instead."

Justin pointed to the page in his hand. "Bedwyr says it right here about 'a beautiful manuscript with references to the Seven Stones in the ancient scroll, but diverting the reader with obscure and often nonsensical allusions.' That's the *Chronicles of the Stone*. We thought it was so important, but it's not—it's all made up. The only part that was true was the first bit about the sacred scarab."

Adam quickly felt for his scarab and squeezed it so hard the pointy bits dug into his palm.

Justin continued, "Dr. Khalid's chasing the wrong things." He pulled a sour face. "Well, I hope he is."

"What about the book of dragons, the *Codex Draconum*?" asked Kim.

"I think it's a big clue," said Adam.

"No, it's not a clue," replied Justin. "It was just a nice book to read. That's what Bedwyr thought."

"No," insisted Adam. "He thought wrong. The pilgrim said Bedwyr must read it carefully. But he didn't. So he might have missed something."

"If the family kept everything," said Kim, "then it should still be here. Look at all these books. Some of them are so old. You can see they never threw anything away."

Justin gazed slowly around the room. "Yeah, zillions of books. Where do you want to start looking?"

Kim bit her lip.

Adam scanned the walls of shelves. The late afternoon sun shone through the skylight, softly illuminating the thousands of book covers. "Where would we even begin?"

Thumbelina and Athena Sound the Alarm

That night they went to bed early. Although Sheldon offered to tell them another blood-curdling tale of horror from the family archive of ghosts, Adam politely declined, saying they were all tired after such an exciting day. Justin and Kim agreed. Archie said he was also exhausted. He tottered up to bed after polishing off an enormous meal and drinking some of Mrs. Grant's special nerve tonic, which made him rather giggly.

Adam decided to put the translated pages of Bedwyr's diary in the secret hideaway in the Narnia cupboard. It seemed the safest place for now, at least until James and Isabel returned.

Once he and Justin had cleaned their teeth, said goodnight to Kim, and jumped into bed, Adam really did feel tired. Kim hadn't said much, but Adam thought she seemed as nervous as he was about what might happen next.

"So, what do we do now?" Adam asked Justin, who was thumping his pillow into a more comfortable shape.

Justin stopped thumping and looked at Adam, one eyebrow raised. "What do you mean?"

"I mean what should we do while Ink's away?"

Justin returned to pummeling his pillow. "This thing feels like a rock. There must be mediaeval feathers inside."

Adam prodded his cousin with one finger. "Are you listening to me?"

Justin gave the pillow a final thump before settling back against it. "Well, what can we really do? I have no idea where to start looking for the scroll—or anything, in fact. Ink said he'll be back soon so we should wait for him. If anything happens, well, we'll just have to deal with it." He gave a loud yawn and closed his eyes.

Adam prodded him again. "So aren't you scared anymore?"

Justin opened his eyes. He looked indignant. "Scared?" He sat up. "*When* was I ever scared?"

"You looked scared when Ebrahim's letter said peril was hard at our heels. That could be now."

Justin lay back on the pillow again. "I can't worry about something that hasn't happened yet. I just hope those monk creatures don't come back. Ink told the one that broke in we haven't got the secret book of that guy Arthy-peeus, or whatever he's called."

"Ar*the*pius. The guy's name is Ar*the*pius."

"Whatever." Justin rolled over and grabbed the quilt, pulling it onto his side of the bed. "Let me sleep."

Treading with care, Hamish moved toward what he thought was an intruder. He gripped a heavy saucepan, the first thing he had grabbed from his little kitchen when he heard scuffling in the mews. He wondered how the intruders had managed to get past the alarm system. A black shape hovered in front of the door leading to the incubators. Intent on his target, Hamish took another step and raised the saucepan. Before he could bring it crashing down on the back of the intruder's head, a punishing blow struck him from behind. As he fell face first to the ground, he smelled something … the raw odor of gasoline.

Then he heard a muffled exchange of words in a language he didn't understand, followed by footsteps retreating. He touched the back of his head and felt wetness. When he looked, his fingers were covered in blood. These attackers were no ordinary rare egg thieves; they had more sinister intentions.

Almost fainting with pain, Hamish dragged himself to the cages. He managed to reach up and grasp the wire front of Athena's cage. He fumbled at the clasp and then fell to the ground, groaning in agony, his eyes closed. The cage door swung open and Athena hopped onto the bottom of the doorframe, giving a few soft, questioning hoots. Hamish opened his eyes and waved a feeble hand.

"Fetch the boy, Athena. Fetch him before it's too late." His hand dropped to his side.

"Fly," he whispered to the empty cage as he drifted into unconsciousness. Athena was already gone.

Adam didn't go to sleep right away. Holding his golden scarab, he watched the sky change color, the delicate pink and purple shades of evening finally giving way to a velvety darkness speckled with stars. Only then did he put the scarab under his pillow for safekeeping. He fell into a deep and dreamless sleep, but eventually the sound of tapping woke him. He sat up in bed and listened. There it was again.

Tap-tap. Tap-tap.

In the bright moonlight, a small shape fluttered at the window, silhouetted against the pane.

Ugh, it's a bat. I hate bats. Adam pulled the quilt up to his chin and watched the little creature flapping against the windowpane. A larger shape kept swooping past the window. *I bet the big one is a vampire bat.* He wished they hadn't teased Kim about the *Twilight* movie. All the stuff they'd laughed at before, like ghosts and vampires, seemed somehow scarier in an old castle.

Then he heard a soft *hoo-hoo*. Bats didn't hoot. Adam scrambled out of bed and ran to the window. Taking care not to knock the owl off the sill, he opened the window and stuck out his hand. Thumbelina ran up his arm and onto his shoulder. She chirruped as she gave his ear an affectionate peck.

"What are you doing out?" Adam tickled her head. "Hamish will be so angry."

He turned to see Justin awake. "Look who's here."

Justin threw back the quilt and came over to the window. "What's up?"

Adam showed him the little owl. "She must have escaped." He placed her back on the windowsill. "You'd better go home, Thumbelina, before you get into trouble."

Justin pointed at something outside. "Why's the other one flying around like that? It looks like Athena."

219

As he spoke, Thumbelina gave an excited hoot and launched into the sky, following Athena. The boys hung out of the window, watching Athena flying away with Thumbelina flapping beneath her. Then Adam noticed a strange glow coming from the direction in which Athena was heading. The glow was a fire and the direction was the stables.

"Fire!" Adam yelled. "The stables are on fire."

The boys quickly put on sneakers and pulled sweaters over their pajamas. They ran down the staircase, screaming at the tops of their voices, "Fire! Fire!" Mrs. Grant had left a light on in the hallway downstairs so this time they could see their way clearly.

When they reached the entrance hall, Adam grabbed Justin's arm. "We're wasting our breath shouting. Sheldon and Mrs. McLeod and Mrs. Grant live on the other side of the castle, in the staff quarters. They can't hear us. What do we do?"

Justin looked around in desperation. His glance fell on a huge brass gong Mrs. Grant had told them Sheldon used at banquets to alert late guests. "This!"

He seized the wooden mallet used to sound the instrument and gave the gong a hefty whack. The boom echoed through the entire castle, the sound amplified by its thick stone walls.

Justin gave the gong one more whack and threw down the mallet. "Let's go. The door key's there, on the table next to the suit of armor."

Kim ran down the stairs after them. She had also put on sneakers and a sweater over her pajamas and robe.

"Hey, wait for me. Where are you two going? What's happening?"

"There's a fire at the stables," said Adam, struggling to turn the huge key in the front door. "We have to get help."

At the same time, he wondered how they were going to raise the portcullis. Mrs. McLeod had said they raised it electronically. He hoped the switch was visible.

"You stay here," Justin said to Kim. "It's too dangerous for you to come with us."

"No way," Kim said. "Just try to stop me."

"Okay, but don't get hurt or Aunt Isabel will kill me. She put me in charge. And while Ink's not here, I'm the one who'll get blamed if anything goes wrong."

"I can look after myself," Kim replied tartly.

Between them, Adam and Justin managed to turn the key and open the front door. They raced to the portcullis and, after searching for a few minutes, found a red button on the inside of a supporting pillar. Justin pressed it.

The portcullis slowly creaked upward and the trio shot under it, across the drawbridge and down the driveway, heading for the stables. The moon was bright enough to light their way. Even before they reached the stables, they could smell smoke and hear terrible screaming and thudding as the trapped horses kicked at their stalls.

Adam felt chilled to the bone. What kind of a person would want to kill those beautiful animals?

When they arrived, thick smoke was pouring from the tiled roof, but they couldn't see any flames yet. They looked for some way to put out the fire. The fire extinguisher they had seen the previous day was no longer there. Although the buckets remained, the garden hose that had hung next to the main door had also disappeared. Adam tried to open the door, but a padlock held it closed.

Justin disappeared around a corner and returned a few seconds later, waving an axe. "Look what I found! Get out of the way."

"Wait," said Kim. "We can't go in there like this."

Justin stared at her. "Like what?"

She yanked off her sweater and cotton robe, and tore a piece from her robe to make a rough mask. "Here, wet this and tie it over your mouth and nose."

"Good thinking," said Justin, snatching the swatch out of her hand. "You're not so bad for a girl."

Kim made a face at him, but she looked pleased to be part of the team.

Adam began filling a bucket from the outside tap.

"I haven't even got the door open yet," Justin said to him. "What are you doing?"

"This." Adam poured the water over Justin's head, soaking him. "You don't want to fry in there."

The shrieking and banging from inside the stables grew louder, and a tongue of flame shot from under the door. Once they had soaked their clothes and tied makeshift masks over their noses and mouths, Justin hacked at the padlock until it broke. Adam and Kim yanked open the door. The fire was blazing just inside the entrance and at the far end, where the hayloft was located. The flames

221

hadn't reached the horses yet, although sparks were already drifting in their direction.

The six animals, maddened by fear, kicked at their stalls to escape. Ducking low to avoid the flying hooves, Kim and Adam opened the doors. The horses galloped off into the night. Justin began filling a bucket to douse the flames in the front section. The inside fire extinguisher had also disappeared. Flames began to rise near the hayloft as a terrifying wall of orange and yellow tongues licked hungrily at the hay.

"Where are Billy and Terence?" Adam yelled above the roar. Smoke choked his lungs, burning his nostrils, and he could hardly see.

Kim and Justin were also struggling to breathe. Their wet clothing and hair warded off flames, but the sound of sizzling meant they were drying fast. They dashed outside to drench themselves again.

"Where have the horses gone?" Justin said, shaking his head to get rid of the excess water pouring from his hair.

"I don't think they'll go far," said Kim. "Maybe to the paddock." Her singed plaits hung limp and bedraggled, making her look like a drowned rat.

A faint cry came from inside the stables.

"It's Billy," said Kim.

They ran back to the hayloft ladder, where a tousled sandy head peered over the top, surrounded by leaping flames.

Justin grabbed the ladder. "I'll fetch him. I'm the strongest so I can lift him down. You two go find Terence."

"My dad," cried Billy. "He's in the cottage."

With a last backward glance at Justin, who was starting up the hayloft ladder, Adam and Kim raced out of the stables. Dashing to the front of the cottage, they stared, aghast. Here was the source of the glow seen from the castle window: a flaming wall shot up the front of the cottage, making it impossible to enter. The fire was well established and burning fiercely. The intense heat drove Adam and Kim back.

Shouts came from the path behind them as Sheldon, Mrs. Grant, and Mrs. McLeod hurried forward, all still in pajamas, slippers, and robes. The two women, their hair in curlers, had blankets slung over their shoulders and each clutched a bottle of water in one hand and a bucket in the other. Sheldon held a long, thick stick and a flashlight. He threw both aside when he saw the flames. Running to a small shed at the side of the cottage, he emerged a minute later with a garden hose, which he connected to an outside tap.

"Better than nothing," he cried. "Fill up the buckets, Mrs. McLeod."

As Sheldon began spraying water onto the flames, Justin emerged through the trees, a smoke-blackened Billy clinging to his back.

Mrs. Grant dropped her bucket, ran to Justin, and hugged them both. "Billy, where's your father?"

Mute, Billy pointed to the cottage, the front now almost engulfed in fire.

"We can go through the back door," said Adam.

"No," cried Mrs. McLeod, "it's too dangerous."

"Did you call the fire station?" asked Kim.

Mrs. Grant, her cheeks ashen, replied, "I tried, but the telephone line is *still* down even though Sheldon reported it this afternoon. Besides, Haddley doesn't have its own fire service. We usually have to get them to come from Westchester. It's a town very close by, no more than a few miles."

"Someone must ride to the village," said Mrs. McLeod briskly. She glanced at Billy. "You'll have to go, Billy. You can ride one of the horses."

"Sirius." Billy's voice sounded hoarse from the smoke. "There he is."

He pointed behind the group. Sirius loomed through the trees, a massive shadow, tossing his head and whickering when he saw Billy.

"Isn't it too dangerous?" asked Kim. "Billy's so small and Sirius is so big. He hasn't got a saddle or reins either."

"Billy can ride anything on four legs, can't you, my pet?" said Mrs. McLeod, patting the boy on the head. "Ride to the police station and tell Sidney Parrott to call the Westchester fire brigade."

She pulled a face as she spoke. "I knew Sidney's mother. Not local, and it shows."

The horse trotted right up to them when Billy whistled. The boy scrambled onto Sirius' back with Mrs. Grant's help. He grasped the horse's mane with clenched fists.

"Be careful now, Billy," said Mrs. Grant.

Billy grinned, showing white teeth amid a soot-masked face. He clicked his tongue and cried, "Yah! Come on, Sirius."

Horse and rider galloped off into the night. While Mrs. Grant and Mrs. McLeod watched them go, Adam and Justin sneaked to the rear of the cottage, with

Kim behind them. Despite the roaring flames in the front, the back was quiet, with masses of smoke pouring from under the door.

"Remember to stay as low as you can," Justin instructed, taking charge of the operation. "Smoke rises so there'll be cleaner air near the floor. Put your masks on."

Kim and Adam did so.

"Here goes," said Justin, and he and Adam slammed at the door with their shoulders, breaking the flimsy lock.

The trio fumbled their way into the kitchen, coughing and wheezing from the thick smoke billowing around them. On hands and knees, they felt their way along the passage until Adam stumbled on something. He looked down. Terence lay sprawled on the floor.

"Here he is!"

Adam grabbed what he thought was a leg, but it was an arm. Kim and Justin scrambled toward him, each grabbing a limb. Having devoured each room with alarming speed, the flames had almost reached them now and the heat was intense. The fire made unearthly sounds, roaring and growling like a hungry beast. The thud of timber falling as the roof began to cave in spurred them on.

Adam couldn't believe they were in such a terrifying situation. He struggled to breathe, even with his dampened cotton mask. His eyes stung and watered from the smoke; he could barely see as they hauled Terence from the passage and into the kitchen.

Kim and Justin were just shapes crouched in the thick smoke next to him. Justin screamed, "Pull!" several times. They heaved repeatedly until finally they fell out of the kitchen door, dragging Terence's body. The kitchen windows exploded behind them in a shower of blackened glass.

Mrs. McLeod and Mrs. Grant helped them tug Terence clear. As they looked back, the entire roof caved in with a loud crash. Flames, sparks, and huge columns of smoke rose into the night sky, lighting up the area with an eerie glow. The two women took over, wiping Terence's face and helping him sit up for a drink of water.

"Billy? Where's Billy?" he croaked.

"Don't you worry now," said Mrs. Grant. "He's gone for the fire brigade."

Terence closed his eyes and moaned, his head falling to one side. He looked terrible, his face pale and his breathing labored. Mrs. Grant covered him with a blanket and sat holding his hand.

The kids ran to the front of the cottage where Sheldon was staring at the all-consuming flames as they leaped continually higher. The garden hose lay useless at his feet, dribbling a trickle of water. Blackened roses hung from the devastated porch. The windows had also shattered from the heat, leaving splinters scattered on the ground.

"The cottage is gone," he said. "Nothing more I can do."

"What about the horses?" Adam asked. "Are they safe?"

"Yes, I checked on them. Rowan is the leader and she took them to the paddock. Clever beasts. There's a big old shed nearby that's not used these days, so I'll put them in there later tonight with food and water. Tomorrow I'll ask Mr. McGillivray on the estate next door if he can keep them for a bit, until we're all sorted out. But I think Sirius should stay, just to give Billy something to make him smile. He's so attached to that horse."

He glanced at them. "Well, you three look like a dirty bunch of ragamuffins."

They were streaked with soot from top to toes, and their clothes and hair were scorched. Kim's plaits were singed at the ends. Her once-pretty pink pajamas were filthy. Adam felt utterly exhausted. But the night was not over.

Kim clapped one hand to her mouth. "What about Hamish?"

They ran to the mews, which had not caught fire. Hamish lay in front of Athena's cage with Athena and Thumbelina perched in the open doorway, gazing at him and uttering soft hoots.

Sheldon turned Hamish over and checked his pulse. "He'll be all right. Just knocked out. Lucky the fire didn't get this side because the wind's blowing in the opposite direction. He and the poor birds wouldn't have stood a chance. Let's hope the fire brigade arrives soon."

Adam felt a familiar coldness creep over him. Who could be so ruthless as to almost kill six beautiful horses and attack two innocent people? He didn't want to acknowledge the bitter truth to himself, especially when he caught Justin staring at him. There was only one person who would stop at nothing to get what he wanted. Their enemy was closer than they had imagined.

Sheldon managed to carry Hamish back to the cottage and laid him next to Terence.

"Shall we try to get them up to the castle?" asked Mrs. McLeod.

"No," Sheldon said, "I think we should wait for the medics. Maybe a nice cup of tea will help?"

Mrs. Grant said she would put the kettle on and prepare some sandwiches.

"Do you think Billy will make it to the police station?" asked Kim.

"Of course he will," Mrs. McLeod replied, but her ashen face and uneasy demeanor suggested she was not convinced. She looked up at the sky. "Thank heavens, here's the rain. Just in time. Get the blankets."

Miraculously, the sky opened and rain poured down hard, dampening the flames. Smoke rose thicker as the fire sizzled under the pelting drops.

Kim sighed as she huddled in a blanket. "I hope this is the worst that'll happen."

But Adam knew that if Dr. Khalid was the instigator of this near tragedy, it would only be the beginning.

CONSTABLE PARROTT TAKES CHARGE

Billy galloped through the woods toward the village, taking a shortcut that he and Sirius knew. Sirius, now calm, raced as if he understood the danger that beset the group at the castle. Billy laughed as the wind ruffled his hair and small branches brushed his cheeks. His heart pounded with excitement. He felt important. So many people were depending on him and Sirius, including his dad. He couldn't let them down. Hooves thudding, mane and tail flying, the great horse thundered into the village, taking the boy right up to the police station door.

Constable Sidney Parrott dozed at his post. With his collar unbuttoned, his feet up on the desk, his head thrown back, and his hand still grasping a now cold cup of tea, he snored loudly, unaware of the furor that awaited him. It was unfortunate for Sidney, but he did rather resemble a parrot, a fact that had brought him much grief while growing up. Now in his late twenties, Sidney had a large beak of a nose, a pinkish face, and jutting ears. Under his helmet, thin strands of mousy hair were carefully combed over what was fast becoming a bald patch atop his head. Loud thumps at the door woke him from his nap. He jerked his head up violently, at the same time pouring the tea into his lap. His helmet flew off and hit the wall behind him.

"Wha—? Whassa—?"

"It's me, Billy Burns, Mr. Parrott," Billy screamed from outside.

"It's *Constable* Parrott to you, young Billy," the irate officer yelled. "And if this is a practical joke, I'm a-gonna arrest you for wasting police time."

Yanking open the door, he beheld an awful sight. Both horse and boy were covered in soot. Billy's hair and eyebrows were singed, and his clothes were

227

charred where burning wisps of hay had fallen on him. Sirius, usually handsome and well groomed, looked even worse, his silvery coat now blackened from smoke. Rearing up on his hind legs, he rolled his eyes wildly, snorting and whinnying. His flailing hooves seemed the size of buckets to Sidney. The unlikely pair looked as if they had just escaped from the fires of hell.

Sidney banged the door closed and leaned against it, trembling. He didn't like horses, and especially not the one prancing about on the doorstep, snorting and rolling its eyes in such a fearsome manner.

"Take that wild beast away, Billy, right this instant," he shouted through the door, "or I'll tell your dad on you and you'll get the whipping of your life."

"*Please*, Mr. Constable Parrott," Billy screamed even louder. "There's a fire up at the castle. The stables are on fire and my dad's hurt—"

"A fire? At the castle? Why didn't you say so before?"

The door flew open. Sidney reappeared, his uniform now neatly buttoned in place, although still damp with tea. His thoughts raced in wild triumph. This was the moment he'd been waiting for all his life; an opportunity to take charge in a crisis, to shine, to show the village he wasn't the butt of jokes, but the stuff of which heroes were made. Promotion was at his fingertips. Now he would attract the attention of his superiors. He would be vindicated.

Beryl Winkworth, the plump local beauty, wouldn't turn him down at the village dance after this. Already, he could see the adoration in her blue eyes, and her full pink lips curling in an admiring smile. He could almost hear her cooing, "Oh, Sidney. You're my champion."

Sidney forced himself to push aside this pleasant daydream, as it was difficult enough to concentrate with such a big animal leaping about on the doorstep. Holding the telephone in one hand while fumbling for car keys with the other, and between yelling instructions into the receiver and trying to question Billy, he managed to inform the fire brigade in Westchester of the fire.

He put on his helmet and raced out of the station, banging the door closed behind him. Speed was essential so he jumped into his dilapidated old car and quickly reversed with a horrible grinding of gears. His predecessor had driven the official police car into a tree the previous year during a particularly exciting car chase involving a runaway baker's van. Nothing had been done yet about purchasing a replacement. Sidney was thus obliged to use his own vehicle. Uncomplaining, he viewed it as just one more example of his unswerving duty to

Her Majesty. Revving the engine, he stuck his head out of the window and waved Billy toward the castle. Billy saluted and galloped off.

It was between sips of hot cocoa and the munching of sandwiches that a loud clanging heralded the approach of a fire engine. An ambulance followed, siren blaring. Somehow, the vehicles had managed the bumpy track leading to the stables, though by now the cottage fire had diminished. The heavy rain, which had since turned to fine drizzle, had almost completely extinguished the flames in the stables. Two paramedics attended to Hamish and Terence, while the firefighters unrolled hoses to deal with the last of the cottage blaze. Billy scrambled off Sirius, and the horse trotted away to the paddock.

When the medics examined Terence, his head lolled about alarmingly. Billy burst into tears so Mrs. McLeod took him away from the scene to calm him down. Sidney stalked over to her and they exchanged a few angry words. The officer grabbed one of Billy's arms and Mrs. McLeod grabbed the other. Soon, the two adults were pulling the bewildered boy from side to side. Finally, Mrs. McLeod gave a huge heave and Billy flew to her side.

"No, you're not taking him," she said, "and that's flat."

Adam wandered over, with an interested Kim and Justin close behind. "What's the matter?" he asked.

Sidney adjusted his uniform collar, his lips pinched with anger. "Well, I shouldn't say, but you might as well all know. It's Billy what's done this."

"Rubbish," hissed Mrs. McLeod. "He's just a wee bairn. He's done nothing except be a hero and go fetch you." She lifted her shoulders in a gesture that somehow smacked of contempt. "Much good that's done, I see."

"That may be," said Sidney, clearly annoyed that the scruffy urchin in question should tarnish his own moment of glory, "but he's done it before, and now he's done it again."

Justin spoke up. "What's he done before?"

Sidney pressed his lips together a second time.

Mrs. McLeod put on a mutinous expression. "Billy's mother died in a fire a few months back, and now the *officer* ..." she spat out the word as if it were something disgusting "... has decided that this helpless little boy is capable of setting fire to the cottage."

"Yes, and that's why he's to come with me," said Sidney. "It's as plain as a pikestaff that the boy is a juvenile delinquent and can't be trusted. Same thing has happened twice. No coincidence. It's obvious he couldn't resist the opportunity to set the place alight again."

"Where are you going to keep Billy? In the cells? His father is going to the hospital in Edinburgh. Who's going to look after a child?" Mrs. McLeod waved to the paramedics who, having strapped Terence to a stretcher, announced their departure, along with the firefighters. The ambulance and fire engine rumbled off.

"See? There they go."

The constable looked uncomfortable, but stood firm. "The law's the law."

He dug into his top pocket and pulled out a small notebook and a pencil. Flipping the notebook open, he licked the tip of his pencil and looked defiantly at Mrs. McLeod. "I am ready to take statements," he announced.

Mrs. McLeod drew herself up to her full height, which wasn't very tall, and went a weird purple color because she was so angry.

"Well, I never," she burst out. "When I think of all the times you used to sit in my kitchen and tuck into a nice tea. I never thought I'd hear you talk like that about a poor defenseless little boy, Sidney Parrott, and I don't care if you're now the Lord Mayor himself, you're not touching this boy."

Mrs. McLeod did look funny with the curlers falling out of her hair and her face all covered in soot. Yet, at the same time, she was rather scary. She took a step toward the constable; he took two quick steps back.

"Arrest him?" she said. "I never heard such nonsense in all my life. He's only eight years old. Why don't you catch some real criminals? What would your poor mother, bless her departed soul, think of your behavior?"

There was an awkward silence. Sidney went bright red at the mention of his mother.

Mrs. Grant folded her arms and interjected, "That's right."

Mrs. McLeod continued her tirade. "Just because you used to run wild about the castle when you were a little boy, Sidney Parrott, don't think that gives you leave to come here putting on airs and graces and try to arrest people who haven't done anything."

Sidney then drew himself up to his full height, which also wasn't very tall, and said, "Are you obstructing me in the course of my police duties? Because if so, Mrs. McLeod, I'm afraid I'll have to place you in custody as well."

There was a frightening silence. Mrs. McLeod's face turned even more purple, as if she were about to explode with rage. She made strange sputtering noises.

Sheldon, distinguished in spite of his smoke-blackened robe and muddied pajamas, stepped forward. "Good evening, Constable Parrott. I can see we have a difficult situation here."

Sidney cast a nervous glance at the angry housekeeper before giving Sheldon a curt nod.

"However," Sheldon continued, "I think I may have a solution that will prove acceptable to all parties concerned."

With the tiniest pinching of his lips, Sidney indicated his willingness to hear the solution.

Sheldon pointed to Billy, now cowering behind Mrs. McLeod, peering around her ample frame with large, frightened eyes. "It would be unwise to lock up this little boy. That sort of thing makes the police appear … er … unsympathetic to the young. You know how the press jumps on these incidents and blows them out of proportion." He frowned. "Police brutality doesn't sound good."

Sidney nodded; Sheldon was right.

"May I suggest you release him into the … ah … custody of the castle household, where he'll be looked after and supervised by three mature staff members? That is, until the matter has been investigated to your satisfaction or until what remaining family he has is advised of the situation. His lordship will be back soon from his fishing trip. I'm sure he'd want to know we *all* did the right thing."

Relieved for a solution that would keep everyone's dignity intact, and mindful that the old earl was particular about matters affecting his staff, Sidney frowned and took a few moments to think.

Then he announced in a solemn voice, "Mr. Sheldon, do you accept the responsibility of Billy Burns until such time as his lordship returns and the matter can be resolved?"

Sheldon replied in an equally solemn voice, "I do."

"There *will* be an official investigation, Mr. Sheldon."

"I should certainly hope so, Constable Parrott."

"Humph," Sidney said, but then he hesitated for a moment.

Sheldon raised a questioning eyebrow.

Sidney straightened his collar and said, "That's that, Mr. Sheldon. I'll be in touch." He strutted off to his car.

They watched him leave, the ramshackle vehicle backfiring as it jolted up the bumpy track.

"Did the constable really play at the castle when he was a little boy?" asked Kim.

"Oh, yes, he did," Mrs. Grant replied. "The old master loves young people and many's the time he'd let the village children ramble about the place, playing hide-and-seek and having fun. Sidney's mother came once a week to help with laundry. She brought Sidney along."

She snorted. "He got into everything. Nosy little beggar."

Mrs. McLeod clutched the trembling boy. "Come along, Billy. How about a nice hot cup of cocoa and then into bed?"

Billy took her hand. "And can I have some cookies with my cocoa?"

"'Course you can, my darling, you can have anything you like."

Hand in hand, the housekeeper and the little boy walked along the path to the castle, two lonely figures silhouetted in the moonlight.

Mrs. Grant dashed after them. "Wait for me, sister."

She caught up to them and slipped one arm around Mrs. McLeod's shoulders as the bedraggled trio trudged back to the castle.

Sheldon coughed. "Sidney was a real handful, pardon my expression."

"What do you mean?" asked Adam.

"Like an eel he was, getting into all the nooks and crannies. He found places we had no idea existed. A couple of times we found him up on the roof, jumping about on the battlements. It was a relief when he outgrew all that." He chuckled as he reminisced. "You wouldn't think he was such a naughty little boy when you see him now. A pillar of the community."

Sheldon suddenly looked tired and much older. His usual sprightly step seemed slower—not surprising after what they had all been through. He gestured toward the cottage. "I think we see how Hamish is doing."

Hamish! Adam suddenly remembered the old man.

Hamish sat alone, a huge bandage covering most of his head and one eye. He wore a large padded neck brace.

Adam dashed up to him. "Are you all right, Hamish?"

Hamish flapped Adam away, his face twisted into a frightening scowl. "I told 'em to leave me be. I don't need no fancy new-fangled stuff. Neck brace, indeed. Huh. I got a bit of a bump on the back and front of my head, that's all. Nothing my bird ointment can't fix."

Kim wrinkled her nose. "Ugh. Do you put smelly bird medicine on yourself, Hamish?"

He glared at her with his remaining good eye and she quailed beneath the ferocious gaze.

"Yes, missy. I put smelly bird medicine on myself. What's good for the birds is good for me, I say." He pulled Adam's sleeve. "The birds came to get you? I was right," he whispered. "I knew it."

Adam wanted ask what he knew, but Hamish staggered to his knees, saying, "The birds need me."

He tried to stand up, but sank back to the ground with a loud groan.

Sheldon arrived just in time to grab his arm. "Come along, Hamish, bedtime for you. The birds are fine. Now if you don't behave yourself and rest, I'll have to ask Bob Hosking from the village to feed your birds."

The explosion that followed indicated Hamish wasn't going to let anyone else near his birds. After securing Athena and Thumbelina in their cages and saying goodnight to the other birds, he and Sheldon tottered off to Hamish's quarters. Strange Scottish words that sounded like bad language floated behind the pair. The kids, filthy, wet, and tired beyond belief, stumbled back to the castle. When they got inside, they heard Mrs. McLeod chivvying Billy off to bed. The kitchen was dark and Jasper's snores indicated the dogs had slept through the commotion. No one had seen Archie, so he had also probably missed the night's excitement.

As they went past the library, Adam noticed the door ajar and a few books on the floor. He stopped, curious, because Sheldon was particular about locking all the doors at night. Neither would Sheldon, in a million years, leave a book on the floor. Adam pushed the door wide open and the most terrible sight met his eyes. The library was a shambles. Books lay scattered on the floor, pictures hung askew, the standing globe was knocked over, cushions were strewn about, and desk drawers lay overturned on the carpet. A set of muddy footprints was clearly visible on the carpet.

"Oh no," Adam whispered. "They've been here already."

exploring the chapel

Adam spent the night tossing and turning. He kept thinking about the ransacked library, and Justin and Kim's shocked faces. What had the person who trashed the library come to steal?

Even Sheldon had looked visibly shocked by the intrusion, but beyond remarking, "The old master will be livid," he had not let anyone into the library to investigate the damage. He had shooed the kids to bed with the advice that things would look better in the morning. Adam wasn't too sure of that. Justin said grumpily that the same huge mess would still be there in the morning and would probably look worse in daylight.

Adam thumped his pillow for what felt like the thousandth time. Although his body was exhausted from the night's events, his mind was awake. Confused thoughts whizzed about in his head, and scenes from the fire played again and again in his mind. Whenever he managed to doze off for a few minutes, the same image materialized—he was bending over a pool of water, looking at his reflection. Behind him was the battle-grimed face of Arthur, leaning over his shoulder and pointing into the water, as if to show him something. But when Adam peered deeper into the water, he woke up.

No one said much at breakfast. Kim and Justin looked as if they had not slept well either. Adam fought back several yawns as he ate his bacon and eggs. Even the usually chatty Mrs. McLeod seemed to have other things on her mind. When she asked them to take care of Billy for her, Justin didn't look too pleased about babysitting, but Billy didn't need much looking after anyway. He seemed recovered from the ordeal of the previous night, and only cried a little when Mrs.

McLeod told him Terence would be in the hospital for a few days and that he was to be a good boy and listen to his new friends.

Sheldon didn't say much more about the mess in the library, except that he would drive down to the village later that day to inform Constable Parrott.

Mrs. McLeod clicked her tongue in annoyance, remarking, "A fat lot of good that will do."

In response, Sheldon mumbled something about an "opportunistic attempted robbery."

"The thieves were probably trying to create a diversion by burning the cottage," said Mrs. Grant as she stacked the breakfast dishes. "I'd bet they were after the silver."

Mrs. McLeod snorted in disbelief. "Nonsense, sister. Anyone who knows the area knows the best silver is locked in the bank vaults in Edinburgh until the castle opens for the tourist season."

Adam thought the thieves had tried to create a diversion by burning the cottage, but they weren't after silver. They were after something much more valuable. The bad part was that no matter who was behind the fire, he and Justin didn't have what they were looking for. They did not have the second stone, if it was Dr. Khalid, and they did not have the book of Arthepius the strange monk was looking for. They also had not found the Scroll of the Ancients yet. They were threatened by enemies and had a whole of nothing on their side. Adam caught Justin staring at him and knew his cousin was thinking the same thing.

The three politely offered to help tidy up the library, but Mrs. Grant said she and Susan —who had popped back from her friends for a few hours to help— would tackle the mammoth task, instructing them to go off and explore the castle grounds some more.

Just before he and the others went off, Adam stuck his head inside the library and spotted Archie sitting on the floor, surrounded by books. Susan was quietly sorting volumes in one corner.

"Come in, Adam," cried Archie, looking pleased about something. He waved a book in the air.

"What's that, sir?"

Adam stepped carefully over the books and cushions strewn across the carpet. He noticed the muddy footprints again. They were much fainter now, mere outlines in fact, because someone had brushed off the surface mud. But they were still visible enough for Adam to see that the footprints led to a bookshelf and then stopped. There were no footprints leading away. It was as if the person had vanished after reaching the shelf. Archie called to him again and Adam forgot about the footprints.

"What a lucky find," Archie said, glowing with excitement. "I've been looking for this rare edition of Horace for years. I always thought James had it, but he said he couldn't remember."

Adam murmured something polite in response and escaped as soon as he could. Rare editions of Horace, whoever he was, were not going to be any use to their quest.

The cousins, Kim, and Billy wandered down to the burnt-out cottage with Sheldon. He had to speak to the investigators who had arrived to track the source of the blaze. They could hear brief fragments of conversation as Sheldon and a few of the firefighters huddled together. The men all looked serious and muttered words like "accelerant," and "burn trail," and "fire barrier." To Adam, it sounded as if someone had poured what one firefighter called "liquid accelerant" (which must be gasoline) through the cottage, along the passage to the front door in a "burn trail," and out onto the porch, creating a "fire barrier" that prevented anyone from escaping. Another firefighter said the smoke had overcome Terence before he could escape through the kitchen door.

Billy hung his head when he saw the blackened shell of his home. He took Kim's hand. His distressed expression showed how he felt.

"Let's get Billy away from here," Kim whispered to Adam. "This is upsetting him."

Sheldon came over. "I think you young people should do something else today. How about visiting the chapel?"

"Sure thing," said Justin, sounding anxious to get away from the depressing scene. "Can we go alone? I thought someone had to row us over."

"Hamish is feeling much better," said Sheldon. "He can take you and then collect you later. Why don't you get Mrs. Grant to make up a picnic basket?"

"Yay!" said Billy, a grin spreading across his freckled face. "I love picnics."

Sheldon said, "It'll take the boy's mind off things, and I'm sure Terence will appreciate your help. Mr. McGillivray's coming this morning to take the horses until the stables are put to rights."

"But not Sirius," said Billy.

237

"Of course not," said Sheldon kindly. "He'll be lonely without you."

On the way back to the castle, Kim and Billy ran ahead so that Billy could show her how fast he ran.

Once they were out of earshot, Adam said to Justin, "This is our chance to check out the hidden passage."

"What hidden passage?"

"The one I saw on the castle plans. Remember, there was a line running from the castle to the stables and then one running from the stables to the chapel. I'm sure there's a passage straight from the castle to the chapel as well."

Justin stopped. "You heard what Ink said. It was just a crease in the paper, not a line. Anyway, the line from the castle to the stables was marked, so it definitely exists and everyone has heard of it. The other lines are just your imagination."

Adam felt his cheeks burn. "It was not my imagination. I know what I saw. I saw two lines, real lines. Okay, they were very faint, but they were there."

Justin gave a scornful laugh as he continued walking. "Ink didn't believe you. That's why he didn't bother to get a magnifying glass from Sheldon to check it out properly. Don't make things up."

Adam wanted to shake Justin hard. He got so mad when Justin put on his mocking voice, as if he were years older than Adam.

"No," Adam reminded him, "he didn't ask Sheldon because that monk guy broke in and then we found Bedwyr's diary, which started a bunch of other things. And then Archie arrived. Ink just forgot."

Justin shrugged and walked faster. "Whatever."

He sounded bored.

Mrs. Grant was happy to make them a picnic basket. Justin supervised the packing of the contents, making sure she included all his favorite treats.

"Do you want some of this bottled water or fruit juice?" she asked.

"Bottled water?" Justin pulled a face. "No way. We'd rather have juice." He looked at the others who nodded.

Mrs. Grant held up a bottle of water. "I don't know what the world's coming to these days. Paying for water in a bottle when the council supplies perfectly good water already, straight from the tap."

"Money, Mrs. Grant," said Sheldon, who was busy polishing yet another candlestick. "It's all about money, and people are such sheep they'll go for any new trend. Baaa!"

They all giggled at his sheep imitation. Then Adam asked, "Did you buy this water, Mrs. Grant?"

"*Buy?*" She gave a disgusted snort. "Of course not. What an idea. Some young lad dropped a whole crate of it off this morning. Said he was delivering for a company called Highland Spring Bottled Water. It's a free sample, he said, for a big promotional launch later this month."

"If it's for free, then we'd better drink it," said Sheldon, peering at his tiny reflection in the base of the candlestick.

Mrs. Grant closed the picnic basket and folded up a tartan rug for them to sit on. "All packed. Enjoy yourselves."

Hamish was unusually subdued as he rowed them across the lake. His neck brace must have been uncomfortable because he kept tugging at it. He still wore the bandage on his head.

Once they had hopped out of the boat and onto the shore, Hamish said, "I'll be back here in a few hours. Don't be late. The mist rises quickly. It'll be as thick as pea soup by four o'clock."

Although it was a bright, sunny day, a cold shiver ran down Adam's spine when Hamish mentioned mist. He thought about Arthur's face reflected in the water in his most recent dream.

They walked up shore until they found a shady tree, and left the picnic basket and rug underneath. The island wasn't large; they walked around it in about half an hour. Billy dashed ahead as if he knew the place well. The chapel sat right in the middle of the island, surrounded by occasional trees, shrubs, and masses of wildflowers. A section of well-tended lawn fringing the chapel separated the property from the outlying vegetation. Adam imagined it could be quite spooky at night, especially wherever the trees clustered together, creating dark shadows.

Justin led the way along a white-pebbled path to the chapel. "Okay, guys, this is it. One haunted chapel coming up."

Adam looked up at the front of the building. Gargoyles lined the rooftop, waterspouts jutting from their mouths. They had hideously ugly faces, with eyes staring blindly ahead. A sinister aura hung about the stone guardians.

Kim looked frightened. "What do you mean by haunted?"

"The whole area is haunted, judging by what Sheldon says. If it isn't the Headless Horseman, it's the Gray Lady, and the other one he mentioned."

Kim shivered. "I'm sure ghosts don't come out during the day."

"This place is haunted, too," said Billy. He went red when Justin stared at him.

"How do you know? You're just a kid," said Justin.

"Yeah, but some nights a funny light goes around the tower," said Billy.

Justin rolled his eyes and glanced at Adam. "A funny light? Yeah, right, little ghost buster." He strode into the chapel.

"Don't be so mean," Adam said, keeping pace with his cousin. "He's only eight."

"Exactly. What does an eight-year-old know? He probably thinks his bedtime stories are true and there's a troll under the bed."

Adam shrugged. Justin was in one of his moods again. It was no use talking to him then. Adam looked about. They were standing inside the main entrance. The chapel was actually a lot bigger than Adam had imagined. This building was unusual, not like their local church back home. Only Billy didn't seem to notice anything special. They walked through the arched doorway and into the cooler interior.

"Why is it called the ruined chapel?" Kim said. "This place looks fine to me."

Kim had a point. The chapel didn't look at all ruined. In fact, it was in good shape. Adam noticed a pile of brochures inside the doorway. He grabbed one.

"Maybe this will tell us." He quickly scanned the pages. "It says here, '*The chapel, believed to have been built in AD 1000 along with the original castle donjon, was a simple structure with little adornment. In 1303, while Scotland struggled to achieve independence, the castle and surrounding areas were taken by the English.*'"

He continued reading silently for a few seconds, and then said, "The Scots thumped the English and the earl took back the castle. Somehow, the chapel was damaged. '*A stray cannonball flattened part of the South Aisle, and a section of the*

240

Baptistery collapsed. Locals continued to call it the ruined chapel, even though it was rebuilt forty years later, in 1343, to what it is now. Most of the original chapel still exists, the stones dating back to AD 1000.'"

"That's no help," said Justin. "If Bedwyr was alive in 1296, like he mentioned in his diary, then the place was rebuilt years after he died. So, if he hid the Scroll of the Ancients here somewhere, it's likely to be covered in paving stones or tombs."

He pointed to a side section where carved stone effigies of several knights and ladies lay on the ground. "See? Mediaeval graves. Those guys could be buried on top of Bedwyr's hiding place."

"What makes you think the scroll is hidden here?" asked Kim. "There's a whole castle we haven't even explored properly yet."

"Because, dummy," Justin said with exaggerated patience, "this is the most likely place. People have been living in the castle since the year 1000. If the scroll was there, I'm convinced someone would have found it by now."

He glanced around. "I wonder which parts are original, not rebuilt."

"I can show you." Billy had an impish expression.

Justin gave the boy a cold stare, but Billy didn't flinch. "Don't make up stories now, Billy."

"Come with me." Billy led them toward the altar.

As they walked, Adam noticed that every inch of the chapel was bursting with carvings, depicting everything from Biblical scenes to leaves and vines, and from angels to devils and gargoyles. Ornately decorated fluted columns lined the various sections.

Kim frowned and then stopped. "This is a really odd church."

Adam went to her side. "What's up?"

"Don't you think it's strange to see all these angels and Biblical things and then right next to it fairytale stuff?" Kim pointed to a pillar. Above the length of the column was a series of carvings. "Look there. Weird carvings on the top bit, whatever it's called."

They all looked up to see unicorns, dragons, grotesque goblin-like creatures, and several strange, grinning faces with leaves around them. Lichen had grown over some of the leaves, giving the impression of living foliage.

241

Adam consulted the brochure again. "The top bit of the column is called a 'capital.' Those leafy faces represent the Green Man, which is a pagan symbol of life. He's kind of cute."

"That's nothing," said Justin. "Look up higher."

Four sets of eyes turned toward the ceiling, which had been carved by craftsmen of centuries ago into patterns of stars and flowers.

"This is a strange place," said Adam, "but it's magnificent."

The sun blazed through stained-glass windows along the sides of the chapel, casting smudges of jeweled colors onto the flagstones.

Billy tugged at Kim's hand. "Come on." He led the way to the altar, and then turned sharp left and went down several stairs. Facing them was the wall of an ancient tower, its stones pitted and marked by time. But it had no doorway.

Justin walked toward the section jutting into the chapel. "What's this?"

"It's a tower," said Billy. "It's from the old part of the chapel. If you go outside, you'll see it looks just like this all the way around. It's closed up, though. You can't get inside."

"Then what's the point?" Adam asked.

Billy shrugged. "Dunno."

They walked back to the central section of the chapel and looked up at the ceiling again. Something hung from the middle of the ceiling. It looked like an arrowhead aiming down at them.

Billy pointed to it. "That's also an old part."

"How do you know all this?" asked Kim.

Billy blinked, as if surprised. "Hamish told me, of course. He's my friend and he knows everything about the castle."

Adam read from the brochure. "That's called the 'pendant keystone.' I wonder what it's for."

They all squinted hard, trying to see the carving on the keystone.

"If it's a keystone," said Kim, "then maybe it's a key."

Justin laughed. "Don't be silly. How can it be a key?"

"I meant a *symbolic* key, dummy," said Kim, rather coldly. "Not a real key."

Justin stopped laughing. "Yeah, of course. You may be right."

Although they looked at it for several minutes, no one had any ideas about its true purpose.

Adam glanced down at his feet. "That's it." He pointed to the floor. "There's the key. Kim's right. It's symbolic."

A large, seven-pointed star was carved into the flagstones. The star extended several feet in all directions. The star sat in a circle, and in each section formed by the arms of the star were strange symbols. However, hundreds of years of feet walking on the surface had worn away the carvings so they appeared too faint to distinguish any details.

The keystone pointed directly at an image in the middle of the star, but none of them could make it out. The star shape seemed somehow familiar to Adam, but he couldn't think why.

"This is a dead end," said Justin. "Let's eat."

Kim and Adam laid out the tartan rug on the grass while Billy and Justin unpacked the food. Mrs. Grant had provided a feast. For the next thirty minutes, there wasn't much talking as they ate and drank. A sense of peace enveloped the little group. Sunshine filtered through the branches overhead, birds sang, and waves lapped gently against the lakeshore. Dr. Khalid and any other growing threat seemed far away.

When Adam had finished eating, he paged through the chapel brochure again.

"What are you looking for?" asked Kim.

"Some information on the crypt with Bedwyr's memorial stone."

"I can show you the crypt," said Billy, stuffing his mouth full of hard-boiled egg. "But you can't go in."

"Why not?" asked Adam.

"'Cause it's locked up now." He swallowed the egg and wiped bits of yolk off his chin with the back of one hand. "There's a gate with a notice."

"Billy seems to know the place well," Kim murmured to Adam.

Justin had fallen asleep with a half-eaten slice of cake in his hand. A curious bee buzzed above his head. Kim, Billy, and Adam tiptoed back into the chapel, where Billy led them through the ranks of ornate columns to another shallow set of stairs. At the bottom was a padlocked wrought-iron gate. The notice on the gate said that due to renovations the crypt was closed until further notice.

Adam was disappointed. "I wanted to see Bedwyr's memorial stone."

"But he's not there," Billy said.

Kim shot a worried look at Adam. "Who's not there?"

243

"Bedwyr."

Adam remembered their first conversation about Bedwyr with the adults. No one had seemed willing to say anything about where he was buried.

Curious as to what Billy's answer would be, Adam asked, "So if he's not there, then where is he?"

Billy shrugged. "Dunno. But I've seen his ghost."

A chill ran down Adam's spine.

"There are no such things as ghosts, Billy," he said gently. "It's just made-up stories for fun. Maybe you heard Sheldon telling his ghost tales and thought you saw a ghost."

A wide, buoyant grin stretched across Billy's freckled face. "'Course there are ghosts. I saw Sir Maulsby once. Phew! What a big horse he's got."

Kim and Adam glanced at each other over Billy's head. Kim tapped the side of her head and rolled her eyes. Adam wondered if maybe Billy wasn't all there. He must have heard Mrs. Grant talking about the last time anyone had seen Sir Maulsby, back in 1998. Obviously, he must also have heard Sheldon tell the story.

"Now, Billy," Adam began, "you know that's impossible—"

"No, it's not," Billy interrupted. "It's best at full moon. Easier to see ghosts. I also saw Bedwyr once."

Adam froze. Behind Billy's back, Kim was shaking her head and twirling one finger in the air.

"What did he look like?" Adam asked.

Billy shrugged again. "Dunno. He had a hoodie on."

"A hoodie?"

"Yeah." Billy looked up at Adam. "You know, a hoodie. A brown one."

"Was he scary?" asked Adam. "Were you afraid?"

"'Course not." Billy gave another grin. A confident grin. "He wouldn't hurt *me*."

"Okay, Billy," Adam said kindly to appease him. "Wow. That must have been amazing."

"Yup," said Billy. "I want more cake."

Kim and Adam stared after the small figure as Billy dashed off.

"That kid has some serious problems," she said. "He must have seen a tourist in a brown hoodie and thought it was Bedwyr's ghost." Her eyes widened.

"Or … hey! Maybe he saw one of the monk creatures. The guy with the poison powder?"

"I hope not," said Adam. He couldn't quite shake off the feeling that Billy was telling the truth. But was it the real truth or simply what Billy had thought he'd seen?

They heard Justin calling, "Hamish is here. Come on, let's go."

Long shadows fell across the shore as they ran down to the boat. It seemed as if no time at all had passed, but they had been on the island for most of the day. Mist covered the lake in a pale blanket that grew thicker and colder with each stroke of Hamish's oars. Hamish didn't say much besides a mumbled, "Enjoy yourselves, then?" When they reached the mainland, he hauled the boat onto the shore and stumped off in the direction of the mews.

Adam felt incredibly tired after their day out. The others looked exhausted, too. Billy kept yawning and Kim's eyelids were heavy. They trudged over the drawbridge with leaden feet. Adam wanted to collapse into bed and sleep for a week. Dusk was falling and the castle was quiet. Too quiet. No pots and pans clanging in the kitchen or Sheldon whistling as he often did. No delicious smells wafting from the kitchen as usual. They dropped the picnic basket and rug in the hallway and went through to the library to find Archie. The place was empty. Archie must have gone up to his room. Most of the books had been put away, although several shelves were still empty. The furniture and cushions were back in their rightful places. Mrs. Grant and Susan must have worked the whole day tidying up.

Justin flopped into a chair and yawned.

"Wow, I'm pooped." He stretched out his arms. "I don't think I can manage dinner after all I've eaten today."

He leaned back and eyed Adam. "I could go to sleep right here."

Adam had a bad feeling. "Where's everyone? Where are the dogs?" A cold sensation clutched his heart. *The dogs!*

He ran to the kitchen, calling, "Jasper? Smudge? Here, boys, we're back."

When he reached the kitchen, the shock of what he saw hit him like a massive blow in the chest. His knees went weak and he clutched the edge of the kitchen table to steady himself. Mrs. Grant and Mrs. McLeod lay next to each other on the floor. Sheldon was slumped in a chair, with his head on the kitchen table and a cup of tea near one hand, as if he had fallen asleep while reaching for it. For one terrible moment, Adam thought the adults were dead. Then Sheldon gave a gusty snore. They were unconscious. Kim, Billy, and Justin burst through the door together. Billy's freckled face was bobbing under Kim's elbow. Adam stepped in front of Kim so Billy couldn't see the adults.

"Get Billy out of here," Adam told her.

Kim hustled Billy back into the hallway. "Billy, I need you to run down to Hamish as fast as you can," she said. "Tell him we need him right away."

"Okay." Billy ran off.

Justin and Adam knelt next to the two women. Justin said, "I can hear them breathing so they must be all right."

The cook and the housekeeper were sprawled on the floor, but looked as if they were simply dozing. Their faces were peaceful and their breathing steady as they slept. Mrs. Grant gave an occasional gentle snort. Susan must've left already.

Adam got to his feet and opened the scullery door. Both dogs lay curled in Jasper's basket, fast asleep. Adam stroked their heads, but neither animal stirred. He looked at Justin. "They must have been drugged … but with what?"

Kim pointed to where a large bottle of Highland Spring Bottled Water lay on the floor, its contents flowing onto the tiles.

"It must be the water. Didn't Mrs. Grant say some guy dropped off a crate for us to sample?"

Justin sat down on a kitchen chair. When he spoke, his voice quavered. "So, if we'd taken water with us instead of juice, we'd also be unconscious."

Adam wanted to add "and defenseless," but he didn't say anything. He swallowed. His throat suddenly felt dry and tight. He grabbed a chair before his knees totally gave out.

Just then, Billy burst into the kitchen. "Hamish is sleeping. I shook him hard, but he won't wake up."

Adam met Justin's frightened gaze. So whoever had done this had gotten to Hamish as well. Everyone must have tasted the water, and Hamish had done so just minutes earlier.

"Why's everyone sleeping?" Billy was puzzled. "Are they all tired?"

Kim gave a big yawn, sat on a kitchen chair, and extended her arms above her head. "Yes. Me too."

She looked at Justin and Adam. They both immediately gave huge yawns and exaggerated stretches as well.

"Hey!" Kim grabbed Billy by the shoulders. "I just thought about Sirius."

At the mention of the horse's name, Billy's face, which had been crumpling into tearful confusion, cleared.

"He must be so lonely down in the old shed by himself," Kim said, "without all his friends. Maybe you should spend a bit of time with him before you go to bed."

The boy grinned. "Sure thing, Kim. I haven't seen Sirius today."

"I bet he's missing you," she said. "You can tell him about our picnic."

Billy grabbed an apple from the fruit bowl on the table. "I'll take him this. See you later." He dashed out of the kitchen.

There was the light thud of his feet down the hall and the bang of the front door closing. Then all was quiet.

"Well done," said Adam. "That gets him safely out of the way for a while." He looked at Justin. "What are we going to do now?"

Before Justin could speak, Kim leaned forward. "I know. I think—"

Justin stood, almost knocking his chair over.

"I don't care what you think. No one cares what you think. I'm sick of you butting into stuff that doesn't concern you. You shouldn't even be here anyway. This is our adventure and you're in the way."

Adam opened his mouth in protest, but Justin turned on him. "Stay out of it, Adam. You're always sticking up for her."

Kim looked stunned at Justin's outburst. Her chair scraped the floor loudly as she stood. "I can see you have a big problem with me, Justin."

Her voice was cold. Adam thought she might burst into tears at Justin's nasty words, but she didn't.

"I knew you'd never accept me being on this trip," she said. "That's okay. You and Adam can sort out this mess because actually I don't even want to be here."

Adam jumped up, but Justin pushed him down hard in his seat.

"Thanks for being my friend, Adam," Kim continued. "But you don't need to take my side anymore."

She gazed at Justin with a look of pity. "I wish you could hear yourself bossing people, throwing your weight around, saying hurtful things." She looked him up and down, her expression scornful. "It's sad because I think that without your super-size ego getting in the way, you could possibly be a nice person. Looks like there's not much chance of that." Kim turned on her heel and left the kitchen.

Adam jumped up again. This time, Justin left him alone.

"What's wrong with you?" Adam burst out. "There was no need to be so nasty to Kim."

Justin went red. He sat in his chair and folded his arms on the table. "I'm glad she's out of the way."

Adam felt an unstoppable wave of anger rising inside him, making his head pound. Why was Justin was acting so oddly?

"She's not out of the way. Kim is only going to her room so, in case you hadn't thought that far ahead, she is still in as much danger as you and me and Billy." He waved one hand at the sleeping adults. "In as much danger as everybody else."

Justin glared at him. "Oh, I see now. We used to be friends, but I'm not good enough since Kim's been around." Justin's face had a shuttered look, as if nothing would get through to him. "She's turned everyone against me, including you."

"No, that's not true, Justin. In fact, the only one who has turned anyone against you is *you*." Adam went to the kitchen door. "Now I'm going to do what you should be doing."

"Oh? And what's that?"

"I'm going to apologize to Kim for what you said. You're so stupid, you haven't even thought about what she'll say to Aunt Isabel. You were supposed to be in charge of both of us, remember? Short memory you have. All you care about is telling people what to do. I can see you don't want any *real* responsibility. Anyway, I'm not getting into trouble just because you don't have any manners."

Justin laughed sarcastically. "Run off then and say sorry, you groveling little traitor. Scared of Aunt Isabel, hey?"

Adam suppressed the urge to give Justin a big punch in the nose. "No, I'm not scared of Aunt Isabel. I just know how it feels to be bullied and laughed at. You can do as you please."

He glared at Justin. "I don't know what's the matter with you these days, but you aren't the same as when we were in Egypt. One minute you're fine, then you're mean. It's no fun being with you anymore."

Adam headed for the staircase and then heard footsteps behind him. Justin gripped his arm.

"Wait. I'm sorry."

Adam shook off Justin's grasp. "No, you're not. You just want me back on your side."

Adam dashed up the stairs. As he reached Kim's door, Justin grabbed his arm again. "I really am sorry. I shouldn't have said those things."

Adam slapped Justin's hand away. "Leave me alone. I don't believe anything you say. If you know you shouldn't have said those things, then why did you?"

Justin's face was ashen. "I didn't mean it."

Adam ignored Justin and knocked gently on Kim's door. "Hey, Kim. Open up. It's me, Adam. Let me in and we can talk."

No answer. He turned the door handle. The door was locked.

Justin knocked a few times. "Kim, it's Justin. I'm sorry I was such a moron. Please come out."

Silence.

He looked at Adam. "See? Now she's being unreasonable. You can't say I didn't try."

Infuriated by Justin's smug tone, Adam exploded. "Just shut up! Shut up, do you hear me?" He pushed Justin hard in the chest. "When are you going to stop being such a jerk?"

Justin stepped back. "Okay, okay. Cool it." He raised his hands. "Look, I surrender."

Adam let out his breath in a big angry puff. "She might be asleep. Let's open the door through our room."

"Yeah, okay, good idea."

They went to their room and opened the interleading door, using the key hanging on the hook by the door. Kim's room was empty.

"Where'd she go?" Justin asked. A worried frown furrowed his brow.

"I don't know," said Adam. "This room's a mess. That's not like Kim. She's super-tidy."

A chair lay on its side and one curtain hung off the rail. The quilt was half on the floor. It looked as if there had been a struggle.

"She's been kidnapped," Adam said, voicing this terrible thought.

"How?" asked Justin. "The door is locked."

"The kidnapper must have locked the door on his way out. Maybe to delay us, to make us think Kim didn't want to come out for a while."

"To gain time," Justin said.

"But who is it?" asked Adam. "Is it those weird monks or is it—" He didn't want to acknowledge the fact that Dr. Khalid might be the kidnapper.

Justin said, "But why would the monks even bother with Kim? We know what they want. They said if we give them the book of Arthy-whoever, they would leave us alone."

"They also said if we don't give it to them, which we can't because we don't have it, they would do something horrible," said Adam. "Not to me because of the mark, but they said my friends must beware."

Adam suddenly remembered Archie. "We haven't seen Archie for hours, not since this morning. We'd better check on him."

They ran down the passage to Archie's room. It was empty but also showed signs of a struggle with clothes and books scattered across the floor, including the rare edition of Horace that Archie had been so excited to find.

Justin glanced around. "Seems like the intruder was looking for something. I wonder why they thought Archie would have it."

The plump historian had been terrified at the thought of confronting Dr. Khalid, which meant that somehow Archie knew something about their rival.

"There must be some sort of connection," Adam said slowly as he sat on the rumpled bed. He rubbed his eyes. "If only we knew what it is. Maybe it's Archie's knowledge of history? Humphrey said he's an expert on fifth and sixth century Britain.

Justin sank onto the bed next to him. "Yeah." His voice sounded so forlorn that Adam decided to patch up the quarrel.

"Let's be friends, okay? There's no time now to fight about who said what. We need to rescue Kim and Archie from whoever has got them before something worse happens."

Justin flashed him a huge, happy smile. "Cool." Then his smile faded. "Thanks," he added.

"No problem." Adam gave him a light punch on the arm. "Billy will be back soon. We're going to have to get him out of the way again."

"How?"

Adam gathered up the quilt from the bed. "I have a plan."

Justin raised his eyebrows.

Adam winked as he shoved the quilt into Justin's arms. "Didn't you just love camping when you were little?"

They went back to the kitchen. The adults and dogs were still sleeping. Adam shoved a carton of fruit juice, a few apples, some carrots, and a packet of ginger cookies into a large canvas carrier bag. He also popped in several muffins and a small meat pie. He was just in time; Billy came running through the front door as the cousins strolled into the hallway.

Adam ruffled Billy's hair. "Hey, Billy. How's Sirius?"

"He was so happy to see me, Adam." Billy's face glowed. "I wish I could stay with him tonight. I could make a bed in the straw."

Adam glanced at Justin. "That's exactly what we were thinking." He held up the carrier bag. "Why don't you have a midnight feast with Sirius and sleep in the old shed tonight?"

Billy's eyes widened. "Can I? Wow! But won't Mrs. McLeod say no?"

Justin folded up the quilt and put it into the carrier bag.

"She says it's fine because poor old Sirius is alone," said Adam, feeling horrible for lying.

"Yay," Billy squealed. "Can I stay the *whole* night?"

Justin feigned a mock serious expression. "You won't be scared, will you?"

"'Course not," said Billy loftily. "I'll have Sirius to protect me. My dad *always* lets me sleep in the big stables."

Justin just looked at him.

Billy grinned. "Okay. Sometimes." He grabbed the carrier bag and ran off, yelling, "Woo-hoo." The front door banged behind him again.

"So that's why he was in the stables when the cottage was set on fire," Justin said. "Lucky his dad let him sleep there that night. I don't think we could have gotten both of them out in time."

What if something had happened to Billy? Adam shuddered to think. *Something could still happen.*

Justin read Adam's expression. "Don't worry. No one will try anything with Sirius. Have you seen the size of those hooves?"

When Adam didn't reply, Justin added, "He's a country boy, remember? He knows this place better than either of us." He looked about. "Where should we start looking for Kim and Archie?"

Adam remembered the faint footprints he had seen on the library carpet, footprints that stopped right at the bookcase. "The library."

Justin grabbed his arm. "Before we go, let's check on the others. We should cover Mrs. Grant and Mrs. McLeod. They'll catch cold lying on that stone floor."

They took the picnic rug from the basket they had left in the hallway and went to the kitchen. They covered the two women, who continued to sleep peacefully. Adam leaned over Sheldon to check he was still breathing.

The butler opened one eye. His voice was hoarse as he tried to speak. "The gree ... ma ... the gree ... ma ..."

"Don't worry, Sheldon, we'll get help as soon as we can," said Adam. "Archie and Kim have been kidnapped so we're going to rescue them first."

Sheldon gripped Adam's hand hard as he lifted his head a few inches off the table. "Gree ... ma ..." He slumped back down, his eyes closed.

Adam stared at the unconscious man. "Do you think they'll be all right?"

Justin said, "If anyone wanted them dead, they would have killed them, not drugged them."

"I wish we could call the police or an ambulance," Adam said.

"The telephone is still not working. Anyway, look what happened last time the police came. Constable Parrott wanted to arrest Billy. If we called him this time, he'd lock *us* up and then we wouldn't have a chance to rescue Kim and Archie, and solve this mystery."

Adam nodded slowly.

"Come on." Justin pulled Adam's sleeve. "We can do this."

The boys ran to the library where Adam pointed to the footprints on the carpet. Mrs. McLeod and Susan had brushed most of the mud off, but faint outlines remained. They followed the prints to the bookcase and stopped.

"This leads nowhere," said Justin. "The guy must have flown away."

Adam noticed something carved into the back panel of the shelf, level with his eyes. A grinning, impish face, surrounded by leaves and vines, looked back at him.

"The Green Man."

"What?"

Adam touched the carving with trembling fingers.

"That's what Sheldon meant. The Green Man. I read about him in the brochure at the chapel. Some kind of nature spirit."

Justin peered at it. "Great. What now?"

Adam pressed on the carving and wasn't at all surprised when part of the bookshelf swung inward, revealing the top step of a stone stairway that led down into total blackness.

INK LEARNS THE TRUTH

Ink pushed open the door of Humphrey's hospital room. Amelia sat next to the bed, leaning forward, her head and one arm resting on the quilt. She was asleep. Humphrey lay still and white. He seemed to have shrunk, now smaller and frailer than Ink had ever seen him. His arms, as withered as two old sticks, rested on top of the quilt. On the bedside table sat a basket of uneaten fruit. Sudden tears pricked the inside of Ink's eyelids. He blinked hard several times.

As he approached the bed, something glittered in Amelia's hand. A gold locket dangled off the edge of the bed. He gently pulled the chain out of Amelia's fingers to stop the locket from falling to the floor. Curious, he opened it. The picture inside came as a shock. It could have been him. The same thatch of black hair standing on end, the same dark eyes, and the same long face and pale skin. Then it dawned on him. He knew who it was. He closed the locket and gently shook Amelia. She lifted her head, still sleepy. Her eyes widened when she saw what he was holding. She reached out for it, but Ink pulled his hand away.

"This is my real father." He said it as a fact, not a question, as he dangled the locket in the air. "And you're my real mother. Aren't you?"

Amelia nodded and he gave her the locket. Amelia clasped the chain around her neck and tucked the locket beneath her blouse. She looked exhausted and strangely untidy, as if she had flung on her clothes higgledy-piggledy.

"I should have told you years ago, but you were so happy with Humphrey that I didn't see the need. I also thought you weren't ready to know the truth about your father."

Ink pulled up a chair. "I'm ready now."

255

Although his voice was calm, Ink's insides were churning. Would he hear good or bad?

Amelia cast a quick glance at the bed to check that Humphrey was still asleep. She lifted her shoulders in a tired gesture. "Where do I begin?"

"The beginning is usually a good place."

Amelia reached down for her handbag on the floor and fumbled in it for a tissue. "Twenty years ago, I was just married to Bartholomew Blott, a researcher of ancient Greek manuscripts."

"My father."

"Your father."

Ink felt strange, slightly dizzy. Amelia, whom he had known all his life, who had turned out to be his mother, was now sitting next to him telling him about his dead father. Somehow, the news didn't surprise him. It was as if he had always known the truth deep down. In a weird way, it even seemed to be the most natural thing in the world. He was glad about that.

"How did he die?"

Amelia dabbed her eyes with the tissue. "He was killed during a research trip to Greece. An explosion occurred while he was working in a library in Athens and the bookshelves collapsed on him. People said it was a gas explosion triggered by an earth tremor, but I wasn't convinced."

Ink frowned. "Why not?"

"Your father's last letter said he'd made an astounding discovery that would transform our lives and circumstances. He said it would change history and that some people might not like it."

Ink felt uneasy. "What people?"

Amelia shrugged. "I don't know, but after what I've seen working all these years for Humphrey, I know some people would kill to get their hands on valuable manuscripts."

"Where was I?"

Amelia gave him a watery smile. "On your way. I didn't know I was pregnant. It was a scary situation because my parents didn't even know we were married."

"Why not?"

"It was a long time ago and my parents were extremely conservative. Your father had nothing and that's why they would never have approved of our marriage.

I thought that your father's discovery would bring him the recognition he wanted and my parents' acceptance. Then it would be all right that we were married."

Ink shifted in his chair. "But it didn't work out that way."

"Does it ever?"

"What happened next?"

"I stayed with an aunt of mine, who was happy to help, and after you were born I decided to find you a new family. Someone who could give you a better life."

Ink sighed. "I know the rest of the story."

Amelia looked away. "Yes, you do." She tucked a stray curl behind one ear.

Ink said, "Did you come to work for Humphrey to keep an eye on me?"

"That's right. I was confident he and Pandora would give you a wonderful life, but I didn't want to miss out on seeing you grow up."

At her words, Ink broke into a smile, remembering how, puffing and panting, Humphrey had once struggled to kick a football with him, and then had opted to go inside and teach him to read from old books.

"I guess you were still there as my mother. I mean, I always tell people you're like a mother to me."

"Are you angry with me?"

Tears finally broke through and trickled down Ink's cheeks. He rubbed his eyes with the back of one hand. "Don't be silly."

He gave her a quick hard hug. "Must I call you Mom now?"

Amelia sounded almost indignant. "Of course not. What would people think?"

"Did you ever tell your parents? My grandparents, I mean?"

Amelia smoothed out several creases in the quilt. She didn't answer right away.

"No, it didn't seem necessary. I was so happy when Humphrey adopted you. You were doing well in your new life. Then once they died, I realized I had kept the truth from everyone for too long—including you. And I just kept putting it off. Until now."

Ink rocked back in the chair, with his hands behind his head. "I wonder what my father discovered that was so important."

"I don't think you should worry about that now." Amelia sounded flustered. "I mean, after so many years it probably isn't as significant as he imagined."

Ink looked at her. "How can you say that?"

"I mean—" She flapped her hands in a nervous gesture. "I mean there's so much happening that it's not important right now. Anyway, the people he was working with sent me a box of his books, some artifacts, and documents he had collected in Greece. They were so kind. You can dig through his stuff and keep whatever you like."

Ink grinned. "Cool. I'd like that." Then he noticed a large buff envelope on the bed. Amelia must have been leaning on it. "What's that?"

"It's for you."

Ink wrinkled his nose. "And the cheesy medallion?"

Amelia carefully peeled the sticky tape from the envelope and handed the pendant and chain to him. "I think that's meant for you as well."

Ink laughed. "There's no way I'm wearing this horrible thing. It looks like a hippie emblem."

Amelia peered at it. "No, it's not. It looks like a kind of dog." She hastily added, "I think Humphrey wanted you to have this. You see, he hid it away before the intruder came in and attacked him. I found it behind the sofa cushions when I tidied up. It's probably important."

Ink slipped the chain over his head and shoved the medallion out of sight under his T-shirt. "Well, if that's what Dad wanted." He stopped and looked at Amelia. "I meant to say …"

"I know what you mean. Bartholomew was your father, but Humphrey's your dad."

Relieved, Ink smiled at her. "How's he doing?"

They both gazed anxiously at the still form on the bed.

"The doctors say he is stable, although not out of danger yet. We'll have to wait and see."

Amelia gave him the envelope. "I'm glad you came, but quite frankly I'd feel better if you went back to Scotland to finish what needs to be done. Those children must be at risk."

Ink slipped the envelope inside his jacket. "I'll leave right away. I just had to check on Humphrey myself."

He hugged Amelia and tiptoed out.

Amelia sat down again and clasped Humphrey's hand. His wrinkled fingers were cold and still in hers.

Pandora came into the room. "Was that Ink I saw running down the passage in such a hurry?"

Amelia nodded. "He's on his way back to Scotland."

"Did you tell him?"

"I had to, Pandora."

Pandora plumped down on the chair next to Amelia. "Well, I'm glad. It's about time the truth came out." She stared at Amelia. "You didn't tell him everything, did you?"

"No, I couldn't. Not with what he's facing back in Scotland."

"Good girl." Pandora opened her bulky handbag and shook out the large gray mass of wool. "I've brought my knitting. Why don't you get some rest? I'll watch Humphrey."

the secret passage

Justin stuck his head into the dark aperture behind the bookshelf. "Phew. Cold and damp down there. We'll need a light."

He went back to the desk and rummaged in the drawers. "Here." He held up a small flashlight. "This must be the only one in the whole castle."

He shone the faint beam down the stone steps. "Remember Sheldon said the tunnel began under the old tower?"

Adam nodded. "Yep."

Justin glanced at him. "Well, I bet one of James' ancestors found that tunnel and dug this one to join up with the original tunnel."

Adam eyed the opening. "Maybe it was the guy who divided the banqueting hall into the library and ballroom. That could be the reason for all the wood paneling and bookshelves in the library—to hide the entrance."

"Could be," said Justin. "That's what Kim thought."

Adam and Justin trod carefully down what seemed the narrowest flight of stone steps in existence. It reminded Adam of how they had sneaked into the basement of the Egyptian Museum in Cairo and had discovered Dr. Khalid's antiques smuggling ring. But this stairway seemed to go on forever and the farther down they went, the colder and damper it became. The chill raised goose bumps on Adam's arms. Like Justin, he was only wearing a light T-shirt and jeans. He wished he had thought to grab a jacket before they had wandered through the secret door in the library.

Justin led the way, the beam from the flashlight casting a feeble glow in the enveloping blackness. The crumbling steps were slippery with moss. Adam nearly lost his footing several times. Finally, the stairs ended in a narrow passageway leading into impenetrable darkness.

"Okay?" Justin's voice sounded hollow in Adam's ear.

"Sure."

However, Adam felt unsure of what awaited them. He put one hand in his pocket and felt the comforting shape of his scarab.

"Then let's go." Justin disappeared ahead into the gloom and Adam hurried to catch up. His left hand trailed against the wall nearest him. After walking for a while, Adam noticed the stones felt wet in places where moisture trickled down the walls. Their sneakers squelched as they tramped through puddles.

"There's water down here," said Adam.

"Yeah, I also noticed that." Justin didn't seem concerned. "We must be near the lake."

Adam stopped. "The lake?" A drop of water plopped onto his head. He looked up. The next drop hit him on the cheek.

Justin's voice grew fainter as he strode ahead. "There *is* a secret passage leading from the castle under the lake to the chapel. This must be it."

He sounded excited, as if it was all his idea in the first place.

Adam walked faster. He imagined water pouring through the walls, flooding the passage and drowning them. "What if the passage collapses? What's stopping the water from leaking in?"

Justin sounded confident. "If it was built so long ago and hasn't conked in yet then it's not likely to, unless someone blows it up with dynamite." He thumped the wall next to him. "Feels solid enough to me. The Romans built under water, remember?"

Adam couldn't remember, but it sounded promising. "What did they use?"

"They invented a kind of cement that hardened under water by adding crushed volcanic ash to lime. They used it for building harbors."

Adam saw water dripping everywhere. "Uh … do you think the Middle Ages builders used it as well?"

Justin's laughter floated back to him. "Stop worrying. What's the worst that can happen?"

Adam could think of a whole list of terrible things with drowning at the top. He said nothing, however, as he didn't want Justin to make fun of him. He shivered, wishing it wasn't so cold and wet in the tunnel. Strangely, Justin seemed to be really enjoying himself.

After a while, they came to a circular area with several narrow passages leading off from it. Justin flashed the beam around. Adam looked up. He could just make out a design in the gloom. He pointed to it. "Look there. I think we're somewhere under the chapel."

Justin shone the flashlight upward. A circle was carved into the stone above their heads. Inside the circle was a seven-pointed star. It wasn't as elaborate as the one inside the chapel, but it was the same design.

"You're right," said Justin. "So where should we go now? Looks like a network of passages. They could lead anywhere."

Just then, the sound of voices came toward them. A raucous laugh and a few words in the same strange language they had heard in Egypt. Arabic! It must be Dr. Khalid's men. When foreign beams of light danced over the floor and walls, the boys shrank back against a wall. Justin switched off his flashlight and slipped it into his jeans back pocket.

Two men strode past, so close that one man's sleeve almost brushed against Adam. Faint with fear, Adam squeezed his eyelids closed. When he opened them, the men were heading into another passage. They were dragging a small figure between them. It was Kim. She stumbled and almost fell, but the men yanked her back onto her feet. Adam was about to scream Kim's name when Justin clapped one hand over his mouth.

"Keep quiet." Justin's voice was low and angry.

"We have to rescue her," Adam sputtered in an equally angry whisper.

"Yes, but let's surprise them. We can't barge in like idiots."

Adam felt like a fool. Of course, they needed a plan.

Justin beckoned Adam to follow him. Crouching low, the boys crept quietly behind the men. After a few minutes, the men disappeared into the blackness and so did their beams. In the dark, the boys slowed down, feeling their way along the walls. Adam's heart was pounding so hard he was sure someone would hear it. He was about to ask Justin to put on their flashlight when Justin stopped.

"I can hear breathing," Justin whispered.

There was a sudden blinding flash of light. The boys raised their arms to shield their eyes. They were in another circular space, surrounded by a blaze of beams. The light came from several strong lamps, the kind used for camping. A

263

dark-clad figure stood in front of Adam. Although Adam had been expecting this encounter, it was a shock to see their enemy again in the flesh. His stomach did a kind of flip-flop and, for a few seconds, he couldn't breathe. Justin gasped in fright.

"Going somewhere?"

Just the sound of that familiar voice made Adam feel sick. It was as if Dr. Khalid had materialized out of nowhere. Their enemy looked quite different from their encounter with him in Egypt. He wore a dark suit, with a black cloak casually draped over his shoulders. The cape was lined with ruby-red silk, giving their nemesis an air of sinister elegance. A dark gray hat with a low brim shadowed his face and a black eye patch covered his right eye. He wore a red scarf knotted around his throat and his lips stretched in a thin smile. When he spoke, his voice sounded rougher than before.

"You notice my wounds from our memorable encounter in the tomb of the Scarab King." He gestured at his face. "The loss of my eye, thanks to Justin here, and my damaged vocal cords, thanks to your scarab, Adam. Perhaps you thought I would not survive?"

Adam's throat went dry; his head swam. Instinctively, he slipped his hand into his pocket and clutched his scarab. It felt warm and reassuring. Memories crowded his mind of the dramatic moment in the tomb of the Scarab King when Justin had used his slingshot to stop Dr. Khalid from shooting him. The sacred scarab had seemed to jump at Dr. Khalid, burying its pincers in the man's throat.

Justin clenched his fists at his sides. "Cockroaches survive anything."

"So, we meet again, my dear young archaeologists, and already I see your manners have not improved in the interval." Dr. Khalid gave one of his exaggerated sighs. "What do they teach you at school these days?"

"Have you got the Pyramidion?" Adam asked, remembering the alabaster shape spinning down into the abyss that had claimed the sarcophagus of the Scarab King. The Pyramidion contained the Stone of Fire, vital to uniting all Seven Stones of Power and reading the *Book of Thoth*.

Dr. Khalid clenched his jaw, struggling to control himself. "No, I have not," he spat. "Just one more inconvenience caused by you two little troublemakers."

Adam sagged with relief. As long as the Pyramidion remained at large, they had a chance to beat Dr. Khalid.

Dr. Khalid tapped Adam on the chest. "Let's not waste any more time. Hand over the second Stone of Power and I'll release your little friend."

Their enemy waved one hand and his henchmen stepped forward. Kim stood between them, her face pinched with terror, her eyes wide. One of the men held a knife against her throat. The other man, holding a flashlight, looked just like Aziz, the Egyptian they had seen drown in the collapse of the Scarab King's tomb. This second man glared at Adam, hatred contorting his face.

"You see me?" He tapped his forehead. "My name is Hussein. Because of you, my brother Aziz is dead. I will avenge myself on you." He drew one hand across his throat. "*Zzzzzt!*"

Aziz had made the same gesture several times in Egypt and Adam got the message. He took a step back as Dr. Khalid uttered a sharp command in Arabic. Hussein growled under his breath; the man with the knife said nothing. Adam glanced at Justin. His face was tight and angry.

"Don't worry, Kim." Justin sounded confident. "We've come to rescue you."

Dr. Khalid's shoulders shook as he laughed. "Oh, here we go again. Didn't you two dunces learn anything from our last encounter?" His gaze hardened. "Where is the second Stone of Power?"

"We haven't got it." Adam hoped his voice wasn't trembling as much as his body. He knew Dr. Khalid's temper and this time they didn't have anything to bargain with. In Egypt, they'd had the sacred scarab. Now they had nothing but themselves.

"Rubbish." The man's expression was grim. "I haven't come all this way to play silly games. Turn out your pockets, Adam."

Adam knew that the sight of the scarab, even though it was only a replica, would cause a whole lot of trouble so he said, "No, I won't. I don't have the Stone of Power. Somebody stole it from the Ashmolean Museum a few days ago, but it wasn't us."

Dr. Khalid frowned as he gnawed his lower lip. Then he flung out one hand dramatically. "Search them."

Before his henchmen could make a move, someone stepped out of the shadows.

"They don't have the second stone. Maybe you should ask the thief who stole it."

When Dr. Khalid saw who had spoken, he staggered back as if the someone had struck him a deadly blow.

"Aaargh!" He flung up his hands in defense. "It's not possible … you're dead. I saw the body myself."

As Ink came into the light, Adam and Justin exchanged astounded glances. Ink was the last person Adam had expected to see. He must have returned to the castle and found the entrance to the secret passage in the library. Adam had forgotten to close it behind him. The situation had taken a weird turn; Dr. Khalid was staring at Ink in shock, as if he knew him.

Ink's voice was cold as he glared at Dr. Khalid with loathing. "My name is Benjamin. Just your reaction tells me you must be thinking of Bartholomew Blott, my father, the man you murdered years ago by blowing up the library in Athens where he was working."

Dr. Khalid gave a shaky laugh. "What? Who told you?" Then his normal self-control returned. "Of course. Bartholomew would have been much older had he survived."

"I worked out your part in his death for myself," said Ink, "and I'm here to protect whatever my father discovered—whatever it is you wanted so badly you had to kill him for it."

"But I never got it," Dr. Khalid screamed at Ink. "After he discovered it, he hid it from me." His face went red and the veins stood out in his neck. His voice rasped horribly in his throat. "The naïve fool. He wanted to share precious information with the world so he wouldn't tell me what he'd found. He just said it would change history."

He raised his arms in a dramatic gesture. The black cloak slithered back, revealing the ruby-red lining. "No, I … Faisal Khalid … *I* will change history."

Then he lowered his arms and composed himself. "I'm wasting time. If you lot don't have the second stone, then who has?"

He gestured again to his henchmen. Hussein scurried away and returned a few moments later herding two prisoners, their hands tied behind their backs. One was fat and covered in mud. The other looked disheveled, although he had clearly once been well dressed.

"Archie?" Adam was astounded.

"And Florian Boldwood?" Justin goggled at the museum curator. "What are they doing here?"

Dr. Khalid folded his arms. "Now that we have all the players on hand, will someone tell me where the second stone is?" He glared at Florian Boldwood. "Mr. Boldwood, I thought we had an agreement."

Adam felt the breath whoosh out of him as all the pieces in the puzzle began to fall into place.

Archie swelled up like a turkey. "What?" he screeched at Florian. His eyes bulged in their sockets. "You had an agreement with this scoundrel? What agreement?"

Florian bit his lip. His golden curls flopped awry and his face was smeared with blood from a cut above one eye. His smart suit was torn and filthy. "I ... I didn't know this would happen," he whimpered. "I just wanted ... so ... I ... er ..." He looked down as he shuffled his feet.

"*You* left the room to the relics unlocked." Adam shook his head in disbelief. "So that Dr. Khalid could steal the second stone from Arthur's sword."

Dr. Khalid's triumphant expression was just as Adam remembered.

"The fool fell for the bait once I told him I could advance his career and his book using my network of connections," said Dr. Khalid. "You academics are so naïve."

"But someone else stole it first," Justin said. "Serves you right." He took a quick step back when Dr. Khalid glowered at him.

Archie's face went completely purple. "If I wasn't tied up, Florian, I'd give you such a punch in the nose. You ... you ... turncoat."

"Well, you are tied up," Dr. Khalid said, "and you're going to stay that way so keep quiet. You've been a great nuisance to me, Archibald Curran. Not at all as helpful as I would have expected from a man of your vast knowledge. After our previous encounter, you should know that I am not a patient man."

Adam felt sorry for Archie. His shoulders were sagging in defeat, his chins wobbled, and his lips trembled. He hung his head and mumbled an apology.

"But you're not entirely useless," Dr. Khalid continued. "You've let slip some very useful information about our young friend Adam, so I won't be too hard on you."

Adam felt a chill run down his spine when Dr. Khalid spoke his name.

Justin burst out, "I know what you told him." He scowled at Archie. "Humphrey said you should keep quiet about it, but you just couldn't resist scoring over Florian Boldwood because you're jealous of him. You told him about Adam's ability because you wanted to seem important, and of course he told—"

"Shut up, Justin." Ink cut Justin short. "Don't say any more."

Ink stared at Archie. "So that's why you were worried about Adam's safety at the castle. You tried to say something before we left on the train. You'd *already* boasted to Florian Boldwood what you knew about Adam. Later, you realized Adam might be in danger if Florian told anyone."

Archie looked as if he wanted to sink through the floor. He gave a faint moan.

Dr. Khalid's wolfish grin revealed his perfect white teeth. "It's too late, Benjamin. You can stop trying to be the hero. I always had a feeling that Adam might be useful." He smirked at Florian and Archie. "Now, thanks to these two bickering fools competing with each other, I know just how valuable he'll be to me."

Archie turned on Florian. "You self-centered scoundrel. You—"

"Blabbermouth," Florian snarled back. "If you'd just kept your own mouth shut, I wouldn't have known this boy could sense things about ancient artifacts just by touching them. I couldn't have said anything because I wouldn't have known it to say anything in the first place. How was I to know that Khalid was after the boy?"

Archie glared at Florian. "Weasel."

Florian glared back. "Fat pig."

"Traitor!"

"Idiot!"

Each man heaved against his bonds, as if he would jump hard on the other if he could get loose.

"Omar." Dr. Khalid waved at his henchman. "Get rid of them. They're boring me."

The man with the knife pushed Kim toward Hussein, and then herded the two sputtering men down one of the dark passages. Hussein grabbed Kim by one arm and waited for Dr. Khalid's orders. Adam glanced at Kim. She still looked terrified.

Dr. Khalid folded his arms as he leaned against a wall, tapping one foot impatiently. For once, he seemed nonplussed. Then he spoke as if thinking aloud. "These children do not have it. The two fools do not have it. So, who has it?"

268

Dr. Khalid thrust his face close to Adam.

Adam flinched as the enemy's scarred countenance hovered only inches away, the black one-eyed glare boring into him.

"*Who* has it?" Dr. Khalid repeated.

The answer emerged from the darkness: "We do."

The Eaters of Poison Return

The voice from the darkness was one Adam would never forget. The last time it had spoken, it had conjured up fear, loathing, and horror, and it did the same now. As before, a moldy, rotten smell pervaded the air at the same time. Dr. Khalid raised a fastidious hand and covered his nose for a moment. Hussein, who still held Kim by the arm, flattened himself against a wall, his face twisted into a mask of terror. With a muffled wail, he followed the direction Omar had taken, dragging Kim with him. Dr. Khalid took several steps back, while sliding his right hand into his coat pocket. Adam was sure he had a gun, like their last encounter in Egypt.

A monk stepped out of the shadows, his dark robe rustling. He appeared to be the leader of the group as several monks clustered behind him. Adam wasn't certain how many because the deep shadows made it difficult to count them.

The head monk slipped back the cowl of his robe, revealing a long, pale, skeletal face, and gleaming dark eyes with purple shadows beneath. His thin lips stretched into a triumphant smile.

"We have it," he repeated. "We have your second stone, your Stone of Power."

Strangely, Dr. Khalid did not appear surprised to see them. He took a gun from his pocket and waved it at the head monk. "Then hand it over. It's no use to you."

The monks did not flinch at the sight of the gun. Again, the head monk's lips twitched in a cheerless smile. "It is very useful to us. After all, you want it and we want something else. Something of great importance to us."

271

Dr. Khalid scowled. "I thought you people might arrive sooner or later, but I didn't know you stole the stone."

The monk shook his head. "We utilize all opportunities."

Dr. Khalid curled his lip. "Traitors."

The monk hissed and lifted both his arms in a strange gesture. The other monks edged closer, hissing as well.

Dr. Khalid stepped back, visibly shaken. "Don't try your conjuring tricks with me."

Adam just had to ask. "Do you know these people?"

Dr. Khalid swung his one-eyed gaze to Adam. "They are the Eaters of Poison. They are deceivers, fatal to the touch. They are fed poison from birth so that by adulthood they can kill others merely by scratching their flesh." He shuddered. "They are also betrayers. Thousands of years ago, an ancient Egyptian priest, a renegade, sold the secrets of the Stone of Fire to this"—his mouth twisted in scorn—"motley crew of charlatans and vagabonds."

Adam remembered they had read about the Egyptian priest in Bedwyr's diary, the one who had sold information about the Stone of Fire. Then something else popped into his head.

"Are they the Dark Brothers?" Adam's heart sank when he saw the effect his question had on both the monks and Dr. Khalid. It was too late to retract his words. The monks gave a collective moan and clustered in the shadows, hands raised as if to fend off his words. Dr. Khalid glanced behind suspiciously, as if expecting to see someone behind him. Then he grabbed Adam's arm so hard he pinched the boy's flesh.

"Ow, let go," Adam cried out. "You're hurting me."

"What do you know about the Dark Brothers?" Dr. Khalid snarled in Adam's ear. "You know too much, boy, far too much for your own good."

"I don't know anything." Adam pretended to whimper, hoping Justin and Ink wouldn't mention Bedwyr's diary. "Uh ... Archie said something, but I think he was talking about the ... the Dark *Ages*."

Dr. Khalid's glare was hard and cold, but he seemed to believe Adam's story. He released Adam's arm. "Archibald Curran is a fool that talks too much."

He gestured toward the group of monks. "As I was saying about this rag-tag group of tramps. In a feeble attempt to blend in with the twenty-first century, they call themselves the Ancient Association of Antiquarian Book Collectors. However, their real name is—"

"The Ancient Association of Alchemists," the head monk said, "descended from the Priests of al Khem." A proud light glinted in his dark eyes. "We are invincible."

Dr. Khalid gave a contemptuous snort.

"What utter rubbish," he said. "You never *descended* from them at all. Your thieving, ignorant, peasant ancestors *bought* information from an order made up of sham priests and fake magicians who found themselves out of work when the Egyptian Empire collapsed. When the great libraries and temples closed, these bogus Egyptian priests—the so-called Priests of al Khem—sold information to the highest bidders. Sacred knowledge, including information about the Stone of Fire, left Egypt and trickled into Europe."

"Al Khem?" Adam said, forgetting his fear of the monks because he was interested in what they had to say. "The land of Khem was the old name for Egypt."

"*Al Khem* means 'from the land of Khem,'" the head monk replied. "The word *alchemist* comes from the same place. And our great leader is the Alchemist."

"They tried to poison us on the train with some kind of powder," Justin blurted out. He shrank back when the head monk stared at him, but defiantly held the man's gaze. "I bet you guys drugged that spring water, too."

"On both occasions we did not try to kill you," said the head monk. "We just needed to get rid of you for a while so we could continue our search. Making everyone sleep was the best way."

Justin snorted. "Gee, thanks! But you tried to kill Ink on the train."

"That was different. We did not have enough knowledge at that time to decide who was an enemy." The baleful eyes fixed on Ink. "Yet you live still?" There was a note of grudging admiration in the head monk's voice. "How can this be?"

"I can tell you," Adam said quickly. "Our friend Dr. Mercury Jones is a scientist and he's looking for a special ingredient that's in your poison. He is trying to make a universal antidote for all known poisons. He said it's a mirthi … uh … something to do with an ancient king. His antidote saved Ink and our dog Smudge."

The head monk stroked his chin with long, bony fingers. He glanced at his fellow monks and then returned his gaze to Adam. "A *mithridate*. A universal antidote? How interesting." His eyes gleamed. "We do not share our secrets with outsiders, but this Mercury Jones … is he a practitioner of the ancient arts?"

Adam didn't know what the "ancient arts" were, but yes seemed to be the best answer. "Yes, he is, and he's about to make the greatest scientific discovery in the world. But he needs your help."

The head monk turned to his companions and they muttered among themselves.

"Just a minute," Dr. Khalid burst out. "We're not cooks exchanging recipes. I am here to collect what I came for—the second Stone of Power."

"And we are here to collect what we came for," replied the head monk. "The secret book of Arthepius."

"What is this book?" asked Justin. "One of you guys … er … one of your friends mentioned it when he broke into the castle the other night."

"We believed you and your companions had it because, overhearing your discussions, we heard what we thought was the name of the great adept and teacher, the master of the art of prolonging life … Arthepius."

Adam was astounded. Kim had been right all along. The monks were on their own mission, completely unrelated to the Seven Stones.

"But what is it?" asked Justin. "And who is Arthepius anyway?"

"When the Greek philosopher and alchemist Arthepius wrote *The Art of Prolonging Human Life* in the twelfth century, he had already lived for one thousand years. Our task," the head monk said, indicating the monks clustered behind him, "is to find the original manuscript for our leader, the great Alchemist—the Master Poisoner."

"Is your leader still alive?" asked Adam. The monks dressed and acted as if they had stepped out of the pages of a history book, but they weren't hundreds of years old.

The head monk shook his head. "He died seven hundred years ago."

"Then why are you still looking for the book if he is dead?" Justin asked, frowning. "It doesn't make sense."

"Perhaps not to you but for us it is our mission, our quest, our reason to live," the head monk said. "This task has been handed down from our ancestors, the original companions of our great master. There will be another leader soon enough. When the time is ripe."

Adam stared at the head monk. The monk's words reminded him of Ebrahim and his friend Hamid's mission. Ebrahim had told Adam in Egypt that, as the last descendants of the original priests of the Scarab King, they had sworn to protect the king's tomb at all costs. He could understand why the monks continued with their strange quest.

"But you know everything about the Seven Stones of Power because of the secrets that were sold to your ancestors hundreds of years ago?"

The head monk nodded. Adam longed to ask if that was the reason the monk in the Chamber of Curiosities knew about the mark on his back and his vision of the temple destruction, but he dared not. He couldn't let Dr. Khalid know any more than he already knew. But the history of the monks and their ancestors meant they must know about his role in the quest for the Seven Stones of Power. For some reason, the monks weren't saying anything about it.

"You could keep the second stone for yourselves and try to use it."

The head monk's smile was tight and grim. "But we have sworn a blood oath and we are bound by it, as were our ancestors. We cannot deviate from our mission until it is completed. Our goal is to locate the secret book of Arthepius."

"Well, I haven't got your blasted book," said Dr. Khalid irritably. "Just give me the stone before I blow your head off."

He pointed his gun. The head monk raised a clenched fist.

Dr. Khalid retreated, his cloak swirling around him in a black and ruby cloud as he shouted, "I place upon you the curse of Sekhmet, lion-headed daughter of Ra, and the goddess of destruction." He threw his arms up in a grand gesture. "Let the eye of Ra descend that it may slay the evil conspirators."

The head monk staggered back with a cry, clutching his chest as if struck by a blow.

Dr. Khalid gave a triumphant shout. "I see you have not forgotten the ancient ways. You know the power of the curse."

Ink stepped forward. "Wait."

Justin grabbed Ink's shoulder. "Ink, stay back or you'll get hurt."

With the force of Justin's grip, Ink's jacket pulled open and his T-shirt tore at the neck. The medallion swung into view.

The head monk stared at Ink with wide eyes, gasped, and fell to his knees. He placed his forehead on the floor. "Lord Anubis, the Keeper of Poisons."

The other monks dropped to their knees and covered their heads with their arms.

Dr. Khalid also stared at the medallion. "Where did you get this?" His voice trembled.

Adam had never seen their enemy so shaken. Even when the tomb of the Scarab King had collapsed, Dr. Khalid had shown no fear. Now he looked distinctly panicky.

"I don't know," said Ink. "Someone sent it to me."

He held the medallion up. The kneeling monks moaned and huddled together. Adam saw it clearly now. It was the crouching figure of Anubis, the dark jackal god of the underworld. The image looked just like the tattoo on Ebrahim's wrist, which was the emblem of the Seal of the City of the Dead. The monks' reactions clearly showed their historical connection with ancient Egypt.

Ink reached inside his jacket and pulled out a large buff envelope. "I have what you seek."

The head monk scrambled to his feet, his expression hopeful.

"This was sent with the medallion," Ink told him.

The monk cocked his head, now mistrustful. "How do we know you speak the truth?"

Ink slid a wad of papers out of the envelope and read from the first page: "*I, Arthepius, having learnt all the art in the Book of Hermes, was once, as others, envious, but having now lived one thousand years or thereabouts ...*"

He looked up. "Is this what you seek?"

The head monk let out a gasp. Behind him, his companions uttered cries of joy. Ink slid the pages back into the envelope.

The head monk held out one hand for the envelope while he felt inside his robe with the other. "Give it to us and I will give you the second Stone of Power." He pulled something out of his robe, and, as Ink held out the envelope, chaos erupted.

Launching himself at the head monk, Dr. Khalid howled, "The stone is mine!"

The head monk tried to leap aside, but, still holding the gun, Dr. Khalid crashed into him. They rolled around, wrestling and knocking over the lamps in their struggle. With lightning speed, the other monks lifted their arms high into the air and swung their fists down. An emerald fire erupted from their fingertips, spreading across the floor, and a deafening explosion reverberated through the tunnel.

As the smoke cleared, the figure of Dr. Khalid materialized. He held the second Stone of Power aloft in triumph. It glowed vibrant red. The head monk lay slumped at his feet, clutching his shoulder. Had Dr. Khalid shot him? Then Adam glimpsed one of the monks shoving the envelope inside his robe.

"I have it now," screamed Dr. Khalid, throwing his head back. His hat fell off, revealing the full extent of his injuries. Livid scars streaked across one side of his face.

He shook his fist at the monks now kneeling at their leader's side. "A mere flesh wound. He will live and you have what you want. So, get back to the dark hole from whence you came."

One of the monks snarled something incomprehensible as he fumbled inside his robe.

Ink suddenly jerked into action and pulled Adam and Justin to one side. "Let's get out of here. These monks seem to have a few tricks up their sleeves … the kind that explode."

"What about the Stone of Power?" Justin cried.

"Do you want to die?" said Ink. "Dr. Khalid will have to escape, too. We'll catch him on the outside. These tunnels weren't built to withstand explosives."

The trio raced down one of the passages just as another terrible blast sounded behind them. The force knocked them off their feet.

Dizzy and covered in mud, Adam hauled himself up and ran after Justin and Ink, who stumbled along in front of him. Then they heard the sound that Adam dreaded most: rushing water. After the second explosion, the contents of the lake had begun to pour into the labyrinth of passages.

Ink raced ahead with Justin close behind, waving his pitifully small torch against the overwhelming blackness. Adam was last. They splashed through ankle-deep water, trying to keep ahead of the torrent gathering momentum behind them. Small freezing cold waves lapped against their legs. They seemed to be running for miles.

"Where are we going?" Adam yelled. His sides ached.

"I'm trying to find Archie and Kim," Ink shouted back. "Dr. Khalid's men went in this direction."

A faint cry came from the left. Ink veered off into the darkness. Justin and Adam waded after him, struggling in the rising water. Then, in the bobbing beam of light, they saw two large bound figures and a smaller one. Dr. Khalid's men were nowhere in sight. Ink quickly untied everyone and heaved Archie to his feet.

"Where are Khalid's men?" he asked.

"They've run off," said Archie. "Scoundrels. Poltroons."

"Are you okay?" Justin asked Kim.

"Yeah." She rubbed her wrists where the rope had chafed the skin. "Thanks, guys. I knew you'd come get me."

Adam looked about. "We're in a dead end. There's a wall in front of us."

Water gushed along the passage. Though not deep enough to drown them right away, soon the level would rise. Then came the weirdest noise.

Thunk! Thunk! It sounded as if someone was banging a large, heavy object overhead.

Justin pointed the flashlight upward. "Do you think there's someone above us?"

Adam felt near his feet in the icy water for a stone. His numbed fingers closed over a sizeable rock. He thrust it at Ink. "You're the tallest. Knock back."

Ink half-laughed in disbelief. "This is crazy."

He reached up and banged the rock against the tunnel roof three times. To their amazement, three loud bangs sounded in return.

Ink shook his head. "It's a miracle. Who can it be?"

By now, the water was swirling around Adam's knees. His legs felt frozen. They all stared hopefully upward. Then came a sound like stone grating against stone and a chink of light appeared overhead, shining into their watery prison. A figure appeared in the illuminated sliver that opened up in the stone ceiling. Archie lifted Kim onto his shoulders and she strained to see.

A second later, she nearly toppled off Archie's shoulders in surprise. "I can see Sirius."

Justin and Adam stared openmouthed at each other and then burst into wild hoots of laughter.

"Billy," Adam sputtered. "Who'd have guessed it?"

Ink, Archie, and Florian craned their necks to see into the aperture that gradually widened as the stone slab slid back. Then Billy's freckled face appeared above them.

"Hello," he said. "Isn't Sirius clever? He told me exactly where to find you."

As the icy water surged higher, Billy dangled one end of a rope down into the cavity. He had already tied the other end to Sirius' halter. Ink scrambled up first and pulled with the horse to get each person out. Kim went next, then Adam, Justin, and Florian. Archie was the last person.

Adam looked down at Archie's girth and the size of the cavity. Would he make it?

"Leave me to die, Ink, dear boy." Archie's voice, tinged with sadness, rolled upward in a hollow echo. "Send my fondest regards to your father."

Ink called down. "Come on, sir, let's just try."

"No, no," Archie wailed, big fat tears splashing down his plump cheeks. "My life is over." The brackish water lapped against his chins. "What a way to die, like a rat drowning in a sewer."

Florian elbowed Ink aside. "Archie, listen to me."

Archie turned his face away. "Get thee behind me, quisling. You ruined my career. I have nothing left to live for. You can crow over me all you like now."

"Archie, the museum needs you."

Archie stopped sobbing. He gulped, gave a small hiccup, and looked up at Florian. "What?"

Florian nodded sadly. "Yes, it's true. I'm not just saying it. I'm a rotten administrator. The catalogue is in a complete mess, the books won't balance, I take too many long lunches, and there are relics missing after the Byzantine Gallery renovation."

Archie blinked. "Relics missing? I can't believe you let it come to this, Florian. You should be ashamed of yourself. And after all I did to get the place running perfectly."

Florian sounded dejected. "Yes, you're quite right, as always. I'm the wrong man for the job. You'd better come back, Archie, before Britain's oldest museum shuts its doors."

Archie closed his eyes. "It's against my better judgment, but I'd like to think there is a shred of sincerity in your statement."

In a voice tinged with urgency, Florian said, "I *am* being sincere, Archie, maybe for the first time in my life. We all need you."

Archie's eyes flew open. He glared at Ink, who had thrust his head into the cavity next to Florian. "Get me out of here right away. I have work to do."

With Archie's cooperation and barely inches to spare, they all heaved at the rope and slowly raised the plump academic from what might have been his final watery resting place.

Once Archie was safe and the stone slab replaced, Adam looked around. "It's the old shed."

The place was warm, with straw on the floor and even a lamp to give some light. Sheldon must have left it there when he had stabled the horses after the fire.

"Yes," said Ink. "Amazing. This must be part of the original stables that isn't on the estate drawings."

"So this is where the tunnel really comes out," said Justin. "It's just as we all thought—the tunnel did lead to the stables, but centuries ago the stables must have been rebuilt where they are now. And somehow only this old shed stayed." He said apologetically to Adam, "You were right."

Kim patted Sirius' neck. "How did you find us, Billy?"

"Well," said Billy, "Sirius and me ate all the food from our midnight feast and then I went to sleep, but Sirius said he couldn't sleep. He kept walking around, thumping one hoof on the ground, and then pushing the straw with his nose."

Billy looked at the circle of interested faces and swelled with pride. "I helped him push away all the straw and we found this big stone on the ground with a metal ring in it. Sirius thumped it twice with his hoof as if he knew it was important. Then you banged three times and we banged three times, and that's how I knew someone was stuck down there. I tied one end of the rope to Sirius and the other end to the ring, and Sirius pulled the stone away."

He went bright red. "Sirius is the hero."

Kim gave him a hug. "No, Billy, you're also the hero."

"Okay, heroes," said Ink. "Time to catch up with our friend Khalid."

"I'll stay here with Florian," said Archie, placing a firm hand on Florian's shoulder. "We have a few things to thrash out."

Florian gave a muffled bleat at the word *thrash*.

Archie made shooing gestures in Ink's direction. "Off with you lot now. Go get 'em and show no mercy."

Then Archie said, "Pass me that quilt, Florian, I'm freezing to death. Billy, dear boy, are you sure you and Sirius ate *all* the food?"

As they dashed from the shed, Adam chuckled; Archie always was thinking of food. Then his smile faded. There was no one to help them now—no police, no Gran to the rescue with her Turkish friends Suleiman and Ictzak, no Egyptian army like before, and no Ebrahim. There was no one in authority, no force of law and order. It was just him and the others. Dr. Khalid had the second Stone of Power and was possibly going to get away with it.

They ran out into pelting rain. Icy drops smacked their faces. Within seconds, their already half-sodden clothes were drenched again and clinging cold and heavy against their skins. Adam saw the castle up ahead, his vision blurred as the rain began pouring even harder. Lightning struck in long jagged flashes, lighting the way.

"Where are we going?" Adam shouted to Ink between the deafening peals of thunder.

"The castle."

"But why?" Justin asked. "Dr. Khalid must have a car or some kind of transport. And he won't go to the castle."

Ink pointed up at the sky. "There's his transport and the castle roof is the only safe place it can land."

Thwukah! Thwukah! Thwukah!

For the first time, Adam heard the deep throbbing sounds and lights appeared above the castle.

"It's a helicopter," Adam screamed.

Hopelessness enveloped him. What chance did they have now to stop their enemy?

DR. KHALID'S ESCAPE

Constable Sidney Parrott sat at his desk, writing a report. As hard as he tried, he couldn't prevent his thoughts from straying back to the recent antics at the castle. Finally, after chewing the top of his ballpoint pen right off, he spat out the bits of plastic, buttoned his uniform collar, wedged his helmet firmly on his head, and marched out of the station, with his truncheon tucked under one arm. There was nothing else to do but return to the castle and do a bit of sleuthing on his own. He was undeterred by the fact that it was late at night and pouring with rain. He knew the countryside and castle surroundings like the back of his hand.

"Those kids are up to something and I'm going to get to the bottom of it."

He jumped into his battered old car and sped off, feeling rather guilty about driving ten miles over the speed limit, but when duty called a Parrott, it called in a trumpet blast. He struggled to see the road ahead because the windshield wiper on the driver's side wasn't working properly, so he had to lean out of his window, getting drenched in the process. But a fervor blazed within Sidney that night. A sense of rising euphoria eclipsed the triumphant feelings he'd had on the night of the fire. This time he knew he would be a hero. It was as if fate, destiny, and all the things he'd read about in Madame FiFi's "Stargazer" column at the back of the *Haddley Herald* each Tuesday were joining forces tonight.

His latest horoscope had read, *"Be prepared for a momentous change in your career and love life."*

Sidney was prepared.

As he drove up the winding road to the castle, he heard a helicopter overhead. He looked up as it hovered above the castle and then slowly descended behind the battlements. There was ample space on the roof. During World War II, a big *H* had been painted in yellow on the roof in case the castle was needed for emergency aerial landings. Instantly, Sidney's mind filled with thoughts of international criminals engaged in illegal activities, such as narcotics, weapons, or diamond smuggling. He frowned as he wondered how a few kids could be involved in such unlikely doings, but then thrust speculation aside as he stamped his foot on the accelerator.

Within a few minutes, he pulled up to his destination and parked behind a clump of bushes near the moat. He could enter the castle and reach the roof through the front way, but that would be too easy. No, he would go the secret way. From now on, he was an officer on foot, fulfilling his duties to the crown.

When Adam and the others reached the castle, they went first to the kitchen to check on the adults and the dogs. All were still asleep, snoring loudly. Ink ran up the staircase with the cousins and Kim close on his heels, their wet sneakers squelching loudly as they crept along the main upstairs passage. It wasn't even worth trying to keep quiet. Ink indicated a small side door that led from the old nursery up a narrow stairwell to the battlements. He pushed the door open just wide enough for them to scuttle through the gap on all fours.

The helicopter hovered overhead. The door of the craft opened and someone inside it began to lower a rope ladder. Then, through the driving rain, a figure became visible on the opposite side of the roof: Dr. Khalid. Adam tried to wipe his face dry with his hands, but it didn't help much. The rain was pouring, running through his hair and then down his cheeks in chilly trickles. Lightning flashed above them. The storm seemed even more horrible and scary up on the roof.

"What's the plan?" Adam whispered to Ink.

"Uh … no plan yet. I'm still thinking. I want to see what Khalid does first."

Just then, as the rope ladder swung low enough to reach, Dr. Khalid made a dash for it. The rope ladder swayed wildly in the wind as he grabbed at it. His black cloak flapped around him, getting in the way.

The most amazing sensation of courage rose inside Adam, pushing him to do something. It was almost as if he couldn't stop himself, despite the fact that he was just a boy and Dr. Khalid was his sworn enemy.

"He's getting away," Adam screamed. "I've got to stop him." Without thinking, he ran toward Dr. Khalid. "You won't get away," he yelled, reaching out to grasp the man's cloak.

Dr. Khalid reeled back, shocked, but only for a moment. Then he grabbed Adam by the shirt, yanking him almost off his feet.

"How fortuitous our paths should cross so soon, Adam. You've saved me the trouble of having to look for you."

He pulled Adam against him with one hand and turned to face the others. Peering through the heavy rain, he yelled, "Stay out of the way and you won't get hurt."

Then he grabbed the end of the rope ladder with his free hand. The helicopter hovered lower, enabling Dr. Khalid to get one foot onto the bottom rung. He managed to hoist himself up several rungs of the rope ladder, dragging Adam with him by one arm. Adam nearly threw up as the ladder swayed violently from side to side with the motion of the helicopter. A bitter taste rose in his throat.

Dr. Khalid screamed at the pilot, "Stop rocking about, you idiot. Try to keep this thing still."

"Sorry, sir," the pilot yelled back, "but there's a terrible crosswind. You must hurry or we'll never make it. I can't hold it for much longer. We could crash any minute."

Adam struggled frantically to get free. Dr. Khalid's lips curled into a frightening grimace as his fingers closed tighter on Adam's arm in an iron grip.

"*Climb* before I shoot you."

His heart pounding with fear, Adam began to climb upward. Then he felt a hand grab his ankle. He looked down to see Ink standing below the rope ladder, grinning up at him.

Dr. Khalid looked down as well. "You're going to end up like your father, you stupid fool."

Ink laughed. "I had a good role model," he said, as he grabbed Adam's ankles and yanked hard. Adam fell into Ink's arms.

Dr. Khalid swore loudly. "Omar, Hussein. Get over here or I'll leave you behind."

There was no reply.

"Omar? Hussein?"

A voice yelled, "I'm afraid your men have been detained pending further investigation into your activities, sir, one of which is the unlawful use of a helicopter above a residential dwelling."

Dr. Khalid squinted into the gloom. "Who are you?"

"Constable Parrott of Her Majesty's Scottish Police Service."

Dr. Khalid groaned. "I can't believe it. The village Plod."

"The name is Constable *Parrott*, sir, not Plod, and I'll thank you to remember it in future."

Dr. Khalid was so enraged he almost fell off the rope ladder. Hoisting himself up a few more rungs, he took something out of his pocket and shouted into the darkness, "Feast your eyes on this, Adam Sinclair, because it's the last time you'll see the second Stone of Power."

He thrust his arm out. In his hand was the second stone.

Adam wasn't sure why, but he took his scarab out of his pocket and held it up as well. At the same instant, a tremendous flash of lightning struck the battlements and the second Stone of Power glowed red. Adam's scarab flashed a bright yellow light. An arc of blinding brilliance shimmered around the helicopter. Dr. Khalid's foot slipped and he slid down a few rungs. Then, above the noise of the storm and the helicopter, Adam heard a strange wild cry.

"*Keeiah!*"

The piercing shriek came out of nowhere, followed swiftly by the rushing of giant wings. An enormous eagle flew past Dr. Khalid, its claws striking his outstretched hand. Dr. Khalid fell further down the rope ladder. As he grabbed for the ladder with both hands to stop himself falling, he let the second Stone of Power drop over the battlements. Adam closed his eyes in despair. He couldn't bear to see it plunge into the moat. This was the worst thing that could have happened. If it fell into the water, they'd never find it.

He opened his eyes as a second shriek came, higher and shriller, but this time there were no large rushing wings. Instead, there was only a quiet whooshing as a slim raptor shape swooped past just in time and caught the stone in its claws. Both birds disappeared into the night.

Dr. Khalid shouted in rage, but hung helplessly from the swaying ladder as the helicopter lifted higher into the air.

"Un-flipping-believable," said Justin. He put one arm around Kim's shoulders, gazing into the sky with the rest of them as the helicopter became a mere speck of light and then disappeared.

Tying up Loose Ends

After that, things happened very quickly. Constable Parrott explained how he had sneaked up onto the roof using the secret way he had discovered while playing at the castle as a child. He had found Omar and Hussein in the shadows, waiting for Dr. Khalid to summon them to the helicopter. Two swipes with his truncheon soon dispatched the henchmen, who now lay trussed up in the hallway.

Just as he was finishing his story, barking, and voices from the kitchen heralded the arrival of Mrs. Grant, Mrs. McLeod, and Sheldon with the dogs. The ladies were irate that someone had drugged the drinking water. Mrs. Grant vowed that in future she would set Jasper on any tradesmen arriving unannounced, especially ones with free samples.

Mrs. McLeod admitted that Sidney had been brave to tackle two ruffians, especially when one was found in possession of a large knife with a wickedly curved blade. She seemed to have forgotten her previous bad opinion of Sidney since she extended him an immediate invitation to visit any time he chose.

Hamish arrived with Archie and Florian in tow, demanding tea and sandwiches. When Mrs. Grant realized it was way past midnight, she shooed the kids off to bed. Justin was so tired that he didn't even say goodnight. He began snoring as soon as his head hit his pillow. Adam put his scarab safely under his pillow as always, and fell asleep.

The next morning, they overslept, which wasn't surprising after all the excitement the night before. Justin pulled his side of the bed straight and dashed off downstairs. Adam quickly pulled up the covers on his side. It wasn't really making the bed properly, but there was no time for that. When he reached under his pillow to check on his scarab, Adam found a small, black velvet bag there as well. He opened it and found several fragments of what looked like reddish brown clay. How had the velvet bag got there? Someone must have put it there during all the commotion the previous night, but who and, more importantly, why?

Adam shoved the velvet bag back under his pillow, but popped his scarab into his pocket. He would ask Ebrahim about the clay bits when they saw him, which hopefully would be soon. Ebrahim was the only person who could possibly make sense of everything.

At breakfast, Florian and Archie were in the library, their voices raised as they argued about some obscure reference to Horace. Billy, Ink, Justin, and Kim were shoveling food down their throats as if they hadn't eaten for a week while Adam pushed his breakfast around with a fork, feeling inexplicably despondent. Justin and Kim were telling Ink how exciting Bedwyr's diary translation had been, until Justin noticed Adam.

"What's up?" asked Justin through a mouthful of scrambled egg. "Have some toast."

The two women were busy at the stove and Sheldon had disappeared into the pantry. Adam waited until Billy left the table to get more toast from Mrs. Grant before he spoke.

"Nothing." Adam shrugged. Then he put down his fork. "No, there is something. We went to all that trouble and now the second Stone of Power is missing. We didn't even find the Scroll of the Ancients."

Just then, Sheldon emerged from the pantry. "Oh, I almost forgot," he said, with a mischievous twinkle in his eyes. "What do you think I have here?"

He placed a stone on the table. Nothing special—just an ordinary, round, brownish stone. But Adam knew what it was. His fingers closed over the stone and he felt breathless for a few seconds, as if all the air had whooshed out of his lungs. He wondered why he felt something now when he touched the second stone, but hadn't felt anything in the museum.

Sheldon placed one hand on Adam's wrist, interrupting his thoughts. "Hamish came to me this morning and said he'd found this in one of the bird cages." His gaze was steady. "Be careful. Keep it safe."

Adam wasn't sure how much Sheldon knew so he didn't reply. He just smiled, nodded his thanks, and slipped it into his pocket next to his scarab. When

Sheldon returned to the pantry, Adam turned to the others. "Aquila and Horus saved the stone last night."

They nodded while chewing. "Yeah, good old Aquila and Horus," Justin mumbled through a big mouthful. "What would we do without them?"

"I wonder how they knew to come and save it," Kim said, looking bewildered. "I mean, clever or not, they are still just birds."

Justin leaned over to grab more toast. "Genius birds, I guess."

Adam couldn't figure it out. Yes, the birds were clever, but how had they known exactly what to do? Had Hamish sent them? Did Hamish know more than he was saying? He had mentioned the green language, the ability to understand birds, and those scars on his wrists covered up old tattoos.

"Aren't you surprised?" Adam asked Ink.

Ink gave a snort of laughter. "Eaters of Poison, underground passages, monks who blow up things with strange explosives, a helicopter on the roof ... now why would two smart birds rescuing the second Stone of Power surprise me?"

Sheldon popped his head around the pantry door. "Hamish said you might all like to visit the chapel today."

"We've already seen it," said Kim. "What's the point?"

Sheldon winked. "Hamish isn't given to inviting people out in his boat so perhaps you should go." He disappeared again.

They finished eating and then wandered down to the mews where they found Hamish busy with the birds.

"You'll be wanting to row over today, then," he said. It wasn't a question. "You need to see something."

"Uh ... thanks for the stone, Hamish," said Adam.

Hamish stared at him, unblinking. "What stone?" He walked quickly ahead to the boat.

"But—"

Ink poked Adam's back as he went past, giving a quick shake of his head to indicate Adam should say nothing more.

When they arrived at the island, Hamish said he would be back shortly. They wandered up to the chapel with Billy racing ahead as usual. He disappeared around the side of the building. Suddenly, they heard screaming. Everyone broke into a run. They turned the corner of the chapel and found Billy standing in front of the strange tower with no entrance. Half the tower lay in ruins, clearly the result of a lightning strike from the previous night's storm.

Billy pointed at something in the debris so Adam and Justin clambered over the stones to look while Kim took Billy to one side. Adam spotted it first: a long, thin shape, half-covered in rubble, and wrapped in brown hessian much like the fabric of the robes the monks wore. Brownish sticks poked out from under some folds on one side of the fabric. Adam pulled back the hessian and recoiled in fright. A lop-sided skull grinned back at him. The brownish sticks were the arm and shoulder bones of a skeleton. He knew instantly the identity of the skeleton.

"It's Bedwyr," he called out. "It must be him."

Ink climbed over the broken masonry and gently pulled the brown robes all the way back. The skeleton clutched a book to its chest. Ink slid the book from under the clinging finger bones and handed it to Adam so he could climb back down. Adam held it out to Justin, who gave a soft whistle of surprise.

"Look at the cover. It says *Codex Draconum*."

Ink peered over Adam's shoulder. "Isn't that the book the old pilgrim gave Bedwyr as a gift?"

Adam nodded. He stared more closely at the skeleton. The skull looked lop-sided because it was at an odd angle from the body. Bedwyr's neck had been broken.

When Hamish came to collect them, he wasn't shocked at their news, but said he would get Sheldon to call the coroner.

When they reached the castle, they found another surprise: Isabel and James had finally arrived. The archaeologist looked paler and thinner than when the boys had last seen their friend in Egypt, but James said he felt fit.

They sat together at the table in the library and pieced together their stories. Florian and Archie had taken their argument to the kitchen, where they were enjoying an early lunch and an animated discussion about somebody named Pliny the Younger. Billy had run off to the old shed, taking a bag of fruit and veggie snacks for Sirius.

Ink let Adam and Justin do most of the talking. Hearing of their adventures, Isabel didn't hit the roof as Adam had feared. Instead, when they were finished, she got up from her seat and hugged them both.

"I knew you two would manage just fine," she said.

"Uh … don't forget Kim, Aunt Isabel," said Justin. He pulled Kim forward. "She was amazing with her ideas and finding clues."

Isabel raised her eyebrows. "That's very generous of you, Justin."

Justin went red. "It's true. We couldn't have done it without her." He nudged Adam. "Right, bro?"

"Absolutely," said Adam. He glanced at his aunt and caught the twinkle in her eyes.

"We're sorry about the tunnels under the chapel and the secret passage being flooded," Justin said to James.

James was taken aback. "Sorry? But it's not your fault." He leaned forward and ruffled Justin's hair. "Hey, at least you found them after hundreds of years of various family members looking in vain. The water can be easily pumped out and the walls mended."

"Are you going to bury Bedwyr now?" Kim asked James.

James' expression became solemn. "Yes. He'll join the family in the Ancient Burial Ground, where he should have been these last seven hundred years."

"Didn't everyone believe he'd gone back to the monastery and died of poisoning?" asked Adam. "That's what you told us in Egypt. You said the monastery just sent back a few of his things."

"I've been thinking about that," James replied. "It looks as if he never made it. He must have gone to the chapel to pray for the last time before setting out on his journey and been accosted by someone. I think whoever was slowly poisoning him counted on Bedwyr being too weak to defend himself."

"So his body was here all the time," said Isabel, with a note of sadness. "That's why the monastery never returned it to the family. They couldn't."

"The family must have thought he'd been buried at the monastery," said James. "That explains why there's just the memorial stone and not a proper grave."

"He was definitely murdered," said Adam. "His skull wasn't straight on his spine." Adam didn't want to say it aloud, but he hoped that with a proper burial the monk's spirit would be laid to rest. After what Billy had said about seeing Sir Maulsby Dredwell and Bedwyr, Adam didn't want to face any ghosts while he was here. He'd had enough excitement for one holiday.

"I think his neck was broken by whoever attacked him," said Ink. "Then the murderer bricked up the body in the tower. I'm guessing here that no one

293

investigated because Bedwyr's father died at that time and, well, it was just left that way."

James didn't reply, but he looked gloomy, wrapped in his own thoughts. Then he said, "Tell me more about Bedwyr's diary."

"Yes," said Adam eagerly, keen to cheer James up. "It's amazing. It explains everything. It turns out the *Chronicles of the Stone,* Bedwyr's poem that Dr. Khalid stole, is actually a fake.

James burst out laughing. He laughed so hard he even slapped the top of the library table. "Now that's what I call good news. Maybe this will slow Khalid down and get him off our backs while he goes off in the wrong direction, searching for the next stone."

Justin added, "There's just so much information about the Scroll of the Ancients—and the Stone of Fire, as well. You have to read it. It's too much to explain."

James grinned and glanced at Ink. "Ink says you all helped him translate it, but that Justin hit on the right cipher to crack the code."

Justin glowed with pride. "Yes, actually it was my idea. I just knew from the start that it was the Caesar cipher."

"Incredible." James shot a sideways grin at Isabel. "I don't know how they do it."

"I told you how bright they are," she replied. "Now you know I wasn't exaggerating."

Adam placed the second Stone of Power and the *Codex Draconum* on the library table. "Now what do we do?"

James touched the stone with reverence. "This must go straight back to the Ashmolean and be restored to Excalibur."

"So you think the sword is Excalibur?" asked Justin.

James nodded. "I know it's Excalibur."

"Shouldn't this stone be locked up like the first Stone of Power?" Kim looked worried. "Dr. Khalid already tried to steal that so won't he try again?"

"It's safer in plain sight with museum security guards, state-of-the-art technology to protect it, and round-the-clock surveillance," James said reassuringly.

Adam thought privately that Dr. Khalid was far too clever to let any of that deter him from his mission, but he didn't say anything.

"And the book?" Kim asked. "When you read Bedwyr's diary, you'll see that someone gave it to him and said it was very important, and that he must read it carefully."

James turned the pages, glancing briefly at the images. "It's charming, but I can't see anything important here. Just pictures of mythological creatures and lots of dragons. We'll put it in the antique book collection."

Sheldon walked into the library with a tray of refreshments.

Adam winked at him. "You were right about the secret passage, Sheldon."

"Was I, Master Adam? How so?" The butler cracked a small smile.

"The secret passage *was* there and we found it just like the saying."

The butler raised his eyebrows. "What saying, Master Adam?"

"You know," Adam persisted. "You told us that when the castle inhabitants are in danger, the tunnel will be revealed for their safety."

Sheldon coughed. "Did I say that? Goodness me, Master Adam. I really can't remember."

"But—"

Justin kicked him under the table. "Can we have chocolate cake as well, please, Sheldon?"

"Right away, Master Justin." The butler disappeared and Adam felt he hadn't wanted to explain further.

James stretched. "I don't know about the rest of you, but I'm for a hot shower and a long sleep."

Aunt Isabel said, "That goes for me as well. There's a lot to catch up on, but I'm so tired that my brain is turning into mush. See you kids later."

The adults exited the library, leaving the cousins and Kim alone with Ink.

"There are too many loose ends," grumbled Adam. "Just like in Egypt. I've got so many questions and no one seems to be able to answer them." He frowned at his companions. "Actually no one seems to *want* to answer them."

Ink pointed to the *Codex Draconum*. "Let's have a look at the book since it was mentioned in Bedwyr's diary. Didn't he say that he'd given it to his father because it was just a book about mythological animals?"

"That's right," said Adam. "But remember when we found Bedwyr's body, the book was tucked into his robe and he was holding it, as if he was trying to protect it."

"So maybe he found something important in it after all," said Justin. "Let's see."

Adam pulled the book across the table at the same time Justin reached for it. As they both grabbed, there was the sound of tearing.

"Be careful," said Ink.

Justin glared at Adam. "Look what you did."

Adam glared back. "It wasn't me. You pulled it too hard."

"Guys …" Kim's voice was quiet. She pointed to the book. Part of the leather cover had torn away from the binding, revealing a yellowish piece of parchment tucked into where the cover folded over.

Ink carefully teased it out and unfolded the parchment. "This is interesting."

The argument forgotten, Justin and Adam leaned forward.

"Is it in code?" Justin asked. "I like code."

Ink scanned the lines. "I don't think so. It doesn't look like the writing in Bedwyr's diary. There's a diagram here … but without the wording, I don't know what it means."

Adam peered at the diagram and the strange writing. "That's the same kind of star that was on Arthur's sword."

Ink examined the document closely. "Really?"

"What language is it?" asked Kim.

"Beats me," said Ink. "But I think it's extremely old, like Aramaic or some kind of ancient text."

"We should give it to Ebrahim," said Adam. "I hope we see him soon. He'll be able to tell us what it means."

"And what do the animals and those squiggly things mean?" Kim indicated the strange symbols.

Ink pointed to the images. "These are symbols of the various planets. Here are the alchemical signs for different metals. Then in the corners, you can see the images of a bird, a stag, a salamander, and a fish, which I guess are for air, earth, fire, and water. This is incredible, but I have no idea what it all means."

Adam scrutinized the diagram. At the top of the picture was a winged image. It looked Egyptian. "What's this?"

Ink examined it. "I think that's called the winged disk of Akhenaten." He pointed to the image in the middle of the diagram. "This looks like the Egyptian all-seeing eye."

In the center of the strange diagram was the *udjat* they had heard about in Egypt. It was the all-seeing eye of Horus and was supposed to give protection. On the sides of the diagram was the *ankh*, the Egyptian sign of life—just like the unusual mark on Adam's back. Adam felt a strange excitement stealing over him. This all led back to the quest for the Seven Stones of Power and the *Book of Thoth*. All these bits of information just needed someone to put them together, like pieces in a puzzle. He wished Ebrahim were here right now to make sense of things.

"What shall we do with this?" he asked.

Ink said, "I'll show this to James as soon as he comes down and he must send it to Ebrahim right away. It's too precious for us to keep, I'm sure." He folded the paper carefully and slipped it back inside the *Codex Draconum*.

Sheldon came into the library with a large chocolate cake. He bowed and handed the plate to Justin. "All yours, Master Justin."

Justin went red when the others burst out laughing. "No, I didn't mean all for me."

"Just my little joke, Master Justin. Mrs. McLeod asked me to remind you there's a small ceremony down at the village square this afternoon."

Ink raised his eyebrows. "What kind of ceremony?"

Sheldon's eyes twinkled. "I believe we have a local hero. Constable Parrott is getting a commendation for bravery from the station commander for his part in apprehending the ruffians the other night."

On their way to the ceremony, they stopped off at the vet for Ink's final check up. There was no one else in the waiting room because everyone was probably down at the square, waiting for the ceremony to begin. Even the receptionist had left early. Bruce invited them into his office and closed the door. To their surprise, Mac was there. The scientist looked as shabby as ever, but something seemed to have happened to him, something amazing that had transformed him. His face glowing with excitement, he sat at Bruce's desk, staring with disbelief at two thick parcels. Mac had unwrapped the contents and they lay on the table, half-covered with brown paper.

"It's wonderful," he stammered. "Amazing ... even miraculous."

"What is it?" asked Adam.

Bruce stared at them with narrowed eyes. "Do you know anything about these?" He indicated the two parcels.

Adam shook his head, Kim shrugged, and Ink said, "Nothing to do with us."

"So what is it?" Justin asked impatiently.

Mac lifted a bundle of yellowed pages, bound with twine, and held them out. "This is something I thought was lost in the mists of time." His voice quivered. "It's a copy of the *Book of Venoms*, written by Magister Santes de Ardoynis. It was the average assassin's most sought-after guide throughout the fifteenth century. And this"—he lifted another bundle of pages from the other parcel—"is a copy of the *Book of Antidotes*, written by Peter of Albano."

"Are they important?" Kim asked.

"Are they *important*?" Mac echoed. "This is the completion of my work. In these historical documents, I know I will find the information I have been seeking."

Something suspiciously like tears glittered behind his oversized lenses.

Bruce folded his arms. "What *I'd* like to know is how these two ancient manuscripts arrived at my surgery with Mac's name written on the wrappings."

Adam put on his most innocent look. "We're as puzzled as you. Maybe someone heard about Mac's research and wanted to help him anonymously."

"Yeah, you know," Ink added, "maybe a collector of ancient manuscripts who just wanted to do something for science."

"They're right!" Mac leaped up from his chair, took off his glasses, and began cleaning them with the corner of his jacket. "I've been writing to museums and libraries for years, asking for information and now, finally, some Good Samaritan who doesn't wish to be named has sent me the information I desperately need." He looked at Bruce. "That's it."

"Well," Bruce said, "if you kids haven't got anything to do with it then I guess it's the only answer. Come on, Ink, let's do your check up." He held up his stethoscope. "Take a deep breath in."

He sounded so skeptical that Adam was glad when they finally escaped to make their way to the village square.

"The monks helped Mac," Adam told the others as they walked. "I didn't think they would, but they did. Ink gave them the secret book of Arthepius and in exchange they gave Mac those two manuscripts about poisons and stuff."

As he spoke, he thought about the velvet bag under his pillow. He was certain now it had also come from the monks. He could have asked Mac about the little pieces of clay, but that would have just aroused Bruce's suspicions even more. He would have to wait until they saw Ebrahim again.

When they arrived, they saw a makeshift podium and a band nearby, getting ready to play. Apparently, news about the event had travelled fast as a number of flea market stalls had mushroomed overnight, selling homemade items, food, and various goodies.

At precisely 2:00 p.m., the station commander called for everyone's attention and Sidney, his face bright red, stumbled onto the podium to receive a medal and a written commendation. He was so thrilled he could hardly concentrate on the station commander's words. Out of the corner of one eye, he spotted the gorgeous Beryl Winkworth, and, to his amazement, the rest happened just as he had imagined. Beryl took a tiny lace-edged handkerchief from her cardigan sleeve and fluttered it at him, while smiling in a most encouraging way. As she glanced up at him from under her long black eyelashes, her blue eyes sparkled with the promise of amazing possibilities. Madame FiFi had been right. His dreams had come true. A promotion and love—all in one day.

Adam and the others clapped loudly after the station commander's speech. Sidney became so tearful that he could barely stammer out a few words of thanks. The band struck up an energetic tune and people began dancing in the square. Ink spotted someone he knew and left to go chat.

Justin pointed to a small caravan parked at the edge of the village green. "Hey, a fortuneteller." He elbowed Adam. "Remember the one in Egypt? Boy, she was weird."

"Cool," said Kim. "I'd love to hear my fortune. Maybe she can tell me if I'll pass math this year."

Adam felt uncomfortable. He didn't want another experience like in Egypt when the old fortuneteller had told him his life was in danger. From then on, they had plunged headlong into a series of life-threatening events and Adam had nearly died. For him, even one near-death experience was too much.

"Naah," he said, trying to sound casual. "Let's give it a miss."

Justin read the sign outside the fortuneteller's caravan aloud. *"Madame FiFi's amazingly accurate and true predictions. Find out what the stars hold in store for you."* He winked at Adam. "No palms this time. Madame FiFi does tealeaves."

Justin and Kim ignored Adam's protests as they strolled over to the caravan. Madame FiFi was showing out a smiling visitor, who then trotted down the caravan steps.

"Look," said Justin. "A satisfied customer."

Madame FiFi was a buxom woman, dressed in a traditional gipsy style with a frilled white blouse and a long, multicolored skirt. Dark curls tumbled from the confines of the bright red turban on her head. She wore clinking gold bracelets and big, round gold earrings. Heavy black makeup ringed her eyes, giving her a mysterious look. When she spoke, however, she rolled her *r* sounds, just like Mrs. McLeod.

"Hullo, me darlings," she cooed. "Want yer fortunes told then?" She looked them up and down before naming her price. "I'll do a group discount. Five pounds."

"Sure," said Justin, feeling in his pockets.

"Come along then, kids," said the fortuneteller. "Pay me after the reading."

They squeezed into her cramped caravan and sat down on a rickety sofa. Her bracelets jangling with each gesture, Madame FiFi poured hot water from a kettle into three cups and then spooned tealeaves into each cup.

Adam watched the dark flakes of tea swirling in his cup.

"Now," she instructed them. "Turn yer cup round nicely a few times before the first sip, drink the tea, and then turn the cup upside-down on the saucer."

The tea tasted slightly bitter without milk or sugar, but wasn't unpleasant.

Madame FiFi looked at Kim's cup first. "Ooooh, dearie," she trilled. "It says words and numbers will be your friends."

Kim looked puzzled. "What does that mean?"

Madame FiFi made a small impatient noise. "I don't know, dearie, it's just the message I get. You must make of it what you please."

She took Justin's cup. "You next, luv." She peered into the cup. "This one says the position you desire will be yours."

"Yes!" Justin gave an air punch. "I know I'll be a prefect next year."

The fortuneteller giggled. "Maybe even head boy some day if you play yer cards right."

She turned to Adam. "Now let's see what's in store fer this young man."

Adam felt a sudden wooziness when he put his cup down. He closed his eyes as a fierce wind rushed past him. When he opened them again and looked down, he was standing on the top of an immense tower. A soft, brilliantly hued garment covered his arms. It was a cloak made of iridescent feathers, their colors sparkling in the sunlight. He lifted his hands to his head. He wore a strange headdress. It was heavy and, from what he could feel, elaborately decorated.

Where am I?

Miles and miles of forest spread out in front of him in a vast expanse of greenery. He heard faint cheering and then the *whoomp-whoomp* of mighty wings. A giant bird circled him, the beating of its enormous wings sending gusts that lifted his feathered cloak, causing it to float behind him like beautiful wings. Now the excited crowd was screaming, roaring, cheering. He turned his head to see a dark shadow falling across him.

Cold liquid splashed onto his face. As he looked up from where he was lying on the caravan floor, three anxious faces stared down at him. He blinked and rubbed his eyes. Madame FiFi was holding a jug.

"Are you all right, dearie? It's just ordinary tea from the supermarket." Madame FiFi picked up his cup and sniffed it. "This has never happened before. I always use Typhoo Tea."

Kim and Justin helped Adam to his feet.

"I'm okay," he told them. "I just felt dizzy."

Madame FiFi nodded in sympathy. "It's warm today and a bit crowded in here. Best get back home. Maybe have a little lie-down?" She ushered them out of the door and down the caravan steps.

Justin turned back. "But I haven't paid you."

However, just like the fortuneteller in Egypt, Madame FiFi didn't seem to want payment. She shook her head and waved. "Toodle-oo."

"Didn't you see anything for Adam?" Kim called to her.

"Er … just a big bird," said the woman. "Maybe his mum's going to buy him a parrot."

As they wandered back to the village square, Adam didn't say anything about his fainting fit until finally Justin asked, "What happened back there?"

Adam shrugged. "It was nothing. Like I said, I felt dizzy." He looked ahead. "Hey, there's Aunt Isabel and James. Let's catch up to them."

In her caravan, Madame FiFi picked up the cup the boy had used. She stared at the pattern of tealeaves for a few minutes, then sat down heavily on the sofa, wondering if she should call them back. Then she shook her head. It was probably an anomaly, something that hadn't happened for a long time. How could she explain to a young boy that in his future she had seen travel to a distant and dangerous land, a giant bird, and a blood sacrifice?

The Excalibur Stone Returned

Standing in the Ashmolean Museum, Adam tugged at his stiff collar. Isabel had bought them all smart clothes for this special occasion—the unveiling of the statue of King Arthur. Justin stood next to Adam, also in his suit and tie, looking as uncomfortable as his cousin felt. Kim, on the other hand, was radiant with excitement. She and Isabel looked very nice in their new outfits.

Isabel had even bought a hat for the occasion, causing the boys to raise surprised eyebrows. To their knowledge, their aunt had never worn a fancy hat like that before. Justin had said quietly that all those feathers made the hat look like a bird perched on her head. Kim said he should be careful about what he said because the hat was actually called a "fascinator" and cost a lot of money.

With them were James, Ebrahim Faza, his friend Hamid, Ink, and Humphrey. Amelia wasn't there because she had decided to watch it all on television with her friend Mildred Perkins and Pandora. Everyone looked splendid. Ebrahim had joined them at last, as he had promised. Adam thought it was a pity their friend had missed all the exciting parts of the adventure. Ebrahim wore his official suit with the red sash and his array of medals, which Justin and Adam had seen before when he came to their school back home with an Egyptian delegation to give them medals. Hamid, his tall, thin Egyptian friend, wore the long red robes he favored. Humphrey, reeking of mothballs, looked a little less crumpled than usual, but his shabby tweed suit obviously hadn't been worn in a long time. Ink wore his usual jeans and skull-and-crossbones T-shirt. He only put on a jacket after Amelia threatened to make him stay home.

Archibald Curran and Florian Boldwood stood a little way off, surrounded by museum directors. Florian was subdued, unlike his usual brash, publicity-loving self. Archie had bought a new spotted bowtie in hideous bright yellow and lime green for the occasion. He looked so happy, his round face shining with pride and enthusiasm, his chins wobbling and his expression animated as he greeted and talked to everyone.

As it was the biggest event Oxford had ever seen, the *Who's Who* of British society and politics had all arrived. The place was crammed with stylishly dressed important guests and dignitaries, as well as newspaper and television reporters waving cameras. Adam recognized the presenter Nigel Smith who had interviewed Florian when the second stone had first disappeared. People mingled, greeting each other and chatting, while harassed waiters darted among the crowd, balancing trays of drinks and snacks.

Adam tried to concentrate on the deputy prime minister's speech. The gray-haired Sir Reginald Swank was in his sixties. Of medium height and build, he had a weak chin, which detracted from his otherwise pleasant face. He seemed in awe of his wife, Lady Clarissa Swank, who looked much younger and more ambitious than her husband. She was a tall, big-boned woman, dressed in a sophisticated suit of pale pink silk, with a string of large pearls around her neck, and pearl drops in her ears. Her jet-black hair was set in an elegant twist atop her head. She graciously posed for the eager swarm of reporters. As the cameras flashed, her rouged smile was poised and practiced, but her pale green eyes were cold and calculating.

Skilled decorators had transformed the Special Exhibitions Gallery for this important event. A range of exhibits showed life in the Dark Ages, along with cases of artifacts, weapons, and ornaments. A tall rectangular shape covered with a red velvet cloth stood in the middle of the floor. At the appointed moment, Lady Swank would pull on a gold-tasseled cord and the cloth would fall away, revealing what the museum's sculptors and artists had been working on tirelessly for several weeks.

"And so," said Sir Reginald with a proud smile, "we are delighted that the stone stolen from Arthur's sword, Excalibur, has been found and returned to its rightful place. We'd like to thank the Oxford police for their unflagging efforts in the case, as well as several members of the public who provided vital information."

He gave Detective-Inspector Bradley a nod of acknowledgment. Adam was surprised to see the police officer there and hoped like crazy the police had forgotten about the CCTV tapes on the day of the burglary.

Justin whispered in Adam's ear, "Vital information? For Pete's sake, we *gave* them back the stone."

Apparently hearing him, Lady Swank glared while Kim said, "Hush!" and Isabel poked him with a sharp elbow. Detective-Inspector Bradley looked in their direction and a small smile appeared on his face. Evidently, the police had *not* forgotten the CCTV tapes. Adam wondered how much they really knew.

"Let us not overlook," Sir Reginald continued, "what Arthur means to Britain and its people. Arthur is the ideal of kingship during both peace and war. He stands for everything that is true and good in a leader. He is a symbol of just sovereignty, one we can all aspire to emulate in our own way, however great or small. Perhaps one day he will be in our midst again."

As the crowd applauded, Sir Reginald peered at a group of reporters clustered nearby. "Any questions?"

Justin put up a hand. "I have a question."

An aide sprang forward as Sir Reginald raised his eyebrows. The aide muttered in the deputy prime minister's ear.

Sir Reginald looked around the room. "Well, I was expecting to field a barrage of questions from the press so this is a surprise. Maybe this young man is planning to be a reporter."

Justin went red when the room erupted into gales of laughter. "No, I'm not, sir. My question is what would you do if Arthur returned like all the legends say?"

Sir Reginald ran a finger under his collar to loosen it. He coughed and then flashed a diplomatic smile. "I'm not sure I can answer that, young man. It would not be up to me to decide what to do. We are, after all, a constitutional monarchy."

He gave an embarrassed *haw-haw* and everyone tittered in agreement.

A reedy voice came from the back of the room. "Why, Sir Reginald, Arthur promised he would return to save Britain from dark destruction in her hour of need. If indeed he did return, then would that mean the present government isn't doing its job properly?"

"Who is that?" Sir Reginald muttered to his aide. The aide consulted a list and then shook his head.

The voice continued. "The upholders of a corrupt and incompetent government would not welcome the return of Arthur, a noble and faultless ruler whose reign would rescue the nation."

A collective gasp sounded throughout the room and there was a murmur of shocked voices.

Sir Reginald bristled with anger. "Who are you to make these accusations? Show yourself, sir."

The crowd parted as a scrawny man limped to the front. Sir Reginald, who towered over his inquirer, glared at the wrinkled, almost shriveled figure.

"Caractacus Blight," the man said. "Curator of the Romano-British Collections at the British Museum."

Sir Reginald gave a thin smile. "Well, Mr. Blight, since you are an academic, I will assume your question and comments are merely rhetorical conjectures of an intellectual nature and do not require an official answer." He gave a nervous chuckle and the crowd broke into small bursts of laughter.

The tension passed and Sir Reginald beamed. "Now, I think it's time for the unveiling." He turned to Lady Swank. "My dear, will you oblige?"

Lady Swank stepped forward and pulled at the gold-tasseled rope. As she did so, the foyer lights dimmed and a spotlight shone directly onto the red cloth. It swished to the floor in velvety folds, revealing the statue of King Arthur in a huge glass case. Another gasp erupted from the spectators.

"*Arturus Rex Quondam, Rexque Futurus*," said Sir Reginald, with an elaborate flourish of one hand. "Arthur, our once and future king."

Everyone clapped loudly and several people touched handkerchiefs to the corners of their eyes. It was a moving moment. Sir Reginald looked suitably solemn as he gestured for the lights to be turned up again. Waves of chattering voices rose and fell as people clustered about the glass case, *oohing* and *aahing* in admiration.

Adam felt as if he could burst with pride. "It's fantastic," he breathed.

"Yes, it is." Humphrey spoke quietly. "And exactly as you saw it in your dream."

It was true. Once they were back in Oxford, Adam had spent some time with Humphrey and Archie, describing his vision of Arthur on the eve of the Battle of Badon.

He had also drawn a picture of how he remembered Arthur's battle dress and the sword. To his amazement, the museum artists and sculptors had recreated his vision down to the last detail. Arthur sat astride a white horse that was rearing up on its hindquarters. The figure held aloft a magnificent sword with dragons decorating the hilt and a small seven-pointed star under the crossguard, just as he had seen it in his dream.

Adam felt in his pocket for the golden scarab. "But that's not the real sword, is it?" he asked Humphrey.

Humphrey laughed and shook a reproving finger. "No, son, of course not. There are many months of restoration ahead of us. This is only a replica."

"And the stone?" asked Justin. "Where's the second Stone of Power?"

"Safe," said a familiar voice behind them.

Justin and Adam turned to see a smiling Hamid with Ebrahim next to him. "And so ends the second adventure," Hamid said.

Adam felt an inexplicable pang of disappointment. "Yes, and we still don't know so much."

Ebrahim raised his eyebrows. "More questions? Let us try to answer them."

"I know we rescued the second Stone of Power," Adam said, "but we didn't find the Scroll of the Ancients, which I thought was so important. So we failed."

Hamid looked surprised. "Failed? You did not fail, my dear Adam. The scroll will be found when the time is right. Perhaps we have all been too hasty and things were not meant to happen as we envisaged them."

Ebrahim chuckled. "James already told us the interesting news that Bedwyr's *Chronicles of the Stone*, that Dr. Khalid stole and believes in so fervently, is actually a fake, a red herring as you say." He put his hand up to his mouth to hide his amusement, but his shoulders quivered. "And we all know that Dr. Khalid believes the scroll is lost so we have that advantage as well."

"Aren't you worried that it will be harder to find more Stones of Power now?" Adam asked.

Ebrahim shook his head. "We told you in Egypt that the first Stone of Power, the sacred scarab, exerts a compelling magnetic influence on the other stones. Look how quickly those archaeologists found Arthur's war regalia. I believe they were actually digging for something entirely different at the time. The remaining five stones will surface and we must be there first to find them when they do."

"However, your search for the scroll unearthed more information about the entire quest," Hamid continued. He took a piece of paper out of his robe pocket. "This document you and Justin discovered hidden in the cover of the *Codex Draconum* offers clues that will ultimately trace the Scroll of the Ancients."

"We don't know what the writing means," said Kim.

Ebrahim and Hamid exchanged satisfied smiles.

"But we do," said Hamid. "When James sent it to us with the translated copy of Bedwyr's diary, I summoned my best historical and archaeological experts to work on it."

Everyone, including James and Isabel, drew closer to Hamid.

"That's not the original," Adam said, noticing how new the document appeared.

Hamid shook his head. "No, the original document is fragile and, of course, too precious to carry around. It's safely locked away. I have copied the drawing and the translated text."

Adam peered at the diagram. "What does it mean?"

"Let me read the text to you," said Hamid. "The English translation is on the back." He turned the page over to reveal writing.

"*This picture, plain and insignificant in appearance, concealeth a great and important thing. Yea, it containeth a secret of the kind that is the greatest treasure in all the world. Now there remain only the Seven Signs. Hear further what they mean. If thou dost understand this well, this knowledge shall nevermore fail thee. Seven realms with seven kings; seven times with seven spheres; seven ciphers, seven beasts, and seven metals. Also, seven arts and the Seven Stones. Well for him who findeth this. Herein is a secret thing of the wise in which is to be found great power.*"

Hamid looked up at a ring of blank expressions.

Ebrahim said, "Hamid and I believe—"

The answer hit Adam like a ton of bricks. "I know what it means. This is the whole quest in a nutshell." He pointed to the paper in Hamid's hand. "Seven realms means seven places we'll have to visit on the quest, like Egypt and then Scotland and then wherever is next. 'With seven kings' means—"

Justin interrupted. "Those must be the seven kings that last used each Stone of Power before they were lost."

"Seven times would be the era or time period each stone was last used," James said slowly, "and *with* seven spheres would be the seven planets significant at that time."

Ebrahim's expression was somber. "So that likely means the alignment of those planets within the next eighteen months."

He glanced at the cousins. "Do you remember in Egypt that I explained about the confluence of the planets at that time? The person who reunites all seven stones with the Stone of Fire will be able to read the *Book of Thoth*."

He patted Adam's shoulder. "What else do you make of this mysterious text?"

"Seven beasts are easy." Adam grinned. He took the page from Hamid, turned it over, and pointed to the diagram. "Here's the sacred scarab that came first and then I saw a red dragon on Arthur's banner."

"Seven metals—we already know about the gold for the Scarab King and meteoric iron for Arthur's sword," said Justin.

"Don't forget the actual symbols for the planets and the metals in the diagram," Ink said, pointing to the paper. "There are more clues in the drawing itself."

Justin said, "Seven ciphers means seven codes. We already translated hieroglyphics in Egypt and the Latin Caesar cipher in Bedwyr's diary."

Ebrahim and Hamid applauded softly.

"What are the seven arts?" Adam asked.

Ebrahim looked solemn. "Well, this has baffled us because it seems there are two answers."

James raised his eyebrows. "Two?"

Hamid nodded.

Ebrahim placed one hand on Adam's shoulder. "Whatever the meaning in this text, it concerns you. We think the seven arts could be the *artes magicae* ... either the *artes liberales* or the *artes mechanicae*."

Adam remembered the head monk asking them if Mercury Jones practised the ancient arts. Could it be the same thing?

Hamid continued, "The *artes liberales* are good qualities you will discover in yourself, Adam. As the chosen bearer of the sacred scarab and finder of the Seven Stones, your journey will test you in such a way that you will need these qualities."

Adam's stomach turned over. He looked up into Ebrahim's face, which wore a gentle smile.

"What are these qualities?" Adam asked.

"I think you have learned the first two already. Compassion—or mercy—which you showed in Egypt when you saved Ismal from the shifting sands. Then courage, which you displayed when you helped rescue Terence Burns from the flames of his cottage, and on the rooftop when you tackled Dr. Khalid."

"But it wasn't only me," Adam protested. He glanced at his cousin and then back at Ebrahim. "Justin shared in all the dangers in Egypt, and he and Kim were with me on this last adventure. They also helped save Terence."

"That's not quite true," said Justin. "In Egypt I was ready to let Ismal die because I was so angry. You talked me out of it. You also tried to stop Dr. Khalid from escaping in the helicopter by yourself. I know we all helped Terence, but Kim and I didn't do anything else."

"And the other qualities?" Kim asked.

"I do not know in what order they will manifest," said Hamid, "but they are healing, wisdom, teaching, humility, and power."

Adam flipped the page and read aloud, *"Herein is a secret thing of the wise in which is to be found great power."*

"Exactly. The merging of the Seven Stones of Power with the Stone of Fire, and the ability to control time, the universe, and ..." Hamid sighed. "You know the rest."

Adam tried to give the paper back to Hamid, who pushed his hand away. "No, this is your copy. You will need this to guide your future steps."

Adam stared at him. "Aren't you going to help us work it out properly? Tell us what all the other things mean?"

Hamid shook his head. "No, Adam, that task is one you and your companions will complete."

Before Adam could protest that they didn't really know much more about all the mysterious things the diagram portrayed, Isabel butted in.

"What are the *artes mechanicae*?" Isabel asked. "You said the *artes liberales* are good. Does that mean the *artes mechanicae* are bad?"

Before Ebrahim could answer, Archie surged up to them, breathless with excitement. He had someone with him—the shriveled little man who had been rude to Sir Reginald. Up close, Caractacus Blight was not an agreeable sight. Frown lines crisscrossed his forehead, while deep furrows of discontent pulled down the corners of his mouth. Even his balding head looked wrinkled. He hunched his shoulders as if he had a crooked back, and he walked with a slight limp.

"Hello, everyone!" Archie looked so pleased. "Allow me to introduce my good friend Caractacus Blight. We were at Oxford together as students. We had such happy times." He put his arm around the man's shoulders. "Our paths have crossed again. How fortunate."

When Adam saw Caractacus Blight's sullen expression, he knew instinctively that Caractacus was no friend to Archie.

Poor Archie, can't he see how jealous this man is of him?

"Come along," Archie said, dragging Caractacus off. "So many people I'd like you to meet."

Isabel turned to Ebrahim as if to ask her question again, but Hamid tapped his watch.

Ebrahim nodded in response. He took Isabel's hand and bowed over it. "So nice to see you again, Isabel. I look forward to reading your forthcoming article about the theft and rescue of the Excalibur Stone, no doubt with a thought-provoking political or social angle. We must be off now."

James drew Isabel aside to speak to someone just as Nigel Smith pounced on Humphrey and Ink, babbling questions and demanding a photo. He beckoned frantically to a photographer. No one took any notice of the kids. Adam, Justin, and Kim stood with Ebrahim and Hamid.

"B-but what's going to happen next?" Adam stuttered.

The corners of Ebrahim's mouth lifted in a familiar, secretive smile. "Be patient. The next chapter will begin sooner than you think."

"But when?" asked Justin. "How will we know?"

Hamid patted Justin's shoulder. "James will inform you when the quest resumes. Ebrahim and I are working on getting as much information as possible on the whereabouts of the third Stone of Power."

Justin broke into a wide grin. "Cool. I can't wait."

"I have one last question," Adam said.

Ebrahim and Hamid exchanged glances and then looked quizzically at him. Adam sensed they really wanted to go, but were staying to listen just to be polite.

He reddened a little. "Actually it's two questions in one. Where did the monks come from? I mean why did they suddenly appear and if they're *not* the Dark Brothers, who are the Dark Brothers?"

Ebrahim and Hamid reacted exactly as the monks and Dr. Khalid had done. They looked around in a furtive manner, as if someone might be listening, and then moved closer.

Ebrahim wasn't smiling when he spoke. "I told you in Egypt that the discovery of the first Stone of Power had stirred the universal ether and that soon the other stones would manifest, drawn by the magnetic force of the first stone."

Adam nodded.

"Alas," Ebrahim continued, "other strange and sometimes unwelcome creatures may also come to light, with their own plots and ambitions."

He glanced behind him and said, "As for the Dark … er … the other people that Bedwyr mentioned in his diary. They are a truly malevolent and dangerous group. They make the Eaters of Poison seem harmless."

As the words from Bedwyr's diary popped into Adam's head, he whispered them softly. "Seek not the kingdom of darkness, for evil will surely appear; 'tis only the Master of Brightness shall vanquish the shadow of fear."

To Adam's astonishment, Hamid replied, "Know that light is thine heritage. Know that darkness is only a veil. Sealed in thine heart is brightness eternal, waiting to turn night pale."

Adam gasped. "But that wasn't in the diary! How do you know …?"

Someone called Adam's name and he looked around. When he turned back, Ebrahim and Hamid had disappeared.

Sir Reginald approached them. "Ah, our young heroes. Come along now."

He then beckoned to several aides, who sprang forward and began to escort the cousins and Kim out of the room.

"Hey," Justin protested. "Where are we going?"

"Please come with us," said one of the aides, placing a firm hand on his shoulder.

Adam saw Isabel and James standing with another group. They merely waved and Isabel called, "See you in a few minutes." Even Ink and Humphrey seemed to know something he did not because they also smiled and waved. Nigel Smith pointed to them and mumbled to his photographer.

315

They went down some stairs and reached a room just off the main foyer. Sir Reginald studied Adam with a grave expression. "You have done us all a very good service, young man. A great day for Britain. Perhaps you will become a politician in the future and serve your own country."

Adam shook his head. "No, sir, I have a much more important task ahead of me." •

"And what's that?" Sir Reginald asked with an indulgent smile.

"I have to save the world," Adam said solemnly.

Before Sir Reginald could reply, the door to the room opened and an aide came out. He whispered something to Sir Reginald, who then ushered them inside. The aides stayed outside, leaving them alone with Sir Reginald and the single occupant of the room: a small, elderly woman, wearing a turquoise dress and matching coat, and a perky hat with lots of feathers and netting. She sat in an armchair, her hands clasped in her lap, and a large handbag at her feet. A fat Corgi dog lay fast asleep under her chair. Adam had seen her before, but he wasn't sure where.

"Omigosh," Kim hissed. "It's her. The queen of England. I've seen her picture in one of Gran's overseas magazines."

"Come along," whispered Sir Reginald. "Don't be nervous. You may address Her Majesty as Ma'am."

His throat dry, Adam stumbled as he walked forward. The monarch stood and shook hands with him, and then with Justin and Kim.

When she spoke, her voice was low and pleasant. Kim stared at her, mesmerized and tongue-tied. Justin, who had gone bright red, made a sort of gargling sound and then kept quiet.

"I believe we owe you three young people a huge debt of gratitude," she said. "For rescuing the Stone of Excalibur at great risk to yourselves."

Justin and Kim were still speechless so Adam did the talking. "Uh … you're very welcome, Ma'am," he croaked. His voice also seemed to desert him. "It was nothing."

The queen gave them such a sweet, charming smile that she seemed as warm and caring as Gran. She shook her head. "It was a brave and selfless act."

She beckoned to Sir Reginald. He reached into his pocket and took out three small, flat, maroon boxes.

Her next words were surprising. "In the interests of national security and your own personal safety, we have made this a private occasion, just between us."

Her meaningful glance meant they couldn't tell anyone … well, not any adults anyway.

Sir Reginald flipped open the lid of the first box. He handed it to the queen, who shook Adam's hand and gave him the box, saying, "With our sincere thanks and gratitude."

Adam examined the medal inside while she gave a box each to Justin and Kim.

"I think it's rather a delightful interpretation of the Arthur legend," the queen said in a chatty tone.

Adam looked up at her and felt his cheeks turn red. What did you say to the queen of England? "Er … yes, Ma'am."

The medal was a small gold circle attached to a blue ribbon. In the center of the medal was the seven-pointed star he'd seen on Arthur's sword. Engraved along the circumference of the medal were the words *Companion of Arthur.*

Sir Reginald coughed.

The queen looked at him and said, "Yes, I know."

An aide entered the room and began to usher the kids out.

As they walked toward the door, Adam heard the queen say to the deputy prime minster in a low voice, "Are you sure it's safe?"

"Quite safe, Ma'am."

These were the last words Adam heard before the door closed and the aide pointed the way back to the Special Exhibitions Gallery.

Most of the crowd had disappeared by the time they returned to the exhibition. Those remaining were chatting or finishing off the food. After examining the kids' medals, Humphrey, Ink, James, and Isabel stood with them in front of the statue of Arthur, admiring it. Adam gazed at the sword. For a fraction of a second, the stone in the hilt gleamed strangely. No one else seemed to have noticed it. Adam slipped his hand into his pocket and felt the scarab. The scarab had blazed with a weird light on the battlements, but it could have been the reflection of lightning that struck at the same moment. After all, it was only a replica and not the real scarab. He moved closer to the statue and stared at the stone in the sword again. The stone remained dull. Obviously, it was a copy, just as Humphrey had said. The strange gleam must have been a trick of the light.

"Will they have extra security?" he asked.

Humphrey said, "Yes, of course. They have installed state-of-the-art infrared beams and alarm systems so that when the real sword is ready for installation, it will be safe—safer, in fact, than locking it in a vault."

When a museum security guard approached them, Adam realized they were the last people left in the museum. He had a strange feeling of yearning, of not wanting to leave the statue, but when the man pointed at the wall clock, Isabel bundled everyone down the stairs and out of the main door.

What Adam and, in fact, no one else had noticed was the strange ring on the security guard's right hand. Roughly made and a mere crude representation of a master ring far more finely wrought, the design was still visible. It depicted a snake writhing around the hilt of a dagger. The dagger was piercing an intricate knot.

Later that night, Sir Reginald, wrestling with the bowtie that had annoyed him during the presentation, contemplated the evening's events.

"Interesting young boy," he said to Lady Clarissa, who sat at her dressing table while removing her jewelry.

She turned her head as she took off one earring. "What young boy?"

"Adam, the one who seems to be the hero of this whole affair."

Lady Clarissa gazed into the mirror, admiring her reflection. "You should have gotten a medal," she remarked sourly. She wiped off her pink lipstick with a tissue.

Sir Reginald gave an exasperated snort. "For heaven's sake, Clarissa, I'm the deputy prime minister. I don't need medals. He's a brave lad who helped return a precious artifact to the nation."

She gave him a cold stare. "The *deputy* prime minster."

Sir Reginald flushed. "Some women would be proud to be the wife of the deputy prime minster."

Lady Clarissa turned back to the mirror and began removing the other earring. "And what did you say to this little hero?"

Sir Reginald ignored the sneering note in her voice. "I asked him if he was going to be a politician."

Her silence prompted him to answer the unspoken question. "He said he had something more important to do."

Her laughter struck him as unkind.

"And what was that?" she asked.

"He said he had to save the world first."

"Ridiculous!" And with that, Lady Clarissa dismissed the topic. "I think you should speak to your secretary about getting more influential people to attend the French ambassador's dinner on Thursday. The present list is a bunch of old fogeys. No one I'd consider significant."

"When I was his age," Sir Reginald said softly, "I wanted to save the world once."

Lady Clarissa heard only a fragment. "What?" she said sharply.

Sir Reginald dropped his cuff links into a small leather box on the nightstand. "Nothing, my dear. Nothing at all."

the enö of this aöventure

That night, Adam snuggled deep into his pillows. This was their last night in Oxford and they spent it at Pandora Brocklehurst's cottage. Isabel and Kim shared a room while Adam shared as usual with Justin. What a fantastic day. The unveiling of the statue of Arthur, receiving a medal from the queen of England herself, and being called a Companion of Arthur. Who could ask for more? He drifted off to sleep, hoping he would have another dream about Arthur, but one that was more positive. The memory of his last dream—the sight of Arthur's haggard, battle-weary face—still troubled and haunted him.

He did not dream of Arthur that night. He awoke to the most delicious smell of bacon, eggs, and sausages wafting up to their room. Justin wasn't there. Adam heard the sound of china rattling, and Justin and Kim telling Aunt Isabel something. Aunt Isabel called for him to hurry up or there would be no food left. He quickly showered and dressed. Before going downstairs, he grabbed the small velvet bag and shoved it into his pocket, along with his scarab. He had forgotten to mention the strange bits of clay to Ebrahim, and then Ebrahim and Hamid had had to leave. Humphrey might know what the bits were.

Although they ate an enormous breakfast, Pandora insisted on giving them second helpings because everyone knew, she said, that airline food was inedible. Then they would walk the short distance to Humphrey's cottage for a last visit before catching the plane home. By now, their bags were packed and ready to go. They left their luggage just inside the garden gate, to collect when their cab came. Kim and Isabel strolled on ahead with Pandora. Isabel had her arm around Kim's shoulders, and she was bending her head down to listen to Kim. Kim was talking and laughing, obviously telling their aunt something funny. They looked so comfortable with each other. Adam felt strange, left out—maybe even jealous.

"What's up?" asked Justin.

Adam shrugged and dug his hands into his pockets. "Nothing."

"You're just a bit down because all the excitement's over," said Justin.

Adam glanced at him before kicking a stone out of the way. "Think so?"

Justin nodded wisely. "Yup. It's the big nosedive after the big adventure. I felt like that when we got back from Egypt."

Adam felt a bit better after hearing he wasn't the only one. "Me too."

They walked on farther. "So this is normal?" Adam asked.

"Oh, completely," Justin said with a knowledgeable air. "I just think of what's ahead of us and then I get excited again. I mean, we have such fantastic adventures still to come."

Adam shot him a puzzled look. "Even though you don't know where we're going next?"

Justin grinned. "That's the fun part. I can't wait for James to send us another invitation. Hey, wasn't the rest of holiday great?"

Adam thought about how the adventure at Strathairn Castle had ended. They had stayed another two weeks and lots had happened in between. When he had shown Justin and Kim the small velvet bag with pieces of clay, they both shrugged and said he should ask Humphrey. Justin didn't seem to think it was that important anyway. Terence had made a full recovery and, to everyone's astonishment, announced his engagement to Diana Kingston, Billy's therapist. Now Billy would have two parents again. The little boy was over the moon with happiness. Kim had decided that Smudge should stay at the castle. He and Jasper were such firm friends it would be a shame to part them. Jasper needed company when James was away. James had begun rebuilding the stables and Terence's cottage. When Omar and Hussein finally confessed to the Edinburgh police, they revealed they had started the fires. Between sobs for mercy, the two thugs said they had only meant to create a distraction so they and Dr. Khalid could get into the castle unnoticed. They said the fire had gotten out of control, but they hadn't meant to hurt anyone, and *especially* not the horses. They also confessed to trashing the library, searching for the second Stone of Power.

However, Adam still felt depressed about saying good-bye to their new friends. Mrs. Grant and Mrs. McLeod had given them all big hugs, shed tears, and made them promise to come back soon. Even Sheldon had sniffed when he shook their hands. Hamish had just mumbled something about knowing they'd be back to get under his feet, and then blinked a few times as if there was something in his eyes.

James had returned to Edinburgh that morning and Adam missed him already. Voices and laughter brought Adam out of his gloom as they arrived at the cottage. Humphrey gave them a warm welcome although he looked sad. Amelia and Ink were there, of course, as well as Archie. Now that he had his old job back, the plump academic seemed utterly transformed. Gone were the signs of discontent and resentment. He glowed, he effused, he sang the museum's praises; he even put in a good word for Florian Boldwood, whom he said had buckled down to some real hard work for a change. Apparently, Florian had even exchanged his designer suits for more ordinary gear.

After swopping news and catching up, Isabel said she couldn't believe the amazing story of Amelia and Ink.

Amelia hugged a red-faced Ink. "Finally, I could tell him the truth about his parents."

"But only after I had to work most of it out for myself," said Ink.

The grin on his face showed just how much the new knowledge meant to him. While listening, Pandora touched the corners of her eyes with a tissue.

Ink slapped Justin on the back. "How about that ride I promised you? I've got an extra helmet."

Justin looked as if he could explode with joy. "Really? I thought you'd forgotten."

"Never," said Ink. He glanced at Isabel. She was engrossed in conversation with Amelia. "C'mon, let's split while we can."

"This is so cool," said Justin. He and Ink dashed off before Isabel noticed.

Meanwhile, Humphrey approached Adam. "I can see you still have questions troubling you."

Archie sidled over to join them, clutching a cup of tea and, even at such an early hour, a cream bun that he stuffed into his mouth.

Adam shifted in his seat, feeling a bit uncomfortable, but Humphrey's expression was encouraging so he said, "Arthur told me to restore the Stone of Caledfwlch, lest the land descend into ravening darkness. Well, we did restore it but …"

323

Humphrey nodded. "I know what's bothering you. You never saw any results."

"Yes," Adam burst out. "I had a terrible dream of Arthur being defeated—that must have been his final battle, the Battle of Camlann—so now I don't know if what we did made any difference."

"Of course it made a difference," Archie said gently. "You have no idea just how much of a difference."

"And I will never know unless I dream about Arthur again, but since that last dream, I haven't." Adam felt miserable.

"Sometimes we cannot know," said Humphrey. "We just have to believe in what we're doing and press on."

"I don't know if I can do that," said Adam.

Humphrey patted his shoulder. "You can and you will."

Then Adam remembered something else that had been bothering him since that dreadful dream. "Why did Arthur fight his final battle against his nephew Mordred? I mean, Arthur was king, right?"

Humphrey waved at Archie. "You're the expert."

Archie's eyes gleamed. "Well, no, actually Arthur wasn't a legitimate king."

Adam was horrified. "But everyone says 'King Arthur' when they talk about him."

Archie put on a smug expression, set down his teacup, and pushed his glasses higher onto his nose. "Ah, well, here's the story. According to legend, Uther Pendragon was madly in love with Igraine, Duke Gorlois' wife. He asked Merlin to help him win her affection. Merlin was a bit rascally here and used his magic. Igraine didn't know that Merlin had cast a spell on Uther, enabling him to assume the likeness of Duke Gorlois, her husband. So when she conceived Arthur, she was actually still married to the duke, who was later killed in battle."

Adam frowned. "Merlin using a spell on people is like cheating."

Humphrey shrugged. "Legends ... you know how they are."

"Let me finish." Archie flapped one hand impatiently at Humphrey. "That's why Arthur was known in the historical records of the time as *dux bellorum*, or the 'commander of battles'—not a king. He was illegitimate and a king had to be the legitimate heir to rule."

"So why was Mordred fighting him?" asked Adam.

"Medraut was his correct name," said Archie. "You see, Uther ended up marrying Igraine after the duke died. Together they had Anna, Arthur's younger sister. After Anna grew up and married King Lot, she gave birth to Medraut. Therefore, Medraut had a legitimate claim to the crown through his mother and he was willing to fight Arthur for it. They fought at the battle of Camlann."

"Did Arthur die in the battle?" asked Adam, remembering Arthur's weary, battle-worn face.

Archie first nodded, but then shook his head. "Well, if legends are anything to go by, Arthur was taken to the magical isle of Avalon to heal his wounds and wait until Britain needed him again."

"*I perish by this people which I made,*" Humphrey quoted, "*though Merlin sware that I should come again to rule once more; but, let what will be, be …*" He coughed. "Tennyson. *Idylls of the King.* It's a lovely legend, but one wonders can it be true?"

"I don't know," said Adam. "But my dreams about Arthur were real." Then he remembered the velvet bag. He pulled it from his pocket and handed it to Humphrey. "I found this under my pillow the morning after we met the strange monks in the underground tunnel. I wanted to ask Ebrahim about it but I forgot. I think the monks left it for me."

Humphrey opened the bag and shook several earth-colored fragments onto his palm. He peered at the reddish bits.

Archie picked up a sliver and nibbled on it cautiously. "What's this?"

"I wouldn't eat that if I were you," Humphrey said.

Archie peered at Humphrey through his thick lenses. His eyes rolled owlishly. "But you're *not* me, Humphrey Biddle. Why shouldn't I eat this?"

"Because," Humphrey said, with a sly glance at Adam, "it's *terra sigillata.*"

Archie nibbled a bit more. "And? So?"

"It's made from goat's blood."

"Paaah!" Archie spat the bits into his handkerchief and took a huge gulp from his teacup. "Why didn't you tell me?"

"I've been trying to do just that," Humphrey replied patiently.

"What's it for?" Adam asked.

Humphrey turned one of the fragments over in his palm. "In the fifth century BC, a substance called *terra sigillata*, meaning 'sacred sealed earth,' was said to be a universal antidote. It consisted of red clay found only in a particular hill on the Greek island of Lemnos. The clay was retrieved once a year in an elaborate ceremony and mixed with goat's blood to make a paste. It's thought that the substance acted like activated charcoal, absorbing toxic chemicals and thus decreasing the amount of toxin absorbed by the gut."

Archie continued to make choking sounds. "I could be poisoned."

"Hardly likely, Archie," Humphrey replied drily. "It's an *antidote* to poison."

Archie stopped choking. He looked disappointed. "Oh. Well, why didn't you tell me before?"

Adam's gaze met Humphrey's mirthful twinkle and he almost burst out laughing. Humphrey continued to examine the pieces.

"What are you looking for?" asked Adam.

"The stamp or seal." Humphrey held a piece up for Adam to see while Archie made disapproving noises. "Look, this is a seal to show it's genuine. Virtually any kind of clay could have been passed off as the real substance from the island of Lemnos. To prevent fraud, this special clay was often prepared in tablets and stamped with a seal, thus giving the substance its name."

He shook the fragments back into the velvet bag. "This is the real stuff." He gave the bag back to Adam.

"The Eaters of Poison must have left it for me," said Adam, "because they gave our friend Mac two important manuscripts as well. Stuff to do with poisons and antidotes." He jiggled the bag up and down. "I wonder why they gave me this."

Humphrey looked at Adam over his gold-rimmed pince-nez. "Maybe you're going to need it later." He rubbed his forehead as if it pained him.

"Does your head still ache after the attack?" Archie asked with a sympathetic look.

"I almost forgot," said Adam. "One more thing. Who attacked you that night? And who left the manuscript for Ink?"

Humphrey and Archie exchanged glances and then both shrugged.

"We have racked our brains, dear boy," Archie said, "and come to a dead end."

Humphrey nodded. "The Oxford police investigated further and even sent someone up to Edinburgh to interrogate Dr. Khalid's men, Omar and Hussein. They flatly deny ever having been near the cottage, so they could not have been involved either in the attack or in leaving the envelope addressed to Ink on the doorstep."

Adam grinned. "A secret friend, maybe?" Then he thought for a moment. "Also a secret enemy, I guess? I mean, the guy who attacked you. Maybe the guy who attacked you was looking for the envelope the other guy delivered to your cottage."

The look that passed between Humphrey and Archie was strange, almost sly, but it was so brief that Adam thought he had imagined it.

"Yes, maybe you're right." Humphrey ruffled Adam's hair. "So it's lucky we have someone on our side, eh?"

"Don't you mind not knowing all the answers?" Adam asked.

Humphrey smiled. "All the answers? At my age, I consider myself lucky if I get *some* of the answers."

Archie said, "When you're as old as we are, dear boy, it's easier to be patient."

"My goodness," Isabel almost shrieked. "Look at the time! Where's Justin?"

The cab arrived at the gate, the driver honking impatiently just as Justin and Ink roared up to the cottage on Ink's bike. After a flurry of collecting bags from Pandora's cottage, checking tickets and passports, and giving hugs and promises to stay in touch, they were back at Heathrow Airport with Isabel.

On the plane, Justin sat next to Adam, Isabel sat on the other side of Adam, and Kim took the aisle seat because she said it made her feel safer.

Adam drifted off, his eyes closed.

Justin nudged him. "Hey."

Adam opened his eyes.

"What's up?"

Adam wriggled to get more comfortable. "Nothing. Just thinking."

"That's your problem," said Justin. "You think too much about things and you don't enjoy what happens. So, what *are* you thinking about?"

Before Adam could reply, Justin made a grand gesture, smacking his own forehead. "No, wait. Don't tell me." He peered into Adam's face. "Let me think. Unanswered questions?"

Adam gave a wry grin. "Yeah, no prizes for guessing, huh?"

When Justin lifted his eyebrows in inquiry, Adam said, "The Eaters of Poison, those monks, said that Arthepius wrote his manuscript in the twelfth century."

Justin nodded. "Yes, and they also said he'd been alive for about a thousand years, which I find a bit hard to believe."

"This is a crazy idea," said Adam hesitantly, "but maybe there's a connection between them, Bedwyr and the abbot, and Bedwyr's monastery."

Justin sat up as if electrified. "Because Bedwyr suspected he was being poisoned and his family also thought so?"

Adam nodded. "And maybe the abbot got Bedwyr to do all that research into old books and stuff because he was looking for Arthepius' manuscript about living for a long time. Remember Bedwyr said something in his diary about the abbot's purpose being revealed. I mean, maybe the abbot was also trying to find the Scroll of the Ancients, like we originally thought, and he figured that living for a very long time would be a huge plus in helping him find the scroll."

Justin looked astounded. "Maybe the *abbot* was really the Alchemist, the Master Poisoner, and the ancestors of the Eaters of Poison worked for him as assassins."

Adam frowned. "Could be. It's all terribly complicated."

"Then the abbot poisoned Bedwyr because he thought Bedwyr knew too much. It's scary how many people are willing to kill to get what they want," Justin replied. He finished off his complimentary packet of peanuts and pointed to Adam's snack. "Can I have your peanuts if you're not going to eat them?"

Adam passed him the packet. "Knock yourself out." Then he said, "I forgot to tell Ebrahim the monks knew about my vision of the destruction of the temple, the mark on my back, and they called me the Chosen One. It must all be connected."

Justin allowed himself a big smirk as he stuffed the last peanuts into his mouth. "Yep, it's all linked, see? I mean, everyone so far is connected to Egypt. Remember Bedwyr's diary? He described how the Brotherhood of the Stone was formed and the great secret of power was kept hidden until someone betrayed them.

328

The traitor who sold the secret of the Stone of Fire sold it to the ancestors of these Eaters of Poison. Remember? It was a lot of information. Whoever blabbed would have told everything—the *Book of Thoth*, the Stone of Fire, the Seven Stones of Power, what it all means. That's why the monks were so scared of Dr. Khalid when he used the curse of Sekhmet against them."

Justin wasn't joking; now he looked serious.

Adam nodded. "It all leads back to Egypt and the *Book of Thoth*."

"That's the whole point of it all. When one of the Eaters of Poison came to the shop the first time, didn't he ask Humphrey about mediaeval texts that mentioned Egyptian writing?"

Adam looked thoughtful. "If there's a connection between the ancestors of the Eaters of Poison and Bedwyr, maybe that's why they knew about the passages under the chapel. But I wonder how Dr. Khalid and his men discovered the secret door."

"He'd been to the castle before, remember?" Justin said. "Snooping around when he stole Bedwyr's *Chronicle* poem, which we now know is a fake. Anyway, when his men trashed the library looking for the second Stone of Power, they threw all the books down. They must have accidentally revealed the carved face of the Green Man that was probably hidden behind those books for hundreds of years."

Justin frowned as his own thoughts led him to another conclusion. "So, if Khalid's men opened the secret door, it would have been easy enough for the Eaters of Poison to follow after and hide away. Those funny footprints, remember?"

Adam did not reply. He was still puzzled about other details: the strange scars on Hamish's wrists that might conceal Celtic tattoos and him talking about the language of the birds, which the person who read the *Book of Thoth* would be able to understand. Then there was the fact that Sheldon seemed to know more than he was telling anyone. It dawned on him that there were weird similarities between the seven-pointed star on Arthur's sword, the worn carving on the chapel floor, and the diagram they had found inside the cover of the *Codex Draconum*. Oh, yes, and what about the creepy feelings they'd had in the Star Maze that also had seven points in a star shape. Had the pilgrim chosen Bedwyr randomly as the best person to hide the Scroll of the Ancients or did James' family have a deeper historical connection with the quest? And how did Hamid know those things he said, stuff about darkness being a veil? That was definitely not in the translation of Bedwyr's diary, but it sounded as if it could be part of the bit about the Dark Brothers. It was all too much to unravel at once. His brain felt stuffed with ideas and theories that might not even be true.

He dug in his other pocket and pulled out the diagram Hamid had given him. It was filled with weird symbols and signs, but this was a map in a way, a guide to what was coming.

Justin leaned over and peered at it. "You know what this is?"

Adam shook his head. "No, what is it?"

Justin smirked. "It's the Mystic Star, the one Bedwyr mentioned in his diary. It was bugging me last night and now you've reminded me. When we get back, we'll really look at it carefully. I'm sure all those squiggles mean something. Ink said something about signs of planets and metals."

Adam felt like an idiot as he folded the paper and put it back in his pocket. He was supposed to be the bearer of the sacred scarab and maybe he was the Heroic Child, although he wasn't too keen on that, and he didn't even recognize what Bedwyr's diary had told them.

"Hey, cheer up," Justin said. "I also don't know how it all adds up, but the good part is that we saved the second Stone of Power, we got a medal from the queen of England herself, and we're going on another trip soon."

"Doesn't it bug you when we don't get answers right away?" Adam asked. "It bugs me."

Justin laughed. "Naah! We'll find out as we go along, I'm sure." He leaned forward so he could see Isabel. "So must we keep quiet about this adventure, Aunt Isabel?" He put on a naughty, crooked grin.

Isabel laughed. "For a start, let's keep quiet about the Eaters of Poison. I think that would send your mothers into orbit."

Adam said, "But we can't tell anyone anything this time, can we?"

Isabel looked down at him, a gentle smile playing about her lips. She patted his hand. "No, I'm afraid not. I mean, when the queen of England asks you to keep a secret, I think it would be a bit like treason to talk about it. I guess you could tell your friends about the fun parts of your trip, like exploring Oxford, visiting the Ashmolean, seeing Edinburgh Castle, and spending your holiday at a real old Scottish castle. I'm sure there'll be something in the papers about the sword and the robbery at the museum, so you can talk about that. But not the dangerous stuff and certainly nothing about the queen."

Adam sighed. "I suppose as the quest continues we'll have to keep everything a secret, won't we?"

Isabel nodded. "I'm afraid so."

Kim folded her arms, a satisfied smile on her face. "I just worked out what Madame FiFi meant." She looked at the others. "What do you think she meant?"

Justin shrugged. "Dunno."

"She said words and numbers will be my friends."

Adam looked blankly at her. "So?"

"That means I'm going to pass English and math."

Adam grinned as he leaned over to give her a light arm punch. "Cool. You deserve it after beating us at deciphering Bedwyr's diary."

"Aunt Isabel," Justin asked, "have you got any idea where we're going next?"

She shook her head. "Absolutely none at all. We'll have to wait for James to contact us."

Then somehow things all came together for Adam—Kim's interpretation of her fortune, Justin's question, and his vision at Madame FiFi's. Standing on a tower, hearing the *whoomp-whoomp* of great wings beating and the rush of air as the giant bird flew past him, seeing miles and miles of green stretching out in front of him. Where could that be? He was sure of only one thing—that's where they would be going next.

Two weeks later, Miss Briggs, Adam's class teacher, needed to discuss something with Mr. Fry, the school's headmaster. She pushed open his office door as she called out, "Good morning, Headmaster."

Mr. Fry crouched at the window overlooking the sports field. In fact, *hunched* was a better word because he appeared to be gazing out of the window and holding something to his face. He whirled around as she entered and hid the something behind his back.

"Miss Briggs! You startled me."

"Headmaster?" Miss Briggs cocked her head at an angle in a gesture her pupils knew all too well as she studied the headmaster. "What are you doing?"

Mr. Fry's face turned a deep red at her suspicious tone. He sheepishly waved a pair of binoculars in front of her. "Just keeping an eye on things, Miss Briggs. Very necessary in a school of this size with so many different personalities at play here."

She frowned and moved closer to the window. "What are you looking at?"

He handed her the binoculars. "There, at the edge of the rugby field. Adam Sinclair. He was sitting alone for a few minutes and then half the class arrived, headed up by that fat boy. You know the one who's always in trouble."

"Wilfred Smythe."

Mr. Fry scowled. "That's right, Wilfred Smythe. Can't stand the little monster. I wish his parents would keep their promise about removing him if he fails another subject."

Miss Briggs expertly adjusted the binoculars. "I don't think that's going to happen soon, Headmaster."

Mr. Fry stared at her. "What do you mean?"

Miss Briggs continued to scrutinize the group. Then she straightened up and handed him the binoculars. "Here, take a look. I think you'll see better now."

"Oh, thank you." He squinted through the lenses. "They're all laughing. The fat—I mean Smythe—has just sat down next to Sinclair. He seems to be telling the other boys to sit down as well. Now Sinclair's talking. Now he's jumped up and he's waving his arms above his head." He turned to Miss Briggs. "What's going on?"

"I think Adam's telling them about the overseas trip he just had."

Mr. Fry raised his eyebrows an inch. "*Another* trip? He and his cousin just came back from Egypt. What gadabouts. My parents didn't take me anywhere, let alone overseas."

"Well, times have changed, Headmaster, and I believe in travel to broaden the mind." Miss Briggs' tone was tart. "Clearly, their parents have the same opinion."

The headmaster mumbled something in agreement.

Miss Briggs continued, "Ever since Adam's talk on Egypt, most of the class really pulled up their socks and did better in their term history test."

Mr. Fry raised his eyebrows another inch. "Really? Even Smythe?"

"*Especially* Wilfred Smythe," said Miss Briggs firmly. "He passed with flying colors. I was very impressed with his effort. He got a gold star for 'Most Improved Marks.'"

"Oh." Mr. Fry sounded disappointed.

They both stared out of the window at the circle of school kids who were paying close attention as Adam spoke.

"I wish they'd listen to me like that when I'm teaching," said the headmaster. "Where did he go this time?"

"I believe he and his cousin Justin went to England and Scotland. He said something about helping the police find an old relic that was stolen from the Ashmolean Museum in Oxford."

Mr. Fry blinked. This time his eyebrows shot up. "Really? The police *again*? What excitement at such a young age. Yes, I remember the Egyptian Embassy came to the school and gave him and his cousin those medals after they went to Egypt and got involved in cracking that smuggling ring."

Mr. Fry nodded as he recalled the occasion. "And what's next on the syllabus for your class, Miss Briggs?"

Miss Briggs handed him the subject file he had asked for.

"The Dark Ages," she said primly as she walked out of his office.

epilogue

C aractacus Blight limped up the garden path, his left leg aching more than usual. The deep furrows of discontent lining his face seemed even more pronounced. The gate squeaked shut behind him as he fumbled with the key in the front door. He stopped. Some instinct made him turn his head to glance at the bushes on either side of the path. Nothing. He looked across the road. Only a man at the bus stop.

Idiot, he'll be waiting a long time.

As he closed the front door, he froze in the shadowy hallway, his senses alert. Something felt different. The place seemed empty, but Caractacus knew his home of fifty-five years. Someone was there. He tiptoed slowly forward, treading with care on the worn carpet. He reached the living room and slid his hand around the doorjamb, fumbling for the light switch. A strange smell teased his nostrils. Cigar smoke? He stared into the gloom where a pinprick of orange glowed.

"Stop creeping about, Caractacus, my good fellow. Yes, do put on the light."

Stunned, Caractacus obeyed. The man sitting comfortably in an armchair wore a dark gray hat pulled down low to conceal most of his face, but Caractacus saw the thin black mustache and he knew that voice. It was rough, almost hoarse, and sounded different, but there was no mistaking his unwelcome guest.

"*You*? But … but—"

"Yes, yes, I know." The visitor waved one hand nonchalantly. He held a black cheroot between two fingers. "I'm supposed to be dead. You must have read the news report a few months ago. The eminent Dr. Faisal Khalid died in a tragic accident at one of the newly discovered digs near the Valley of the Kings. As you can see, I'm not dead, although being thought dead does have its uses."

He beckoned the bewildered Caractacus into the living room. "Come, sit down. Take off your coat. You look tired. Hard day at the museum?"

Caractacus obeyed as if in slow motion, first taking off his coat and letting it slide to the floor, and then sinking onto the sofa. He loosened his tie.

The man rose and went over to a nearby drinks trolley laden with bottles and glasses. "Whisky? Ice?"

Speechless, Caractacus nodded. Keeping his gaze lowered, he heard the cold tinkle of ice against glass and the gurgling of pouring liquid. The visitor must have been here for a while; he'd had time to fetch ice from the kitchen. This felt like a horrible dream from which he would never wake.

He looked up as Dr. Khalid handed him a glass, with a sympathetic nod. "I do understand. It's such a battle every day to get things done. You're surrounded by idiots who don't appreciate what you're doing."

"Yes," Caractacus burst out. "But how—" He stopped and then set the glass down on an end table. "What do you want from me?" he asked in a sulky tone.

Dr. Khalid strolled around the room, taking occasional puffs from his cheroot. "Nice cozy little place you have here."

"Just get to the point," Caractacus snapped. "I haven't any money so I don't know what you're after." He half rose. "I should call the police."

Dr. Khalid threw back his head in a roar of laughter. "Money? Is that what you think I want?"

With his visitor's head thrown back, Caractacus caught a glimpse of the man's face under the brim of his hat: there was an eye patch and dreadful scars. He was too afraid to ask what had happened in Egypt.

Then Dr. Khalid tilted his hat back further to glare at his trembling host, revealing even more of his ravaged face. "Money is not at the top of my wish list."

Caractacus shrank as far as possible into the sofa, trying to avoid the ghastly, blazing one-eyed stare.

"I have plenty of money, thank you. No, I want something else, something you'll help me get when the time is right."

"I don't know what you're talking about," whined Caractacus. "If you don't want money, then—" Again, he stopped as realization dawned. "I won't be involved in any of your tricks." He folded his arms and pushed out his lower lip in a heavy pout. "I can't help you and you can't make me."

Dr. Khalid, who had begun pacing the room, turned. "You can and you will help me."

Caractacus put on a mutinous expression. Then he tossed his head in an offhand way. "You can *try* to make me. What's the worst that can happen? You'll kill me? I'm not afraid of death."

Dr. Khalid made a wry face. "How dramatic you are. Contrary to popular opinion, I don't kill everyone who doesn't obey me." He drew on his cheroot and blew a smoke ring. "I would simply make an anonymous call to Interpol, the division dealing with stolen antiquities."

At first, Caractacus didn't know what Dr. Khalid was talking about. Then he shot a frightened glance at the glass-fronted display cabinet behind his visitor, who burst into mocking laughter.

Dr. Khalid wagged a disapproving finger at Caractacus. "Being involved with museums has its advantages and I can see just how well you have utilized those opportunities. You've been a very naughty boy indeed." He stroked his mustache as he studied the contents of the cabinet. "Now, what do I see here? Aha, Cleopatra's ring. A pretty piece stolen … let me see … several years ago from an exhibition at the British Museum. And, my goodness, so many other delightful pieces … small and easily missed."

He walked over to Caractacus and stared down at him. "I could go on, but need I do so?"

Mute with fear, Caractacus shook his head as he cowered against the cushions. He had stashed an uncomfortably large number of stolen treasures, including paintings, in his house. He would go to prison for dozens of years if the authorities found out.

"What do you want?" he finally asked. His throat felt so dry and sore he could hardly speak. He gulped the drink in his glass, coughing as the liquid burned his throat.

Dr. Khalid sauntered back to his chair and sat, calmly crossing his legs. After sipping his drink, he puffed several times at his cheroot, blowing another large smoke ring into the middle of the room.

Caractacus flinched. His mother would turn in her grave if she could see this imbecile polluting her living room. He didn't smoke and avoided people who did.

At last, Dr. Khalid spoke. "I want the Stone of Excalibur."

Caractacus blanched. His mouth fell open. "You must be mad," he croaked. "You can't steal the sword. It's a national treasure."

Dr. Khalid sighed as he stubbed out his cheroot in a glass bowl. Caractacus flinched again. It was his mother's favorite rose-crystal bowl. By now, she was probably spinning in her grave.

"You're not listening to me," said Dr. Khalid. "I don't want the sword—just the stone in the hilt."

Caractacus frowned. "What's so important about the stone?"

"Nothing that concerns you," Dr. Khalid replied smoothly. "However, I would have thought that the sword might interest you."

Caractacus frowned even more. "What do you mean?"

Dr. Khalid settled himself comfortably into his chair. He sipped his drink again. "Tell me more about your unusual name. You are named after someone famous."

Caractacus' thin lips stretched in a bleak smile. "Yes, for some obscure reason—possibly our Welsh roots—my mother thought we were descended from the chieftain of the Catuvellauni tribe, who led the British opposition to the Roman conquest. That chieftain, Caractacus, fled to Wales to continue the resistance, but was defeated at the Battle of Caer Caradoc in AD 51 and taken to Rome in chains. He was sentenced to death as a military prisoner, but made such a moving speech before his execution that the Emperor Claudius spared him."

"And why should your mother have been wrong?" Dr. Khalid's voice was soft, hypnotic, and persuasive. "I think she was right. Your noble lineage makes you the rightful possessor of the sword that made Arthur great. He was a Welsh commander in battle, a *dux bellorum* and an *imperator* in Latin—or, in your native tongue, an *amherawdr*. You are Arthur's true and rightful heir. His spiritual heir, at least."

Caractacus closed his eyes, allowing the coaxing voice of the world's greatest antiques thief to wash over him. *Yes, maybe Mother was right.* For years, she had drummed it into him. He could almost hear her voice. He could almost see her sitting right there in the chair that his uninvited guest now occupied, her crochet

338

hook flying in and out of the lace as she created yet another tray cloth. *"You're destined for greatness, my son. That's why I named you Caractacus, after your famous ancestor."* Then again, maybe it was just another of his mother's romantic fancies. He thought of the piles of rubbishy novels she had loved to read.

He opened his eyes. Dr. Khalid's smile was triumphant.

Caractacus scowled. "There's no proof the sword is even Excalibur. I think it's just a publicity stunt. Downing Street's grab at the popular vote. The government is desperate to win back the confidence of the people."

Dr. Khalid shook his head. "The sword is one of the Thirteen Treasures of Britain."

Caractacus sat bolt upright. "What?"

"Tsk tsk." Dr. Khalid wagged an admonishing finger again. "You haven't kept up with your history, have you? Your friend Archibald Curran let that nugget of information slip out." He leaned forward. "Tell me, what is the Knowledge of Britain?"

Caractacus replied automatically, "The Knowledge of Britain is the knowledge of the properties of the Thirteen Treasures of Britain."

"What are the Thirteen Treasures of Britain?"

Dumbfounded, but speaking quickly in a low whisper, Caractacus recited the poem he knew by heart:

> *The burning blade one cannot hold,*
> *The whetstone will prefer the bold,*
> *The cauldron to reveal the brave,*
> *The horn that many drink might have,*
> *The hamper whereon a hundred feast,*
> *The halter to tame the wildest beast,*
> *The chariot fleet for the journey's wish,*
> *To please the hungry man's need, the dish,*
> *The knife serves twenty-four places laid,*
> *The coat for the wellborn man is made,*
> *The board of silver and of gold will deal,*
> *The warrior ring can a man conceal,*
> *The mantle will not him reveal.*

Caractacus explained, "The Whetstone of Tudwal Tudglyd: if a brave man sharpened his sword on the whetstone, then the sword would certainly kill any man from whom it drew blood. If a cowardly man used the whetstone, his sword would refuse to draw blood at all. The Cauldron of Dyrnwch the Giant: if meat for a coward was put in to boil, it would never boil, but if meat for a brave man was put in, it would boil quickly. The Horn of Brân Galed contained whatever drink might be wished for."

Caractacus closed his eyes again. "The Hamper of Gwyddno Garanhir. Food for one man would be put in it and when it was opened, food for a hundred men would be found inside. The Halter of Clydno Eiddynd: whatever horse he might wish for, he would find in the halter. The Chariot of Morgan Mwynfawr ... if a man drove in it, he only had to wish for his destination and he would be there quickly."

He stopped, opened his eyes, and watched his visitor. Dr. Khalid did not speak; he merely gave an imperious wave for Caractacus to continue.

"The Dish of Rhygenydd—whatever food you wished for would appear. The Knife of Llawfrodedd Farchog would serve enough for twenty-four men to eat at table. The Coat of Padarn Beisrudd: if a well-born man put it on, it would be the right size for him; if a peasant, it would not fit."

He sucked in a deep breath. "The Chessboard of Gwenddoleu ap Ceidio—if the pieces were set, they would play by themselves. The board was made of gold and the men of silver. The Warrior Ring of Eluned: whoever wore this ring became invisible. The Mantle of Arthur: whoever was under it could not be seen, but he could see everyone."

He stopped. After a brief silence, Dr. Khalid applauded softly. "Well done, Caractacus, but haven't you left out the most important item? The burning blade."

Caractacus swallowed nervously. "White-Hilt, the Sword of Rhydderch Hael. Also known as Dyrnwyn, the flame blade. If anyone but its owner drew it, the sword burst into flame from its hilt to its tip."

"The Sword of Rhydderch Hael is Excalibur," said Dr. Khalid, with a note of urgency in his voice. "And your spiritual birthright. The sword is yours. The stone is mine."

Caractacus picked up his glass. He swallowed the remaining liquid to ease his parched throat, but it burned all the way down to his stomach. "You're right. They all think I'm a loser, a nobody, a nothing."

Dr. Khalid leaned forward, his remaining dark eye burning with a black fire. "You're not. You're a hero, and Britain will thank you when you lead this country out of darkness and into the light."

Caractacus said in a dazed voice, "It was Suetonius Paulinus, the governor appointed by Nero. In AD 61, two legions crushed the Druid sanctuary in Ynys Mon. They killed the Druids, bards, and priestesses. They cut down the sacred groves. They destroyed ancient Britain."

"That's right." Dr. Khalid's voice was compelling. "When the Romans slaughtered the Druids, they broke the bond between Britain and the old gods. It's up to you to repair that bond and save Britain. You must remake ancient Britain, the *real* Britain, and restore its age of splendor."

Caractacus squirmed under that one-eyed glare.

"*Restitutor Orbis*, Restorer of the World," said Dr. Khalid firmly.

"Wh-wh-what's that?" Caractacus' voice quavered.

"As the Roman Empire tottered in the third and fourth centuries, and crumbled in the fifth, a few good emperors restored the order for short bursts of time and delayed the barbarian onslaught. Aurelian, Diocletian, and Constantine the Great were such leaders. As a result, the Romans were known for this tradition: in the hour of darkness, a hero, the *Restitutor Orbis*, would rise up to dispel the chaos and restore *Romanitas*, the traditional values of Roman nobility. Arthur was clearly a British *Restitutor*."

Dr. Khalid patted Caractacus' shoulder. "And you, my friend, are his successor."

Caractacus gazed at him, mesmerized as if under a spell. He was convinced. "What must I do?"

Dr. Khalid stood, his cloak swishing around him. He adjusted his hat, pulling it down to hide his face. "Nothing. Do nothing … yet. I will tell you when the time is right."

Caractacus closed his eyes for a fraction of a second, a glorious vision of Excalibur floating before him. When he opened them, Dr. Khalid had gone and nothing remained of his presence except an empty glass and the lingering smell of a stubbed-out cheroot.

Caractacus remembered one unusual thing about his sinister caller. The ring on his right hand was unforgettable. The design depicted a snake writhing around the hilt of a dagger. The dagger was piercing an intricate knot.

341

Caractacus wondered what it meant. Then he thought of his visitor's last words.

Restitutor Orbis, Restorer of the World.

He rather liked the sound of it.

The End

READERS' GUIDE TO KING ARTHUR & THE DARK AGES

There is extensive information on Arthur and Roman Britain in *The Companion Guide to The Search for the Stone of Excalibur* but these endnotes will help booklovers enjoy the story even more while reading.

WHO WAS ARTHUR?

King Arthur is without doubt the greatest legendary figure in the western world. Countless poems, books, screenplays, and material have been written about him, speculating on his birth, his exploits, his legacy, and what he has come to represent to the world. Even death cannot touch him since legend says he is not dead, but sleeping in a cave on the isle of Avalon, waiting to be awakened in time of his country's direst need. Mystery and magic surround the story of this man who became a leader, a kingly figure, a symbol of hope and renewal. Who was the real Arthur, the man who lived and fought in the tumultuous period in history called the Dark Ages?

The Dark Ages (also called the Early Middle Ages) was a period of chaos and warfare that lasted from the 5th Century to approximately AD 1000. It is appropriately called the Dark Ages because, not only was it a time when civilization collapsed, but very few records survive from this era. That is why we know so little about the period in which Arthur is said to have lived and why there is such debate concerning his historical existence. There was a real Arthur, a great

343

and skilled war leader who performed many brave and epic deeds. He most likely was a nobleman of British-Roman ancestry. Arthur was believed to have had extensive knowledge of Roman military strategies and warfare, which he successfully used against the Saxons during the late 5th and early 6th Centuries. His possible birth date was circa AD 478. An important aspect of Arthur's heritage, whoever he was, is that he was a Celt by tradition and history. At the time Arthur lived there was no distinct 'England' to speak of. He was a Briton, of Celtic stock, the product of a Celtic society.

By AD 410, Rome had withdrawn from Britain, leaving it vulnerable. It wasn't long before the barbarian tribes that the Roman troops had kept at bay began to reappear. Soon the invasions increased in size and number as the news spread that Britain was easy pickings and practically defenseless since the British clans and kingdoms were unable to unite for their own protection. It is here that history starts to merge with legend and the famous names of Vortigern, Ambrosius Aurelianus, Uther Pendragon, and Arthur appear.

By AD 500, Britain had fragmented into a number of smaller kingdoms, a situation intensified by the tendency of rulers to leave their realms to be divided amongst their sons, instead of direct inheritance to the eldest. Thus tribal groups became even more splintered. The largest and strongest of these kingdoms was Powys. It is against this background that the figure of Arthur emerges. Arthur is thought to be one of the princes in South-Western England who fought in an alliance of British leaders against the Saxons and their allies, the Angles, Jutes, and Frisians, as well as the Picts and Scots who came from the north after the Romans left. The fighting continued until circa AD 516 when, at the Battle of Mount Badon, the united Britons inflicted a severe defeat on the Anglo-Saxons. This victory turned the tide of the barbarian advances for the next fifty years, permitting a final 'golden age' for Celtic civilization in Britain. The utterly defeated Saxons did not attack the Celts again until 571.

WARFARE IN ARTHUR'S TIME

Every king or ruler had his war-band or personal retinue who would fight with him, sometimes to the death. One can see how easily this rather idealized concept of a band of loyal warriors was adopted by 12th Century writers to become a band of knights in shining armor who embarked upon quests to prove their worth and adherence to a code of chivalry. Forget any idea of thousands of horsemen streaming across a battlefield, armor glinting in the sunlight, pennants flying—a ferocious sight indeed. In Arthur's time, a war-band of 300 men would have been considered impressive.

Legend describes Arthur as being skilled in warfare. Arthur's innovation, probably, was mounted cavalry. It is clear from war poetry of the time that British warriors could fight mounted. No Saxon line could withstand a charge by lightly armored cavalry, and the Saxons would have had no experience with this. The British warriors would charge the line, break it up into segments, and either finish off the enemy while on horseback, or get off their horses and fight on the ground. The horse gave Arthur the mobility to be where the Saxons were, wherever they were. It was a true revolution in warfare at the time. The British method of fighting was varied. There was no rigid division between 'cavalry' and 'infantry'; the trained post-Roman warrior was skilled in several types of fighting. He could fight on horse and on foot; individually and in formed squads; at a distance and hand-to-hand. This was also before the introduction of the stirrup, which is important in striking downward blows and anchoring a rider more securely. (Dark Ages riders would have used a simple toe loop or anchored their feet under the girth of the saddle.)

Most of us probably picture Arthur riding out from a huge, imposing stone castle ahead of his knights in shining armor. The truth is far from this movie-inspired image. Instead, his castle would have been a hill fort. This is an elevated site with one or more ramparts made of earth, stone, and/or wood, with an external ditch. Hill forts in Britain existed from the Bronze Age. In Britain, the Bronze Age was from about 2100 to 750 BC, but the great period of hill fort construction was during the Iron Age, between 200 BC and the Roman conquest of Britain in AD 43. The British Iron Age lasted until the Roman Conquest and until the 5th Century in non-Romanized parts (Wales, Scotland, and Ireland). The Romans fortified many Celtic Iron Age hill forts for their own use by building wooden palisades and gateways. They occupied some forts, but others were destroyed, and then abandoned when the Romans withdrew from Britain in AD 410. These strongholds provided post-Roman Britons with a network of defenses in the absence of Roman military power. Post-Roman buildings were wooden with thatched roofs, although stone-built buildings are more common in Wales and Scotland. The fortresses of at least the highland kings and their chieftains were fortified strongholds. These would have formed the foci for campaigning.

ARMOR & WEAPONS

The armor and weapons of the 5th Century Britons would have been modelled on those used by the Romans; in fact, some troops may have used actual old Roman equipment, given the length of time Britain was a Roman colony. The weaponry and armor of post-Roman 'British' warriors remains an enigma. Because of the lack of weapon burials in the highlands, very little weaponry is known from these regions. This, as well as the practice of offering weapons to the spirits of the water, would explain the complete lack of the distinctively crafted Celtic swords after the Roman invasion. The Celts had stopped manufacturing their unique swords because under the Roman occupation (AD 43—410), only Roman soldiers were allowed to own swords. Given the Romanized nature of 5th Century Britain, and the fact that the Britons preserved Roman technology and methods of warfare long after the Roman exodus in AD 410, it is more likely their weapons and armor would have retained a strong Roman influence. Military leaders of this era would have used the *spatha*, a cavalry sword originally designed by the Romans. It would have been two feet long with a stunted crossguard.

Most foot soldiers would have had very basic (hardened) leather armor, their only protection against weapons designed to brutally hack a man to pieces. Most warriors would have been armed with a circular shield and a spear. The small amounts of available armor, helmets, swords, and chain mail at that time would have been reserved for the highborn or professional warrior class. Shields were often quite small targets with 'bosses' (raised, round portions) aimed at catching and deflecting blows. Warriors used shields for attack as well as defense. Shields could smash the enemy to the ground or clear the way for arrows and spears. Armaments included a large number of missile weapons, such as throwing spears and javelins, and throwing axes.

Why is Arthur Important?

Arthur is important to us because he appears as the ideal of kingship during peace and war. He stands for all that is true and good in a leader. Writers of the High Middle Ages (from AD 1200 to 1500) tended to use ancient myths and legends and place them in a context of knighthood and chivalry. Thus, it is hard to achieve a reasonably accurate chronology of Arthur's life as the chaotic 5th and 6th Centuries were the darkest period of the Early Middle Ages. Although exact dates are hard to pinpoint, a hazy outline of events emerges.

- Year c. AD 478: claimed to be Arthur's birth date. Legends say he was the son of Uther Pendragon and Igraine (Ygerne) of Cornwall. Tintagel Castle in Cornwall is thought to have been his birthplace. (see front map)
- Year c. 495: Uther Pendragon was drawn into a renewed war with the Northern Angles. When his commander, King Lot of Lothian, was unsuccessful, the ailing and aging king was carried to St. Albans (*Caer-Mincip*) to besiege the Anglian princes himself. He won through, but the Germans poisoned the water supply and Uther, along with many of his men, died in the days that followed. Arthur became a military leader in the fight against the Saxons.
- Year c. 516/7: Battle of Mount Badon in the war against the Saxons. Arthur was victorious. A long peace ensued.
- Year c. 535(-7): Battle of Camlann (Camlaun), where both Arthur and his kinsman and antagonist Mordred (Medraut) fell.

One distinctive aspect of Celtic culture was that, although the Celts sought and praised victory, they remembered the longest and empathized the most with defeat. The leader of the losing side became the hero and impressed himself onto the imagination of the common person. Such was the case with Arthur after the disastrous Battle of Camlann.

Following Arthur's death at Camlann, his fame spread all over Europe. Arthurian tales helped to define a new way of thinking in Europe. A code of chivalry emerged that emphasized how one should live and conduct oneself with honor and bravery. During the centuries following Arthur's death, Arthur's role changed. From a local chieftain he became a conquering hero, a champion of peace and justice, a king of kings. No matter who or what Arthur was originally, the essence of what he came to represent both to his own people and to those living centuries later will always be remembered.

Arthur's Battles

The 9th Century Welsh historian, Nennius, records twelve great victories in battle during Arthur's time as *Dux Bellorum* (leader of battles). He says: *'Arthur fought ... together with the Kings of the British; but he was Dux Bellorum.'*

This would seem to confirm the popular view today that Arthur was a professional soldier; a brilliant military leader heading an alliance of British kings to engage in warfare against all coming enemies. Some historians believe Arthur headed up a war band of cavalrymen, traveling around the country and championing the British cause, hence his widespread popularity. You can follow Arthur's battles on the map in the front of the book.

❖ *'The first battle was at the mouth of the river called Glein'*: This might be one of the two Rivers Glen in Britain today—one in Lincolnshire and one in Northumberland. Unfortunately, *Glen* stems from the Celtic for 'pure' so there were probably many rivers thus named in 6th Century Britain.

❖ *'The second, the third, the fourth and the fifth were on another river, called the Dubglas, which is in the region of Linnuis'*: The *River Dubglas* is modern Douglas, meaning 'black water.' It might be any one of the many Rivers Blackwater in Britain today. The better-known Roman *Lindum* is now the city of Lincoln. The surrounding area would be *Linnuis*: it is still called Lindsey today.

❖ *'The sixth battle was on the river called Bassas'*: Cambuslang in the southern suburbs of Glasgow, Scotland, already has Arthurian associations as the burial place of the great king's Northern British enemy, Caw. Perhaps Caw was killed in the battle.

❖   *'The seventh battle was in the Caledonian Forest, that is, the Battle of Celidon Coit':* The seventh battle site is almost certainly the Caledonian Forest in modern Scotland: *Coed Celyddon.*

❖   *'The eighth battle was in Guinnion fort ... the heathen were put to flight on that day, and there was great slaughter upon them ...':* The name *Guinnion* is very similar to the Roman fort of *Vinovium* at Binchester, Durham, so this is possibly the location.

❖   *'The ninth battle was in the City of the Legion':* The *Urbe Legionis* or 'City of the Legions' could be Chester. It was actually recorded in the *Annales Cambriae* as *Urbs Legionis* and was the site of a Battle of Chester in Dark Age times.

❖   *'The tenth battle was on the bank of the river called Tribruit':* The battle is mentioned in an 11th Century Welsh poem from the Black Book of Carmarthen, *Pa Gur.*

❖   *'The eleventh battle was on the hill called Agned':* Geoffrey of Monmouth identifies *Monte Agned* as Edinburgh and the rock of Edinburgh Castle was certainly occupied at this time.

❖   *'The twelfth battle was on Badon Hill and in it nine hundred and sixty men fell in one day, from a single charge of Arthur's, and no-one lay them low save he alone.'* It was at the Battle of Mount Badon that tradition says the Saxon advance into Britain was finally halted. It was Arthur's greatest victory. The battle site is possibly Bath, *Caer Baddon,* or, at least somewhere in its vicinity.

❖   Nennius does not mention Arthur's last battle, where he was fatally wounded. We learn about it from the *Annales Cambriae* as: *'The Strife of Camlann in which Arthur and Medraut perished.'* Generally, however, modern historians recognise the battle site as the Roman fort of *Camboglanna,* on Hadrian's Wall. The place is now called Castlesteads in Cumbria.

EXCALIBUR & THE SYMBOLISM OF THE SWORD

The sword is the perennial symbol of empires, knighthood, chivalry, and fantasy. But it is also one of the world's most ancient technologies, connected with breakthroughs in metallurgy that would change the world. There are even some types of ancient swords so strong that modern science still can't work out how they were made. Legendary figures throughout the world have long been associated with magical swords or weaponry with special powers—the sword is often the symbol of kingship. The names given to many swords in mythology, literature, and history indicate the significance of the weapon and the wealth or importance of the owner. Celts were the first people to name weapons and attribute special powers to them. The most famous example is the legendary Excalibur, sword of King Arthur, often also associated with the rightful sovereignty of Great Britain.

In many ancient legends, magical swords are usually forged by a deity or fairy blacksmith. As the 'people of iron,' it is only natural that the Celts would have a smith-god as one of their primary deities. His name was Gofannon.

As the sword has historically been a weapon of status, it has become symbolic of warfare or state power. Thus the surrender of a sword is a well-known universal symbol of defeat, perhaps even symbolising death itself. Depositing swords, weaponry, and other valuables in sacred lakes and rivers was a popular practice among the Celtic peoples, often as an offering to the goddess of the water. Perhaps this is how the 'Lady of the Lake' legend developed, when (according to lore) Sir Bedivere, after defying Arthur's request to throw the sword back into the lake, finally obeys his lord. To this day, many rivers in England have been the best source of Celtic swords and artifacts.

Celts were well known for their fierce fighting and placed a high value on fine weaponry. Many Celtic swords had richly decorated hilts, inlaid with amber, ivory, or gold leaf. Scabbards, shields, and helmets were similarly decorated and often adorned with an adder (thought to have mystic powers). The Celtic warriors were renowned swordsmen, using both heavy, long-bladed slashing swords and one-handed short swords. Their human-shaped hilts easily identified both versions of early Celtic swords. This sword design is unique to Celtic swords and incorporated matching upper and lower guards, which curved away from the grip (symbolizing the arms and legs), and to complete the figure, a head-shaped pommel was used. However, what would the historical Arthur's sword really have looked like? In the Arthurian romances, Excalibur is often depicted as a mediaeval broadsword. However, if Arthur lived circa AD 500 then his sword would have been of a very different design.

Given the Romanized nature of 5th Century Britain, the sword that the historical Arthur would have used is a *spatha* with a hilt constructed by a local British craftsman, maybe carved with decorations. In all the later myths and legends that developed around the figure of Arthur, descriptions of Excalibur certainly give rise to the belief that this was a sword with almost magical powers. In Welsh legend, Arthur's sword is known as *Caledfwlch* ('Hard-cleft'), a Welsh word derived from *Calad-Bolg*, meaning 'Hard Lightning.'

Even Excalibur's scabbard was said to have powers of its own. Injuries from loss of blood, for example, would not kill the wearer. In some tales, wounds received by someone wearing the scabbard did not bleed at all. The scabbard is stolen by the sorceress Morgan le Fay and thrown into a lake, never to be found again. As a result, when Mordred wounds Arthur, the king receives a mortal wound, and without the healing properties of the scabbard, must surely never recover.

Who Succeeded Arthur?

Who took Arthur's place after the Battle of Camlann? Geoffrey of Monmouth says: *'He handed the crown of Britain over to his cousin Constantine, the son of Cador, Duke of Cornwall.'*

Geoffrey of Monmouth (1100—c. 1155) was a cleric and one of the major figures in the development of British historiography (the writing of history) and the popularity of tales of King Arthur. Given Geoffrey's tendency to elaborate on the Arthurian legends, one might wonder if this was another literary invention. Cador (Latin: *Cadorius*) was a legendary Duke of Cornwall. Cador is said to be King Arthur's relative (a cousin?). Cador (or Cado) was the historical son of a Dumnonian king named Gerren Llyngesoc, and succeeded him as monarch. According to literary tradition, Cador was a good friend of Arthur and the two fought together many times against the Saxons and other enemies. At the famous Siege of Mount Badon, Cador commanded the British contingent that chased the invaders back to their boats at Thanet. Cador probably died at the beginning of the 6th Century. Traditionally, this was at the Battle of Camlann, after which he was buried in the Condolden (or Cadon) Barrow near Camelford in Cerniw, Wales.

Constantine III (c. AD 520—576), the son of Cador, was a legendary king of the Britons, as recounted by Geoffrey of Monmouth. Constantine fought in the Battle of Camlann and was apparently one of the few survivors. Arthur, about to be taken to Avalon, passed the crown to him. Geoffrey says that Constantine continued to have trouble from the Saxons and from the two sons of Mordred, who were Melehan and Melou. He eventually subdued his enemies, however, and chased Mordred's sons into churches where he murdered them. According to Geoffrey, he was struck down by God for killing them while in sanctuary, and was buried next to Uther Pendragon at Stonehenge.

The Dragon in Celtic Mythology

Stories of dragons appear all throughout history and almost every culture has their own idea about dragons. One reason for this could be the finding of dinosaur fossils. Dragons could be used to describe the bones of gigantic unknown creatures.

In Celtic mythology, the dragon was believed to inhabit a world that was parallel to the physical world. Druids believed that the dragon's power affected the 'ley' or energy of the land. They believed that the path the dragons took, called a 'vein,' was important to the flow of energy through the physical world. Where dragons trod, magical power flowed, and where they laired were invariably places of great sanctity and mystical harmony. Areas where a dragon passed often, where dragon paths crossed, or places a dragon stopped to rest became more powerful than the areas surrounding it. Druids hunted for these lines and made ley lines maps for their people, instructing them to build their temples and homes along the lines in order to harvest the energies. Stonehenge is thought to be one of those places. In addition, some believe that the Celtic cross surrounded by a circle is a symbol of the crossing ley lines and that the circle of life is centered on that power.

King Arthur himself was burdened by dreams of dragons, although it is unclear which color he saw. He saw them specifically at the time of Mordred's conception and before his death. He is eaten by dragons in his final dream and it is at his next battle that Mordred kills him. It is said that when a king sees dragons then ruin will come to his kingdom and himself.

There are two types of dragons in Celtic lore. There is the standard winged version with four legs that most people are familiar with and there is a sea serpent that is depicted as either a giant wingless serpent or a huge serpent with wings, but no legs. The dragon was a gatekeeper to other worlds and guardian to the secrets and treasures of the universe. They were often depicted side by side with the Celtic gods. As creatures that protect the Earth and all living things, Celtic dragons are considered the most powerful of all the Celtic symbols.

Dragons are used as a symbol of power and wisdom among leaders. Dragons are seen on many coats of arms. The Welsh flag proudly displays the Red Dragon and their motto reads: *Y Ddraig Goch Ddyry Cychwyn*, meaning 'The Red Dragon Leads the Way.' *Y Ddraig Goch*, the red dragon, was derived from the Great Red Serpent that had represented the Welsh god Dewi.

JOURNEY WITH KING ARTHUR

There are so many places in Britain associated with King Arthur that it is hard to know which ones are real and which are legendary. Follow Arthur's journey from birth to death. The places you will read about are listed on the map (see front of the book).

TINTAGEL CASTLE (CORNWALL): Was this Arthur's birthplace? Though it is said that King Arthur was born at Tintagel, early literary sources only ever actually say that he was conceived there.

CAMELOT: Where was the real Camelot? Was there even a real court of King Arthur? Some historians think it actually existed at Cadbury Castle and here's why. Cadbury Castle is an Iron Age hill fort in the parish of South Cadbury in the English county of Somerset. When considering that Arthur flourished late 5th to early 6th Century, it is entirely possible that he made one of these earthen strongholds his headquarters.

THE LADY'S LAKE: The Lady of the Lake supposedly gave Arthur the sword Excalibur after he had broken his original sword (from the stone) in battle with King Pellinore. Legend says Bedwyr (or Bedivere) threw the great Excalibur back into the swirling waters after King Arthur fell at the fateful Battle of Camlann.

Pomparles Bridge, *the Pont-Perles* or 'Perilous Bridge' just outside Glastonbury, once guarded the southern approach to this well-known Dark Age settlement.

ARTHUR'S LAST RESTING PLACE: The mystery of Arthur's grave remains unsolved and, according to legend, Arthur was fully healed at Avalon and he lives today, waiting for the time when his people will have great need of him. Then he will appear and restore his kingdom. Three possible places exist: Glastonbury Abbey, Glastonbury itself, and the Island of Bardsey. Which one do you think is the most likely last resting place of Arthur, the once and future King?

GLASTONBURY ABBEY: When Avalon became linked with Glastonbury in the 10th Century, Arthur was assumed to have been buried at the ancient Abbey there. This was an eminently suitable spot for the last resting-place of the High-King. It is the most holy place in Britain, for Glastonbury's *Vetusta Ecclesia* or 'Old Church' is said to have been founded by St. Joseph of Arimathea himself.

GLASTONBURY AREA: Why is Glastonbury identified as the ancient and mysterious Isle of Avalon where King Arthur was taken to be healed of his fatal battle wounds? Glastonbury lies in the middle of Somerset, miles from the sea, so how could anyone ever consider it an island? Glastonbury is built on high ground surrounded on all sides by the Somerset Levels, some of the flattest land in the country. In the Dark Ages, the Levels were marshland and Glastonbury stood proud as an island towering above them. Hence, its ancient British name was *Ynys Witrin*, thought to translate as 'Island of Glass.'

BARDSEY ISLAND: Could this be Avalon? Legends claim that after the Battle of Camlann the wounded Arthur was laid in a barge and sailed to the Isle of Avalon (*Avalonia* means *Apples* in ancient British) for his wounds to be healed. In most of these accounts, though the island is described in detail, its exact location is rarely pinpointed. What better place for King Arthur to eventually be buried than the *Insula Sanctorum*. A little-known 14th Century manuscript known as '*The Death of Arthur*,' does actually state that Arthur '*gave orders that he should be carried to Gwynedd, for he intended to stay in the Isle of Avalon.*'

COMING NEXT

THE TEMPLE OF THE CRYSTAL TIMEKEEPER

Continuing the adventure that ended in Britain just a short while ago, cousins Adam and Justin Sinclair, with their friend Kim Maleka, are now hunting for the third Stone of Power, one of seven mysterious stones lost centuries ago. The third stone might be located in an ancient city, hidden in the depths of the Mexican jungle. Of course, their old adversary Dr. Khalid is close behind as the trio travels through the jungle in search of the lost city of stone gods. This time Adam will clash with a terrible enemy who adopts the persona of an evil Aztec god, Tezcatlipoca. Will they emerge alive from the jungle? Will Dr. Khalid find the third Stone of Power before they do?

CHAPTER ONE
CRASH LANDING IN THE JUNGLE

Adam opened his eyes. The terrible thudding noise, the screaming sounds of metal tearing, and the rush of branches breaking had finally stopped. Still strapped into his seat, he hung at an angle, the seat belt being the only thing preventing him from hurtling through the gaping hole in the roof of the plane to the jungle floor below. The strap cut into his chest as his whole weight pressed against the fabric. He craned his neck upward, twisting awkwardly to see the others. His body ached after the awful jarring and jolting when the plane fell. The first thing he did was shove his hand into his right side pants pocket to feel for his golden scarab. Phew! He let out a sigh of relief. It was safe. He squeezed the scarab for a few seconds to get his courage up. It felt warm and comforting in his hand.

"Justin? Kim?" he called, hoping like crazy they were all right.

"Uhh." The groan came from Kim. "Ow! My head."

"What the *flip* happened just now?"

Adam grinned. Justin was okay. He could tell by his cousin's angry tone.

"Are we alive?" Kim's voice was faint. She sounded dazed. "Why am I the wrong way up?"

"I think we've crashed into the jungle." Adam tried to look around. He couldn't see much because the interior of the plane was shadowy. Everything looked weird upside-down.

"That's just flipping great," Justin exploded. "Just great! The jungle is only thousands of miles big. We might as well be dead."

"Don't say that," said Kim, almost crying.

"It's true. What else do you want me to say?"

Adam called out, "Cool it, you two. Let's think about how to get out of here."

Even as he said this, he figured Justin was probably right. James had told them they were flying over the Lacandon jungle, measuring roughly 1.9 million hectares—a lot of jungle. Maybe it wasn't so big in actual miles, but nearly two million of anything sounded enormous. He remembered looking out of the window and admiring the vast expanse of greenery that stretched like a gigantic carpet as far as the eye could see. He also remembered James saying how difficult it was to see things on the ground because of the density of the tree canopy and vice versa. Things couldn't be worse than they were right now.

By holding his head at an angle, Adam could just make out James, their archaeologist friend, slumped against the instrument panel in the cockpit. He looked in a bad way; his head lolled to one side and his eyes remained closed.

"James! James!" Adam called out, even though James must be unconscious. Blood trickled down the side of James' face.

"What do we do now?" cried Kim.

The plane shuddered. Then, with the same awful tearing noise as before, the plane fell a few feet. Adam's heart pounded somewhere between his throat and his stomach. The sensation felt like being in a lift going down very quickly. James had mentioned some of the trees were between one to two hundred feet high. How far had they had fallen already? Soon there wouldn't be anywhere to go except hit the ground.

"Hang on," Justin yelled. "It's shifting."

Adam clutched the sides of his seat as the plane dropped like a stone. The metal cylinder of the fuselage was all that protected them from being smashed to pieces as the plane shuddered and bumped downward. The most horrible shaking reverberated through every bone in his body. Even his teeth rattled. Then, amazingly, the nose of the plane hit a branch, the fuselage rotated, and everything turned right side up. Adam looked at Justin. They burst out laughing, a nervous "thank-goodness-we're-alive" kind of laughter. Kim didn't laugh.

Justin unsnapped his seat belt and motioned for the others to stay in their seats. He stepped carefully into the cockpit to check on James. Adam looked up: the huge hole in the roof of the plane revealed massed tree branches with an occasional tiny flash of blue sky. They had fallen far down, near the ground. He wondered if that was good or bad.

Justin poked his head back into the compartment. "James is alive but knocked out. He looked around. "We have to get out of here right now. I can smell fuel."

Adam sniffed. Justin was right again. They would roast alive if the plane caught fire. He glanced at Kim. She sat with a frozen expression, her fingers digging into the sides of her seat.

"Hey, Kim."

She didn't reply, just stared ahead, as if too terrified to move.

Adam carefully eased out of his seat and inched over to her, praying that his movements wouldn't dislodge the plane. The plane settled into the branches with more screeching sounds as the metal tore into the bark of the tree. During those few long seconds, Adam clung to the top of Kim's seat. When the movement stopped, he looked at Kim and grinned ... a big fake grin that he hoped would convince her he wasn't worried.

"Narrow escape, huh?"

She gave him a weak smile in return, but her wide eyes betrayed her total terror. Adam glanced at Justin. They exchanged grins and Justin made a thumbs-up sign.

"We can climb out of the windows," Adam said. "We're not far off the ground."

"What about James?" Kim said. "We can't leave him."

"No, of course not," said Justin impatiently. "But let's get out first and check our surroundings. Then we can rescue him."

Kim climbed out of the window nearest the trunk of the tree. The glass had shattered in the crash so it was easy to squeeze through and scramble down the side of the plane to the ground, using branches to hang onto as they dropped the last few feet. They looked up at the plane, resting in the crook of two massive tree branches. It was actually higher than Adam had imagined. He wondered how they would get

James down to safety. He could just see the top of James' head resting on the instrument panel. By some miracle, the plane's windscreen remained intact. He and Justin took a few steps back.

"Oh, no," Justin muttered angrily. "It's so much higher up than I thought."

"You guys said planes never fall out of the sky," Kim said in an accusing tone. She slumped to the ground in a forlorn heap and then pushed aside some fern fronds, trying to make herself more comfortable. "Ow! This stuff is prickly."

"They don't usually," said Adam. "Not the big planes anyway."

"I just knew James was making a mistake hiring this beat-up old plane," Justin said sourly. He folded his arms in a huff. "No wonder it fell to pieces."

"No, it's not the plane," said Adam. "This is a Cessna 185."

Justin shrugged. "So? What's so special about it?"

Adam looked up at the battered carcass of the plane, its once-bright yellow and silver paintwork now scarred and scratched from the tree branches.

"They're solid planes. Most of the air forces in the world use them. James told me this model has a strengthened fuselage. They're used in bush flying, reconnaissance, and even in the ice-fields in Alaska and Canada."

Their skeptical expressions said otherwise. Justin raised his eyebrows and gave a disbelieving snort.

"I'm telling you this is a good plane." Adam was convinced the problem lay elsewhere. Planes like the sturdy Cessna 185 didn't just fall apart for no reason.

Kim sniffed and tossed her head in scorn. "It can't be all that good." She pointed at the plane. "Look, the wings have fallen right off."

The wings and tail had sheared off completely. Some parts lay on the ground and bits of wreckage hung in the surrounding trees. It looked like a scene from a disaster movie.

"That's not surprising," said Justin. "The wings got torn off when the plane hit the trees."

"It's a good plane," Adam repeated doggedly. "Someone must have sabotaged it."

As he finally voiced his fears, a cold sensation clutched at his chest. Fearful thoughts chased around in his mind. They had only been in Mexico a few days. Had Dr. Khalid caught up with them already? Did he even know they were here? James was an experienced pilot. What could have gone wrong?

Justin laughed. "That's impossible. It must have been some kind of malfunction. Maybe something broke. I heard a bang and then things went crazy."

Adam didn't say anything more about sabotage. He replayed in his mind James' last words: "Hang on, kids."

As Justin said, a loud noise had come from the rear and then the plane began to bank left as James fought to keep control. Adam pushed those horrible memories aside, trying to focus on the present and getting back to safety. Well, getting out of the jungle for a start.

Kim rolled her eyes in an "I'm bored with this" look. "Can we please stop talking about stupid planes and think about getting James to safety?"

"You started it," Justin snapped. His face was tight and tense with worry. Justin always got bad-tempered when he felt stressed out.

"Let's think about the best route back to civilization," Adam said. "There's no point in us arguing."

A quick glance about him showed trees, trees, and even more trees surrounding them. Adam looked up. The gigantic trees formed a thick green canopy overhead, with an occasional brief glimpse of blue sky. Long creepers and lianas hung down from the branches. Monkeys screamed and chattered above their heads, while brightly colored birds whooped with strange cries. Something crashed through the undergrowth nearby. It sounded like a large animal. James had mentioned the wild animals that inhabited the Mexican jungle. Jaguars, wild pigs, crocodiles, and deadly snakes instantly sprang to mind, not to mention the large variety of poisonous insects and spiders, including tarantulas, scorpions, and *bird-eating* spiders. How big could that spider be? As big as a side plate or a dinner plate? Adam tried to remember which size scorpion James had said was the poisonous one: was it the smaller one or the larger one?

Just thinking about these wild creatures gave Adam the shivers, especially the jaguar which was an apex predator. When he'd asked James what that meant, James looked serious and said, "It's at the top of the jungle food chain with no predators of its own. Man is its only enemy."

Man, not three helpless kids without weapons, who had just crash-landed in the jungle, many miles away from civilization. Then Adam remembered the stalk and ambush part of James' lecture, and the fact that jaguars had an exceptionally powerful bite. They also had a way of crushing their prey's skull bones with one bite. Maybe it was better not to worry about jaguars, even though one might be stalking them at that very moment.

The big leafy plants surrounding them looked menacing. Moss and lichen grew on the tree trunks and branches, giving them a creepy look. Something moved … a snake lazily uncoiled from a nearby low branch and slithered away. Insects buzzed incessantly. Everything was so loud. This was no Disney movie jungle with friendly talking, singing, and dancing animals like Baloo and Bagheera from *The Jungle Book*. The undergrowth consisted of masses of ferns and shrubs, with no sign of a path, a beaten track, or any shred of evidence that people might be nearby. It was hot and muggy. Although they had felt the heat the minute they arrived in Mexico, it seemed to be even hotter in the jungle with all the trees and vegetation creating a dense green mass. Sweat rolled down Adam's forehead in warm drops and his damp shirt clung to his back like a clammy second skin. He felt suffocated.

Justin wiped his forehead with one arm, leaving wet patches on the sleeve of his khaki shirt. "I'm dying of heat here. I'm sweating like a pig, too."

Adam wondered if pigs actually sweated. He'd used the same expression often before, but hearing it now in the middle of a vast jungle, Justin's words sounded weird. In fact, the whole situation was so weird that he wondered if he was dreaming. Maybe he was still back in the hotel room, in the middle of an awful nightmare, and all this was unreal. He pinched his arm hard, digging his nails into his skin so that he felt pain. He looked down. His nails made white half moon impressions that slowly turned pink. Nothing changed. He didn't wake up because he was already awake and this hot, scary jungle was real.

"Don't just stand there, Adam. We should get the stuff out of the plane first," said Kim, scrambling to her feet. "There's a first aid kit in the back, and some food and water. Justin, don't forget the signal flares. Maybe the radio still works." She spoke in an organizing, bossy voice.

"I doubt it," said Adam. "The nose hit the trees first."

He headed for the plane, but Justin grabbed his arm and pulled him close.

"Don't look at those bushes. I think there's someone there," Justin hissed.

As Adam turned his head toward the bushes, Justin yanked his arm. "I said don't look."

Adam stood still. Slowly Justin's hand fell away from his arm. The cousins stared at each other, rigid with tension.

"What did you see?" Adam whispered, not wanting to hear.

"Lots of eyes looking at us. *Human* eyes."

"What shall we do?" Kim whispered.

Adam's heart sank. He wanted to crawl away into the undergrowth and hide. This trip was a complete disaster. Even before arriving in Mexico, they'd had no idea where they were going until they got to the airport in Johannesburg and met their aunt. Aunt Isabel had arranged their passports and visas because James wanted to give them an incredible surprise. Their parents, who were used to their expeditions with Aunt Isabel by now, were also in on the secret. Since the boys' first trip to Egypt, their parents thought travel improved young minds and were keen for the cousins to experience the world. Of course, they didn't know anything about the quest for the Seven Stones of Power; or that each trip involved a possibly deadly encounter with their mortal enemy, Dr. Faisal Khalid, who was also in pursuit of the stones. Adam could just imagine his parents totally freaking out if they knew what was really happening.

James had flown to Mexico a few days earlier to start his investigations and to hire an expedition guide. How James had laughed when he met them at the airport in Mexico City. His infectious smile made everyone giggle as he said he was going to make this the ultimate treasure hunt, only revealing clues as they went along. Of course, they were looking for the third Stone of Power, but this time they had no details, just his mention of a "lost city." James said the reconnaissance trip over the jungle was to get an idea of distance, but he hadn't said distance to what or where.

Adam recalled thinking Mexico would be the most fantastic adventure with real jungles and ruined ancient cities. Well, now they were in a real jungle and it was more frightening than fantastic, especially when the only adult was hurt and unconscious, and they had no way of getting back to civilization.

Everything had seemed all right to begin with. Aunt Isabel remained in Mexico City to do extra research at the National Museum of Anthropology. She was always preparing articles on some interesting subject or other. James knew the director of the museum very well. The director was delighted to assist the well-known investigative journalist Isabel Sinclair. The kids and James flew first to a place called Comitan, where they stayed overnight. It was about 500 miles away from Mexico City. The next morning, James had hired the Cessna from a small air charter company at the Copalar Airport in Comitan. The owner of the plane, Juan, had smiled at them through his glossy black mustache as he wiped his oily hands on a rag. When he gave James the keys, he'd told James to look after his "beautiful senorita." Juan didn't seem the treacherous type. Juan had shown them a photo of his family: his two small children holding Chico, their tiny Chihuahua dog, and Juan's plump, pretty wife called Carmen. But their enemy Dr. Khalid had intimidated people in the past, people who had betrayed them in the end.

Adam squared his shoulders and tried to act brave. Unfortunately, at that moment he felt about as brave as the biggest coward this side of the Rio Grande.

"Maybe we can make friends with whoever is in the bushes."

Adam wasn't very confident as he spoke. People who lived in the jungle were not like people who lived in cities. Jungle dwellers usually had weapons for protection … or attack. They mostly wanted to be left alone. He had heard about uncontacted tribes that definitely didn't want anyone from the outside world to intrude in their lives. He'd also read a terrible story about a tribe in Papua, New Guinea that ate some missionaries a few years ago. He thought he shouldn't mention it right now. Kim would freak out if anyone mentioned the word "cannibal."

"You can do that. You're good at making friends with the locals," said Justin, sounding hopeful.

Justin's words reminded Adam how, in the search for the first Stone of Power, Ismal, their kidnapper in Egypt, became their friend after Adam saved the man's life.

Kim let out a piercing scream as a group of Indians materialized out of the bushes. They must have been there all the time. Adam was amazed at how they blended in with their environment. The men were not much taller than Justin and him, but they were muscular and looked strong. They wore loincloths and carried spears and bows. Black paint daubed across their eye sockets formed a mask on the men's faces. The warriors' skins were a light brown color, with tattoos and weird ritual scars ornamenting their bodies. Some wore armbands, and decorations around their ankles; a few wore elaborate necklaces made of colored stones. Most of them had thick ear plugs through the lobes of their ears. They all had longish black hair cut so that their fringes came down to where the paint mask began. Their dark eyes glittered strangely as they stared back at the trio.

Adam swallowed. Justin made a loud gulping sound that he tried to turn into a cough. Kim stood with her hands pressed against her mouth, her huge brown eyes wide with shock. Then, a boy about Adam's age stalked closer. He stared at them with proud eyes and a sneer on his face. His eye mask had red dots along the edges. He was different from the rest because the older men deferred to him. The boy looked up at the Cessna and gestured with his spear. Instantly, several men laid down their weapons, ran to the wreckage, and swarmed up the tree in a flash.

"Hey," said Justin. "You can't go there."

He took a step forward and two warriors crossed their spears in front of his chest.

"Okay," he said, stepping back and raising his hands. "You can go there."

Kim sidled up to Adam. No one tried to stop her. The rest of the group stared intently at the men as, one by one, they slipped into the fuselage through the hole in the top. The boy shouted orders in a strange language.

"Are we prisoners?" she whispered, clutching Adam's arm.

Adam glanced about. The Indians were focused on the plane and paid no attention to them.

"I don't think so," he replied. "They're just ignoring us."

"For now," Justin muttered.

Somehow, the men managed to maneuver James out of the plane. They tied him onto the back of one of the men, who climbed nimbly down the tree. James' left leg hung at an angle. It must have been broken in the crash. His head and arms flopped over the much smaller man's shoulders. The men laid James gently on the ground at a safe distance from the Cessna. His face was white and, although he breathed deeply, he showed no signs of coming round. A few seconds later, the nose of the plane tilted downward and the creaking wreck slid to the ground with a crash that certainly would have killed James if he had remained inside the cockpit. Kim caught her breath. Adam tried to go to James, but the two men with spears crossed them in front of him.

Adam had the creepiest feeling he was still in a very bad dream, one that seemed endless. This shouldn't be happening. They should have been flying back to the airfield by now, then having lunch with Juan, who had promised them genuine Mexican tortillas, and talking about their trip. Instead, they were trapped in the jungle, surrounded by tribesmen with spears, who acted as if they weren't afraid to use their weapons, and James was badly hurt. One of the rescuers made a rough leg splint with two spears and pieces of liana. Then several men picked James up, holding his body above their heads, and trotted off.

Justin grabbed Adam, his face white with fright. "They're kidnapping him. They're going to kill him. They're going to kill us as well."

Adam said with a forced composure, although his heart thundered, "I don't think so. They weren't aggressive and they did rescue him from the plane."

"How do you know?" asked Kim. Her eyes were wide as saucers again. "They might be cannibals."

"I don't know, but I think if they were going to kill us, they would've done so already."

"Ha," Justin scoffed. "No, they wouldn't."

"Okay, why not?" asked Adam.

Justin bugged his eyes. "Because then they would have to carry our three dead bodies back to camp, that's why."

Adam felt a stab of fear, although the men hadn't acted hostile and only put up their spears to stop him and Justin interfering with what they were doing. The men had melted into the jungle. One minute they were there; the next they were gone. Then the boy reappeared and beckoned impatiently to them. Adam looked at Kim and then at Justin.

"What shall we do?" he asked.

"I'll take my chances with them," said Kim firmly. "I'm not staying here by myself in a jungle full of hungry wild animals."

"Me neither," said Justin. He sounded relieved that, in a way, Kim had made the decision for them.

He pulled Adam's arm. "Come on, let's go. What's the worst that can happen?"

Adam didn't know, but staying alone in a jungle wasn't top of his list of possible solutions to their predicament. "Coming," he cried.

They ran after the tribesmen into the gloomy depths of the impenetrable jungle.